MW01069913

GREEN LANTERN

SLEEPERS · BOOK THREE

SLEEPERS · BOOK THREE

By Christopher J. Priest and Mike Baron

ibooks
new york
www.ibooks.net

DISTRIBUTED BY PUBLISHERS GROUP WEST

An Original Publication of ibooks, inc.

Copyright © 2004 DC Comics. All rights reserved.

Green Lantern and all related titles, characters and indicia are
Trademarks of DC Comics © 2004

An ibooks, inc. Book

Distributed by Publishers Group West
1700 Fourth Street, Berkeley, CA 94710

ibooks, inc.
24 West 25th Street
New York, NY 10010

The ibooks World Wide Web site address is:
www.ibooks.net

The DC Comics World Wide Web site address is:
www.dccomics.com

ISBN 159687-103-2

First ibooks, inc. printing August 2005
10 9 8 7 6 5 4 3 2 1

Front jacket art by John Watson
Jacket design by Georg Brewer

Printed in the U.S.A.

For Lillie Mae
Who believed enough to buy a ten-year-old a typewriter.

SLEEPERS · BOOK THREE

CHAPTER

1

Sid hadn't been home thirteen seconds before Maybelle started in with the nagging. The roast had been warming in the oven since six and it was nearly eight-thirty before her thoughtless, useless husband found his way home. Which missed the point that Maybelle had been married to Sid for thirty years and by now should have learned two things: First, the more you nagged Sid the later he came home. Second, you don't keep a roast warming in the oven because that will dry it out. Better to keep it wrapped in a broiler bag so the juices keep it moist, and then flash broil it with a brush of butter at about 350 degrees, slice the meat thinly on the bias against the grain, then ladle on gravy and garnish with the julienne vegetables once Sid finally and reluctantly arrived home for his nightly flogging.

Not that any advice would help. Maybelle's argument wasn't about dinner, it was about process, about her life. The oversized muumuu with Snickers candy bars shoved in the pockets and hair curlers were a cry for help. This was a person who actually told time by whether Montel Williams or Judge Judy was blaring out of the idiot box. One of those sad pumpkins destined to be buried with a *TV Guide* clutched by a rigor mortised claw. Wearing big panties with the little ducks on them. On the days she actually mustered the strength to get dressed, she wore sweatpants and loud, oversized floral blouses that made her look like the Rose Bowl parade, well toward the Roseanne Barr end of the Jennifer Lopez/Bea Arthur teeter-totter.

Maybelle was a miserable, lost soul who lived vicariously through Sid and all but held her breath until he came home. Her venting at him was not about him so much as it was about her inability to exist whenever he stepped out of the door.

In the end, arguing was all they had left and, as Sid came home later and later, the whole thing became a vicious cycle: Maybelle preparing dinner at six knowing Sid wouldn't be home anytime before eight. But she set him up anyway because she had nothing else in her life that required her to keep breathing. And even an argument from Sid was attention.

And so it was that the nightly battle in the Hoffmeister apartment was well under way, the two of them going at each other while I stood less than four feet away, staring out of their window at the apartment on the other side of the monorail tracks where Tavares was about to be murdered.

I was wearing an ankle-length black duster, baseball cap and dark sunglasses, like a refugee from one of those Matrix films. My skin was bleach white—inhumanly white. Which was apropos since I was, in fact, no longer human. I stood facing the Hoffmeister's bay window, the nightly rain spattering off of it, in full view of the apartment on the other side of the Seattle Center Monorail tracks. Across the way, Tavares was talking to his doorman for the last time in this life, telling him to send his murderers upstairs.

Neither the battling Hoffmeisters nor Tavares could see me. People could only see me if I chose to let them, so the Hoffmeisters battled on while I concentrated on the job at hand.

Eddie Stengle and Brad Walker entered Tavares' plush luxury apartment. The two men had much love for Tavares, their partner in various business enterprises. The three men had made a fortune helping each other out, and tonight would be no different. Three workaday guys punching the clock.

I didn't flinch when Maybelle threw the dry roast to the floor. The Hoffmeisters' yammering threatened to distract me, but I just screened them out. All things in Creation have a purpose, even the annoying things. My focus was Tavares, who was offering Eddie and Brad a duffel bag I knew contained $300 thousand in unmarked bills. Eddie and Brad backing off, hands raised, as if they had no idea what Tavares was doing, should have been a hint. But Tavares kept to his game, pulling out a fistful of bills as the Monorail blurred past and Sid punched Maybelle so hard she spun into the counter, sending dishes and spices and all manner of things to the floor.

The Monorail passing would obscure normal human vision, but I clearly saw Brad shove Tavares backwards because I was there, in the room with them, and there, in the room with the Hoffmeisters, at the same time. It's a kind of omnipresence, tapping into Creation, being in harmony with it, that frees you of the human constraints of time and place, neither of which having had much meaning for me in a long time. I was once here or there. I was once this person or that person. Now I simply am. Now I understand my place in Creation. My purpose. All of which allowed me to stay focused on Brad and Eddie even as Maybelle plunged a butcher knife into Sid's chest behind me.

Sid screamed as he staggered back, knocking over the dinner table Maybelle had meticulously set earlier at six o'clock. I didn't move. Saving Sid's life—once a natural reflex for me—was never a consideration. There is a Natural Law that suggests natural processes always tend toward disorder. Another expression of the same process is *entropy*. That is, all ordered matter will eventually approach disorder. Systems of harmony and order—more commonly known control systems—become more complex and more ordered by random, accidental and direction-less chance. Who was I to say it wasn't Sid's time?

Heroism—and I was once called a "hero"—imposes one view of order over another. One view says Sid died tonight. Another says the Spectre saved Sid tonight. My role in Creation is to exact vengeance, not make choices and not impose one view over another. As Sid crashed to the floor, blood spurting from his chest, I considered how much Maybelle's life might have changed if only she'd understood that concept.

Maybelle was screaming, "I hate you! Hate you!" but who she really hated was herself, her reflection in his person. His unwillingness to capitulate to her reality, her powerlessness to change him, to mold him and force Sid to properly fit into the movie playing inside Maybelle's head. The feature film that had them chatting pleasantly over dinner at six, Sid bringing her roses and allowing her to control his every waking thought. Maybelle didn't hate Sid, she hated the choices that had led her to this comfortable but ultimately meaningless existence. The wrong turns that lead so many women to exist only for Oprah and six o'clock meals and the kind of chronic self-absorption that forces them into being incredible pills.

It's taken me a long time, but I've finally come to accept that everyone is entitled to their own reality. In the search for truth, we each have to come to accept that my truth may not be your truth may not be her truth. The more immature you are, the more insecure you are, the farther divorced you become from your place in Creation. Instead of harmony, there is chaos as you flail about trying to mold the universe to your view of it, forcing misery on everyone around you. The Inquisition. The Holocaust. Maybelle cooking dinner every night at six.

The Maybelles of the world tend to sabotage their families' futures by alienating a man from his manhood. The desperate woman married to the man who has emotionally checked out, but choosing to see what she wants to see rather than admit she's actually alone in every way that counts, and, worse, that she's not nineteen and not built like Jennifer Lopez. Her prospects for happiness and security are totally screwed if she lets reality in, so she goes on pretending that this man who barely speaks to her, who spends the majority of his time in the street, who never seems satisfied or emotionally invested–this... child...who once pursued her like a house on fire, who professed love and devotion over and over, who stood before God and made a vow to her, but whose interest in her had waned to dry pot roast–she goes on deluding herself that things are fine. Admitting, even to herself, anything close to the truth would be emotionally catastrophic.

The authoritative, pushy, demanding woman, the edge of threat almost always in her voice, even when she's joking, is a cry for help. This is an enormously insecure person. This is someone who wants to be desired and loved and romanced and dragged off to bed but, failing the J-Lo test, has a self-image hampered by the reality of child-bearing or gravity or the march of time, has had her worst fears confirmed by her mate's capitulation to her Mommy act. She's brow-beaten him into accepting her matriarchal role, and his surrender is a damning condemnation for her, a validation of her worse fear: that she is, in fact, not J-Lo. She's Bea Arthur. She is Maybelle. And, worse, This Is Maybelle's Actual Life.

Brad held a Taurus .40 semi-automatic on Tavares as Eddie ripped Tavares' shirt open, revealing the wire the FBI had forced Tavares wear. This was Tavares' only way out, as he would definitely do tall time in the joint unless he gave up Brad and Eddie. Tavares staggered back with the *pup-pup-pup* of Brad's silencer sending blood spatters to the floor. Tavares left this world without realizing the "FBI" agents he was cooperating with were actually Brad and Eddie's pals.

Maybelle, now completely unhinged, repeatedly buried her knife in her husband's corpse while screaming at him, blaming him and exhausting herself as she baptized herself in Alfred Hitchcock blood. I hadn't turned around. I had absolutely no sympathy for either of them.

Brad and Eddie hit the hallway with their duffel, confident no one had heard or seen a thing, when they spotted me at the end of the hall. The albino in the black trench. Brad snapped his Taurus at me, "What the fugh are YOU lookin' at?"

I gave Brad nothing. I simply was.

Eddie displayed his detective's badge as he dragged Brad away, showing me his Seattle Police Department Detective's shield. "Police business, pal. Clear out." Brad and Eddie left me standing in the hall, only to spot me waiting for them at the bottom of the stairs. And I was still at the Hoffmeisters. It's hard to explain and takes a bit of getting used to.

Eddie pulled a .380 SigArms, "I told you, man—police business!"

I gave them nothing as the two detectives moved cautiously past me. They both considered shooting me, but were confident I had not seen them commit any crime and thus could not testify.

I didn't need to testify.

The detectives started their unmarked police car in the alley and sped off, only to find me blocking their exit.

"Christ, there he is again!" Brad had had more than enough of me. In his mind, he had been fair and noble in his own way. Now it was time to deal me out. He hit the gas, kicking the Ford Crown Victoria to just under fifty miles an hour when the car passed through me.

Time slowed to a crawl as the car passed through me as though I were immaterial. As though I were a projection. Eddie and Brad had long moments as the car passed and seconds clicked off, the men scrutinizing this ghost, this shade in their midst.

In those moments, as our realities briefly merged, I removed my sunglasses. Let them see my eyes.

Gave them the Look.

Eddie and Brad instinctively recognized Death when they saw it. Only, I was much more than Death. I was Vengeance.

As the car slowly passed through me, I said two words to them. "Marie Tunelley." The two men now turned, looking at me out of their back window as they sailed into the busy rain-slick avenue at 52 miles per hour—

—and were hit broadside by a newspaper truck.

The Crown Vic imploded as Brad was crushed, the impact ripping his torso from his legs. Glass exploded from the car as the truck shoved it half a block toward the monorail station.

I walked out of the alley.

Eddie, bleeding, stumbled out of the ruined car as the truck driver rushed to see if he could help.

I walked toward Eddie, my unearthly pallor partially obscured by the rain.

Eddie, drenched from rain and blood, opened fire with his Sig. He was aiming at me but he put four into the truck driver who was coming to help him and whom I did not save because saving people is not what I do.

I kept walking.

Out of ammo, Eddie briefly considered his backup piece, but rushed up the monorail stairs instead.

"Who are you?" Brad screamed at me with one of his few dying breaths. I was about to walk past Brad, whose body ended as a bloody mass just below his navel. Brad no longer existed to me. But, for reasons I can't fully explain, I did notice him.

I stopped long enough to take his Taurus.

A monorail pulled into the station as a half-crazed Eddie raced toward the platform.

I was waiting for him.

A handful of locals and tourists exited the train, one of the last of the evening. Walked past me without noticing me. I didn't exist to them.

"Who are you?" Eddie screamed, half-blinded by glass and blood in his eye. I gave him the name.

"Marie Tunnelly." The six-year-old who drowned when her mother's Pathfinder smashed through a guard rail and into the river after Brad and Eddie sideswiped her chasing down one of Tavares' rivals. Distraught over her daughter's death, Marie's mother took a bottle of pills and joined Marie in Creation.

Eddie opened fire with his backup piece, a .38 snub-nose Colt Chief's Special, and bodies began dropping all around me. Shots I could have pulled out of the air or turned back on Eddie with a simple thought. But, as I said, saving people was no longer my purpose in Creation.

There was screaming. Panic. Disorder. A breakdown in the entire system.

Eddie dashed to his left, leaping over a barrier and climbing onto the monorail tracks as the train pulled out of the station. Eddie made a leap for it, barely holding onto sheet metal slick with rain before pulling himself in between the cars.

He smiled at me as he passed by on the monorail. Gave me the middle finger. *So long, sucker.*

I watched Eddie go.

From the platform.

From the alley.

From the Hoffmeisters.

Eddie's panic subsided in waves as he sucked air and tried to steady himself. He was nearly thrown from the monorail when the train suddenly jerked to a dead stop from a speed of forty miles per hour.

Eddie looked up, mouth agape with disbelief.

The Spectre was nearly 100 feet tall, a giant impossibly walking through the elegant Seattle City Center. The rain was now a downpour, clouds blocking out the moonlight and casting the giant in an even more horrific moodiness. The Spectre had stopped the monorail with the simplest hand gesture, the huge train being just a toy to him. Pale white, with a flowing green cloak attached to an ominous emerald hood. The insignia of the Green Lantern Corps was emblazoned upon his chest for no good reason as the Spectre was no longer a Green Lantern and was no longer Hal Jordan. The Spectre was the Spirit of Vengeance; immortal, invulnerable, invincible. The Spectre was, ultimately, all that was left to me, and I took an odd comfort in the curse. Of the variety of evils I had been and evils I had done, joining my essence with the Spirit of Vengeance was most definitely the lesser.

With each step the Spectre took, the railway shuddered and swayed and Eddie was forced to hang on to the slippery wet metal for dear life—an increasingly meaningless gesture. I stooped down to face him.

Let him see my eyes.

"The Spirit of Vengeance has come for you, Detective. Your evil has found you out!"

Eddie threw up, hurling all over the beautiful monorail. He thought he had a move. He knew nothing about the Spectre, but he saw the super-hero trunks—the classic super-hero costume design—and the cloak. He thought, whoever this is, he must be a hero. Heroes don't kill.

"Y-you—you're a Green Lantern, right? Right?" Eddie smiled, rain spattering off of his face: *let's make a deal.* "Look—I can help you! I can point you to a lot of criminals—I—"

I gave him the Look. Even scarier at thirty feet across.

"Wait—you can't—I mean—"

"The stench of evil men demands an answer, Detective! Your destiny waits! So swears—the Spectre!"

"No!" Eddie screamed as the Spectre's massive hand snatched up the Monorail car he was clinging to. The remaining cars jumped the rail but did not fall off. Massive electrical sparks leaped from severed connections, illuminating the giant in Frankensteinian hues.

Eddie scrambled inside the empty Monorail car while screaming at the giant. "Please! Please! I'm begging—"

The Spectre lumbered ominously across the city, heading for Puget Sound. Eddie screaming from the Monorail car in the giant's grip.

I watched the Spectre from the Monorail platform. From the alley. From the Hoffmeisters. I am he and he is me, the Spirit of Vengeance and Hal Jordan, disgraced former Green Lantern, one and the same. A nearly omnipotent being, the Spectre is quite capable of being in two places at the same time. Two time periods at the same time. It is a difficult concept to explain. I simply am.

Maybelle was weeping, now. A mix of tears, blood, saliva and mucus covered her face and neck. I still hadn't turned around. It wasn't my concern.

The Spectre waded out into Puget Sound, displacing several small boats, as Metro Police helicopters approached, shining spotlights on the implausible giant. I ignored all of that. Ignored Eddie. Ignored Maybelle. I kept the harmony of the universe.

I stooped into the Sound and drove the Metro car under water, holding it there while Eddie tried to escape the crushed metal, much like little Marie Tunnelly had tried to escape her car. Even though I was not there, with her, her cries were heard across Eternity—as are all things. The Spirit of Vengeance knew how to tap into Eternity and thus could know things Hal Jordan could not know and see things Hal Jordan could not see. It was a kind of omniscience that allowed me to know the smallest details of events long past or yet to come. As I said, it's difficult to explain.

As the police chopper closed in, I found the monorail car with my heel and smashed it flat, twelve feet into the bedrock below.

The helicopters buzzed around my head at eye level, not sure whether to offer help or open fire. I was unconcerned with either.

I gave them the Look.

I put nothing out in the universe for them. No emotion, no sympathy, no empathy, no hope. I simply was.

And, having done what I came to do—

—I withdrew to the Hoffmeisters, where I finally turned around. the Spectre was no longer in the bay and the news crews, arriving both a day late and dollar short, were already shifting into Talking-Head Mode, speculating what that was about.

The Spectre was both an honored member of the Justice Society and a cruel dealer of death. While this reality puzzled and disturbed a great many people, there was no inconsistency to it. The Spectre, as he existed during the Society days, had his mission and the team provided means to that end. The Spectre, as I now existed, had no use for such contrivances—sitting around tables with gaudily dressed do-gooders. I required no companionship. My mission needed no validation or assistance. I simply am.

I stopped briefly to consider the weeping, pathetic bloody woman at my feet. I let her see me. Maybelle, in shock and grieving, saw me but did not see me. Saw me, but I no more existed to her than she existed to me. She had her reality, I had mine. I sneered down at her in a superior fashion. I despised the damage the Maybelles of the world did to the universe.

Maybelle's noisy grief was completely selfish. The woman, so lost in her own self-absorption, could not possibly realize the grief she was experiencing was more about her own needs. She needed Sid to fight with. To live through. Without him to torture and abuse, she was nothing. She didn't permit Sid even the dignity of death, as even that became about her and her needs.

Maybelle had no concept of the Spectre, the near-omnipotence of my power. She had no concept of that moment, that place in all eternity. And, why should she? After all, I wasn't God. I was just some albino in a trench coat.

For purely selfish reasons, I decided to explain it to her; to reveal some of the mystery of the universe, of systems of harmony and order and the second law of thermodynamics.

I pulled out Brad's Taurus. Aimed it at her bloody face.

Okay. Now I'm God.

This Maybelle understood. Brad's .40 Taurus existed in her reality. Now we were communicating. She seemed relieved. Grateful that her judgment would be so swift.

I put the Taurus in my coat pocket. I wasn't a judge. This business between Sid and Maybelle had less to do with evil and more to do with communication. The Spectre didn't exact vengeance over bad communication. Despite all my power, I couldn't muster enough of an opinion about her one way or the other.

I left her there, wallowing in her chronic self-absorption.

I hoped my next death would be better than Sid's.

2

I was cold.

It was one of those days you hate. One of those days that refused to make up its mind. Are you fall or winter? Are you going to rain or snow? Gray day. The kind of weather that saps the life out of you and turns your thoughts to things like suicide or questions like why Weebles actually don't fall down or why Tony Danza has a talk show. Gray day, and all of Star City was now Hell's Waiting Room.

And I was cold.

The convenience store was hardly that. The cold in there came not from the lack of heat—the cheapskate-tubby-chain-smoking-heart-attack candidate behind the counter kept the thermostat down around 40—but the lack of human kindness. A friendly smile or kind word would go a long way to buttress the sticker shock of Heart Attack's price gouging. Here, on these streets, it's either pay Heart Attack's prices or shiver while you wait on a bus that's never on schedule to take you cross town to Big Mart. Most people on these streets can't afford the time and energy it takes to get to Big Mart unless they are pushing a broom there. Most people on these streets have crying babies only Heart Attack's inconvenience store can deal with. And, rather than be a help to these streets, to these hopeless people,

Heart Attack levies his Bitterness Tax. His Self Loathing Tax. His I'll Never Score With Avril Lavigne Tax.

Heart Attack never saw me, even though I practically lived there, in that raggedy inconvenience store. Aisle three, section two, by the corn chips. Pretending to warm up from Gray Day. But he never saw me. If Heart Attack could see me, he'd never let me in his store, for, surely, a guy who dressed the way I did was hiding a 12-gauge under his coat, waiting to punk Heart Attack for his Old English and Twinkie money. But I wasn't there to rob him, and I was, in the end, completely unconcerned about Heart Attack or his place in Creation.

I was simply cold.

The warmth I was seeking had nothing to do with Heart Attack or with the ratty, smelly little universe of which he was indeed master. The warmth I sought—and sought often—was in Janelle. Janelle was not quite eighteen. She was a black girl with bad hair. She never really fixed herself up before going to work there every day. She was not Halle Berry. She was not Alicia Keys. She was poor. She had a baby. Her baby had no father. She was never leaving those streets.

Janelle spent most of her day bent over doing this and that. Doing Heart Attack's job. Beads of sweat ran across her forehead and her hair became sticky and unmanageable. Heart Attack stole glances at her butt, and she accepted his occasional pawing as the price of working close to home, but Janelle was not for sale. There were lines and Heart Attack knew crossing those lines meant a broomstick in his colon. Janelle had that kind of strength.

More than that, she had that kind of warmth. Janelle smiled. Janelle smiled for me. In the midst of her suffering. In the midst of the hand life had dealt her. She looked at me, and I let her see me. I allowed her to see the hollow shell of a man I had become. Black coat. Baseball cap. Sunglasses. Inconceivably

14

white skin. Not pale skin, sheet white skin. Skin so white it should have sent Janelle stumbling back toward the beer coolers. Instead, she smiled. She shared herself with me.

She named me. Called me Gabby because I talked so much. Which was to say I didn't talk at all. And I already had a name. My name was Hal. But I was ashamed to tell people that. You see, Hal was the name Marty Jordan gave me. And I've dishonored his memory with every choice I've made. Choices that have left me homeless, friendless, and utterly hopeless. A man with no flesh tone and no body heat. Burning with lust for this precious girl who named me.

Not lust as Heart Attack lusted after her. I lusted after her humanity. Her light. Heart Attack's rat factory became the one place on these streets where I could touch just the smallest part of who I used to be. Catch just a glimpse of the humanity I'd left behind long ago. I was cold, and she warmed me. I was lost, but she found me. I no longer knew who I was, but she knew. She took my hand—something most people never did anymore—and she named me Gabby. I had become Gabby, the Spirit Of Vengeance. Cursed to walk the earth doing the bidding of some unseen voice. Forced to fulfill some indentured-servitude contract of uncertain origin and duration. And, there, in the most hateful place of those streets, of Ollie's streets, I found the one pinhole of light fate would allow me. I was cold. Janelle warmed me.

That was why the shattering glass really ticked me off.

The irregular burp of a Tech-9 machine pistol sent the patrons sprawling to the floor as the glass doors in the soda and beer cooler created a fanfare actually louder than the gunfire itself. K-Dogg, hyped up on Crystal Meth and Alpha-Bits breakfast cereal, was grabbing cash out of Heart Attack's register. Cypress Hill blared out of an iPod clipped to his belt, which made me briefly wonder how K-Dogg—whose name was actually Alfred

Terrywood—could hear the police sirens. Then I remembered there would be no police sirens. Police only came through these streets when absolutely needed and only came at platoon strength. On these streets, getting robbed was part of your licensing process. It was as organic as the pervasive hopelessness that enveloped everything and everyone there. The fact was, if you charged five bucks for a quart of milk, this kind of thing was inevitable.

These were lessons from Ollie. These were Ollie's streets. Things he told me while I tried to drown him out with Knicks highlights. While I flipped through flight manuals or pretended to doze off. Things Ollie tried to teach me back when I used to be Hal.

I let K-Dogg see me. "Jump the eff back, nigga!" he barked in his best Jay-Z baritone. Alfred pressed his Tech-9 against Heart Attack's temple, "Don't go bein' no hero!"

I waited. Waiting was my job. Long ago, when I was Hal, my job was to serve and protect. But there, in Hell's convenience store, I was Gabby The Waiter. The guy who waits. My mission no longer to protect but to avenge. I had absolutely no plans to be a hero. Being a hero was no longer my job. But K-Alfred didn't know that. He stepped back into the rack of Mars Bars, on special at three for five dollars, and the noise startled him, causing him to spin around and assassinate the ATM machine in the corner, Alfred Dogg's Tech-9 spitting some twenty rounds per second as the ATM machine squealed and died.

The noise startled Heart Attack, who actually began having a heart attack, spasming and jerking as he lost control of both his dignity and his bladder. K-Goofball took this as a threat and fired at Heart Attack, only Heart Attack was no longer standing where Alfred thought he was. Heart Attack was already smashing into the Dentyne and heading for the floor. So, instead of blowing Heart Attack's head off, Heart Attack only caught one in the shoulder. Of course, Heart Attack was still having a heart attack, but I digress.

K-Dogg was still in full Dumb Hype Mode, fancying himself, as most of these gangster wannabes do, as Al Pacino in *Scarface*. *Say hello to my little friend.* Wary of a stand-off with the cops who were absolutely not coming, K-Dogg made a field command decision: he grabbed Janelle.

Before I could even ask myself why, I extended my fist toward K-Dogg. The fist that absolutely did not have a ring on it. The fist that had not had a ring on it in a very long time. It was a reflex that died hard, aiming the ring at the bad guy. Creating a giant boxing glove or a man-sized mouse trap out of emerald energy. Back when I was Hal.

But, now I was Gabby. K-Dogg had my light, my beloved Janelle. And all I had was a pale, bony fist. Twitchy, K-Dogg jerked his pistol against Janelle's head as Janelle screamed, and I lowered my useless fist that absolutely did not have a ring on it. I gave K-Dogg nothing, no reason to hurt her. I stayed on mission: I waited.

K-Dogg allowed himself a Tony Montana pregnant pause before vanishing into Gray Day with Janelle. While I waited. As quiet settled once again in Hell's convenience store.

"Ya fraggin' idiot! Why didn't you stop him?" The words echoing inside my head sounded an awful lot like Heart Attack's voice. Until I realized it was, in fact, Heart Attack's voice, echoing my own self-loathing. We have a lot in common, Heart Attack and I. I'll never score with Avril Lavigne, either.

I squatted down next to Heart Attack. I was terribly angry at him for getting robbed. Getting robbed while I was there. Because now, Heart Attack was my problem. Now, Heart Attack was dying—more of the heart attack than the gunshot, but it didn't matter. The waiting was over. Now my mission, my new mission, had to begin.

I had to avenge this fat jerk. This price-gouging sack of misery who exploited people at their weakest, who victimized people who were already victims. This lowlife turd who took my light from me, who had now taken away the tiniest ray of hope from my life. She warmed me. She named me. She was my friend. And now, that was all over. Because of him.

"Call Nine One—" Heart Attack sputtered out his last breaths, his eyes going glassy as vessels all over his chest burst and spilled blood into his lungs. He was drowning in his own blood as he demanded I call for help. I couldn't if I wanted to. It was against the rules. Helping? No good. Preventing? No. I was a near-omnipotent creature. An indefinable being of indescribable power who could not operate a telephone. I could hit somebody with it, but I was not allowed to use the phone to summon help or prevent harm.

I was the Spirit of Vengeance. All I could do was avenge. That's how things worked. That was the deal. Hanging around Heart Attack's smelly flea factory just to get a smile from Janelle was not part of the deal. And this was probably the Boss' way of reminding me.

You see, Janelle was becoming more important to me than my mission. Touching her light was becoming my one hand-hold on humanity as I once knew it. But now, this robbery took all of that away. You see, as the Spirit of Vengeance, I had to avenge Heart Attack. I had to punish those guilty of his murder.

And Janelle was in on it.

The gray day was that much grayer as I stepped out onto Ollie's streets. The cluttered and noisy rent-subsidized world thundered on with icy indifference to me or my plight: I'd lost my light. Lost my hand-hold.

I walked the streets more out of reflex than need. As a near-omnipotent being, I didn't ever need to walk. I actually moved about by willing it. I simply appeared wherever I was motivated to. I could approximate something that looked a lot like flying, and if it made it easier for people to process, sure, call it flying. But flying implied limitations I simply didn't have. Who I was and what I did and how I did it were all quite a bit beyond simple explanations.

I walked. And there was an echo of a human moment—much like the pain of a phantom limb amputees often feel. This emotional speed bump hammered me with a reminder of everything I'd lost. Janelle and K-Dogg were in it together. How did I know? It's one of the things I can't adequately explain unless you're dead. Let's just say it's a "universe thing": I more or less reached into Creation and Creation revealed things to me. Things like Janelle setting up the robbery.

I was walking because I was in no hurry to exact revenge against a single teenage mother who had shown me kindness. Who didn't smoke crack or drink, who didn't have any more nefarious a use for Heart Attack's money than diapers and formula for the baby. But, the rules say, now it's my job to hang her from a meat hook or toss her under a bus. That's the deal.

Losing Janelle felt like being dumped by a girlfriend. It's that knot in the pit of your stomach. The pain no aspirin can help you with. It's just going to hang around until it has done its work—hardening you as a little more of your humanness slips away. It's that flinch, that painful reminder of mistakes, hers and yours. On my way to hang Janelle from a meat hook, to orphan her baby, I went over my own mistakes, losing count somewhere around 35,000. Letting her touch me was a mistake. Needing her was a mistake.

I motivated myself into Janelle's tiny, crowded apartment, where her baby was crying. I stood over the thrift store bassinette and, removing my sunglasses, spent a moment with the screaming child.

"My name is Hal." I did not smile. I was less impressed by babies than I'd once been. Omnipotence tends to rob life of much of its romance. Ninety percent of the people on the planet are morons. Only about a tenth of humanity has any real sense of purpose or love or art. So, ninety percent of all babies are just morons-in-waiting. These wonderful bundles of joy parents are so happy with who grow up to become hateful, selfish and utterly clueless morons painting mustaches on the Mona Lisa.

"I know you can understand me. I'd appreciate it if you'd stop all that noise now." The baby quieted, now curious about the ghost standing over her.

I looked around Janelle's crowded, mismatched studio apartment: clothes in boxes because she could not afford furniture. Photos of kids—kids everywhere. Then, I remembered, Janelle is just a kid herself. These kids were her friends. From another life. A life she'd left behind when she became pregnant. Track and field photos. Martial arts. Band. Janelle was a bright girl on track for any number of possibilities.

Until she got Heart Attack killed.

"I reached into Creation and Creation revealed to me about 37,000 different paths your life can take, Claudia," I said to the baby. "Of those paths, easily 20,000 of them will lead you to a place like this, to a life like this. About 10,000 other paths will lead you to suburbia with a fat husband and a mini van. The rest will do better."

Claudia gurgled and played with her toes. I turned around and looked down at her.

"Are you paying attention? I'm trying to help you, here." Wrong. Help was not the mission. Neither was guilt. But, helping Claudia, I supposed, would help me with what I was about to do to her mother.

"Make good choices, Claudia. Be patient. Don't let your mother's loss embitter you. Find your own way." Claudia smiled and rolled over, but I knew she heard me. Creation told me so, babies not being nearly as inert as adults think they are.

Claudia had light, too. Just like her mother. I wanted to touch her. No, I wanted her to touch me. Like Lazarus. The rich man in hell wanting the beggar Lazarus to dip his finger in water and touch him with it. I was both rich man and beggar. I wanted her light.

But, I'd learned my lesson. Not that I'd brought this fate onto Janelle, but that I'd brought this fate onto myself by allowing her to touch me. By letting myself need her. And, as she and K-Dogg came through the apartment door, giggling over their convenience store robbery, the phantom pain moved me from my foolish fantasy.

It was time to go to work.

3

O ne of the buttons from Hector's shirt caught Carol in the eye as they popped, en masse, when Carol ripped his $125 Bill Blass open. *Great,* she thought, *now I'm gonna be winking all day.* Such collateral damage was a sort of occupational hazard for the Ferris Aircraft CEO, who often conducted business under increasingly less than perfect circumstances since she and her husband separated.

Hector tried to kiss Carol but she slapped him as hard as she had slapped anybody, Hector's face spinning around and slamming into the shelf behind him. Carol pressed the flat of her hand against the side of his face, mushing Hector's pale, bony face into the splintering wood shelves as rolls of toilet paper began toppling off, unraveling in a kind of fanfare to Carol and Hector's violent transaction.

Carol pressed her lips hungrily to Hector's neck while bending him back like a pretzel. Hector was surprised by Carol's strength. A woman of reasonable and normal proportions, Carol exerted the kind of strength Hector would expect in a burly bodyguard rather than in someone with Demi Moore's proportions. Carol's ferocity also took him by surprise, as roll after roll of toilet paper created a kind of snow blindness, preventing him from actually seeing her.

Hector's eyeglasses lost their grip, bouncing onto and off of the floor as Carol's heel found and purposefully mangled them. A trophy. A souvenir. More paper. Tissue everywhere. The strong odor of ammonia choking the life out of them both. More things rattling off of shelves, and then Hector cried out unexpectedly and far sooner than he'd imagined. Something blunt hit his head, and Hector tumbled to the floor, tangled in toilet paper.

And completely alone.

Carol was cold.

She thought, surely, $3,000 of Donna Karan wool should adequately warm her, but she was wrong. She blithely scrutinized herself in the ladies room mirror as she tried to repair the damage to her make-up, but soon realized that the damage was too far gone. Hector was grabby and kissed too much. The makeup was a write-off; she'd have to start over.

She stared at herself in the mirror. *I hate my life.* Hector's cheap cologne all over her. Faint hairs between her eyebrows. *Now I'm getting a unibrow.* She looked for spinach between her teeth. She adjusted her bra, sighing with relief as the underwire was making railroad tracks in her chest. She frowned. She was good at frowning. She cursed at me. "I know you're here. I can feel you." She was wrong. I wasn't there.

I was thirty feet down the hall, inside the courtroom, watching Judge Hector Ramirez squint through legal briefs. Beneath his robe, Judge Ramirez's expensive dress shirt was held together by safety pins, and, during the recess, the judge had accidentally sat on his eyeglasses.

I was still in the black coat and hat, but had removed by sunglasses. Not that it mattered since I didn't allow anyone to see me.

The case was Zekis Manufacturing versus Ferris Aircraft, one of about a dozen pending civil suits against Carol's father's company. Carol was struggling to keep her father's aircraft design plant alive amid stiff competition from Boeing and McDonnell Douglas. With China cutting back orders and the U.S. increasingly unliked among foreign nations, the airplane biz was in a real slump. The military being Ferris Aircraft's biggest customer, Carol fretted over her unibrow and quietly prayed for war. War was always good for business.

Zekis, a small parts manufacturer, was about to go under if they lost the Ferris aircraft contract. Tony Cheung pitched Carol a better and cheaper mouse trap over drinks at Spago's and then one of Tony's 2,000 lawyers found a weakness in the Zekis deal, which Carol used to dump Zekis and his twelve hundred family employees in order to save ten cents a widget from Tony Cheung. Zekis sued because it was that or die, with its twelve hundred workers losing the family Chevy and what-not if the plant closed.

It wasn't that Carol didn't care about the families. It was that Carol cared more about Ferris families and their Chevys than she did about Zekis families or the one-horse town in Minnesota that would become a half-horse or, say, quarter-horse town once Zekis folded. Keeping the doors open at Ferris was increasingly hard work. Crying for Argentina or Zekis meant crying all day, every day. Sometimes being the boss means you have to push a button on somebody, and today was the day Carol Ferris pushed a button on Sam Zekis and his twelve hundred families.

I hate my life. Carol's mantra repeated in her head as she splashed water on her face. There was an emptiness she couldn't fill and couldn't escape. A hollowness that often moved her to the shallow end of the pool, becoming a bit two-dimensional because she had excised that person, that third dimension, long ago.

Drying her face in the mirror, she saw her: Star Sapphire. The villain. The ruthless, evil, hateful counterpart to Green Lantern. The woman who killed and then gruesomely dismembered John Stewart's wife. The villain who lived only to see Hal Jordan dead. Hal Jordan, the man Carol Ferris loved, was also Hal Jordan, the man Star Sapphire hated.

She was the missing piece of the puzzle. The third dimension. The soul Carol excised. The terran Queen selected by the Zamoran race—female counterparts to the Guardians of the Galaxy. And, though she had survived Sapphire's evil influence and renounced the power of the Zamoran jewel—easily as powerful as a Green Lantern power ring—Star Sapphire remained only a thought away. There. In the mirror. In her mind. In her little compromises and shortcuts. In the hardened, ruthless person Carol had become in an effort to contain her. Star Sapphire was to Carol Ferris what twenty-year-old Scotch was to an alcoholic. The lure, the temptation, the seduction of power, was always just a breath away.

Carol kept washing. An alcoholic doesn't want a drink. An alcoholic wants ten drinks. Carol didn't just want to wear the costume, she wanted to feel the power from her nose to her toes, and she wanted to let that power have its way with her like Hector in the broom closet. Carol wanted the world, but chose her humanity. The cost was the icy discipline of a ruthless control freak. A discipline she could not let slip even for a second without tragic consequence.

When she looked again, Star Sapphire was gone. There was only Carol.

Even so, at the crack of Hector's gavel, Sam Zekis's families all lost their Chevys.

I hate my life.

Carol Ferris' penthouse looked out over the Bay, providing a spectacular city view at night. While Carol busied herself in the bathroom, I was in the living room, keeping an eye on Everett. Everett Holtzman, who used the handle "Scorpio," was one of Carol's pilots. After me, Carol had sworn off pilots, but Carol had caught Scorpio on surveillance tapes telling his fellow pilots how he'd planned to bag Carol, so she decided to make an example of him.

A bottle blond, ripped with *Bally's 24 Fitness* muscles, Everett was the kind of overly pretty guy who was so vain it was hard to believe he was straight. Bagging his boss at Ferris Aircraft was the ultimate trophy for a guy like Scorpio, a Tom Cruise wannabe with visions of Kelly McGuiness melting in his arms. A guy who cleaned his nails obsessively and paid too much for haircuts.

I still had the black coat. Not that Everett could tell, as I didn't allow him to see me. I just hung out, like three feet from him, over by Carol's pretentious West African tribal mask. Everything in Carol's $2 million penthouse was cynically calculated to make this look like a $2 million penthouse. All picked out by Tobey, Carol's humorless interior designer. Not only did Carol not know what an André Charles Boulle curio was, she didn't actually know she owned one. Turn the lights off, and Carol couldn't make it across the room without knocking something over. Carol Ferris's lavish Star City penthouse was a place to shower and grab maybe four hours sleep before heading back to her real home, the fishbowl at Ferris Aircraft.

Everett hovered while checking his hair in the reflection of the Louis XV Rococo cabinet. He'd finally worn Carol down and won a date with her. He'd spent five hundred dollars on lobster and Harry Connick, Jr.'s jazz band at La Lune. He'd regaled her with tales of performing his BFM well below the hard deck, flying to the elbow with an HCA that forced the bandit down to 200 knots, where he was bleeding energy and Scorpio could enter the WVR fight—in A-G configuration with Mavericks loaded—with his airspeed at 450 knots. Tech-speak and abbreviations which would impress the La Lune waitress but surely insulted Carol, who'd been breathing jet fumes since she could walk and who'd spelled out $TR=V^2/gG$—the equation for turn radius—with her letter blocks in pre-school.

So Everett changed his mode of attack, opening his soul to her, telling her his dreams, tales of his tough childhood on the streets of Allentown. He didn't flirt. He didn't push. Everett tried the oldest plan in the book: sincerity. Honesty. Truth.

Now all of that was about to pay off. He was going to nail the boss.

Moron. He made the mistake nearly every man makes. He failed to accept that the rules of engagement always favor the woman. The woman knows, long before you arrive to pick her up for the date, just where and how far the date is going. Coercion and mischief and guile exist only to bolster the guy's ego. The woman has decided, long before you pulled up at curbside, what was or was not going to happen there that night.

I had no sympathy for him. Everett had worked for Carol for about eight months, long enough for him to know better. Carol used guys like Everett for sport. She might turn him out like a pretzel just out of sheer boredom. Just as an exercise, keeping her diva skills finely honed.

Only a man who truly loved Carol could come to accept that beneath that cold, mean exterior was an even colder, meaner interior. Somewhere inside, Carol was genuinely evil. And that's meant in a good way. Evil in the sense that she knows what she is about. And, while social custom requires she take a stab at being a decent human being and productive member of society, Carol was a villain. Born to be a villain. It was almost noble; the kind of evil you could actually respect.

Everett was swimming with the sharks. He thought he was calling the plays, but this was NFL football. Carol deliberately left Hector's cheap cologne on her, forcing Everett to pretend not to notice. She had Everett's locker cleaned out while Everett gassed on about his daring escape, despite an ECM lockup and ALQ-131 failure, and Connick crooned *Isn't It Romantic?* The guy was simply out of his league with a woman like Carol. A woman who would leave him crying in the rain, wearing only his underpants, calling her name like Stanley Kowalski, just for the sheer sport of it.

Everett should have escaped while he could. Instead, he loosened his tie and took a hit of Binaca while searching through Carol's Bose system for Barry White. I wanted to warn him, to help him, but, as I mentioned, that wasn't the mission. The boss frowned on such acts.

In the bedroom, Carol thought about going after the stray hairs building a bridge between her two eyebrows. Instead, she took another pass at the underwire and ran a hand through her hair. *I hate my life.* She was trying to change the subject. The subject wasn't Everett, the subject was the news. The local news about the bodega murders in Westville. It was the kind of news that angered Carol because it reminded her of me. Reminded her that, despite my best efforts, I was not, in fact, dead. Well, at least not in a manner of speaking. And, that, whatever you thought of me, I was still playing God; behavior Carol had hoped I would some day outgrow.

The Love Unlimited Orchestra struck up the ominous stutter of *It's Ecstasy,* and Carol exhaled, "Thank God." Torturing Everett would at least give her something to do.

"So, Everett, wanna hit the rack?" Carol blithely announced as she marched into the cavernous living room. "My eyebrows are growing together and I've got spinach stuck between my teeth, but if you can get past that, we can bring a vote to the floor."

Everett, no *West Wing* fan, had no idea what bringing a vote to the floor meant, but he got the general idea. And he could care less about the spinach. "Sounds like a plan," he said, abandoning his more complex Rube Goldberg seduction plan as Carol and her $3000 worth of Donna Karan stepped down into the luxurious sunken living room with the 180-degree panoramic view of nighttime Star City. Carol's too-short skirt got even shorter as she plopped down next to him with the aplomb of a seventh grader, her legs crossing in that annoying faster-than-you-can-see fashion and locking knee over knee as hydraulic clamps of sheer will bolted down the apparatus. The good news: a healthy slice of thigh out there, golden in the subdued light. The bad news: the lockdown, a gauntlet thrown.

"Let's make this special," Everett said as he slipped Carol's jacket and blouse off of one shoulder, kissing her. This she allowed. Everett moved to her neck, kissing the nape of it, enjoying her scent as his hand moved to her other shoulder, gently pushing her blouse off of that shoulder as well. Carol allowed that as well. After all, it was a nice bra. An expensive bra. A painful bra.

Everett's moves were high school clumsy, but he became distracted by something: Carol's woodenness. At first he didn't care. Guys like Everett never do, but it flashed in his mind that this woman was his boss, so perhaps he should actually care that she didn't seem involved in this activity. Everett empathically understood that Carol was...counting. He stopped, moving back enough to appreciate her beauty. A beauty that was impossible to say no to. The jacket and blouse off of both shoulders now, the bra making a brief, teasing appearance.

Carol was amused. Not *I love you* amused, but amused, say, the way one looks at fish in an aquarium. *Oh my, what colorful fish.* And, thundering through Everett's brain: numbers. Counting. Carol was mentally counting. *How long before he realizes this is not going to happen?*

"What's wrong?" he asked.

"Who said anything was wrong?"

"Why did you stop?"

"I didn't stop. *You* stopped."

"I stopped because you stopped."

"I never started. You started without me."

"You said I could."

"Yep."

"But you didn't mean it."

"Oh, no, I meant it."

"But...you're just sitting there."

"What's it matter? You got a green flag. What's it matter to you what I do while you do what you do?"

This was the place where Everett was supposed to assert. Men usually asserted. It made them seem somehow more masculine. But Everett was now wiggling in Venus's flytrap. This wasn't a woman, this wasn't even his boss. This was the devil's ex-wife. And, he *amused* her. Nothing kills a guy's ego more than discovering he *amuses her*.

"I—I—" Everett stammered, caught somewhere between assertive and Richard Simmons. Too much, and he's flying charters for Golden Years Retirement Village. Not enough, and the jacket goes back over the shoulders.

Carol got up, heading for the breathtaking view of the bay and the Star City skyline. "Let me tell you a story, Everett."

Everett hated being called "Everett." He was Scorpio. Test Pilot. Top Gun. Main Man. He was a badass, with all the ego and chutzpah that required. The Right Stuff. But, this was his boss, and he was suddenly hearing his own voice in his head, screaming at him to get out of there.

"A long time ago, in a galaxy far, far away, there was a race of beings who decided to bring order to chaos—to become Guardians of the Galaxy, a race of intergalactic policemen.

These little blue guys had vast power, more power than we can adequately conceive of, and they used that power to create a kind of battery—a centralized power source on their homeworld of Oa." Carol opened the patio door, letting in the gray day which had become the gray night. Cold, friendless weather. She seemed not to notice.

"The Guardians of the Galaxy recruited noble creatures from around the universe to be galactic cops. They gave each of these cops a ring, a kind of power ring, that drew power from the main battery and did whatever these guys needed the rings to do."

Everett was caught between the penthouse front door and the patio. The front door meant escape but a certain loss of dignity, while the patio held out the slimmest hope of his salvaging his evening's mission.

"Now, it so happened that one of these galactic cops crash-landed and died here on Earth. Before he died, he passed his ring and his mission on to an Earthman, who succeeded him in becoming the Green Lantern—the galactic cop—of this space sector—Sector 2814."

Space sectors. The woman was talking about *space sectors*. The front door looked like the better idea to Everett. But his ego wrestled with his intellect. *I'm a fighter pilot, dammit. Fly to the elbow.*

"For years, this guy did his job and did it well, becoming the very best of the entire corps. But, in the end, he became corrupted by power.

"Coast City, his home town, was vaporized by a villain named Cyborg. Seven million people dead. Green Lantern was driven insane by the loss, and first tried to recreate Coast City with his own power ring. When that wasn't enough, he realized he needed more power. He flew to Oa, murdered the Green Lanterns there, murdered Sinestro—the sworn enemy of the Green Lantern corps—and murdered all of the little blue Guardian guys except one, by the name of Ganthet, who flew to earth and gave the one remaining power ring to the first kid he met in an alley."

Everett's intellect headed for the door but his body stepped onto the patio where he shivered involuntarily. Thank God it was cold out so Carol wouldn't immediately realize that his shivering was more about his loony boss than the weather.

"Meanwhile, my guy, the Green Lantern, became Parallax, a being of near-limitless power. His efforts to rebuild the universe—and, in so doing, Coast City—were stopped by his closest friends, and everyone figured that was the end of that.

"He later made a play for redemption by sacrificing himself to destroy the Sun-Eater, a mysterious creature that was putting out the Sun, causing Earth and its inhabitants to slowly freeze to death. He sacrificed his life to save the planet, reigniting Earth's dying star."

Maybe if I jump, she'll stop talking...

"Now, here's where this whole business really jumps the shark: his super-hero buddies eventually found him in Purgatory, of all places, where the disgraced former Green Lantern begged them to trust him one last time. He prevented major villains from merging with the near-omnipotent Spirit of Vengeance by convincing the Spirit he himself deserved the punishment.

"The Spirit agreed," Everett had checked out on Carol's story way back at Abin Sur's crash landing. He was freezing and his hopes for a banner night had faded to nothing, "and, that's how a Green Lantern became a ghost. Well, a Spectre, actually. The Spirit of Vengeance."

"Carol," Everett said, shivering from the cold, "why are you telling me this?"

"Just trying to answer your question."

"But, I didn't ask a question."

"Sure you did. You asked me, 'What's wrong?' Don't you want to know, or would you rather we just got on with it?"

Everett thought, *I'd rather we just got on with it.*

Everett *said,* "No...I want to know what's wrong." No he didn't. He wanted to see the elevator doors closing with him inside. But Carol owned his manhood now. Leaving there without scoring was no longer an option for him if he ever wanted to step onto pre-flight without hearing howls of laughter.

Carol aimed a remote control and her 79-inch Sony high definition plasma flat screen clicked to life. The news was still preempting regular programming, droning on and on about the Westville convenience store murders. The shop owner dead of a heart attack. His robbers—a gangsta wannabe named Alfred and a store clerk named Janelle—found dead, stuffed into an ice machine.

The crime scene guys had to bring blow torches to cut K-Dogg and Janelle out of the ice machine. It would be another two days of thawing before the medical examiner discovered K-Dogg's Tech-9—cut into small pieces and force-fed him—still undigested among his stomach contents.

"See that, Everett? That's something this guy would do. This Spirit of Vengeance. It's his signature: some grossly ironic, over-the-top punishment. Melt them like candles or cut them in half with a giant scissor."

Carol switched over to CBN, where Trudy Woodrow was replaying footage of the giant Spectre in Puget Sound.

Carol was talking to *me* now, but Everett had the instinct of a walrus. "The man I knew, the man I *loved,* would never do something like that. Wouldn't even think it. But this...creature...he's become? Yeah, that's him."

Everett was becoming increasingly antsy. He began caring less and less about his rep or his job. "And, you know what he'll do next, Everett? Know what he *always* does after he pulls one of these?"

Carol looked out over the bay. "He comes here."

"Here," Everett repeated, his sarcasm leaping out before he realized it. No doubt, now: Carol was a loon.

"A guilt thing. He just comes here and hangs around. He thinks I can't tell, but I can tell when he's here. I have a Pathetic Sensor that goes off."

Everett had sensors of his own going off, "Maybe I should be going..."

Carol snapped around, grabbing a fistful of Everett's Versace silk shirt. Carol's strength surprised Everett. She didn't *look* like she could forcibly throw him off of the patio with one hand, but now he knew that she could.

"You really *are* slow, there, Everett," she said, annoyed. "I need you here. To do what you do. To take what you want.

"I figure he's hurting enough as it is. Last thing he wants is to stand there and watch me get it on with another guy."

"Stand there?"

"Yes."

"Stand there, like, right now?"

"Like right now, Everett."

Everett looked over Carol's shoulder, peering back inside the penthouse. "Where?"

"How should I know? He doesn't let me see him. Probably thinks that's for the best."

"S-so...he's, ah...invisible."

"No, well, I guess. More like he just decided we can't see him. There's a difference."

"You're...trying to make a ghost jealous?"

"I'm not sure he's able to be jealous anymore, Everett. And he's not a ghost per se. It's really hard to explain unless you've been there."

Everett's fear of losing his job was replaced by fear of losing his life. "Been...where?"

"Dead."

"Dead?"

"Yeah. Dead."

"You—you're dead?"

"Not at the moment, no."

"But...you...*were* dead...?"

"Yes. But only for awhile."

"And that's how you know when he's around...you've kind of been through it yourself?"

"I suppose."

"And you want me to...you want to hurt his feelings...?"

"I want him to stop coming here. I want him to stop anchoring himself to me. It's done. It's *been* done. It has *so* been done between us."

Carol began yelling at me. Of course, I was on the other side of the room, but she couldn't know that. "You hear me, Hal? It's *so been done!*"

She spun around and began yelling at the drapes. "What do I have to do to finally put an end to this...this...whatever this is?"

Everett mentally updated his résumé as he headed for the patio door, "Maybe...I should leave you two alone..."

Carol grabbed Everett and threw him over the railing, holding him by a fistful of his silk shirt, which began tearing from his weight. Everett screamed like a girl. Sixty-two floors beneath him were The Shoppes At The Bay, couples milling about, huddling in the gray night.

"Think you're funny? Think this is playtime, Everett?" It was Carol speaking, but the voice sounded much like Star Sapphire.

Having never met Star Sapphire before, all Everett could do was dangle and squirm, which made his shirt tear even more

and him sink even farther. "I'm a joke to you, Everett? Is that
it?"

"N-no—! Of course—of course not—!" If Carol was straining
under Everett's weight, it didn't show.

Carol brandished a DVD. "Surveillance footage, Everett. You
telling the boys how you planned to bag me." Everett's shirt
tore a little more and he slipped further toward eternity. Carol
knew I was there. This was as much a test for me as an amusement for Carol: she was torturing Everett and me at the same
time.

But I knew Carol wouldn't drop him. Star Sapphire would,
but she was gone. Carol was, at the end of the day, a pragmatist.
Spawning the urban legend of her dangling "Scorpio" off her
penthouse balcony held much more value for her. It was like
money in the bank.

Four minutes later, Everett's jacket hit him in the back of the
neck as he awkwardly tripped out of the front door. "Your gear
will be waiting for you with security. I'll send you a check for
the lobster."

Carol plopped down on the sofa, arms crossed, a pouting
seventh grader.

I was sitting next to her, but I still didn't let her see me.

"She was a kid, Hal. She was just a kid." Carol referred to
Janelle, dead on the news broadcast. A kid, yes. But a murderer.

"Besides, you're not the Spirit of Vengeance anymore—aren't
you supposed to be the Spirit of Redemption, now?"

Yes. It didn't take.

"I really hate you, you know."

I knew.

"You've got to stop this. You've got to let me go."

I can't.

"Hal—I don't love you anymore."

Really tough to lie to someone who communes with all Creation.

"Hal—" she got tired. She thought about hurling herself off of the patio, but she knew that was something I actually would get involved with.

I don't interfere in her life. I ask nothing of her. I want her to be happy. But letting her go is not an option. Not yet. I move about by motivation. Loving Carol is the one selfish business I have left.

The TV droned on about the murders in Westville and the giant in Puget Sound.

Carol and I sat together a very long time.

She fell asleep with the patio door open.

Hi, Carol. I lost a friend today...

CHAPTER

4

I t begins as a distant thunder, rolling across the heavens with a storm warning's clamor.

It swells to envelop the firmament in grand exclamation.

It climaxes with the stentorian bark of an angry God.

It then retreats in the same subtle fashion with which it arrived, leaving in its wake—

—the brightest day.

The Ferris Aircraft X17, Lieutenant Martin H. Jordan's experimental fighter, dubbed "Stingray," thundered across the Delta flats some 75 miles west of Coast City, banking over The Hangar, Sid and Ellie's dustbowl bar, well in excess of 200 knots. Sid, Ellie and the gang gathered outside with Marty's kids to watch the flyover, the final testing of Ferris Aircraft's latest and grandest achievement.

Hal was cold.

It was cold there on the flats that early in the morning. But Hal didn't care. He never cared when he was allowed to ditch school and watch his dad show off a bit.

"Flight Stingray: we're all green," the flight commander's voice crackled through the static inside Martin Jordan's helmet. "Turn to angels twenty-six left and light 'em."

Martin grinned. He'd been testing the Stingray for twenty-three weeks. He knew what the plane could do. Now it was time to push into the record books. Now they were keeping score.

"Stingray Flight: angels twenty-six left, roger. Turn and burn."

Marty grinned at the photo of his wife and sons, Jack and Hal. Marty wasn't the greatest dad who ever lived. His passion was in the sky. The photo was there mainly to remind him to land the plane.

Downstairs at The Hangar, the ratty old sign slammed against the adobe wall and everyone cupped their ears as Stingray made another pass, this time with the afterburners going full throttle and the plane slamming through the so-called sound barrier. Everybody but Hal, that is. Hal could care less if he went deaf: he wanted the full ride. He wanted to be up there—in the cockpit with Marty. And, he swore, some day he would.

The fighter jet rattled like a subway train as Martin leaned into his turn. The pedals froze up and he had to push down hard on them to get them to move. If he could hear above the noise, he'd hear the plane shaking itself apart. But his mind was on the numbers.

"We're working those up now, Bishop," flight control chopped across the helmet static, "we'll have them for you when you touch down. But I think it's fair to say you've broken a few records today. Hope you're happy."

"Happiness is my default position, Flight."

"Listen, get Sam and Geller to turn wrenches on this thing when I set her down. She's a little pissed off now."

"You'd be, too, Bishop, if you got ridden past design specs the way you just rode ol' gal. C'mon home—I'm buyin' at The Hangar."

"Roger that, Flight." Marty pointed the jet at the landing strip some twelve miles out, dropped below the 10,000-foot hard deck and used his flaps to bleed off energy and cut his air speed. Only, the gauges weren't telling him what he wanted to hear.

Marty tapped on his altimeter, and the needle crashed. A quick glance around the cockpit showed all of the gauges doing pretty much whatever they wanted.

"Stingray, Flight: Got a problem, here."

Crackle crackle, Marty deciphered flight control over the mounting static. "Flight, Stingray: Uh, yeah, we're reading what looks like a main bus failure—"

An electrical problem, likely caused by the trial-and-error of flight testing voltage breakers.

"You're gonna just have to eyeball it."

Marty would need to bring the plane in without gauges because the power to the gauges was interrupted, likely by a circuit breaker closing.

"Roger that." Planes falling apart beneath you was just part of the fun of being a test pilot—a human guinea pig. The closest thing to being a circus performer shot out of a cannon. Neither Marty nor flight control were particularly concerned that their $20 million airplane had just turned into a glider.

They might have been more concerned had they realized the jetwash behind Marty's plane consisted not only of engine exhaust but of vaporized hydraulic fluid. Pressure seals had popped on the flyby, and the plane was venting.

Which accounted for the increasingly sluggish throttle and pedals. Now Marty was pushing so hard on the pedals, he was all but standing on them. "Stingray, Flight."

"Flight, Stingray."

"She's pretty pissed, Flight. Forget the bus—how's the hydraulic pressure?"

"Well, Bishop, everything's dead—all the gauges spinning. Probably just a bus failure."

"Yeah, well, I'm standing on the pedal with both feet, and she's not moving. I think we've got a bigger headache than a blown fuse."

Crackling.

Crackling went on for about forty seconds. Now Marty was a bit concerned. Smartass retorts usually meant it's no big deal. Long periods of static meant they were going around the room.

Marty reached behind his flight couch and grabbed the ejection handle. Without pedals or flaps, he had absolutely no control of an aircraft aimed at the ground and moving fast as a bullet.

Crackling.

"Stingray, Flight."

More crackling.

Marty got a good grip on the handle. He was pretty low and moving too fast. Ejecting this low and this fast might kill him. Staying on board almost certainly would.

"Stingray, Flight."

Crackling.

"Flight, Stingray: ah, crap, Marty, I think we lost her. You'd better get out of there."

Something Marty had figured out without the fifty-nine seconds of radio static. Losing the plane ticked him off, though. It meant the stats were no good. They'd have to start over.

"Bishop?"

"Dammit, Flight, you've gotta be kidding me."

Marty had about twenty seconds to live, but living was beside the point. Test pilots were practically fearless. Bailing out was something you did only if the plane blew up, and then only maybe.

Outside The Hangar, Hal squinted in the sun and shivered in the morning cold as he watched his dad's plane coming in for a landing.

"He's coming in! He's really moving!"

Upstairs, Marty took his hand off the ejection handle, figuring that bailing out might kill him; landing the plane might kill him. Either choice, he could be a dead man. He'd rather be a dead man with stats.

"Stingray, Flight: I'm going for it."

"Flight, Stingray: negative. Eject eject eject."

"That's a negative, Flight. Get rescue to spray the field with foam. I'm dumping fuel now."

"Negative, Stingray. Eject."

Hal bolted away from The Hangar as the crowd cheered Marty's final flyby. "I'm gonna be the first one to see him!"

"Dead man either way, Flight. Let's see if I can at least do some good, here."

"Marty—get out of there!"

Hal raced toward the air strip. "Dad!"

"Flight, Stingray: eject eject eject!"

Hal stopped at the edge of the air strip, blinded by a flash of light and a clap of thunder as the cold morning air cut through him.

It begins as the glorious din of a triumphant army.

It grows with the crescendo of an archangel's shout.

It climaxes with a glimpse of the face of God.

It then dissipates across the valley, ushering in—

—the darkest night.

The sound of my own voice startled me.

It scared the life out of Carol, who had dozed off in my lap.

It had been a long time since I had that dream.

"Ah-*hah!* It *is* you! You *are* here!!"

I had no idea what Carol was screaming about. My heart was racing and I brushed her off as I tried to collect myself.

"Hal!"

Not now.

"Hal!"

I snapped out of my disorientation and sneered at her, "Dammit, woman, what?"

Carol, ticked, said, "I should ask you the same question!"

It took me long moments to remember who I was. Where I was. How long I'd been there. And, most of all, that Carol could actually see me.

"Oh," I said. "That."

"Yes, Hal. 'That.' You...haunting me. 'That.'"

"Look, Carol, I've got a lot on my mind, now—"

"Oh, *really?*"

"Something is wrong." I stood up, ignoring Carol as she rambled on. "Something is very wrong. I must have missed something."

"You missed the door, as in please walk through it!"

I spun around, annoyed at Carol's lack of discipline. "Don't you get it? Carol—I fell asleep."

"So?"

"So stop letting your emotions run you like a teenager and *think*. I'm the Spectre. I'm not even alive anymore. I don't need sleep. I never sleep."

"Hal, I'm going to break something."

"Don't you feel it? You felt me—you sensed my presence. Don't things seem...out of place?"

"I have no idea what you're talking about, Hal. I just want you to leave."

"No, you don't."

"Yes, I really do."

"That's just your pride talking."

"And your ego making you think I want to get it on with a dead man."

"Carol—something's wrong. The world...the universe...is not right." I paced toward the open patio door. It was freezing in the penthouse. "What have I missed?"

"Everything, Hal. You've missed everything." Carol's anger only told me how much she still loved me. "Now, please, do the universe a favor: go hurl yourself into the sun. Again."

My back was to her and I was kind of ignoring her because she wasn't helping. An odd sensation ran up and down my back and I felt a tightening in my chest. It had been so long since I'd felt it, it actually took me a minute to give the sensation a name—

—fear. I was actually fearful. With a gesture, I motivated myself into the Spectre's costume. Why the Spectre needed a costume was a question for Dr. Phil. Force of habit, I suppose, but they were my work clothes. I turned and faced Carol, giving her my iciest Spirit of Vengeance mask.

"Nice try," she said. "Just get out."

My mask didn't work on her any better than hers worked on me. She felt my anxiety and that frightened her, though she was at least as unwilling to show weakness to me as I was to show weakness to her.

It was such a stupid game.

But, Carol knew, for the Spectre to be afraid meant something was terribly wrong with the world. And things would likely get much worse before they got any better.

I stepped onto the balcony and motivated myself twelve feet into the air, the Spectre's cloak billowing in the night sky. "When I know something, I'll get in touch."

"Don't bother," Carol said, her back to me. It was such a stupid game. I didn't need to fly. She didn't hate me.

If anything, my theatrics only made her jealous. Like pouring Scotch in front of an alcoholic. Her back to me, Carol clenched her fists and licked her lips, lusting after just one drink of the power she had renounced, of the evil she'd defeated within herself. She missed it. Her entire body ached for it, and my air walking didn't help matters any.

Carol squinted and grimaced and squeezed it out. "Go away." But she wasn't talking to me. She was talking to *her*—to Star Sapphire. And, spinning around with fire in her eyes and a curse on her lips—

—I was gone.

5

S omething was wrong. I could feel it.

Something I had overlooked. Missed. Forgotten.

I wandered the Earth, retracing my steps of the past few weeks, trying to figure out exactly where the universe went off the rails. Before merging with the Spirit of Vengeance, I'd been Parallax: madman who would be God. So I had a lot of experience in these things. It was never the big things—the sun exploding, a black hole collapsing—that destroyed reality as we knew it. It was the little stuff. A sneeze. A misplaced atom or two. You'd be surprised at how little it took to get the dominoes going.

I looked into Creation and saw nothing. Saw a blue screen, like I hadn't paid the cable bill. Which only confirmed my suspicion that something was off. And maybe somebody was blocking the signal.

So, where had I been the past few weeks? There were the bank robbers I had fed to the wild boars. The Colombian drug lord I had vaporized into dust and packed into his own coke kilos. The terrorists I'd strapped to an Ever Bomb that blows them up and reconstitutes them and blows them up again and again for all eternity. The invasion from the Qwardian universe Kyle Rayner—who replaced me as Green Lantern—thwarted. The drunk driver I had drowned by trapping his car inside a giant bottle of Chivas. The right-wing religious bigot I'd driven insane by showing him a picture of my boss. The embezzler who'd suffered an embolism after ingesting thousands of his own contracts. Puget Sound.

Then there was Janelle. My light. My friend. I motivated to Hartford Children's Hospital, where I appeared in surgeon's scrubs and tanned up my flesh to a more human level. I picked up a patient chart in a Saunders aluminum form holder from the nursing station without anyone blinking, and wandered down the hall while looking at the chart. No one noticed me, which actually disappointed me in a way since I had decided I wanted to be seen that evening. Actually, I wanted to be seen only by one person. By my light.

I shouldered into the nursery where a dozen or so infants were either sleeping or crying. The duty nurse paid me hardly any attention at all as, distracted by my medical chart, I made my way to the young woman I'd come to see.

"Hi, Claudia, you remember me?" Janelle's baby was in perfect health, wide awake in the middle of the night. Attempting to fit a toe into her mouth.

"Just wanted to see how you were." Liar. I wanted her to touch me. I wanted her light; not to merely look human, but to be human. If only for a moment.

"Look, the state is going to take custody of you and place you in foster care for a while. I've looked into Creation and Creation revealed several possible candidates for parents. The ones you want are the Reynolds, so don't be a pain when they visit you." The baby gurgled. Her speech ability obviously hadn't developed yet but there was nothing wrong with her cognitive function.

"By the way—you notice anything wrong? Something seems... different...about the world. I can't put my finger on it." Claudia smiled and gestured impatiently with her hands, which meant nothing. "Well, if you think of anything, just call. I can hear you wherever I am."

"You won't find the answers you seek here." The voice actually startled me, and I spun around the way humans spin around. Spirits of Vengeance rarely spin around, but it's a reflex that's hard to unlearn. My aluminum form holder clattered to the floor and a chorus of crying babies began to fill the nursery.

Behind me, another infant, a male, was sitting up in his bassinette. His arms extended and draped along the lip of the bed, his legs crossed casually. A very grown-up pose for a six-month-old. "You're wasting your time. Besides, it's not your concern."

Keeping my eye on this baby, I picked up my clipboard and estimated about fifteen seconds before the duty nurse arrived. "What's not my concern?"

"That's not your concern, either. That's how much it's not your concern, that it's not even your concern what isn't your concern." The baby looked put upon. Like I was getting on his nerves.

I got annoyed. Okay, not really, since I tended to not get annoyed anymore, but I was in Human Emulation Mode, and annoyance was called for. "Look—something is wrong. Very wrong. I can feel it."

"It has nothing to do with you. Go your way."

"It feels like danger. It feels like grave danger."

"It's not your concern."

"It is if I can prevent—"

Now the baby was annoyed, leaning forward and pointing an accusing finger. "There you go again, Jordan. This is what got you messed up in the first place: your enormous ego. *You* have to be the one to do everything."

I think, at that point, I actually was annoyed. Which was

intcresting. Actually, any human emotion was interesting to me. "I have the power—"

"You have nothing. *I* have the power. It's mine, not yours. We made a deal. I'm holding up my end, you need to hold up yours."

"But—"

"Everything in creation has its role. Its time, its place, its purpose. You keep screwing things up."

"So...I just sit on my hands?"

"You don't even know what you're talking about yet. Could be nothing."

"If it were nothing, you wouldn't be here."

"Jordan—you *can* use the flat side of a wrench to drive a nail into a wall. But that's not what the wrench was designed to do."

I swallowed that one as the duty nurse came in. "Be a wrench, Jordan. Keep your word."

The baby snarled at me, shaking a Robert DeNiro finger, "Don't piss me off."

And then the duty nurse was there. And the baby was just a baby. I apologized for dropping my form holder, but she waved me off. *Idiot.*

I wandered back down the hall rather annoyed that, even in my human emulation mode, I was still, apparently, a spectre. The boss had warned me off. Whatever was wrong with the universe was not my concern. My job was to crush child labor sweatshop owners in giant steam presses.

And that was fine with me. I asked for this curse—this Spirit of Vengeance gig—to atone for the unatoneable. The unforgivable. Evil that would drive me insane to have to live with it. Not life, or whatever this is, seemed a logical solution. Without human emotion, the sheer proportion of the evil I'd done didn't impact me the way it would if I still needed to breathe. If I were flesh and bone, the very concept of *trillions* of deaths by my hand would drive me insane—and I'd become *him* again. *That* guy. The lunatic who nearly destroyed everything.

I stepped into the elevator out of habit, but as the doors closed I was the Spectre again. I motivated myself to Gotham City, where the sign outside the warehouse warned POLICE CRIME SCENE INVESTIGATION.

Inside the deserted, ancient building, moonlight intruding through broken glass and reflected off of my pale skin, making me either an incredibly chilling sight or, say, the ultimate pirate of the Caribbean. I stood outside a closet that was, much to my relief, just a closet, and not a transformer bridge—a star gate built by the Qwardian invaders Kyle Rayner repelled a few weeks ago. Green Lantern—and, yes, it's awkward for me to call him that—shut down all Qwardian star gates and cut off their access to thousands of counterfeit power rings spread throughout time and space. The rings were designed to get into the hands of unwitting accomplices, who would become "sleepers"—enemy combatants planted among targeted populations. The Qwardians could then activate those counterfeit power rings via their star gates, and instantly flank us with a preplaced army of sleepers, each with power rivaling Green Lantern's own.

Kyle Rainer had reported the closet as a star gate, built decades before by the Qwardians, and used by a kind of "Hole in the Wall Gang" to evade police. Kyle chased the gang through this gate and ended up in a wholly different place and time.

But the closet was just a closet now. Not a trace of any known electromagnetic or thermal emissions, and it amazed me with how fast I disregarded the boss. I was supposed to be wandering Earth, shade-like. Avenging wrongs. Instead, I was sniffing around to see if a closet was still a closet.

"It's shut down, I assure you." The voice melting out of the jet black might have most people jumping out of their skin, but beings who are aware—in harmony and community with the universc—are difficult to sneak up on. Besides, I expected Batman, though this was impressively fast.

He chose to be a voice. He was in one of his *I'll just be a voice* moods. My back was to him, but I could see him clearly. "So, you've been monitoring this place...and I tripped some kind of alarm."

"Everything in existence emits some kind of signature, Hal. It's all about knowing what to listen for. About being in the right place at the right time."

Batman, a flesh-and-bone billionaire with a crime fetish, was trying to spook me. Me. A man who's been to hell and back and back again. I had the power to level entire cities. He could bench press about 350. I could destroy the world's most powerful beings with the sweep of my hand. He could punch out tubby losers dressed as penguins and so forth. There are no known limits to my omnipotence. Without water, he's a dead man in ten days.

Sell *spook* somewhere else, pal. We're full up, here.

"Don't you want to know why I'm here?" I asked.

"Not particularly."

I tried to read him, but Batman had had years of practice. He put nothing out into the world. A head full of static. I turned to address nothing at all, jet black.

"Something's wrong. I don't know what. But something is terribly wrong."

"Of course it is..." a half-hiss, trailing.

"How do you know?"

"If it wasn't, neither of us would dress this way."

My best Spirit of Vengeance glare. Nothing. It was like scowling at a brick.

I blinked first. "Could be nothing."

"It's not."

"Could be minor."

"It's not minor."

"But you don't know what it is."

"No," he said. And, upon reflection, "But neither do you."

I'm not sure I ever liked him. When I was Green Lantern, he existed on the periphery of my awareness, which is where we both were the most comfortable. I didn't approve of his methods. He thought I was too much of a boy scout. Neither of us had either problem anymore.

A rustle in the black. *Still here.*

Jim Corrigan, the original Spectre, was a police detective. He had the advantage of deductive reasoning. I was a test pilot. Flying by the seat of my pants.

"The word you're looking for is *process...*" Hiss, trailing. Now I was the one putting too much out in the world, and he was reading me.

"Yes," I agreed.

"The worst thing a detective can have is an *opinion.* Opinion works against process."

Taking me to school, now. "Go on."

"Natural law, Hal. Magic, sorcery, God. The second law of thermodynamics. It's all mathematics. The difference being what we process and what we do not."

"Something's wrong."

"Absolutely."

"And it's bad."

"Yes."

"And you don't know what it is."

"No."

"And, that doesn't bother you?"

"No."

"Why?"

"Because that's my process."

"Mathematics?"

"Two plus two, Hal. It's right there."

Another rustle. I was boring him now.

"Will you help me?"

"I'm busy. But you've helped me, so I'll help you. When it's time."

He was leaving. I knew he was leaving, but only barely. I doubt a human being would have realized it because he'd begun throwing his voice, like a ventriloquist, making it seem he was still six feet away when he was more like twelve.

"Things that seem right are probably wrong. Problems solved probably aren't. Right is wrong, yes is no, victory is defeat. Turn things around and start there, Hal. Won't take all night."

But, it did.

CHAPTER

6

In geosynchronous orbit above the planet, Gotham City looked rather like a handful of dust. The old warehouse was not perceptible to the naked human eye, but a scientist with a good satellite telescope could find it. I could see it clearly and in minute detail from 22,300 miles above the planet. It still told me absolutely nothing.

It's all about knowing what to listen for, the man said. About being in the right place at the right time.

The right *time.*

Motivating myself to the orbit of Phobos, the Martian moon, I briefly marveled at the beauty of Creation. Even the swirling, red sandstorms of the ruined Martian landscape—once a living, thriving, lush utopia and home to an advanced race of philosophers and poets—existed in harmony with everything else. That human beings came to be the dominant species of this star system—at least for now—was an orderly progression of a larger plan. Lines on a manuscript we are not yet evolved enough to read.

Looking at Olympus Mons, the largest volcano in our solar system, and Valles Marineris, the Grand Canyon of Mars, nearly as long as the United States of America is wide, I marveled at how well sorcery or spiritualism—or however regular people think of the source of the Spectre's power—understood the laws of science. At the speed of light, it would take at least five minutes to get to Phobos. But I was there in the time it took me to want to be there. And, in the time it would take me to want to walk along Miami Beach, I would be walking along Miami Beach, with no appreciable time having elapsed.

Moving at speeds approaching or surpassing the speed of light—hyper-fast travel within general relativity or "warp" speed, if you will—creates fundamental problems with things like watches and calendars. But, magic—mysticism, spiritualism—all of that seems to overcome such trivial obstacles as relativistic rules for time and space. *Paper covers rock.*

The hand of God? Or is God simply science we do not yet understand?

I'd spent my entire life being a scientist. And, yet, every time I charged my power ring and pulled on the green leotard I defied logic, reason, method and process to go dashing around the solar system—the *solar system*—and home again during the space of a Super Bowl commercial break.

It actually took years for me to surrender myself to the notion that I could dash to the Kuiper Belt and back and not find everyone I knew dead for centuries. That the Guardians realized how important community—love, family and, yes, spirituality, meaning and purpose—was for temporal creatures. Part of the magic in the rings was immensely complex variables that dealt with general relativity, making us not only space travelers but time travelers: always moving forward and back in time as we traveled immense distances to perform our duties.

Of course, the notion of a magic ring was insipidly childish and utter nonsense. For years, my effectiveness and, frankly, my power, was limited by how smart I thought I was. By how well I thought I understood physics. It wasn't until I stopped wriggling in the mousetrap that I began to actually understand what science is all about: rational inquiry into things we cannot explain. Mysticism. Theology.

The magic Green Lantern ring was only magic because my mind hadn't yet evolved enough to comprehend how complex a machine it was. Even now, in my oneness with Creation, in my grasp of things seen and unseen, I am comfortable with the ring without completely understanding how it works. I have matured to the point that I accept the fact that it does work. That it simply is. And, that simply *being* can and often is sufficient.

That acceptance has made me much more sane. Much more powerful.

Much more dangerous.

From Phobos, the universe still felt off-kilter. I could see more and understood less. The larger the palette, the more detail to process.

Process, the man said.

In Gotham, I was performing Batman's process. Imitating him. Which is faulty process, since I am not, in fact, him.

I simply *am.* And that is sufficient.

Motivating myself to Ceres, within the asteroid belt near the massive gas giant Jupiter, the solar system still seemed wrong. And I still couldn't put my finger on it.

Process.

Don't do Batman's process—do the Spectre's process. *What am I missing?*

I motivated myself to Charon, the icy moon orbiting Pluto near the extreme edge of our solar system. Nothing. Everything. The vastness, the simple incomprehensibility of Creation. The unlikely logic of it all—the *math*—demands not only science but something beyond that.

Architecture. Art. Purpose.

Perhaps, at the very end of intellect and reason, there is a precipice beyond which no rational thought exists. Perhaps faith involves leaping into that abyss and, in so doing, elevating our thinking beyond what we can prove on paper. Without dismissing intellect or reason we can evolve both and, in so doing, find that small piece of ourselves that we've been missing.

Pondering the imponderable took my mind off the fact I was no closer to an answer than I'd been at the warehouse. Something was desperately wrong but I had absolutely no clue what it might be.

As Green Lantern, the trip to Pluto might have taken me twenty minutes. I now realize the trip took twenty minutes to keep me from going insane. The real magic of the Guardians' rings was making interplanetary travel occur along seemingly rational lines flesh and bone types could process. After all, if the power ring could get me to Pluto's moon in twenty minutes—a trip that would take nine years and five months under the most optimal orbit alignment and by the most advanced space craft available to man—it surely could do it in the space of a thought. I could have simply *willed* myself there. And the ring would have automatically compensated for the time there and back—

—then it hit me: *process*. Not Batman's. Not Spectre's. Hal Jordan: what would *his* process be? Hal was a scientist, not a detective. Not a Spirit of Vengeance. Hal's process would be much more empirical.

In special relativity, spacetime does not require the notion of a universal time component. The time component for events viewed by people in motion with respect to each other will always be different. In special relativity, in spacetime, simultaneity exists, but we cannot perceive it if the distances are too great.

Right "now," whatever "now" means, someone standing on Charon, Pluto's moon, would be seeing Earth as it happened five hours ago, since it takes light that long to move from Earth to Pluto. Moving from Earth to Charon in an eye blink would require me to move at many times the speed of light, which is impossible. But somehow I am able to circumvent that limitation. The Guardians' spacetime compensation envelope allows for that—for me to move great distances without the passage of significant time. The trip to the edge of the solar system felt like twenty minutes because, somehow, the Guardians figured that would seem about right to me.

But, as Spectre, the Spirit of Vengeance, that was a crutch I no longer needed.

I spoke to Creation, which was still not revealing much to me but did my bidding anyway. "Turn it off!"

I needed to turn it off. Turn off the magic. The inexplicable compensation envelope for spacetime travel. The logic bubble that kept me from going insane when I moved from Earth to the farthest point in the solar system in only twenty minutes. Even though I was no longer Hal Jordan, no longer Green Lantern, I had instinctively been moving about the universe in a very...Green Lantern way, still using a time/space compensation scheme similar to the power ring's buffers.

I decided to experiment a little, now moving through time as well as space. No longer compensating for faster-than-light travel, I motivated myself to Miami Beach during the time I saw seeing it from Charon, arriving half a day before I'd left Gotham City. The universe was still wrong, still off. I motivated myself back to Charon and back again, arriving in Miami the previous day. Before Janelle. Before Maybelle. The universe still felt wrong.

But, I was on to something.

Process.

I motivated myself to the Pleiades cluster, some 400 light years away. The most famous star cluster visible to Earth, the Pleiades can be seen without binoculars from even the most polluted cities, offering hope and wonder to even the most hopeless among us. The Seven Sisters, a reflective blue nebulae that surround the bright cluster of 3,000 stars and low-mass brown dwarfs, is Creation's gift to us all. A humbling testament to how small we are in the scheme of things, and how great we are, as part of that scheme.

To the Spectre, the Pleiades was merely another rest stop on the Intergalactic Jersey Turnpike. But Hal Jordan had explored only the smallest fraction of what were potentially thousands of cultures just in this one system alone, the Pleiades being one of billions of clusters of systems in the universe. Just being there momentarily overwhelmed me with awe and wonder—further exposing an unsettling vulnerability, a humanity that was, in and of itself, evidence that the very universe I so appreciated was somehow way off-kilter. The Spectre wasn't a space explorer, wasn't an intergalactic defender. This was loafing on the job, and I'd already been warned by the Boss.

With the space/time compensation still off, moving much faster than the speed of light, I motivated myself to Balmerino Abbey, arriving in thirteenth century Scotland. Cold, damp. Gray day. A gentle and winning loneliness that demanded pipers and drums. Mist on the moors. A place of ghosts.

Suddenly, everything was right again. The universe, my place in it: it all made sense. The vibrations, all familiar. The currents of existence and awareness: comfortable and comforting. There, standing in the cobbled courtyard bordered by three arches of the Chapter House near the winding, cobbled Night Stairs, my cloak billowing ominously in the cutting morning breeze, the Spectre was surely that—a vision of God's judgment and wrath.

Drinking in the morning fragrance, the wind whispering by

my ears, I closed my eyes and allowed myself the moment. The humanity. Bread was baking. Children's laughter echoing off of the hills.

Morning.

Like I was noticing it for the first time.

"Ad Deum qui laetificat juventutem meam."

To God, the joy of my youth, I heard a gentle voice say.

"Emitte lucem tuam et veritatem tuam: ipsa me deduxerunt et adduxerunt in montem sanctum tuum, et in tabernacula tua."

I turned to face the terrified young novice. She could not have been quite fourteen years old. Marie Tunnelly. She was crying, her tiny body rigid with fear and awe at this vision. Terror struck through her even as she blessed God for choosing her to receive this theophany.

I translated her words, mostly for my own benefit, "Send forth Thy light and Thy truth: for they have led me and brought me to Thy holy hill," I gently said to the novice, surprised I remembered it from Mass, "and Thy dwelling place."

She fell to her knees, bowing. I'm sure the Boss was irritated. It was a huge distraction.

"Don't be afraid," I said, as gently as I could. I briefly thought of either vanishing or assuming a more human guise, but figured that'd just make things worse. "And do not worship me. I am but a mortal man."

She wasn't buying it. She knew a spook when she saw one.

"Touch me." I extended a pale, bony hand. This was me being selfish. I wanted her light. Just the smallest fraction of it.

The novice looked up with tears welling, completely shaken, my hand close to her. It wasn't enough for me to touch her, I wanted to *be* touched. To warm myself, if only for an instant.

"Go on," I whispered. "Let me show you."

Humbled and shaken, the novice shared her light with me,

completely oblivious to the irony, that, if any soul was being saved it was mine.

I stoically looked down on the novice. I considered smiling but thought she'd pass out. "Now, go in peace."

She paused a respectful moment before scurrying back toward the Chapter House.

I paused to cling to fleeting moments of how glorious, how excellent, my humanity once was. And how I'd squandered it.

I allowed myself regret; the quiet dignity of suffering.

And then I remembered who I was. What I was. My place in Creation. And it alarmed me that, yet again, the Spectre's immortal shell had failed me, exposed me to human weakness. Whatever was wrong in the universe was certainly not my concern, and yet my weakness—Hal Jordan—would give me no rest until I at least figured out what the threat was. Then I could alert the Justice League, or whomever, and it would be their problem.

Having found a point in time where the universe seemed normal and stable, I now had a clue as to how to figure out what was wrong by first figuring out when it went wrong. I finally had a process.

Bells tolled forebodingly in the courtyard as I narrowed my eyes into my very best Spirit of Vengeance glare. I'd found my process: *when's the last time you knew things were true?*

"Turn it back on!" I demanded of Creation and Creation continued to work with me, once again providing the inexplicable time/space compensation envelope as I motivated myself around the universe.

By adjusting both my speed and the depth of the compensation envelope around me—a little more, then a little more than that—I was able to slowly click time forward toward the "present" until I found the last time the universe seemed right to me.

It was moments before Kyle Rayner defeated Sinestro.

CHAPTER

7

Kyle was cold.

It was one of those 'tween days in New York City, the days when the weather refused to make up its mind about what it was going to do. It was cold and damp and unpleasant and Kyle's save-a-nickel landlord had the thermostat locked off at 58 degrees, though the joke was on him because Kyle kept a small space heater going all day by his drawing board and the electricity was included in the rent. Regrettably, fire insurance was not, and the growing pile of discarded paper at Kyle's feet made a dangerous combo with the space heater, but it slipped Kyle's mind because Kyle's mind, Kyle's very soul, belonged to Howard.

Not that Kyle loved Howard or even hated Howard. Howard simply was. Howard was a force of nature and, frankly, if Howard didn't exist, there'd be somebody else Kyle would be obsessing over: Tom. Paul. Nicole. Voices on the other end of a telephone always on the verge of being shut off because Kyle had been immature enough to embrace his artistic side rather than actually go for that nice, union factory gig. He could have been plant supervisor by now, pot belly and dental plan, home at 6:30 to the little woman and the fried chicken. Instead, he was Kyle the Miserable, singing for his supper, making a living by being creative. By being an artist.

Creative expression is extremely cathartic and fulfilling until you actually decide to make a living doing it. Making a living by doing something creative—writing, drawing, dancing, fire-eating—requires a kind of bastardization of the creative impulse. A kind of Caged Monkey riff, where You Must Now Be Creative Every 28 Days Or Else. Whether you feel like it or not. Whether the impulse is with you or not. Bus drivers, for example, rarely toss and turn all night obsessing over where they will drive the next day. They show up, and somebody tells them. They get their bus and that's that. At the end of the day, they park the thing and go home to the fried chicken. Creative types, however, can never leave work at the office.

Kyle could always tell you how long it would take to clean his apartment. It took him three hours and twelve minutes, exactly, to clean his apartment because he had a system; a start-the-dishes-sort-the-laundry-while-he-did-other-things system. Start in the bedroom, work backward. But Kyle could never tell you how long it would take him to draw a duck. I mean, to most of us, a duck is a duck. But an artist, a real artist like Kyle, wants to know the duck's name. Spends three hours Googling duck names, swinging by a few online fan sites hoping for an ego boost only to discover WWW.50REASONSKYLERAYNERSUCKS.COM. Which, of course, now required at least two hours of return fire to the message boards. Kyle then spent another three hours in angst over the duck's breed—the writer clearly being an idiot, having picked a breed that doesn't work for the story. Then Kyle needed to fully understand the duck's motivation.

All of which drove Howard nuts. Howard was Kyle's editor. Howard had been editing comic strips for thirty-two years and had contempt for all freelance artists. To Howard, they were all Kyles. These morons who make all of this money in their paja-mas. Who get paid more than his entire day's salary to just draw a damned duck and they can't even do that within a reasonable time. Howard had absolutely no sympathy for the Kyles of this world and reminded Kyle of that every day when Howard would call and remind Kyle a line was forming outside Howard's door of freelancers waiting to take Kyle's job if Kyle couldn't turn in the damned duck already.

So Kyle was cold. Shivering in a tee shirt and boxer shorts while huddled over his board, wrestling with the duck while fighting the impulse to fly down to New Orleans and fix Trudy Woodrow's hair. A fine and noted journalist, CBN News Anchor Trudy Woodrow had the severe, angled face of a prison guard, and either had the worst taste in hair styles or the network was just having a little fun with her, because, every time Kyle saw her he got a little colder and wanted to hide the Dalmatians.

Kyle was also late on his bills, which kept him glancing out the window for the Comcast truck as he figured any day now the cable guy would make Trudy go away, and one eye on his DSL connection indicator light, making sure it was green and not red.

Next door, Cody the yellow Labrador was barking. Cody was always barking. Usually barking at nothing. Barking was Cody's hobby. Cody's master would leave for work around seven in the morning, and Cody would start barking. And it wasn't the little scrappy bark of a terrier or a toy poodle. Cody's was the meaty, bassy, booming bark of a 125-pound *Dogasaurus rex* who got bored and annoyed at being left home alone all day and would take it out on the world around him.

Stress and indigestion wrecked Kyle's concentration as he went Duck-Trudy-Cody, Duck-Trudy-Cody, bang on wall, scream at dog, look out for cable guy, check DSL, Duck-Trudy-Cody.

I hate my life.

In a tray near his drawing table was the polished emerald metal of Kyle's Green Lantern ring. The ring rather mocked him. *Lets go for a ride.* Kyle sneered at the ring, which he took off while he was drawing because the weight threw his hand off. "No," Kyle said out loud to the ring, "Howard will kill me."

Screw Howard. He'll wait.

"He's *been* waiting."

He'll wait some more. C'mon—put me on! Let's hang out!

Kyle sucked it in, choosing to be a grown-up. "Can't."

Can.

"No way."

Way.

"I need the money."

Go to Africa—grab some diamonds. Screw Howard.

"No."

And lets punk-slap the dog on our way out.

"Can't."

Punk.

Kyle was more than halfway through the sixtieth draft of the duck. Mind you, Howard probably would have accepted Kyle's third or fourth attempt but that's the artistic process. Artists never want you to see how lame their work really is. By the time they turn something in, know at least several earlier drafts have hit the floor dangerously close to the space heater.

If Kyle could just stay focused, he could turn the duck in and begin the second part of the creative process: chasing the check. He'd been keeping Howard waiting for longer than he ever should, and he suspected Howard would return the favor on the other end. See, Howard had been at this long enough to know the only reason an artist ever turns in anything at all is that they are desperate for money. Soon as the duck hits Howard's desk, that's like publishing an announcement in the *Times*. KYLE'S RUNNING FROM THE CABLE GUY. The small victory any editor ever has over the Kyles in this world is making them sweat over the check.

Duck-Trudy-Cody. It was the circle of life.

I'd been sitting in Kyle's cramped work room for nearly two hours trying to figure the guy out. Green Lantern. *This* was Green Lantern. While I was meticulously selected by the dying Abin Sur to succeed him as the protector of Space Sector 2814, Ganthet—the last surviving Guardian—tossed Kyle my old power ring at random. While I spent years struggling with my intellect, with my appreciation for science, Kyle just put the thing on and started flying around. It was a *magic ring.*

The horror of my failures notwithstanding, I did my best and gave my all to protect the universe. And now, some kid not qualified to deliver pizza has the universe's most powerful weapon in a soap dish next to his drawing table.

So, yeah, it took me a minute to let him know I was there. The conversation I might have started two hours ago wasn't the one I'd come there to have.

Two hours, and he still hadn't finished that duck.

Kyle was either too distracted or too inexperienced to realize I was there. His brief stint as the omnipotent Ion had apparently taught him less than it should. Even though he wasn't wearing his Green Lantern ring, the ring was close enough to alert him to my presence, but Kyle had a lot on his mind.

Too bad. Being a Green Lantern is a tough racket, kid.

"You have a problem," sent Kyle's arm sweeping across his desk, knocking bottles of ink and cans of brushes over the side. Kyle spun toward me with a snarl and instinctively extended a fist on which there was no ring.

I was pleased to see I wasn't the only one who did that.

I gently poked a finger in the direction of the soap dish. Kyle turned to see I was pointing at his power ring. "Oh, yeah, thanks."

"You scared the snot out of me, Spectre." *Spectre.* He called me *Spectre.* Guess I had that coming. Ex-senators are called,

'Senator.' Ex-presidents are called, 'Mr. President.' *Spectre.* Guess I should be used to it by now.

"I'm a little busy here—"

"Yes," I said, icily, "the duck."

Kyle was the anti-Batman, spewing so much of himself out into Creation that reading him was less about reaching in than it was screening through "the abundance of Kyle". He felt stupid, telling me how busy he and his duck were. He immediately realized if I was sitting in his studio, all hell was breaking loose.

"Sorry. What's up?"

"The Weaponers of Qward—you foiled their invasion. Defeated their Sleeper—"

"Eddie Roach, yeah. The guy with the Sinestro ring. The ring turned him, literally, into Sinestro—"

"And so forth," which shut Kyle down. Not talking to a chimp, here, Kyle. "The Qwardians planted thousands of these rings throughout time and space—thousands of sleepers. Thousands of potential Sinestros."

Kyle blinked, wondering if it was his turn to speak. "Yeah, but we shut down the transformer bridges—the star gates between the Qward dimension and our own. We cut off the rings from their power source."

"Did we?" I gave Kyle The Look. Kyle swallowed. I enjoyed knowing The Look still worked.

"What are we talking about, here, Spectre?"

Out of habit, I began pacing around. Lots of drawings of some young woman. "The Qwardian universe exists in parallel to this one, on a different dimensional plane. Their physics are startlingly different from ours, even to the point where the Green Lantern power rings have limited capabilities there. They called it, 'antimatter,' and I suppose that description will do for now.

"The Qwardians see most things differently than we do. Music is noise. Art is repulsive—"

"Good is evil," Kyle got to the point. "To Qwardians, evil is the natural order of things. Hating Earth seems logical and useful. Expanding their antimatter universe into this one would probably destroy both, but their goal is a kind of inter-dimensional imperialism."

"Their goal is revenge, Kyle." Jade. The girl's name was Jade. Jennifer-Lynn Hayden. Alan Scott's daughter. "They're mad at us."

"They're mad at *you,* Spectre. Hal Jordan handed them their hats on several occasions."

I studied Jade. Kyle was actually a very good artist. "Qwardians don't make those kinds of distinctions, Kyle. A Green Lantern is a Green Lantern. A human is a human. A human who is a Green Lantern—well, there's your two-fer."

Kyle writhed in his chair. He felt Howard breathing down his neck. "I really don't see where this is going—"

"Neither did I. Took me days to figure it out. To get what was wrong with the universe. But I get it, now."

"You do?"

"Yes."

I waited just to wait. Just to listen to Cody bark. Just to see how long Kyle would sit there without thinking about that duck.

Kyle pounded on the wall, "Cody, shut up!"

That seemed to do it.

"Hal,"—Oh, I was *Hal* now—"what's up?"

"Math, Kyle. It's all about numbers. Zeros and ones."

"Hal—"

"If Qward exists in an antimatter universe. If music is noise. If art is repulsive—"

"—if evil is good," he offered.

"—then why do we believe shutting down the transformer bridges rendered the Sinestro rings inert? Why do we think that, Kyle?"

That one I just let float out there a minute.

Cody started barking and the phone rang as the Comcast Cable truck pulled up outside.

I gave Kyle The Look.

"So, what do you wanna do?" he asked.

"Me? I've got to see an iron worker in Pittsburg who murdered his lover's husband. I'm going to weld him into a steel plate."

"You're joking—" He pounded on the wall again, "Codeeee—!" Kyle gave me the one-second index finger as he answered the phone, "Yes, Howard. Sure, it's done. No, really. I'm gonna drop it off in—yes, Howard. I—no, yes, Howard—"

And then, Howard was gone.

"Hal, I mean, what's our move?"

"'We' don't *have* a move, Kyle. I don't do that sort of thing."

"But—you helped me with Sinestro and the Qwardians—"

"And got yelled at. I've got a boss, too."

"But—your boss is—I mean, he's—"

"Reminding me everything in Creation has a role and a purpose."

On the TV, Trudy Woodrow went to blue screen.

"Hal—we could be talking about *thousands* of Sinestros."

"Which would explain my being here."

"You've got to *do* something!"

"I did. I came to you."

"B-but—how do I stop them? What do I do?"

I moved toward the door. Not that I needed a door. "Change the gravitational constant of the universe."

"What?"

This kid knows nothing. He's got a *magic ring*.

"Gravity arranges matter in thin filaments. High-density regions undergo collapse and ignite bursts of star formations. These proto-galaxies stream along filaments and meet at nodes, causing a buildup of galaxies and creating universal constants, the basic rules of how things work.

"Tell your power ring to emit a wide-spectrum neutrino pulse. The neutrino is an elementary particle. Its mass is very small, so it only interacts through the weak force and gravitation.

"Because the neutrino only interacts weakly, it has no noticeable effect on ordinary matter. In other words, you won't break anything. But the Qwardian power rings—designed and manufactured in the 'Antimatter' Qward universe where the rules of matter and gravity are vastly different—emit an 'Antimatter signature,' if you will, which will likely react with the pulse—"

Kyle looked like a girl scout left in the rain.

I regrouped. "Tell your ring to emit a wide-spectrum neutrino pulse. It'll work like an EM pulse, sending a spike to the Sinestro rings. Then just tune in to Creation to see where the rings all are, and summon them to you."

"How?"

I was really trying not to dislike Kyle. "By your *will*, Kyle."

Out of habit, I used the door. "It's not that big a deal, Kyle. Turn things around and start there. Won't take all night."

But, it did.

So far as I was concerned, the entire matter of the Sleepers clean-up had been laid to rest. So, even though I still felt a great disturbance in Creation, I had every reason to assume the trouble would soon pass, and pass without my intervention, which would please the Boss.

All of which is my way of explaining why, at that time, I had no idea Kyle would fail so miserably after I left. Being nearly omniscient, of course, I eventually knew everything that transpired.

As it turned out, Kyle put his power ring on, and recharged

it by Inserting his fist into the bell of his power battery, which was, as all Green Lantern power batteries were, crafted in the shape of a large green railroad lantern.

In his boxer shorts.

Change the gravitational constant of the universe. Change the gravitational constant of the universe. Change—

I had an oath. A very solemn oath.

Wrote it myself.

Change the gravimetric universal constant. Change the positional consistent gravimetric constant universal. Change—

Kyle merely stood there. In boxer shorts. Fretting over simple instructions.

Then he ran to the window. "Oh, jeez—"

He looked out of the window, hoping to see me flying away. "Where—Hal! Hal!"

As if I actually did that sort of thing. Flying. It's so...pedestrian.

"Crap," Kyle exclaimed as he hastily dropped to his drawing board. "Gotta write this down—change the universal graviton consistently—"

Which was about when he started slamming his head against his drawing table.

"Stupid.

"Stupid.

"Stupid.

"Stupid.

"Stupid."

Which got Cody barking again. About 9.2 on the Richter scale.

"Cody! Cooo-deeeee!"

Kyle pounded on the wall, "Shut Uuupppp!"

In the midst of his panic, Kyle remembered the duck.

"Crap," he spat as he yanked his power ring off. The ring landed with a loud clink in the soap dish as Kyle put the universe on hold for five more minutes so he could get Howard off his back.

This was Green Lantern.

"C'mon," he muttered as panic ripped through him. He was down to the webbed foot, little dashes of grass along the horizon line. All he needed was three minutes, tops.

He wasn't going to get it.

WOOF WOOF WOOF WOOF WOOF WOOF WOOF WOOF WOOF WOOF WOOF WOOF WOOF WOOF WOOF WOOF WOOF WOOF WOOF WOOF WOOF WOOF WOOF WOOF WOOF WOOF WOOF—

Cody was having one of his meltdowns. It sounded like mortar rounds.

Kyle snapped, raising off his seat and pounding on the wall with both fists, cracking the paint. "Dammit, dog! Shut up!!!"

WOOF WOOF WOOF WOOF WOOF WOOF WOOF WOOF WOOF WOOF WOOF WOOF!

Kyle took a moment to focus. To breathe. To sort out priorities in his head. Spinning in circles was what Kyle used to do, when he was the novice tripping over his own feet. But Kyle was a pro now, a real grown-up. Kyle was Green Lantern.

Everything else would have to wait: dealing with the threat of the Sinestro rings took priority. Kyle jumped up from his drawing board—

—and a grotesquely mutated Cody, with several dozen eyes and weighing, at minimum, 1,000 pounds, smashed through Kyle's door. As big and as ferocious as a lion, this mutated dog knocked Kyle back into his own apartment with a deafening growl and a maw that could snap Kyle's head from his shoulders.

"Ghaaaaaaahhhh!!!" Kyle heard himself scream before he actually thought to do it.

The beast pounced and Kyle barely evaded. Lightning fast, the beast twisted and its jaws snapped through Kyle's cabinet like it was made of straw, books raining down on Kyle as he tried to get his limbs to move faster. Panic coming in waves. His mind said 120 miles per hour but his motor skills were doing the speed limit.

All he needed was, maybe, a second to get his bearings. The beast knew that. The attack was relentless, Kyle scrambling to get out of the way of this horrific nightmare.

Kyle twisted and scrambled but this thing from hell was far faster than it looked, and it sunk its maw into the floor—Kyle barely evading a death strike to his neck.

It took Kyle eight or nine entire seconds to remember he was Green Lantern. But, he finally did, extending his fist toward the hell beast.

A fist that absolutely did not have a ring on it.

The Beast pressed its massive, drooling maw right up against Kyle's face, and bared its fangs at him before slowly shaking its head left to right as if to say *Dear man, don't you realize I'm going to eat you?*

And then the beast actually *said,* in a horrific guttural, "Foolish man."

The last thing Kyle actually remembered seeing before blacking out was one of the Sinestro Sleeper rings embedded in the beast's paw.

CHAPTER

8

Lieutenant Martin H. Jordan's photo came to be just another thing for Ellie to dust. Just part of the clutter on the wall of the Hangar. The run-down old pilot's bar on the Delta Flats had, in the ten years since Marty's death, become even older and more run down. But that was actually part of its charm. Sid refused several offers from old man Ferris himself to either buy the old joint or renovate it. As savvy a businessman as Carl Ferris was, he wasn't a pilot. He didn't understand the pilot's creed, that macho crap that enabled flesh-and-bone human beings to strap themselves inside rockets. Any boob with a slide rule could learn to be a pilot. Being a *test* pilot, however, required a level of determination and self-reinforcing delusion many people interpreted as courage. But it wasn't really about courage. A mailman has courage. A New York cab driver has courage. To make it as a test pilot you needed a lot more than courage. You needed arrogance. An ego the size of Texas. You didn't just want to succeed, you wanted to win. You wanted to beat the other guys. Ruin them. Send them, sniveling, to United Airlines, hat in hand, where they'll spend the rest of their days patrolling the friendly skies in a bus. You see, for test pilots, there truly was no second place. There was the guy who did it and the guys who watched. Test pilots were the rarest breed.

The very best of the very best. After all, trying God's patience required a rare insanity.

Hal Jordan never had it. Hal Jordan was a pilot, maybe the best pilot at Ferris Aircraft, but he was a junior assistant stuck deep in rotation. Everybody knew but nobody ever said that Hal would never make it in this game. Besides being overshadowed by his older brother Jack, Hal had a fatal flaw that disqualified him from the big leagues: nobility. Hal was a straight arrow who did his own homework, crossed at the green and ate his vegetables. Hal was the smartest kid in school, the best athlete, the student body president, editor of the school paper. He idolized Marty and wanted to follow in his dad's footsteps, while somehow keeping his father's prolonged absences and inattention deep within Hal's blind spot. In the realm of *I'm sure Dad had his reasons.*

Hal lived, more or less, on Planet Hal. Where honesty and integrity and, yes, faith were the guiding principles and where Marty was Saint Marty—Greatest Dad Who Ever Lived. Meanwhile, everyone around Hal was lying to him. In a kind of misguided respect for Hal's principles, most people in his orbit hid the dirty laundry from him. Made his world safe. Good always triumphs over evil. Cheating on tests is bad. Marty Jordan was a saint.

That was love, I suppose; family and friends reflecting the fantasy of what Hal wanted life to be, when the reality was that people all around him were gently orbiting in a kind of loving deference to his lunacy and innocence. Hal was The Man Who Knew Much Too Little about everyone and everything. Absolutely everyone in his life was lying to him. Gentle lies, for sure. But, everyone from his mother and brother to sports teammates and friends to Carol told him basically what he wanted to hear. Hal was like this mentally challenged twelve-year-old, beloved by a world of liars.

"You're lying."

"It's true."

"Bull."

"Ask Andy."

"Don't drag me into this. Test pilots never squeal on one another. First thing you learn in flight school."

"I've got five bucks."

Andy caved. "It's true."

"Sold down the tubes by a five spot," Hal exhaled. He, alone, at the table in the Hangar was wearing a flight deck uniform. A technician's uniform, worn by mechanics. No test pilot would be caught dead wearing something like that.

"Hal got fired today!" Andy announced, with great fanfare. Trying, I supposed, to lighten Hal's mood by rubbing Hal's nose in it.

"Yep," Jack gloated, "pink-slipped by old man Ferris himself!" Jack told the table something they already knew. At Ferris Aircraft, the only thing traveling faster than the planes was the gossip.

Three other pilots were at the table, along with the odd girlfriend and pilot wannabe. They were in their third round of drinks. Hal had a beer that had not been touched. He was there but not there.

"Then he got mom to call up and beg for him. Ferris caved in when she laid on the, 'For Marty's sake,' stuff." On some level, Jack thought he was helping. On a much deeper level, Jack was torturing Hal, The Golden Child. The Good Son. Mama's Best. Hal being sidelined at Ferris moved Jack even further along in the rotation. *The guy who does it and the guys who watch.*

"So Hal's at a third less pay and he doesn't fly," Jack concluded. "He'll be stuck in simulator runs for months!"

"Leee-user," Biff snorted.

"Hal is, like, *so* screwed," Dee said.

"Feh. Hal's a *girlie-man,*" Andy offered.

Jack emptied a beer pitcher and then rapped the empty pitcher on the table, "So let's take up some donations for the poor slob!"

Hal glared off into the distance, trying to deal with the agony of friends trying to comfort him by torturing him with his mistakes. Still a very young man at twenty-two, a lot was expected of Hal because, well, he was Hal. The Golden Child. Mr. Valedictorian. The Straightest Man Alive.

And because he was Marty Jordan's son. Which wasn't entirely true. Hal was his mother's son. Jack, Hal's sneak-out-at-night, drag-racing, crib notes, win-at-all-costs, juggle-three-girlfriends, hard-drinking, cliff-diving brother was actually Marty's son. It's as if Mom and Dad divvied the kids up—she'd raise Hal, Marty would raise Jack.

Truth was, Jack raised Jack. Jack idolized his dad as much as Hal did, but he didn't use the goody-goody filters Hal used. He wasn't nearly as naïve as Hal was, nor was he as traumatized by his father's death. Marty was a test pilot. It was his turn, simple as that. Jack knew, when it was *his* turn, he wouldn't whine about it. He wanted to go out like Marty. Protecting Hal was Jack's job, and that included protecting Hal from reality. Jack and Mom were like the Reality Police, the DMZ between Hal and the hard truth about life, about love, about Dad.

Hal spent the better part of his senior year in college drumming up the nerve to ask Carol Ferris, daughter of the demigod Carl, out to lunch. Lunch. With friends. With a group. And, to do that, Hal had to practice in a mirror for seven months. Jack and Carol laughed about that while watching *Rocky & Bullwinkle* in their underwear. Jack didn't love Carol, Jack didn't even much like Carol, who had a real evil streak to her. Carol was a means to an end. Carol put Jack in old man Ferris' line of sight, so being Carol's party pal seemed like good Air Combat Technique.

Carol was only marginally aware of Hal because he was Marty's son and Jack's brother. She and Jack kept their casual cartoon watching entirely to themselves because it was so dangerous. If old man Ferris knew, he'd ship her off to nuns in Westminster, and he'd probably drop Jack out of a jet. So nobody knew. Nobody but them.

She blew off Hal's lunch invite because Hal had watered it down to the point of a mousey rambling *some of the gang are going for pizza*. Carol didn't get it that Hal was asking her out because Hal didn't exist for her. Carol was about Carol. About Daddy and Daddy's business. Jack was fun, Jack was useful. Hal was a boy scout. No, a cub scout. Well beneath the radar. Not even in the Friend Zone. Hal was, well, Hal. And Carol would never have paid Hal any attention at all if she hadn't mentioned it to Jack during their next cartoon.

Jack had a great deal of fun at Hal's expense, explaining how he'd been practicing for months and how the guy totally loved Carol. What a maroon that Hal is. Jack went on and on about how straight Hal was and how he believed in nobility and romance and art and chivalry and all of that. What a feeb.

Carol grew increasingly silent as Jack mocked his younger brother's virtues, a laundry list that touched the smallest part of Carol's humanity: a tiny room somewhere where she wasn't the star of her own movie. Carol balled up Jack's clothes and hurled them out of the window, something you just didn't do to Jack Jordan, but Carol knew where the bodies were buried. She and Jack had a Mutually Assured Destruction pact. They each had a missile key: he could get her shipped off to nuns, she could end his pilot career. Neither could make a real move against the other, but it was their last cartoon.

Carol tracked Hal down in pre-flight and made him walk into

a locker, which drew the attention of the milling students. She didn't smile.

"Were you trying to ask me out?"

"Well—" Hal was no good at lying. "That is—"

"Pick me up at eight. Wear something nice."

A year later, Hal and Carol were still an item. Which made Hal's humiliation at the Hangar all the more unbearable.

The pitcher made the full round of the table and came back with three singles, several Canadian coins, a button and a condom. Hal forced a smile even though he didn't get the mean-spirited nature of the joke. And that he never got those sorts of things was the chief reason he was on the road to nowhere.

Biff, Jack Jordan's supremely arrogant rival—Reggie to Jack's Archie—pulled the condom out, "You won't be needing this anytime soon," he mocked. Then he turned to address the woman standing a few feet away with her arms folded, "Will he?"

Carol Ferris glared at Hal. Hal's attempts to be one of the boys were easily as ridiculous as his attempts to ask her out. But she was tired of mommying the guy. Like his career, that was a relationship that was going nowhere.

Biff, on the other hand, was an idiot. A man her father would run over with his car and then back up and finish the job. But he was a damned good pilot. Carol had absolutely no interest in Biff, a moron who would never make it to first base with her. But Hal didn't know that. Carol was hurting and she wanted to spread that hurt around, so she left the Hangar on Biff's arm. And though Biff never got so much as a handshake from Carol, he stayed with her all night—just to torture Hal.

Carol's exit prompted Hal's own. He paid for a beer he never drank and headed for the door alone. Someone at the table smacked Jack, who was content to let Hal leave, but now everybody needed a ride, so the party dissolved into a mass exodus and a pileup into Hal's old Army Surplus jeep.

The ride along the twisting roads in the delta was making the passengers sick. They were all drunk, anyway, and Hal's high-speed weaving wasn't helping. Hal couldn't hear them—partly because of the wind turbulence, partly because Jack's mockery was echoing in his head. Partly because he wanted to dump the clowns in a hurry and race over to Carol's house and make sure she wasn't watching cartoons with Biff.

The best pilots rarely flew with gauges. Gauges were something you used when the runway was fogged over or when Flight called up for data or when your mommy forces you to. The best pilots flew by the G-force against their chest. By the compression of their lungs or how much of their lunch had traveled back up their esophagus. Gauges were for sissies. You knew how fast you were going with your eyes closed.

Hal didn't use gauges while driving. All test pilots drove fast, especially out there in the middle of nowhere. Hal drove by pressure. The wind in his hair. How loud the whistling in his ears was. He heard Jack. He saw Carol.

Hal floored it, kicking the over-loaded Jeep far past safety ratings for speed, especially in a vintage vehicle without seat-belts or even doors. The party in the back slowed a little as one of the pals chided Hal about his driving, but Hal couldn't hear him. Hal just wanted these idiots out of his car. Out of his life.

There, on that deserted, winding road, it finally occurred to Hal that these people were not his friends. They were test pilots. They'd be his friend *after* they beat him. Hal suddenly realized he'd been lied to, all his life, and the dominoes came tumbling down as his naiveté splintered and cracked against his epiphany. He was about to lose everything—his place at Ferris, his future, Carol. And it was all a joke to these drunken free lunch bastards. *He* was a joke.

Hal gave the Jeep more gas, now urgently in need of getting these mopes out of his car. And then he was going over to

Carol's place to beat the crap out of Biff and reclaim his woman. Somewhere, deep inside, Hal discovered the smallest part of himself that actually was selfish. That actually was arrogant. And, for the first time in his life, he allowed himself to be angry. Without apology. Without reservation. *Screw all of you.*

"Hal! Look out! The sign!"

Hal blinked out of his moment long enough to see he was headed right for a jerry-rigged billboard, one of those flimsy roadside signs illegally put up by local businesses. The damned thing was nearly at ground level and was sitting in the shoulder of the road.

"Dammit!" Hal allowed the profanity as he instinctively jerked the wheel. These old Jeeps didn't have power steering, so it was like a scene out of M.A.S.H. as Hal tugged with all of his strength on the wheel, barely missing the sign.

Now the jeep was in oversteer. True to their nature, even in this moment, the pilots insulted Hal's piloting and made light of the fact the vehicle was now out of control.

Hal glanced at his gauges out of habit, but then pulled hard on the wheel, attempting to turn into the skid. But this wasn't a Buick. This was a old Jeep with lousy suspension that had one too many drunken pilots loaded in back. She refused to cooperate and the nose dug under as the rear wheels spun out and the inertia carried the Jeep over on its side and then over again as it skidded into oncoming traffic and was rammed head-on by an eastbound car.

Hal had the mother of all headaches.

Dizziness. Nausea. Congestion.

And then, the bad news—he wasn't dead.

Nurse Broxton violently yanked the blinds up, hitting Hal with the brilliant morning sun. It hit him like a sledgehammer and he almost blacked out again.

"Where?"

"County General," Nurse Broxton gruffly replied. "You were brought in last night."

Hal didn't understand. "Last night? But I—" the room spun around and sledgehammers pounded him. He closed his eyes again.

"Nurse—could you keep the room from spinning—"

Broxton stopped at the door, snarling. "My son was killed by a drunk driver, Mr. Jordan. If you're looking for sympathy, you've got the wrong R.N."

Hal had absolutely no idea what she was talking about. He tried to squint out a reply, "Drunk? Oh...no..."

"Oh yes." Nurse Broxton's voice had been replaced by Carol's. Hal managed to feebly open his eyes and see her, arms folded, by the door. Glaring.

Hal sucked it up, trying to sit up, now, "Carol—look, I can explain—it was an accident"—Hal was having a great deal of trouble assembling sentences—"the sign—"

And Carol was gone.

Leaving Hal to wonder just where the universe went off the rails.

Which was right about when I woke up.

The first and most startling thing was that I'd fallen asleep again. Falling asleep was more or less against the Spirit Of Vengeance rules. It's difficult to claim near-omniscience when you're snoring.

The second thing I noticed was that I was cold. Again. Outside, somewhere. Sitting, leaning forward, my cheek leaning against cold metal. Cold wet metal, as a light mist was in the night air.

Lastly, I remember the light. The brilliant, blinding light. I figured, the Boss. Had to be. It was his M.O.

But I'd found myself in that awake-but-not-cognizant moment

whcre you realize you need to start moving but your motor skills haven't quite caught up with you. It was a surreal moment. And, as the Spectre, I was a leading expert on surreal moments.

"Do not move! You are under arrest!!"

Someone had left the TV on. Carol. Must be at her place.

"This is the park police! You are surrounded!!"

No...probably not Carol's. The motor function kicked in and I slowly raised my head to squint through the light. No dice. The light was far too blinding.

Then I remembered who I was. The Spectre. Immortal, invincible. Spirit of Vengeance. Instead of looking with Hal Jordan's eyes, I looked with the Spectre's eyes and saw a small army of park police and deputy sheriffs about fifty feet below me. The grounds appeared to be an amusement park of some kind. Which was when I remembered Mama Stassi.

Mama Stassi ran a trailer park near King's Island in Ohio. Many of the park workers lived in her trailer park, and the gentle and loveable, apple pie-baking Mama ran a round-the-clock child care service for the workers' kids. But, only the kids knew about Mama Stassi's special playroom with the lights and cameras and the special play clothes in there, or Mama Stassi's special pay-per-view websites and hidden bank accounts.

Nobody believed seven-year-old Charmane when she broke the rules and told on Mama Stassi, and even the sheriff's men failed to find evidence sufficient to convict her. While the rumors pretty much ended her baby-sitting, Mama Stassi and her bank accounts were beyond prosecution.

At least, from everyone else.

By now the sheriff had certainly found Mama baked inside a twelve-foot pie. Her Internet web servers destroyed, her bank accounts emptied, and a warning to everyone else.

None of which explained how I ended up asleep on the jet fighter ride.

About three dozen kid-sized cable-mounted F-18s hung from a fifty-foot spindle. When the ride is operational, the spindle swings the jets around and the kiddies can play Top Gun. Imagine the surprise of the night watch crew when they shined a flashlight on the Spirit of Vengeance asleep in a toy jet.

"Remain where you are!" The park police chief was still barking orders as a police helicopter flooded the ride with light.

Kenny Loggins' *Danger Zone* suddenly blasted from hidden speakers as thousands of multi-colored lights sprang to life and the massive diesel spindle motor shuddered to life. The police had started the ride, intending to bring the lunatic down.

I gave a stretch and a yawn. So very human. It would take several minutes for the spindle to wind back down to the ground, so there was no real hurry. I allowed myself a moment of annoyance. I had fallen asleep again. Things were still somehow out of sorts in the universe.

I was annoyed with Kyle. What kind of name was that for a Green Lantern, anyway? Kyle Rayner. It could have been annoyance, it could have been jealousy. Both emotions were off-limits to Spirit of Vengeance types, but it was what it was. Kyle still got to do it, still got to prevent things and save and rescue and battle villains. I was the after party, my role didn't begin until all the action was already done. While, on balance, I'm sure the Spectre was at least as powerful as Green Lantern, it didn't change the fact Kyle was the guy who did it while I was one of the guys who watched.

None of which explained the sleeping except to say the universe still felt out of kilter. That annoyed me, because Kyle had all day to get this thing done. This simple thing: defeat a thousand Sinestros. I mean, c'mon. That's not even a lunch. Here it was, thirteen hours later and Kyle still hadn't fixed the universe.

"I liked the pie bit. Very inventive." A squirrel scurried down the high-tension cable and perched itself on the nose cone of my toy plane. The Boss. "It had a real Hans Christian Andersen quality to it. The M.E. will be looking for a huge oven for months."

"Just doing my job," I said, an edge of annoyance. "Just like you asked."

"Yes, but you're still obsessing, Jordan. I mean, what was that *'drinking in the morning fragrance'* foolishness at Balmerino Abbey? You scared the novices half to death."

I needed someone to blame. "It's Jordan," I said, referring to half of my composite being in the third person. Only the Boss understood that. "I don't know what's happening to me."

"Yes, you do. You are a merged being, but you are allowing Jordan to dominate."

"Why?"

"Because, on some level, that's what you want. You're still worrying over things that have nothing to do with you."

"Kyle."

"He's the universe's problem, Jordan. You, on the other hand, are mine."

The police grew closer as we spiraled down. I briefly wondered why thirteen men felt the need to aim shotguns at an unarmed spook in a cape, but then I remembered they had, only hours before, found a dead fat lady baked inside a twelve-foot pie. The park police would certainly have alerted the sheriff's office.

I had more pressing concerns, as something the Boss said opened a door.

"I'm your problem?"

"You are, yes. And I need to teach you more about Creation."

"So...this sleep business...is that you withdrawing the Spectre's immortality from me?"

"Withdrawing is a strong word, Jordan. It's more of a training method. Every time you start meddling, you're going to wake up somewhere increasingly unpleasant."

"Now, wait a minute—"

"Who sent you to Kyle? Who told you to get involved?"

"The kid missed it! Missed a big one. Earth—the universe—could be overrun by Sleepers!"

"So what?"

Without realizing it, I became really angry. Without realizing simply becoming angry meant the Boss was draining even more of the Spectre's power from me. "What the hell is wrong with you? How can you let this happen?"

"Jordan, people have been asking that question since the dawn of time. Let me ask you something:

"You're home with a four-year-old. The mailman comes, you go out to get the mail, you come back, the cookie jar has fallen off of the refrigerator and smashed to bits on the kitchen floor. Your four-year-old is there, cookie crumbs all over her dress, her hand bleeding from cut masonry. Now: who broke the cookie jar?"

The officers started barking orders but I was less interested in them than I was in what the Boss was trying to tell me.

"I assume you have some point."

"You ask, 'Who broke the cookie jar?' and she goes, 'I don't know!' Now, tell me, who broke the cookie jar?"

Running out of time. Shotguns being cocked. The chopper coming in for a landing, now.

"The kid, of course."

The squirrel sat up on its hind legs and grinned at me. "Of course the kid broke the cookie jar. But she's four. She doesn't realize sound travels. She doesn't understand the simple math of the situation. But you do."

The park police knew they had a live one: some nut in a Mardi Gras costume talking things over with a squirrel. They ordered me out of the plane as the ride shuddered to a halt. Actually called it a plane. A *plane*. The pilot in me was insulted.

"Make your point, Boss."

"My point is, the scope of an adult's vision is much wider and has much more depth and dimension to it than that of a four-year-old. Your vision, Spectre, is far greater than that of a mortal adult. How much more so, then, is the scope of *my* vision?"

"Put your hands up!" The park police chief blared, "This is your final warning!!"

Faith. The Boss was talking about faith.

"You want me to trust you—is that it?"

The squirrel got out of the line of fire. "Jordan, I honestly don't care what you do. But sooner or later you will have to come to terms with the fact all things have a role in Creation. You're not a super-hero anymore. You're not a Green Lantern anymore and you're not a pilot anymore.

"No matter what you do, Martin Jordan won't be home for dinner."

The squirrel scurried off. The police allowed that as they closed in on me.

I ignored them as I seethed over the Boss' arrogance. I guess it's good to be the boss, because only the boss can get away with cheap shots and lectures. Hal never said Martin Jordan was a saint. Hal made excuses for his dad's long absences because that's what sons do to protect their mothers and protect themselves. Hindsight being what it is, I now know the excuses were an utter waste. Mom and Jack would pretend to buy into excuses I invented, things I knew weren't true—just to protect me. It was a communal brainwashing. The family denial. When we all knew the truth.

We *all* knew Martin Jordan wouldn't be home for dinner.

"All right, sir—we can do this the easy way or the hard way," the chief of the park police said, aiming his Glock at me as he tentatively reached for my arm. A second park officer was climbing through the apparatus, prepared to engage me from the other side.

Such a waste.

I pouted over the Boss for another moment before deciding, heck with him, I was going to go find Kyle and spank him for being completely inept at his job. If Kyle couldn't deal with the Qwardian Sleepers, then I'd take care of it myself, the Boss notwithstanding.

"Don't move!" the chief ordered as he leaned in, grabbing my arm. I turned to him and gave him The Look: the Spirit of Vengeance.

The chief jerked back a moment, the nutty perp suddenly animated, "Jeeez!!"

It was a good look. I'd gotten really good with it.

Of course, it was an empty threat. As the Spirit of Vengeance, I could no more harm the chief than I could K-Dogg back in Westville. At least, not until they'd committed evil of their own free will. The Look was wholly cosmetic.

Now that I had their attention, I gave them 'the speech.'

"Where evil abides, where the wicked dwell, there also stalks the Spirit of Vengeance! So swears—

"—the Spectre."

And, with that, I motivated myself to Kyle's apartment to pick up where I—

Zzzzzzzzzzzzzzzzzzzzzaaappp!

—I screamed, my head jerking back and then forward, slamming my face against the toy plane. It took me long seconds to realize what had happened: an officer had fired a stun gun.

I squinted through the sine wave enveloping me. The entire universe was this high-pitched tinnitus, images and sounds liquefying. I was suddenly aware of my heart beating. My heart hadn't beaten in years, but there it was, loud as a cannon, pounding against my chest as I began hyperventilating. I tried cupping my ears but could not get my hands to my head as one officer had one hand and the chief had the other. Both men were placing handcuffs on.

It was insane. With the merest thought, I could swallow the entire park in a fissure. Explode these yahoos into fine red mist. I tried for the Look, but I was in such agony, I couldn't pull it together. But I struggled against them, swatting them back long enough to perch myself for a leap out off of the carnival ride.

Which was when an officer's baton rapped me across the knees.

The Spectre, one of the most powerful beings in creation, toppled over into the arms of a half-dozen park police and deputy sheriffs, one of whom put a boot in my back as the others cuffed me.

I looked for the squirrel.

CHAPTER
9

Carol Ferris was in the Bubble.

That's what we called her lavish, huge office, a glass-walled wonder suspended above the main archetype production facility. Glassed in all the way around, the Bubble afforded Carol a 360-degree view of the heartbeat of Ferris Aircraft, and Ferris Aircraft had a 360-degree view of Carol—who was always there. Nobody worked harder for Ferris Aircraft than Carol Ferris, and she was willing and eager to remind you of it. I wouldn't say Carol was mean so much as she was evil, if it were possible to mean that in a good way. It wasn't terribly unusual to find her at her desk at 3:30 A.M., especially if there was a rush deadline or annual report due. What made her evil was, in spite of those insane hours, she'd be there, fresh as a rose, when the hangar gates opened at 7:30. Carol never asked anyone to work harder than her, probably because no one could.

While normally a workaholic, Carol became much more so in the months she'd been separated from her husband. Gil Johns was a nice guy. A quiet guy. A safe guy. Just what Carol thought she needed after what she'd been through. After what loving me cost her. But, eventually, the restlessness in Carol sent Gil overseas for an extended trial separation, and it surprised no one that Carol's icy disposition dropped to sub-zero.

Carol's eyes blurred over the gibberish: DILUTED EARNINGS PER SHARE BEFORE CUMULATIVE EFFECT OF ACCOUNTING CHANGE. CUMULATIVE EFFECT OF ACCOUNTING CHANGE, NET OF TAX. She made notes in longhand hieroglyphs only Tony The Humorless Ken Doll, her long-time assistant, could decipher. Biting her lower lip and snarling at her plasma-screen monitor, she scribbled *Die, Jordan, die and STAY dead* across her notepad, something Tony was used to editing out of the annual reports.

I didn't need the Spectre's pseudo-omniscience to know I was distracting her. That her annoyance was as much about my visit as it was about Ferris's numbers. In her own way, Carol was the poster child for denial, as much as Hal had been. She sought her father's approval as much as Hal did. She made excuses for old man Ferris and invented trips to Disney that never happened, plastering her walls with news clipping of her famous dad because she saw those more than she saw him. She had ultimately taken the job at Ferris just so she could at least bump into the old bastard in the halls. And she'd fallen in love with Ferris Aircraft because that's what he had done.

When the Zamoran race—female counterparts of the Guardians of the Universe—needed a queen, it was their custom to select an off-worlder, an alien. It made some twisted logic, I suppose, for the Zamorans to irritate their male counterparts by selecting, for a queen, the mate of the Guardians' star pupil—the Green Lantern of space sector 2814.

Carol was recruited as the Zamoran Queen and given the powerful Star Sapphire—a jewel that approximated many of the characteristics of the Green Lantern power ring. Taking on the name of her power source, Carol became Star Sapphire. And, while the legend suggests Star Sapphire's evil was borne of the Zamorans' resentment of the Guardians of the Universe, I have a different theory. I think the woman is just evil. And the power just amplified the bitterness Carol had been carrying around since grade school. It's sobering to think of the lives that might have been saved if old man Ferris had hugged his kid a little more.

Carol ripped her notes off the pad, her anti-Hal scribbling had covered the figures anyway. She pushed back from her work and rubbed her eyes. Too tired to go home, she got up to stretch and orbit the Bubble, still completely unaware of how much the design of it resembled the very jewel that had once controlled her life.

Carol was wearing silk tap pants—ladies boxer shorts—and bedroom slippers. Beneath the Bubble was the flight deck and, beneath that, the multi-billion dollar X1010 prototype that was drowning Ferris Aircraft in red ink. The night crew putting the refining touches on the new X1010 was used to getting a show from her and she really didn't care so long as it helped them stay awake. At three in the morning she was damned well going to make herself comfortable, so at some point the skirt and heels were coming off. Seated behind her desk, you'd never know what wonderful surprise might be in store when she got up for her 3:30 stretch.

Another look in the mirror, just to make sure Star Sapphire was truly gone. She was. Carol Ferris glared back at Carol Ferris, with nary a super-villain in sight. But she was Jonesing a little. The way a crack addict gets the shakes. The way a fat girl circles KFC. Carol didn't want to be Star Sapphire again. But she wanted to fly. She wanted the wind in her hair and her heart racing. She wanted the power to build or destroy. She wanted to be super-human. Once you've flown to the moon and home again—without a spacesuit—it's really hard to go back to sitting in traffic and standing in line at Starbuck's.

Carol splashed water on her face and mentally changed the

subject. Finishing the X1010—the new hypersonic fighter jet designed to run McDonnell Douglas and their famous Harrier out of business—was enormously stressful. Ferris stockholders would be very anxious about both the jet and the annual report. The Harrier II Plus used the fabulous Rolls-Royce Pegasus F402-RR-408 jet engine, and included the advanced APG-65 radar system. Ferris' X1010 needed to be a Harrier Killer, with stealth capabilities and guidance systems several laps ahead of the Marine Corps' famous jet. But there had been delays and cost overruns, and now the X1010 threatened to consume both Ferris Aircraft and the company's moody CEO. Carol squeezed the X1010 and Hal Jordan and Star Sapphire out of her head and dutifully shuffled back across the Bubble, to the tacit appreciation of the night watch crew. *Screw it. Life goes on.*

That's when the phone rang. Carol despised answering her own phone only because her father had refused to answer his. He'd make Carol do it. Or the damned thing could ring off the hook. Carl Ferris was not a phone answerer. Now Carl was gone and Carol scrutinized her ringing phone with the Ohio area code and wondered who the devil in Ohio had her private number. She thought about letting it go to voicemail, but curiosity got the better of her, and so it was that she heard my voice on the phone.

"No—don't hang up."

"Hal? Listen—I don't have time for this."

"For what?"

"For whatever this is, I don't have time for it. For you just popping in—"

"I promise, I won't be popping in."

"Yeah, right. I'm hanging up, now."

"No, wait Carol it's im—"

She slammed the phone down.

In Warren County lockup, I had used my one phone call. Bill Holmes, the deputy sheriff on duty, was still filling out paperwork and vouchering my Spectre costume. I wore a county-issued orange jumpsuit. Polyester and itchy, but I loved it. I loved that I could itch.

"What're you so happy about?" the deputy sheriff sneered. Mama Stassi and her giant pie were down at the coroner's office and, my guess was, the detectives were working overtime to pin that on me.

I was smiling. "Happiness is my default position," I said, looking around for anything shiny. I found it in the trim of the deputy sheriff's desk leg, and bent over to see myself in the bright reflection. The deputy sheriff coolly leaned over, giving me the skunk eye. "What're you lookin' at?"

God. The Bible says God created mankind in His own image. For the first time in a very long time I was part of mankind again. My skin had toned up to a normal blush, my eyes their normal green.

I was Hal Jordan.

I was *Hal Jordan*.

The Boss was punishing me. This was his idea of a penalty—stripping me of the Spectre's immortality and power to, I suppose, keep me from meddling with things.

Which was just fine with me. "Look, deputy, I was disconnected. Let me try that number again?"

Carol was pacing again. Talking to herself now. Night watch had cleared out. Anytime Carol started pacing and talking to no one at all, pink slips usually followed. Better to be docked for the hours than to lose the job altogether.

I looked at the deputy sheriff. I couldn't stop smiling. "Some night, huh?" Carol wasn't picking up. I nodded my head to the deputy sheriff, "She'll take the call."

Carol screeched something vulgar as she rushed to the phone, ripped the cable out of the wall, and threw it up against the Bubble glass, where the phone shattered into dozens of shards of Bang & Olufsen high tech.

I hit REDIAL, grinning at the deputy sheriff. "So, " I said, "how *about* that McNabb, huh?" The phone rang on the other end. And rang. And rang.

Carol snatched up the extension phone by the sofa.

"Hal, I swear I'll find the Sword of Destiny myself and pin your pasty ass to the wall with it!"

"Carol, I'm serious. Listen—I need you to find Kyle Rayner."

"Why?"

The deputy sheriff stopped typing and the crowded clerical room came to a halt to watch me. "Because we accidentally activated a thousand Qwardian Sinestro rings and now there may be a legion of Sleepers out there ready to conquer the planet"—I finally noticed I'd become the life of the party—"uh, and since I can't make tomorrow's RPG championship, I need you to pick up my power cards from Kyle."

Carol was livid. Traces of Maybelle. *Why won't you just live your life the way I tell you?* I definitely had a stabbing in my future. She jammed her eyes shut and exhaled. "Did you say, Qward?"

"I did."

"As in the antimatter universe—The Weaponers—Sinestro—*that* Qward?"

"That's the one."

Carol chewed her lip. Assuming I wasn't yanking her chain again, this could actually be important. "So, what—you're going up against them?"

"I can't."

"Why, you got a bus to catch?"

"No, I'm—" I looked around the room. All activity had stopped, and amused deputy sheriffs and corrections officers stood around, arms folded. This was the most entertainment they'd had in years. "Carol, I'm under arrest."

"Yeah, sure."

"No, seriously. It's a long story."

"Well, just float out and deliver your own messages—"

Carol was so damned slow on the uptake sometimes. Got to connect *every* dot. "No, I don't think you're following me. I'm in *jail.*"

Carol's slow uptake was even slower because she was tired and angry and wasn't wearing pants. "And?"

She's actually going to make me say it. I looked around at the frozen amusement of the officers. Then I turned back to the phone and, quietly as I was able—

"—and I've lost my powers."

The room erupted with laughter. The kind of spontaneous, knee-slapping, belly-chuckle joy that is just magic when it happens. One deputy sheriff displayed my Spectre costume, another mimed super-hero flying. It was one of those moments that would inevitably become Warren County Urban Legend. *Gee, thanks, Carol.*

"Hal? Hal is that...*laughter?*"

"Carol. Just get to Kyle and tell him to get his head out of his crack and get the job done—the neutrino pulse—"

"That's how you'll find the rings?" Carol asked. "Send out a pulse and then lock on?" I was relieved to talk to somebody with a brain.

"Yeah, but he hasn't done it yet. Or, at least, he hadn't done it by the time I was, uh, fired."

"Hal—is this a joke? 'Cause if it is—"

"Carol, just find the guy, all right? Go through Ollie or

somebody and get it done before all hell breaks lose." The officers were high-fiving now.

"What about you? What will you do?"

"Sleep," I grinned. "And I may even eat something. I hear county jail food is like fine cuisine."

Carol looked at the receiver for a moment. "Hal? Are you...drunk?"

In a sense, yes. "No. But I am tired and hungry—something I haven't been for a very long time. Look, can I count on you with this Sinestro Sleepers business, 'cause I'm really tired now and want to go to my room—ah, cell."

Carol took long moments to take this in. This was either the cruelest and most insane joke I could muster, or I had just placed the fate of the universe into her hands.

And, mind you, she was *evil*.

Carol placed the receiver against her ear. "Okay. I'll handle it."

"Good. Look, I'll check in when I get sprung from here. 'Night." Sideshow over, I hung up and clapped my hands, rubbing them together, "So, what's for dinner?"

Carol sat in silence for long moments, not knowing quite what to make of things. That I didn't sound worried meant either the threat wasn't that great or that I had complete confidence in her.

That, or I had been driven insane.

This called for another trip to the mirror.

The pulse-and-grab idea seemed simple enough. Star Sapphire could do it. She had no idea why Kyle hadn't taken care of it by now, but then she really didn't know Kyle Rayner. She'd met him briefly, but that was it.

Her assignment seemed simple enough, but it also thrilled

her just the slightest. It was, after all, a caper. A super-hero/super-villain caper. And, it had been so very long for her.

Carol stared at herself in the mirror, heart pounding now.

She licked her lips.

She picked up the phone.

CHAPTER

10

O ver the years, the Justice League has had several headquarters, among them, The Secret Sanctuary hidden in a mountain outside Happy Harbor and the JLA Satellite orbiting the Earth. But none made less sense to me than the current JLA Headquarters, the Watchtower, located in the Tycho crater on the surface of the moon.

While this super-advanced, magnificent structure would make a perfect headquarters for the Green Lantern Corps, it never made much sense to me that Earth's greatest defenders would retreat to a clubhouse located 238,900 miles away from it. If I were a super-villain—as I was when they voted this idea through—the first thing I'd do is sabotage the Watchtower transporter system. And then ravage the planet while the heroes spent the better part of a day shuttling to the surface. The Watchtower was one of those ideas that sounds great in the board meeting but, like the 60-Second Abs machine, it's much less practical than you'd think. Given the advanced teleportation technology at the JLA's disposal, that could move living beings from Earth to the moon in the blink of an eye, there was absolutely nothing they could do at the Watchtower that they couldn't do from, say, a loft in Hoboken.

When John Stewart was born in Detroit, Michigan, one of the immortal Guardians of the Universe told the Ancient Reader in the Tower of Talo on the distant planet Maltus that the Opener of Doors had been born. A gifted architect and community activist, John has certainly opened his fair share of doors, including uniting alien cities stolen by a mad Guardian, which became Oa's Mosaic.

Hal Jordan was ordered to find a second alternate Green Lantern for space sector 2814 after Guy Gardner, Hal's original alternate, became injured. Without telling Hal why, the Guardians chose Stewart. While I'd like to say the partnership has always gone smoothly, truth is often much more complex than that. It should suffice that I'm proud to know him and honored to have served with him.

Even though it's quite possible I was his least favorite person those days.

John was on monitor duty, which was to say he was taking messages for the team and babysitting the clubhouse, things he surely could have done from his New York apartment or, say, a loft in Hoboken.

Terrence Blanchard's *Bounce* boomed in 14-channel multiphasing stereo all around the Watchtower as Stewart, in full Green Lantern uniform, glided majestically through the labyrinthine halls. John was probably one of the very few JLA'ers who actually didn't mind monitor duty so much. He never tired of the Watchtower, with its futuristic design and impractical angles. John loved angles. Loved possibilities. The Watchtower was an architect's dream; a steel and crystal puzzle he never tired of trying to solve.

Having, at that time, been separated from the Spectre's power, I found out most of this after the fact; the Spirit of Vengeance's near-omniscience allowing me to see and know things Hal, at that time, could not. But the Spectre could know whatever he was motivated to know and, once rejoined, I knew everything that had transpired while I was trapped in Hal Jordan's mortality.

Green Lantern John Stewart floated into the transportation pod just as Green Lantern Kyle Rayner beamed aboard. An alert was sounding—Kyle was using a priority beam-out to get himself out of harm's way. Kyle emerged from the transporter chamber gasping for breath. His Green Lantern costume was torn in several places and Kyle was bloodied and scarred.

"Kyle!" John caught his fellow Green Lantern just before Kyle hit the deck. John was much more patient with Kyle than I was, likely because when Kyle assumed the role of Green Lantern I was already Parallax—out to save everything by destroying everything. I was never afforded the luxury or the option of getting to know Kyle or even liking Kyle. By the time I was in any position to interact with him, Kyle was a done deal.

But, John liked Kyle. John advised Kyle and was far more patient with Kyle than I could have been. John wanted to spare Kyle some of the suffering he'd experienced himself—such as the murder of his wife by Star Sapphire—and the mistakes John himself had made—such as the destruction of the planet Xanshi, a result of John's overconfidence.

"What happened?" John demanded.

It took Kyle long seconds to catch his breath. It was obvious Kyle had been in the fight of his life and had barely lived to tell the tale.

John held tight as Kyle sucked wind and tried to form words to describe what had happened to him. It took several long seconds before he could spit it out.

"H—Hal..." Kyle sputtered. "He tried to kill me."

Carol Ferris had a new outfit.

A stylized form-fitting black leather deal. Something that bordered on being a *super costume*. Very *Battlestar Galactica*. A pistol of some futuristic design loaded in a holster. Lots of zippers. There, on the flight deck next to the X1010, Carol was almost loopy from paint fumes but she hid it well as she doled out assignments from her Sony *Clié* PDA. Two things kept the prototype crew from snickering at her. One, the suit fit her like a second skin. It was even better than the tap pants. Two, of course, Carol was the boss. And evil.

"All systems ready, Max?"

Carol's chief technician gave his team a few puzzled looks. The ugly yellow paint on the X1010 was not yet dry and Carol had hung the X1010's star pilot over her balcony two nights before. "Uh," he stuttered, "sure." Max had given twenty months of his life to the X1010, but every great French pastry chef realized that, even though it was his kitchen, Zsa Zsa owned the restaurant.

Carol never looked at anybody as she tapped on her PDA. "Okay, everyone, I need all preflight checks done in ten minutes. Get this data over to Newport and have the Torric project prelims on my desk by nine tomorrow."

Tony the Humorless Ken Doll sidled up, passing a clipboard for her to sign as he briefed Carol. "The revised figures for the annual report are on your desk, the X1010 satellite uplink has been completed, I've moved all of today's appointments—oh, and *he's* here."

Carol never looked up. Kept writing, kept fidgeting with the PDA. "Yeah, well, it's about time."

"And he's firing people again."

That got her attention. She exhaled loudly, rolling her eyes as she glanced up at the Bubble overhead.

Polly, a gifted analyst eighteen months out of grad school, smiled as she stopped by the Bubble to drop off papers for Carol to sign. She smiled because she needed to do something to mask her abject terror of setting foot in that accursed place. The Bubble was the place of the damned, the dragon's lair, and you just never knew which side of the bed Carol had gotten up on until it was much, much too late. But, sooner or later, all senior staff had to set foot in there. And today was Polly's day.

She was a bit put off to find a man sitting behind Carol's desk. Black leather jacket, mock turtleneck shirt. Flowing golden hair and stylized goatee.

Earring.

The man was scribbling notes on Carol's leather-bound, personal and pristine copy of the revised annual report. "This thing was put together by some real mutts," he offered without looking up.

Polly, relieved to not see Carol, was puzzled by this sexy guy. "Umm—hello?"

The man ignored her. Scribble, scribble.

"Sir?"

The man finally looked up, realizing Polly wasn't Carol. He considered her for a moment and then went back to ruining the very expensive, finely-printed annual report, waving Polly off with a dismissive gesture, "You're fired."

Polly's eyes went wide with shock. She stammered something incoherent as she backed out of that accursed place. Polly had absolutely no idea what to do.

"Will you stop that," Carol sneered as she brushed passed Polly, oblivious to Polly's existence. "Oliver—you are such a child."

Oliver Queen, annoyed and not intimidated by Carol in the least, sat back, slouching in Carol's $5,000 Mendolo executive's chair. "News at eleven," he offered, unsmiling. "Why am I here?"

Carol allowed the disrespect. She knew Ollie largely through me. But she respected him because Ollie was old school. Ollie was somebody she actually recognized. He'd toured Ferris Aircraft several times, mostly years ago when he was rich. And, whenever he visited, he'd mockingly fire people.

"What have you done to my damned report?" Carol parried, just to give Ollie a little rhythm.

"Chimps wrote this. This is exactly the kind of chimp-osity that cost me my fortune, Carol. Friend to friend: fire everybody. My dog Sparky and three kids from Kinkos could do a better job with this." Ollie tossed the report in the trash. "Why am I here?"

Carol wanted to win. But time was wasting and she needed him.

"Hal asked me to call y—"

Ollie left.

Carol waited a minute. Polly was still standing there, blinking. Nobody walks out on Carol Ferris. And Carol Ferris certainly never chased anybody who did. Running after Ollie would cost Carol dear and precious wicked witch style points. It simply wasn't done.

"Dammit," Carol cursed under her breath as she bolted out of the door in her Galactica battle suit.

By the time she hit the parking lot, Ollie was already letting the clutch out on his Shelby Mustang Special Edition. When he was rich, it was a Porsche. Now it was a pretend Porsche. Porsche Lite.

"Ollie—*wait!*" Carol demanded, but Ollie pretended not to hear her over the engine.

"Look," she yelled, playing Ollie's game, "if it wasn't for Hal, you'd be dead."

She meant to say, *still* dead. Which, actually, was only half true. The Spectre brought Oliver Queen back from the dead after Ollie had been killed in an airplane explosion. However, Spectre was only able to resurrect Ollie's body. Ollie's body was an animated corpse, a set of bioelectric pathways and muscle responses. A hollow, soulless animatron. Restoring Ollie's soul, making him an actual *person* again, was another bit of business that had had nothing to do with me.

Ollie's face hardened into that *don't screw with me* mask. It was better than The Look. It wasn't that Ollie was bitter toward me, it was just that we'd both moved on, and Ollie didn't particularly care for the way the Spectre did business.

Carol leaned into the driver's window, softening but not surrendering. "This is serious. I need your help."

Orin was the king of Atlantis, a legendary city the planet more or less took for granted because it was located well beneath the Atlantic Ocean. Which always seemed stupid to me considering a kingdom located well beneath the Atlantic Ocean could likely develop incredible weapons we'd never thought of, and develop them in complete and total secrecy. Truth be told, my greatest fascination about the Atlanteans was how they got their toilets to flush, and why they slept in beds.

Descended from normal, land-dwelling humans, I suppose much of the incongruity of the Atlanteans' underwater existence—tables, chairs, beds, chandeliers—owed to the deep ingraining of established tradition. I'd only visited the place a few times, but it always struck me how oddly conventional the kingdom was, in a place where "up" and "down" were mostly abstract concepts, and you had to strap your pressure-sealed cup and saucer to the table that was bolted to the floor. It was all television for Ray Charles.

We called him "Aquaman," and, for reasons I'll never understand, he allowed that. He was, hands down, the smelliest JLA member in history—a salty, peaty tinge he never seemed to notice and we never seemed to bring up. And though he vacillated between being quietly noble and thunderously arrogant, he consistently exuded a quiet confidence that he was superior to us in every conceivable sense.

Aquaman swam faster than most ships and faster than some planes. So fast, in fact, that he had a special water run built for him deep below the Watchtower. A twenty-mile course that looped around Tycho and back to the JLA headquarters. No human being could use the course because Orin had it pressurized to four atmospheres—16,000 pounds per square inch, more than a thousand times greater than the pressure at sea level. It was like swimming through mucous and, while I'm certain some of the other super-powered Leaguers could manage it, only Aquaman thought it a fun ride.

The other annoying thing about him was he liked to drip-dry, which left a trail of smelly mucous puddles all the way to sick bay, where the comm-panel said John had taken Kyle. "What happened?" Orin asked.

John was setting up a saline intravenous drip and taking Kyle's blood pressure. Kyle wore a nasal canula which pumped oxygen and was trying to pull himself together, so John spoke for him.

"Hal attacked Kyle. Kyle thinks it had something to do with that Sinestro business from a few weeks ago. We'd better send out a general alert."

On some levels, Aquaman was still making his mind up about Kyle. In fact, I think that, after nearly a decade of serving together, Aquaman had just decided he liked *me* when I had my breakdown and became Parallax. It took Orin a great deal of time to trust someone. And even longer to like them.

"Hal Jordan now has the power of the Spectre," Aquaman said. "And we've never accurately charted what that means."

John continued tending to Kyle. "No kidding. If Parallax has somehow reasserted itself, or if Hal has been taken over by the programming in those counterfeit rings, it could mean—"

John was interrupted by a miniature harpoon puncturing Kyle's neck and pinning his head back to the wall. John dropped the I.V., whirling toward Aquaman, "Whoa!! Hey, man—are you crazy?"

Aquaman locked an iron grip around Kyle's neck, which was now bleeding from the miniature harpoon. Which was yellow.

"Probably," Aquaman sneered. "Don't worry—it's not as bad as it looks."

John couldn't imagine how that could be true. John didn't have a decade invested in Aquaman. The trust, the team play and hand-off wasn't there. John was caught flat-footed, not knowing what was going on or what he should do.

"What—what are you doing?" John demanded.

Aquaman snarled in Kyle's face as Kyle squirmed under Aquaman's iron grip. "Testing a theory," Aquaman said.

Aquaman's free hand had locked Kyle's right arm down at the wrist, pinning Kyle's hand to the bed frame. With great ceremony, Aquaman snorted back mucous into his lungs and spat the Mother of All Loogies onto Kyle's hand.

John winced, a little grossed out. "What the hell?"

Aquaman's finger rubbed the snot all over Kyle's ring, rubbing the fake green paint off of it and revealing the gold faux ring of Sinestro.

"Hell indeed," Aquaman offered. "John!"

John immediately threw up a power ring-generated force field over Kyle as Aquaman backed toward the comm-panel, ready to hit the emergency call button.

"How—how did you—"

"Parasites, John," Aquaman explained, never taking his glare off of Kyle. "There's no light at the bottom of the ocean. You learn to navigate with every sense you have. Go fluoroscopic."

John changed the radiant pattern of his ring's projection, revealing a hideous network of veins and arteries and skin lesions forming on Kyle—things which would not be seen by the naked eye.

"Parasitcs," Aquaman repeated. "I smelled them the moment I walked in."

"I read the logs about that Sinestro business," John said. "I'll bet this virus pattern matches the one that transformed that kid into Sinestro."

Aquaman hit the alert. "A 'Sinestro virus?'"

"Yah. It was Sinestro's final revenge before he died. The Qwardian race flung thousands of counterfeit power rings throughout time and space, knowing they would end up in the hands of sentient beings who would become unwitting Sleepers they could activate when the time came."

Aquaman snarled, preparing to leave. "And, I suppose that time is now."

John, concerned about his fellow Lantern, agreed. "Yeah. I'm betting it is."

And, with that, John turned his ring on Aquaman, unleashing a massive force bolt that smashed Orin back through a console.

Aquaman shook it off, wiping blood from his mouth with the back of his hand, his fierce gaze locked on John as John approached.

"Well now, things really are about to go to hell, aren't they?" Aquaman sneered.

Aquaman focused his vision on the menacing Stewart, compensating for the ambient light. The Sinestro virus was rapidly eating away at John. Aquaman cursed under his breath for not realizing the odor was coming from *both* Green Lanterns.

John trapped Aquaman in a force field but Aquaman attacked John using his telepathic abilities, which enabled Aquaman to communicate with most marine life—including simple parasites. The parasite infesting John was susceptible to Aquaman's power, and the attack momentarily severed the parasite's control of John long enough for Aquaman to lunge forward.

Beneath the ocean, Aquaman was the fiercest hand-to-hand

combatant anyone was likely to encounter. Fresh out of water, at his full strength, and not hampered by the incredible pressure of the sea depths—Aquaman was likely the most dangerous fighter in the League.

Aquaman knew he had mere seconds to take out two Green Lanterns and lock down the Watchtower. Much as he hated to do it, Aquaman tore ferociously into John Stewart, landing a half-dozen punches before John could swing one or regroup with his power ring. Only the Flash could punch faster and only The Martian Manhunter or Superman could punch harder than Aquaman. Not only was he hitting John in rapid succession, he was destroying John's body with each blow, landing one on top of the other.

John folded as his ribs splintered and blood gushed out of his mouth. Aquaman didn't want to risk killing John, but Kyle was already using his ring to sever the mini-harpoon in his neck and, once he did, that would be the ballgame.

Aquaman viciously backhanded John and then propelled a massive telekinetic instruction at Kyle, *"No."*

The telepathic blast slammed Kyle's head back as white light blasted through his skull. Aquaman was on Kyle in an eye blink, yanking the Sinestro Ring off of Kyle before ramming his elbow back into an operation's panel, initiating an emergency lockdown of the tower.

Aquaman leapt out of sick bay as the emergency lockdown threw up force fields and emergency bulkheads, pulling John's power ring off while sealing the two Lanterns inside. Without blinking, Aquaman tossed both Kyle's ring and John's ring into an emergency disposal unit, which beamed both rings into space.

Aquaman slumped to the floor, ripping his uniform off, until he was completely naked. He then shoved his clothes and accessories into the emergency disposal as well, just in case the virus had gotten on him, and initiated emergency decontamination protocol, which flooded the hall with anti-biogens.

Aquaman coughed and winced as the disinfectant—safe to humans but toxic to him—flooded the chamber. The good news was, Aquaman could hold his breath longer than any human and many super-humans. The bad news was, the anti-biogen was getting into his pores and infecting him. He'd need to get to salt water fast or he'd suffocate.

The disinfectant completed its work, leaving Aquaman in the hall, closed in tight by emergency bulkheads. He was clean—no sign of the Sinestro virus. But the tower was locked down: nobody could get off, nobody could get on. He could not leave the hall until someone released the lockdown protocol.

And he didn't have much time left.

Ollie was annoyed. Nothing new for Ollie.

"This is a joke, right?"

Ollie and Carol were standing on the pre-flight deck above the X1010, the single most precious piece of machinery in the entire complex. The company's entire future hung on this prototype that had cost the company billions to develop.

Which was now painted a loud yellow.

Ollie gave Carol a look.

"I thought you'd appreciate the gesture," she said.

In happier times, Oliver Queen, community activist and neighborhood crank, had been Oliver Queen, multi-millionaire. Playing "Green Arrow" was more of a hobby, a whimsical idea to copy the strange bat-fellow and put to use skills Oliver had learned while stranded on a tropical island.

Mimicking the flamboyant and mysterious Batman, Oliver designed and built quite a few odd tools. An Arrowcar. An Arrow Cave. Yes, Ollie actually had a really fake-looking man-made cave dug under his mansion.

He also had an Arrowplane, a modified jet fighter designed by—wait for it—Ferris Aircraft. Carol had the X1010 painted to become the new Arrowplane, including a stylized "A" on the vertical stabilizer.

Which Ollie wanted absolutely no part of.

"Lady, I haven't been a pilot in a very long time."

"Ollie, it's like riding a bike. It's *easier* than riding a bike. It's all touch screens and joysticks. The computer flies the plane."

Ollie got annoyed, got in Carol's face. The crew on deck turned and wandered off. Either he would punk her or she would punk him and, if she won, they would surely be next.

"Missing the point, Carol. The Arrowplane was the last thing I was able to hang onto after I lost my fortune. It meant a lot to me."

"Which is why you crashed it in the Himalayas."

"I crashed it because my life as Green Arrow was finished. I—I killed a man—"

"And you gave that life up and joined a monastery. Yes, I know the story, Ollie, but it's time to suit up."

"Carol—"

"Ollie—I'm, not kidding. Now."

Stalemate. The two of them were so evenly yoked, I'm shocked they never got together romantically.

Ollie put his jacket cuff to his mouth, his glare still locked on Carol. "Arrow to base."

At the Watchtower, Aquaman struggled to his feet to answer the comm-panel. "Base, Arrow."

Aquaman, Ollie thought. *Why does* he *always have to answer the damned phone?* "Base—you seen Kyle around? We got us a situation here—"

"Code red, Arrow. Kyle and John Stewart are locked in sick bay and the tower is on alert status lockdown. They'd been taken over by some kind of parasite, and Kyle was wearing a yellow

Sinestro Ring. I've sent out a priority JLA alert. Get it in gear—this could be a world-level threat."

Ollie continued to glare at Carol, looking for a way to hang onto his dignity. He never found one.

"Hope you drive stick," Carol sneered as she dropped down into the cockpit, taking the rear in the two-seater fighter jet.

Moments later, the hangar doors opened, and the X1010 taxied out onto landing strip four.

Minutes after that, the Arrowplane jetted into the sky.

11

S itting in the X83 cockpit, the morning after nearly killing his friends in a car accident, Hal Jordan couldn't stop blinking.

It was as if his eyes would not cooperate with him. He tried to focus on the gauges—the X83 was all about gauges—but his eyes were having trouble finding their focus and the massive headache and nausea wasn't helping any. The chemicals the Ferris Aircraft had used to treat the vinyl panels inside the X83 gave off a pungent odor, something most people find pleasant and refer to as, 'that new car smell.' But, in the cramped X83 confines, the odor was overwhelming and made Hal's eyes water and continue to refuse to focus properly. He kept looking toward the toiletries locker, a small compartment near the base of his seat that contained things like Pepto Bismol, Alka Seltzer, Saltines crackers, toilet paper and barf bags. There was also a tube of lipstick and a package of panty hose for good measure—a message to the wusses who couldn't hack the simulator runs. Opening the compartment set off a bright red revolving strobe on the pre flight deck, much like an emergency strobe or police car service light. A loud alarm would go off along with the light, alerting the flight crew that the on-deck pilot had just punked out. It was a joke, really, as no *real* man ever, and I mean never, opened that damned locker.

Fearing he'd lose his nonflying third-less-pay job at Ferris aircraft, Hal had checked himself out of County General AMA—Against Medical Advice—the morning after he'd rolled his jeep. By the time the hangar doors at Ferris opened that morning, everyone at the company knew Hal Jordan had put several of Ferris's best pilots in the hospital because he had been driving drunk.

Driving drunk.

Hal Jordan was, in those days, the ultimate boy scout. His main faults were lack of initiative, lack of focus, and criminally excessive fair play—all of which impeded his career momentum as a test pilot. Drinking and driving was not something Hal Jordan was capable of, though his massive hangover symptoms told a different story.

When Hal was brought into County, he smelled like a drunk. His speech was slurred like a drunk's. And he certainly wasn't capable of walking in a straight line. Everyone else in the car was clearly inebriated and witnesses saw all of them drinking heavily back at the Hangar. Inexperienced interns on the night shift either didn't do a blood alcohol test or mislabeled the results. Either way, there wasn't a piece of paper somewhere that could tell Hal whether he'd been drunk or not, and by the morning it was far too late for any test to be reliably done. Still, the accusation stung, hanging on him in the cold and smelly X83.

Drunk driving.

Hal couldn't say for certain that he *wasn't* drunk. He didn't remember much of anything past losing control of his Jeep. And all he remembered about that night at the Hangar was how depressed he was and how he'd spent the entire evening staring at the head of foam on a beer he didn't remember drinking.

"Flight, Falcon," Biff the Idiot's voice snapped over the comm. Biff left the Hangar last night before Hal did. He took Carol

Ferris, Hal's girlfriend, with him, and Carol had spent the night at Biff's place. The whole flight crew knew *that,* too.

"Falcon, Flight," Hal responded, keeping his annoyance in check as he continued flipping switches inside the cockpit.

"You ready or what, Jordan? Getting old up here." Biff didn't mask his contempt for Hal. Then again, what would you expect from a guy named 'Biff'?

"Stand by, Flight," Jordan said as he shuddered back the X83 canopy, which Carol was banging on with her fist. Hal gave Carol a look. It wasn't The Look. That one he hadn't mastered yet. But it was good enough. It was a, *we're going to fight about Biff but talk about the car accident* look.

"You should be at the hospital, Hal. That, or in jail."

"Yeah, well, I didn't want to lose my job, Carol. My one-third less pay job. It's the only thing I have left." *Since you dumped me for Biff.*

"Hal, if you're looking for someone to blame, start with the nearest mirror," Carol said as she sauntered off. And, yes, Hal was indeed looking for someone to blame. Hal Jordan, the good son, the kid who did everything right, was in a downhill slide he couldn't see the end of.

He wanted Carol to step up. Now was the time when people who loved you—who truly loved you—stepped up. The time when people defended you and protected you and, dammit, *believed* in you. It wasn't that Hal wanted Carol to take a bullet for him, but he wanted a hearing. He wanted a little benefit of the doubt. He wanted her to step up and, at minimum, acknowledge that she'd deliberately treated him like dirt, deliberately spent the night with that moron in the tower just to anger him. And that Hal's anger and hurt was at least some part of the equation that led him to biting his lower lip to keep himself from opening that damned toiletries locker.

Hal thought love should be, well, like Social Security. You

pay into the system over time, and then, when it's your turn, you get to collect on that investment. But, truth was, we are all just mortals. Just flesh and bone, struggling to overcome our human frailties. Hal could see past and expect understanding for his own faults, while failing to see past or understand Carol—Benedict Carol—who was moving away from him just when he needed her most.

The truth was that Carol's investment was entirely in her father, old man Ferris. Her attraction to Hal began with cartoons with Jack—a rogue after Carl Ferris' own heart—but continued with Hal because, even though Hal was nothing at all like her father, he was the kind of noble soul her father would have wanted for her. Hal's inexplicable slip-n-slide from grace moved him out of Carl Ferris's favor, and Carol's loyalty to and investment in Hal was fully anchored in the old man's bedrock.

While coming across as unreasonable or unfeeling, Carol was simply in self-defense mode. "Please daddy" mode. Frightened she'd made a mistake and invested too much in a man her father would ultimately not approve of.

But, in those days, Hal was too young and too immature and too out of sync with Creation to understand the concept of the plurality of the universe—that everyone is entitled to their own concept of reality. Like most people, Hal assumed his reality was the correct one and was often puzzled that everyone else didn't think the way he did. This is the kind of thinking that begins with lovers breaking up, escalates to Maybelle killing Sid, and ends with bombs and missiles being dropped on cities. It is naïve and dangerous thinking. A higher plane of thought reveals many dimensions of reality and truth and allows for a universe where Carol Ferris walking out on her boyfriend in his darkest hour is both reasonable and appropriate behavior.

Of course, most of us don't live in that universe. For most of us, Carol was simply a bitch.

"Flight, Falcon, dammit." Normally, Biff would take a rip for using profanity over the comm. But even the old man was cutting everyone slack today. Everyone but Hal.

Hal locked the canopy, "Falcon, Flight. Yeah, let's go."

His pre-flight check completed, Hal throttled up the X83—and went nowhere. The X83 was a sophisticated flight simulator. A massive enclosure suspended high above the flight deck by a series of gimbals and cables. The X83 was capable of accurately reproducing most any flight conditions a pilot might ever face. That day, Biff had programmed a gut-wrenching series of turns and negative-G rollovers, a program custom designed to torture Hal, whom Biff hated not because Hal had put Biff's fellow pilots in the hospital—in the competitive world of test pilots, this was no small favor, as that moved Biff up several notches in rotation. No, Biff despised Hal because, although Carol spent the night with him, nothing happened between them. Carol curled up on the sofa while Biff spent a sleepless night futilely reviewing scenarios for changing Carol's mind. Bagging the boss's daughter would have been a big move for Biff, especially if he could have found some kinky private thing to hold over Carol and force her to intercede with old man Ferris on his behalf.

But Carol had spent a sleepless night worrying about Hal, and for that Hal must now be punished. Humiliated. Sent to the toiletries locker. Biff would not be happy until that siren and flashing light went off in pre-flight, humiliating Hal Jordan for all time.

Hal instantly knew Biff had reprogrammed the training sequence. Hal had taken hundreds of simulator runs before, but none so capriciously violent. His bleary eyes saw double gauges everywhere, double needles on the double gauges.

Drunk driving.

The X83 spun and lurched and pitched so violently, Hal's head slammed against the bulkhead, making him wish he'd worn his helmet. But helmets were for wusses, so Hal tried to man up and act as if he wasn't mere seconds from blacking out.

The X83 hit a simulated air pocket, dropping Hal so abruptly he bit his tongue, sending a sine wave of pain through his brain. He muffled his involuntary scream into more of a guttural howl.

"Flight, Falcon—what's that? Repeat your last."

Hal was not capable of speech. His tongue was swelling to the size of a knockwurst.

"Flight, Falcon."

Hal could cycle his marker lights, the universal *OK* signal, but he wasn't interested in giving Biff the satisfaction of knowing he'd made Hal bite his own tongue.

"Flight, Falcon." Biff just kept calling. He could see Hal in the cockpit, squinting through double vision and clenching his jaw, Hal's cheeks ballooning a bit. He knew Hal was all right.

He just hated Hal because Carol had refused to sleep with him. Because Carol used Biff to send Hal a message. Biff felt used and cheap, having failed to cheaply use Carol the way he'd intended.

"Flight, Falcon."

Oddly enough, nearly cutting his own tongue in half actually helped clear up Hal's double vision. Hal suddenly found he could focus. He could read the indicator clearly. TOILETRIES.

Biff sent the X83 into a nightmare set of maneuvers, things that would have even the best experienced fighter pilots waiting for Biff in the parking lot with a crow bar. The pressure in Hal's head became so great he forgot about his tongue. Blood drops trickled out of one nostril. TOILETRIES.

"Flight, Falcon."

Hal cursed at Biff under his breath. If Hal passed out inside this thing, it would be just as bad as opening the toiletries locker. Completing the simulator run with his dignity intact was simply not possible.

"F-falcon, F-flight," Hal stammered, the pressure pinning him to the flight couch.

"Flight, Falcon," Biff replied, smarmy. Victory in his sights.

"Biff, this is stupid—I'm half a step away from blacking out—"

"Flight requests your DC, Falcon." DC. Discretionary Clearance. In other words, Biff refused to scrub the mission. Hal would have to abort it. And be a *wuss*.

"For crying out loud, Biff, just shut it down! If I abort, it's just as bad as—"

"My heart bleeds, Jordan. Flight request your DC." Aborting a simulator was exactly like ejecting from a plane. It was accomplished precisely the same way, by reaching behind the flight couch and pulling the EJECT handle. And, it had precisely the same consequences to a pilot's career: losing his equipment was the ultimate shame for a test pilot.

"Flight, Falcon." Hal thought it over.

"Flight, Falcon." Hal's ego wrestled with his intellect.

"Flight, Falcon." The words continued to echo in Hal's head. *Drunk driver.*

"Flight, Falcon." Double gauges now.

"Flight, Falcon." If the flight crew had to carry Hal out of the simulator, his career would be over. Spitting curses at Biff, Hal reluctantly reached behind the flight couch for the EJECT handle. He hoped the day would come when he could return the favor.

Hal pulled the handle.

The X83 shook even more violently, twisting and banking harder than Hal thought it could. Hal slammed against the bulkhead, "Biff! Shut this thing down, dammit!"

But, there was no Biff.

"BIFF!!"

Hal was blinded by a sudden burst of light. *This is it,* he thought, assuming he was either passing out or dying. Either would be embarrassing. Double gauges became triple gauges as pain spiked through Hal's head and the light seared into his skull.

And then the light faded to blue sky and clouds. Hal squinted through the pain, at first marveling at how realistic the X83's flight simulation was. The Delta flats broke through the view as the X83 banked around and accelerated toward the desert. A trick, Hal assumed. Biff must have stayed up all night programming this, which was actually good news. It meant nothing could have happened between Biff and Carol.

Hal heard a strange voice over the comm. *Order is a condition of logical arrangement among the separate elements of a group.*

"Biff—what the hell are you talking about? And, what's happening to—"

The rule of law is the custom or the observance of a prescribed procedure.

"This isn't funny, Biff!" Hal had had enough. He was bailing. He slid the canopy back—

—only to find the desert five thousand feet below him.

Order was established at the dawn of all Creation.

Creation's growth was thereafter guided by preordained random elements which were themselves the workings of perfect order.

"Hey! Hey!" Hal heard himself yelling before he could mask it from his hated arch enemy Biff. The wind caught his hair and threatened to steal his breath, the rush of it pinning him back against the flight couch.

Creation soon gave rise to sentient life forms whose sense of logic and reason were flawed. This event in and of itself was a result of the progressive workings of perfect order.

"Mayday, Mayday, Mayday! Falcon Flight—request immediate—"

Soon, however, these sentient life forms began to strive against their predestination. With each forward step in their develop-

ment, they followed the inefficient logic of their underdeveloped minds.

The X83 banked around, beginning a descent into a barren stretch of desert. Despite years of pilot training, Hal had not much of a clue where he was. Detached from its umbilical, the X83's gauges were all flatlined. And, much as Hal wanted to assume he was hallucinating, the wind cutting against his face kept him alert even as the strange voice continued from the radio that shouldn't be working.

Once the life forms became capable of interfering with the development of other beings, there came a great disturbance to the universe's order. Thus was the need of intergalactic order-keepers recognized. Thus was the Corps formed.

Hal squinted through tears to see, up ahead, the X83's landing site.

Now he knew he was hallucinating.

The Corps is the root of all order and knowledge. The Corps is the maintainer of life and guardian of truth. Without the Corps, there would be chaos and disorder. The Corps is without fear. Without anger or corruption. It is the creation of a highly evolved mind and maintained by like beings whose destiny it is to maintain the order of things in the universe.

The X83 set down in the desert next to a huge craft of unknown origin. A huge crater and twisted metal seemed to indicate a crash, and all of the markings were in strange glyphs that made no sense to Hal at all. Anxious and in great pain, Hal scrutinized the ship design, wondering how the thing could have possibly flown.

It never once occurred to Hal the craft could be a spaceship.

The Corps has battled against the forces of chaos for a millennium.

To serve is the ultimate honor.

The voice stopped. Hal sat in the powerless, useless flight

simulator, abandoned hundreds of miles from Ferris Aircraft. It was all too surreal. Too impossible.

Hal refused to get out of the simulator.

Quiet consumed the plain.

The occasional hawk. A prairie dog in the distance.

Hal refused to get out of the simulator. If this insanity wanted his cooperation, it would have to come and get him.

Which it did.

Suddenly, an unearthly emerald glow enveloped Hal, ripping his flight couch out of the simulator.

"Hey! Wait!" Hal realized he was yelling at some unseen force, something that obviously gave less than a damn about what he wanted. The insanity had tired of waiting on him.

The emerald power dragged Hal—flight couch and all—inside the strange craft. Through tight, twisting gangways that seemed to follow no logical pattern, all that yammer about order and logic notwithstanding.

The stench inside was nearly unbearable and threatened to topple the dominoes of Hal's already weakened constitution. Thick, wet, smelly fog—something that almost passed for breathable air—filled the ship, and Hal gagged and choked it through his system as the emerald power snapped his flight harness and dumped him onto a grated deck.

A grated deck that felt like cheese. *I'm on a cheese ship,* Hal thought. Bleu cheese, from the smell of it. Despite the disgusting thickness of it, Hal inhaled deeply, dragging the almost-air into his lungs, his chest heaving and his ribs aching as his respiratory system worked overtime to push in and out the snot-air on the ship of cheese. Hal heaved and coughed and shook off the malaise long enough to raise his head and see, darkly in a far crawl space—

—a man. He appeared injured, covered with blood. Hal's nobility, the very thing that held him back at Ferris Aircraft, kicked in before either intellect or reason and, pulling himself up off of the cheese floor, he forgot all about his horror and moved to see to the injured, bloody man.

"Hey," Hal said, with much difficulty, "what, they get you, too?"

Which was when Hal realized the man wasn't bleeding. The man's skin was an inhuman magenta red. The man was wearing some manner of flight suit, with an insignia Hal had never seen; stylized circles inside an ellipse on his chest. White opera gloves. And some kind of ring—

—which glowed with the very same green energy that had dragged Hal into the cheese vessel. This set off all of the Christmas tree lights in Hal's brain as he finally shook off his disorientation long enough to actually hear himself say it.

"Spaceship!" Panic ripped through him, "I'm on a damned *spaceship!*"

Hal bolted away from the man, making a run for it. Bad enough he busted up old man Ferris's simulator, no way was he gonna take a trip to Andromeda and meet the Jetsons. Hal bolted for the labyrinthine gangway, hoping he could remember his way out of the intergalactic puzzle factory.

Now fully lucid, Hal ran through the maze and did his level best to remember left here right there up two decks over and down and—

—Hal nearly tripped over the alien as he arrived right back where he began.

Hal looked behind him. A trick?

Hal looked to his left.

He thought about trying it again.

I am the Green Lantern of Space Sector 2814.

Hal stepped back. The red man wasn't dead. But he wasn't speaking. Well, his lips weren't moving. But Hal was still hearing him, anyway.

I am dying.

The alien painfully, and with great effort, raised himself up a bit, now looking at Hal. He gave Hal The Look. He was good at it.

You have been chosen to be my successor.

Hal blinked. It seemed the right thing to do. Then, before he could stop himself, he began chatting up the alien life form.

"No thanks, I'm a test pilot. That's all I want to be.

"Besides, you said you guys have to be fearless, and I'm scared out of my wits."

Fear is, for you, an intellectual exercise. It is a method of self-preservation linked to your species' survival instinct.

That the ring singled you out indicates your potential to overcome your fear. To become truly fearless.

The ring. *What* ring? Then Hal looked again. Oh, yeah. The opera gloves.

The red man extended his hand, displaying a ring composed of polished emerald metal.

The ring must be charged at the battery of power at regular intervals—once every one of your planetary revolutions.

The alien gestured toward an empty metal obelisk with some runes on it.

Call for it and it will appear.

Suddenly, a polished green lantern, in antique design like ones used by railroad workers during the war years, shimmered into view, resting atop the obelisk.

Until you have need of it, the battery may be hidden in an alternate dimensional plane to safeguard it from unworthy hands.

Hal backed off. It was all too *Lost In Space* for him. "Look, I appreciate your offer, but I really can't get involved with this—"

Your wants are not my concern.

The ring has decided.

128

Hal focused on the alien...who then crumbled to dust.

Be sober.

Be vigilant.

The polished green ring inexplicably flew off of the dead alien's hand. Hal backed away and swatted at it like a fly, but the ring paid Hal absolutely no mind, firmly seating itself on Hal's right hand as the alien's final words echoed throughout the cheese ship.

Now you are one of us.

Hal tried to pull the ring off of his finger and realized he was wearing white opera gloves.

Startled, Hal stepped back, slamming into a bulkhead, as he looked down and realized his flight suit had been replaced by the alien's strange, green flight suit with the weird chest emblem—

—a lantern. It was a stylized lantern, representing, Hal supposed, this whole business. What did the alien call himself—a, "Green Lantern"?

Hal began to panic. It seemed like the thing to do.

"A dead alien...this ring...this flight suit..."

Hal looked around. Every exit looked like every other exit. He picked up the power battery and looked at himself in the polished bell.

"Yep. This confirms it. I'm completely insane." He looked around again. "And I still haven't found the damned door."

Hal turned this way. And that. And the other. Cheese. Everywhere you look.

Which was just about where he snapped.

"Let me out of here!!"

Thhhwoooooomm! The ship exploded with green energy as Hal was propelled skyward at a ferocious rate. Hal's eyes were wide with panic as he bulleted through the clouds, arcing high over the desert, the crash sight vanishing to nothingness below him.

It was the first time Hal had ever been that high without an airplane.

"Dah—daaaahh—

"—*Get me down!*" Hal exclaimed.

Hal rocketed to earth at nearly twelve G's, faster than his mind could put together a plan. The desert rushed up faster than he could prepare to meet it, and he impacted into the dust, creating a crater some twenty feet in circumference.

Dust. Hal opened his eyes to dust. A fog of sand and dirt in all directions. There was no sky, no mountains, no ship. Just dust world.

It hadn't yet occurred to him that he was still alive.

When it finally did, Hal looked at his fist. White opera glove. And, on his hand—

—the ring.

Hal felt a smile coming and allowed it, allowed himself a moment of calm.

"Wow. What a rush."

Going to jail is a lot like making your bed in the men's room at a bus station. What almost no TV shows and very few movies tell you is prison cells come in two basic configurations, wet cells and dry cells. Dry cells are temporary holding cells, where prisoners get shuttled to the bathroom as needed. But, being criminals, many of them relieve themselves even in dry cells, so most dry cells have a drain built in the bottom of the floor so the cell can be hosed off after some master criminal has gone potty.

Nearly anytime a prisoner is being held overnight, however, they are kept in wet cells. Wet cells have an odd combination sink and toilet in one corner of the cell. Despite its discrete placement, the odor in a wet cell is unbearable. Which made the drunk tank of the Warren County Jail in Lebanon, Ohio, the odd exception to the rule. A relatively new facility, the jail was practically hospital-sterile, which I supposed was either the harsh enforcement of a neatnick warden or perhaps Warren County had a higher class of lowlife than the average jail. Inside a large community pod—a kind of oversized fish tank for bad people, which was actually quite nice so far as jails go—a half-dozen or so super criminals—out of shape, toothless types who'd likely passed out at bars or gotten into pool hall fights—had gathered around me to watch me sleep.

My sleep was epic. Flawless. I was really good at it. Neither the noise nor the stench nor the comings and goings of the Warren County deputy sheriffs made any impact on me whatsoever. After all, it was the first full night's sleep, the first *human* sleep, I'd had in longer than I could remember.

I was human again. At least for now. Although I knew it would only be temporary, the Boss's "punishment" felt damned good to me. Even the smell of six smelly drunks seemed wonderful to me, that my senses were even capable of being assaulted just ratcheted up the wonder of it all. To be a man, a human man, again. For at least the moment—

—I was Hal Jordan. And I was asleep. Reliving the day I became Green Lantern. Reviewing the paths my life had taken since. Going for the ride.

My fellow inmates watched me sleep. Some had tried to wake me. Some had thought about bullying me. But word was already out that I was some kind of super-hero arrested on a kid's ride at King's Island. Sobered up, most of these tough guys weren't actually so tough. They were only tough in their alter egos, as besotted dufusses in bars and pool halls. There, encircling the man who slept too much, they didn't know quite what to make of me. And, on some level, the feared me. Feared the wrath of the Spectre.

I was the main show at Warren until the earthquake hit. A thunderous, loud proclamation threatened to shake the jail off of its foundation as my roommates hit the deck and jail guards raced toward their command posts to see what was happening.

I kept sleeping. I was enjoying it just that much, not realizing all of that world-shaking going on was for my benefit.

12

O llie fired the massive V/STOL jets, which were so powerful the Arrowplane was blown nearly a hundred feet higher before the on-board computer settled the plane into a teeth-rattling, jittery descent toward State Route 48 and Justice Drive in Lebanon, Ohio. The roar of the Harrier-style *Vertical/Short Take Off and Landing* jets sent pedestrians racing across the several interlocking parking lots of the Warren County Government Campus, mothers defending their children at the nearby school, traffic signals and shop signs swaying in the gale-force wind. Multiple fender-benders occurred in the few seconds it took the plane to land, as drivers leaned out of vehicle windows looking with disbelief at an airplane landing in the sheriff's impound lot. Deputy sheriffs manning the impound lot gate yelled into radios while still more deputy sheriffs raced from central control into the impound area, their arms crossing in a futile attempt to wave the plane off. Staffers and detainees at the Warren County Jail looked with awe out of every available window, wondering what the hell was about to happen, as the imposing Arrowplane negotiated the configuration of light poles in the impound lot to land safely without snapping any of them.

The landing gear touched down in a remote area of the impound lot as the onboard computer bled out the hydraulics and ran out the jet engines prior to shut down. Deputy sheriffs swarmed the plane, yelling and waving, but none of them had drawn a weapon yet. The markings on the vertical stabilizer were a stylized "A" insignia, but the fine print along the underside of the fuselage provided proper registry numbers and identified the plane as being registered to Ferris Aircraft of Star City. Since the plane landed more than two hundred yards from the jail and purposefully set down in an unused area of the sheriff's impound, the deputy sheriffs gave the new arrivals a narrow benefit of the doubt, but sharpshooters and special teams were hurriedly assembling on the slick, metallic courthouse roof in case this was the oddest jail break in history.

Captain John Newsom, the watch commander, spoke through a megaphone but was drowned out by the roar of the jets. He was about to give up when the shutdown cycle completed and, suddenly, the noise began dropping. The jet engine roar reduced to the reductive sine wave of cycling turbines as the canopy popped upward, revealing the jet's two occupants.

"Sorry for the intrusion, Captain," Carol Ferris said, "But it's kind of an emergency."

"And, who might you be, Miss?" Newsom asked.

Carol swung a leg over the side of the jet, providing an impressive view of her form-fitting black battle suit. "I'm Carol Ferris, CEO of Ferris Aircraft. I spoke to a Sergeant Anderson at the booking desk. I've come to bail out one of my pilots."

"Well, Ma'am, you can't leave that aircraft there."

"We don't intend to."

"No, you can't take off, either—ma'am, you must know this is completely—"

"Yes, Captain. I'm sure it is. Can we go inside and you can decide whether to arrest us?"

As Carol and Ollie exited the plane, the deputy sheriffs exchanged a quiet relief that, apparently, they weren't under attack, which in turn allowed them to admire the sleek new

Arrowplane. While maintaining the highest standards of professionalism, not a man among them didn't want to go for a ride in the thing.

"I'm going to have to confiscate that sidearm, Miss," Newsom said, reaching for Carol's pistol. Carol had forgotten she had a pistol. She did not flinch when Newsom cautiously removed it from its holster. The pistol had almost no weight to it, like a kid's empty water gun. "Plastic?"

"Polyphenylsulfone—a polymer used in aircrafts for injection molding," Carol said.

Newsom inspected the weapon carefully. "No bullets?"

"No, sir, it's more of a pulse emitter. Nonlethal and completely legal."

Newsom escorted Carol toward the sheriff's office without handcuffs. After all, Carol was cooperating, and Newsom needed to look up the penalty for landing a Harrier jet in his back yard.

"And who might you be," Deputy Sheriff Bill Holmes asked Ollie as he followed Newsom and Carol.

Ollie, still in the black leather jacket but now wearing stylized sunglasses, never looked at the deputy sheriff, as he said, "Abbie Hoffman."

Carol sat with the booking clerk, Deputy Sheriff Sheila Clark, while Ollie paced, annoyed. A pair of deputy sheriffs stood a discrete distance away but did not let the two strangers out of their sight while Captain Newsom conferred with Major Turnbow—who ran the County Jail—and Warren County Sheriff Tom Ariss about what to do with their two visitors. A call had already gone out to the Federal Aviation Administration, who was sending a man down in a couple hours. A call was also made to Wright-Patterson Air Force Base—where conspiracy theorists had long claimed a flying saucer was being held; Ollie's unauthorized landing and the dead, fat, pie lady adding so much sauce to that particular goose.

Sheriff Ariss, in civilian shirt and tie, figured they should certainly impound the plane, which was conveniently parked in his impound lot, anyway. FAA fines notwithstanding, the officers had a call through to the state's attorney to see what Warren County laws had been broken and whether the couple should be arrested or written an appearance ticket.

Carol sipped coffee as Sheila searched her computer for Hal Jordan without much luck. She thought, for being under arrest, these people were very nice. "I'm sorry, ma'am—nobody by that name is in our facility. You sure it wasn't Butler or Clinton County?"

"No, officer. The call I got from Hal came from here."

Sheila wanted to be helpful. She scanned her computer screen without luck. "What was he brought in for?"

"I have no idea," Carol said as she pulled a folded paper from one of her battle suit's many zippers. "Here," she said, offering a certified copy of Hal Jordan's pilot license to the deputy sheriff.

Hal's picture didn't ring a bell for Sheila, but she hadn't been on duty the night before. "Bill," she said, holding Hal's license up, "we have anybody like this upstairs?"

Deputy Sheriff Bill Holmes squinted at the license. "Maybe." Bill put his glasses on and scrutinized the photo. "Say, does this guy wear a *cape?*"

Ollie rolled his eyes. He was not fond of cops. No offense to Warren County, but Ollie had seen Star City cops step over and step on some of Ollie's constituency—the downtrodden of Westville. He tried not to take it out on decent guys just trying to do their jobs, but he really disliked being there.

And he wasn't leaving without Hal.

"Sometimes," Carol offered. "Do you have a guy in a cape up there...?"

I'd been sleeping for fourteen hours. I'd slept through the excitement of the plane landing. Slept through gates locking and alarms sounding. Nothing could wake me.

Until I heard my partner's voice outside the bars.

"Hal."

As a composite being, I'd become accustomed to referring to myself in the third person, making a distinction between the mortal Hal Jordan and the immortal and near-omniscient Spectre. But, this wasn't my voice. Someone was calling my name in a place where no one knew my name.

To the amazement of the assembled drunks and lowlifes, my eyes finally opened. I thought I was still dreaming. I grimaced a bit as I rolled over and focused on my visitor, seeing Oliver Queen through the thick glass wall of the detention pod.

"Well," I offered. "I'll be damned."

Ollie was stoic. "Too late."

Ollie turned to leave, telling Deputy Sheriff Bill Holmes, "Yeah, that's him. Let's get the hell out of here."

Holmes called after Ollie. "Wait—sir, we can't just—we can't just let him go."

Ollie turned, annoyed, wondering why they didn't just bust Hal out and get on the road already. "Why?"

"We have to verify your story—and, well, we're not sure we can let any of you go."

The spirit of Abbie Hoffman rose in Ollie, "Figures," he snorted. "Right now, your bosses are down there *looking* for excuses to arrest us!"

"Sir, it's just that—"

"—if we'd come in a *bus,* you and me wouldn't be having this conversation, right?"

Bill felt cornered. Cops often feel like they have KICK ME written on their foreheads. "Probably not," he said.

"So, what's so hard about pretending that's a big, yellow bus with wings, and let me and my friends go save the universe already!" Ollie had no time nor patience for this foolishness.

Save the universe, Bill thought. *Here we go.* "Mister—are you all right?"

"He's the Green Arrow," Hal offered, pointing at his old friend.

Bill turned with a *gimme a break* look. "A green *what?*"

"Not 'a' Green Arrow—*the* Green Arrow! I never get how people don't recognize him—his mask is, like, two inches tall."

"Sir—who's the Green Arrow?"

Now Ollie was insulted. "Never mind," he huffed.

"He's a member of the Justice League—" Hal offered.

"Was a member—"

"Whatever."

"Hal, will you shut up—these people already think you're a loon!"

"Ollie—I lost my power. I'm human again—"

"Which means you *didn't* kill a trillion people?"

"Of course it doesn't. Ollie—that's something I'll be atoning for the rest of my life."

"But when you were in trouble—when Coast City was destroyed—when you needed help...did you call me?"

"You were *dead.* Ollie."

"Answer the question!"

"You really want to do this now?"

Ollie got in Hal's face, jabbing a finger. "I figger I got me a captive audience."

"Everything's simple to you, isn't it? Everything is Ollie's Way. Behold—Ollie's Way! There Is No Way But Ollie's Way! Everyone Make Room For Ollie's Way! Behold the grand anarchist! Pardon me while I genuflect."

The more these two bickered, the more Sheriff Bill became convinced he should lock everybody up and sort it out later.

"Better 'n tying a dozen flags to your gas-guzzling S.U.V.!" Ollie sneered.

I couldn't *believe* this guy. "Nothing wrong with supporting your country, Ollie!"

"'My' country? When was it 'mine'? When did I have a say in this Stepford Nation—a country swinging so far to the right it's L-shaped? I mean, *look* at this guy—" Ollie jabbed a finger at Deputy Sheriff Bill. "He wants to give me a haircut so bad he can taste it!"

Bill briefly considered shooting them both.

"Everybody is entitled to their own sense of reality, Ollie—I'm sure even you would agree with that!"

"'Even me'? As in, even someone as stoopit—"

"Precisely. And *how* many special interest groups did you support back when you were rich?"

"Enough to teach me a lesson!"

"Ollie, freedom means, for us to be truly free, we must also protect the rights of people we disagree with. Sometimes it's our turn, sometimes it's their turn!"

"You hear yourself? 'Their' turn! Them! Lemme tell you about 'Them':

"All this damned flag-waving has precious little to do with blacks and Jews and Mexicans and certainly Arabs. The greater tragedy of this new war on terror is that this rallying of white America—in a plangent strum that is certainly heartwarming and glorious to behold—is, for too many people, just a spectator event!

"We applaud and cheer and are brought to tears by this great coalescing of America, but it's not *our* America that's being coalesced! The sloganeering all sounds like *code*. Patriotism as observed through a chain-link fence!"

"God shed His grace on thee, pal!"

"'Love it or Leave it.' *et tu, Harold?*"

"So, what do we do? Hang our heads in shame and become the world's apologists? There really is right and wrong, Ollie. Not everything is shades of gray!"

"But whose right? Whose wrong? Who decides?"

"There are universal constants in all Creation, Oliver. Order. Reason. Logic—"

"Kent State. Tiananmen Square. Ruby Ridge. Port-au-Prince. Rwanda!"

"Gandhi. Nelson Mandela. Mother Theresa. Desmond Tutu!"

"Kublai Khan, Adolph Hitler, Idi Amin!"

"Humanitarian aid!"

"Napalmed villages!"

"Tax cuts!"

"Homeless shelters!"

"Middle East peace!"

"Flag-draped coffins!"

"Tony Bennett."

"Bob Dylan."

And then there was silence. I actually liked Dylan a great deal, but I wasn't giving Ollie the damned satisfaction.

Ollie and I glared at one another through the thick pod glass. Sheriff Bill checked his watch. The other prisoners huddled silently.

I gave Ollie The Look. "So...how you doing?"

"Ah, meso-meso," Ollie said, completely calm.

Sheriff Bill now hated the both of us.

Ollie turned to Bill. "Look, man, it's been grins, but we really gotta hit the road."

Bill was increasingly less amused. "As I said, sir—"

"Carol talk to Kyle yet?" I interrupted.

"No," Ollie said, turning back to Hal. "Sounds like the kid has gone nuts. Aquaman said he's got both Kyle and John Stewart on lockdown in the Watchtower. You know anything about that?"

I frowned. Kyle had obviously blown it. Things were going from bad to worse. "Yeah, I'm afraid so. We'd better get up there."

"So, what, I clock ol' Bill here and steal his keys?"

Sheriff Bill folded his arms and gave Ollie a sarcastic look. "The cell doors are electronically controlled." *Besides, I can whoop your ass.*

Ollie turned back to Hal, "Okay. What's Plan B?"

Plan "B" walked through the door of the sheriff's office while the sheriff continued meeting with his senior staff downstairs. Fred Cook was a deputy U.S. attorney based in Cincinnati, which was nearly an hour's drive from Lebanon. Deputy Sheriff Sheila was a bit unnerved seeing Fred pass through security, given that Carol and Ollie had only been at the sheriff's office about forty minutes or so. For Fred—a chain-smoking complain-a-holic political hack—to actually drive to Lebanon himself instead of sending a fax or email, meant something huge was going down. Given that Sheila had now confirmed Carol's identity as CEO of a multi-billion-dollar corporation and Hal's identity as one of her pilots, Fred moving across the building toward the sheriff's office sounded a "cover your backside" alarm for Sheila, who excused herself from Carol and interrupted the sheriff's meeting.

"Sheriff—Fred Cook," she said, leaning into Sheriff Ariss's office.

Ariss waved her off, "Tell him I'll call him back."

"No, sir—Fred's here. Walking fairly rapidly this way."

Furtive glances shot around Ariss's office as Captain Newsom and other senior staff realized their guests apparently had juice with the governor, and possibly Washington, if Fred the Embittered had made the hour-long drive in person. Ariss exhaled loudly and headed out.

Truth was, the sheriff's team wasn't looking for a reason to hold us there. They were simply being responsible. In this time of terrorist attacks, where airplanes had been used as weapons, simply waving bye-bye to three folks you've never laid eyes on as they flew their own private fighter jet around your county was an extremely bad idea. Ariss didn't like being ambushed, especially by political cranks like Fred Cook who would either be on Ariss's team or not come election time, depending on what was in it for Fred.

"Fred." Ariss shook Fred's bony hand. Fred looked a little sunburned, like he'd spent too much time with his head inside a toaster oven.

Fred handed Ariss a writ with a newspaper clipping attached to it. "Sheriff, this is a court order requiring the release of these members of the Justice League of America."

Taking the writ, Ariss shot Carol a furtive look. "These folks never mentioned the JLA," he said.

Carol put on her "charming" face. "Well, we're flying a bit below the radar, sheriff. We're in our secret identities—national security, you understand." Carol's charming face was less a put-on and more about her realizing Fred's appearance was the result of Carol's call to Judge Hector before they left Coast City. Hector had a judge pal in Ohio issue the writ an hour before they'd even landed in Lebanon.

The sheriff looked at the newspaper photo of Green Lantern, Green Arrow and Black Canary "This doesn't look like you," he said.

Carol leaned forward, still charming. *"Secret* identities, sheriff."

The sheriff looked at Carol, then at sunburned Fred, then at

Newsom, who was definitely out of his element, as the whole deal stank of politics.

Bottom line: they had an apparently harmless guy arrested for drunk and disorderly conduct—which required a desk appearance ticket, not the Warren Commission. There wasn't even tangential evidence connecting Hal Jordan to the dead fat pie lady. And, yes, if Carol and Ollie had come in a bus, we'd all have been on our way by then.

The sheriff handed Captain Newsom the paperwork. "Kick 'em. Mr. Jordan gets a D.T., Ms. Ferris gets a hefty FAA fine and we'll be sending our report down to the State's attorney who may still prosecute her for the unauthorized landing, reckless endangerment, and a half-dozen traffic accidents." He turned to Carol, "You may also wanna brace yourself for a slew of civil suits—those fender-benders, broken windows, and ornery locals looking for a deep pocket."

"Where is Mr. Jordan?" Fred asked as he patted his sunburned forehead with a handkerchief. "The judge sent a priority message for him."

"John?" Sheriff Ariss handed the mercurial assistant U.S. attorney over to Captain Newsom, who escorted him back to the cells.

"Friendly guy," Carol remarked to Sheila.

Sheila was entering the writ information into her computer, processing Hal out. "Yeah. Needs a bit more fiber in his diet. The sheriff figures he's gonna run for governor or something."

"Is he always that...unpleasant?"

"Yeah, just about. Though looks like he's got heat rash or something. Fred's usually white as a sheet. And the new pimp jewelry isn't helping, either."

"Excuse me?"

Sheila looked up at Carol. "Didn't you notice that hideous gold ring?"

Carol exploded into Ariss' office, Ariss and his staff spinning around.

"Sheriff—gun!" she said.

Ariss was getting annoyed now, Washington and super-heroes be damned. "Now, look here, miss, there's no way we're issuing you a firearm—"

"Not your gun—*my* gun! Sheriff—now!"

Upstairs, Captain Newsom escorted Fred the Ice Cube through the holding cells. Newsom wasn't a man who ever did anything for political reasons. He was a cop. His dad was a cop. He helped people who needed help, locked up people who needed locking up. And then he went home to his wife and kids and dog. He never tossed and turned all night worrying about garter snakes like Fred Cook, a guy always working both sides of the street in local politics.

Ollie and Hal were still discussing possible jailbreak scenarios, going over them with Sheriff Bill who shot down one scenario after another, explaining why TV show jailbreaks are stupid and couldn't work in the real world, and for God's sake stop comparing every deputy you meet to Don Knotts and David Hasselhoff. Bill spotted his boss coming down the hall and exhaled loudly, "Oh, thank God." Though seeing Fred Cook gave Bill pause, he was still grateful that babysitting those two idiots would now be someone else's problem. "Hey, Captain."

Newsom clicked on his shoulder-mounted hand mic, talking to Control. "Open 214 please, Sally."

There was no answer.

"Sally? Hey, anybody awake down there?"

Suddenly, a loud alarm went off as all open pod doors began sliding shut. Newsom and Sheriff Bill spun about, wondering what the hell had just happened.

Fred Cook, the spindly assistant U.S. attorney, viciously

backhanded the six-foot-two, 210 pound captain, slamming Newsom into the pod's glass wall while extending his fist toward Deputy sheriff Bill.

Fred's fist had a Sinestro Ring on it.

Sheriff Ariss, now wearing a NovaFlex vest, and several deputy sheriffs raced toward the cells with pistols drawn as the jail went into lockdown mode. Carol was forced to pursue them like "the girl." She hated being treated like the girl. They still hadn't given Carol back her ray gun.

"Sheriff—for God's sake!"

"Stay back, Miss—let us handle this!"

The sheriff and his team were suddenly hit by a massive power surge, an energy blast fired from down the hall, which slammed seven grown men through double doors and down a short flight of stairs.

Carol kept moving, yanking her plastic gun out of Ariss' waistband as she passed him. "Put those away, sheriff," she said, referring to the officers' conventional weapons, "he'll just turn them against you."

"'He' who?" Ariss demanded, in pain but staggering to his feet.

Carol hit the landing, aiming her pistol with both hands, *"Sinestro."*

Deputy U.S. Attorney Fred Cook fired his Sinestro Ring at the pod, cutting through the walls and thick security glass as my cellmates and I hit the deck. The Sinestro virus was now clearly evident, taking over Cook and transforming him into a duplicate of the red-skinned sworn enemy of all Green Lanterns.

"Jordan!" Fred-Sinestro screamed as he fired on us again, this time taking out a huge portion of the wall behind the pod.

Sunlight blasted through the opening as debris rained down on the parking lot below, smashing into cars and scattering people.

Deputy Sheriff Bill Holmes charged the Sleeper with his baton, but the spindly Fred caught Bill with a hand under the chin, effortlessly raising the man off the floor while snapping his baton in half with his free hand.

"Jordan," Fred sneered, talking to me as he crushed the life out of Bill, "how I have...longed...for this day."

The virus was rapidly taking Fred over now, transforming his normally pasty flesh into the rubine hues of Sinestro. Fred sneered a villain's sneer. "And all mankind shall follow you...in destruction!" Fred-Sinestro hurled Bill down the hall, the deputy Sheriff bowling over Ollie.

A gas canister exploded near Fred, setting off a bright concussive effect as tear gas filled the hall. Support troops, in riot gear, were racing toward us, wearing masks and aiming assault weapons. "All right, Fred—just put your hands up, *now*," they ordered.

"You men—get *back!*" I yelled to the riot cops as I hit the deck, trying to avoid the gas. "Get out of here! You don't under—"

The Sleeper fired a massive plasma blast from his ring, which hit the approaching corrections officers, incinerating them. The officers' weapons melted, their boots sticking to the floor as they collapsed. The heat was so great the ceiling came down on the officers, smoldering debris burying them in a heap of superhot, liquefying metal and rubber.

The Sleeper then effortlessly dismissed the tear gas, expelling it toward the helpless officers at one end of the hall, Carol and Ariss at the other end.

"*Back!*" Ariss ordered, grabbing Carol by the collar and yanking her off her feet. He pulled her back into the stairwell, slamming the door as the gas rapidly filled the hall on the other side.

I squinted through the smoke and lingering gas to see a dark figure purposefully walking toward me. Emergency lights overhead cast huge shadows on the painfully thin demon who took his time, savoring his moment of triumph. Energy crackled from the gold ring on his finger and mist billowed around him.

"Jordan," Sinestro said, quietly this time. "Old...friend. How it must...pain you...to cower there, on the floor, among...*criminals*. You've always had such disdain for...*criminals.*"

Sinestro was right. I wasn't afraid of him. I wasn't afraid of anything, Abin Sur's prophecy having long since been realized in my life, I had become, in time, truly fearless. But, yesterday I could have destroyed the Sleeper with the merest thought; with a *yawn* I could have reduced him to ash.

Today I was coughing out tear gas and trying to get my eyes to focus.

Light angled onto the Sleeper. Fred Cook's wool blend suit was being eaten by parasites, a sickly bio-genetic transformation that looked a lot like maggots eating flesh. His hands, his face, his clothes—they were all being transformed into the flesh and uniform of Sinestro.

Sinestro sneered down at me, his fist now looming huge in my eyes, the golden ring glowing with power.

"You pathetic man," Sinestro said. "You should have joined me."

Near-blinded by the brilliance of the ring—the ring all but casting a *spell*—I looked into Creation and, seeing nothing, smiled at him. "How do you know I *didn't?*" I had out-done Sinestro on so many levels. My evil had been so much greater than his, my crimes so much worse.

My only regret about dying was doing it on the damned floor. But begging this automaton was completely out of the question.

"Hey!" a voice barked at Sinestro.

He turned to see Carol firing her weapon—a neutrino pulse emitter. Sinestro screamed in agony as the pulse disrupted the hold the Sinestro virus parasite had on Fred long enough for Fred to spin around and see Ollie, snarling, swinging a metal chair with both hands.

"Lights out, pal!" Ollie viciously hit Sinestro with the chair, smashing poor Fred's jaw as blood and teeth arced out of his mouth. The Sleeper tumbled back off of his feet as Carol rushed forward, firing another pulse at Fred for good measure. "Get the damned thing off!" she demanded.

Ollie got the Sinestro ring off as Ariss and his men surrounded Fred, guns drawn. Carol ignored the officers as she pulled a plastic vial out of her battle suit. "You gentlemen are still not getting me," she said as she concentrated on the vial. "You'll just shoot Fred. Your guns are useless against the real threat"—Ollie handed her the Sinestro ring—"these rings." Carol continued. "There are thousands of them, scattered across space and time. Each one of them is capable of transforming whoever wears one into Sinestro—an evil Green Lantern."

Carol dropped the ring into the plastic vial and sealed it. "These polymer vials are lined with lead and filled with corrosive acid. That should buy us some time until we can dispose of these things properly."

"Properly?" Ariss asked.

"The sun, sheriff," I said, stepping through the ruined pod wall. "We've got to find every one of the Sinestro rings and drop them into the sun."

Ariss gave me a look. "The sun. As in, *our* sun."

I gave Ariss the Look. Time was wasting. "Sheriff—the Sleepers know we're here. The longer we stay here, the more Sleepers will come. The more people will be hurt or killed."

Ariss did not fully understand all of it. He had seven severely wounded deputy sheriffs and a million dollars of damage to his jail. He didn't know any of us and, frankly, didn't know what to believe. His duty was to lock everybody up and call the governor.

Ariss looked down at Fred. The Sinestro virus was dying off, leaving scabs of dead tissue, and Fred was out cold—completely unaware of what had happened to him.

Then Ariss looked at me. Played his gut. "Go."

The Arrowplane's massive V/STOL jets fired in sheriff Tom Ariss's impound lot, setting off yet another shockwave in Lebanon, Ohio. Only, this time, Ariss's men had traffic blocked off and the flight cleared with the FAA. Captain Newsom was on the ground, directing the takeoff.

He'd always wanted to try that.

Our slim advantage was that the Sinestro virus parasite was, in essence, a sophisticated bio-genetic sequence programmed into the Sinestro rings. As each Sleeper was activated, they were no more experienced or knowledgeable in the ring's use than any average person who'd just found it on the sidewalk. For each Sleeper activated, it was Day One. Which was why Fred-Sinestro's hatred of Hal Jordan blinded him to the fact he should have eliminated Carol first. Should have blown up the Arrowplane first. Game Over. But, at their awakening, all the faux Sinestros had was hatred of all Green Lanterns, most especially Hal Jordan.

Ollie was piloting. He knew the plane better than I did, but the cut went through me, anyway, just the smallest echo of Biff and the X83. *The guy who does it, the guys who watch.* The plane only seated two, which landed Carol on my lap; something a lot less fun than you'd think it would be.

Nobody was talking.

It was time to suit up.

CHAPTER

13

C ody was at it again.

WOOF WOOF WOOF WOOF WOOF WOOF WOOF WOOF WOOF WOOF WOOF WOOF!

Jennifer Lynn Hayden screened out the dog's barking as she leaned against the door to Kyle Rayner's Greenwich Village apartment. In a midriff-length suede bolero jacket, hip-hugger jeans and Sketchers, Jennifer's sensual beauty and her startlingly emerald skin were both in abundant evidence, proof indeed that sexiness was beyond skin color. The woman was green as a popsicle and drop-dead gorgeous, which irritated Kyle to the extent that, whenever he and Jade—as she called herself—went to restaurants or clubs, all eyes would be on her. I mean, the *fish* would stop swimming. And the very next reaction, every single time, would be a mass pivoting of heads toward Kyle and a quizzical look, as if to say, *How'd a dweeb like him get a girl like her?* Kyle loved Jade. Loving her was easy enough to do. But she was rough on Kyle's already shaky self-esteem.

I hadn't yet arrived, but all events are recorded in Creation, and the Spectre's near-omniscience allowed him to speak to Creation and know what he was motivated to know. It was a lot like doing a Google search. Things Hal could not know at the time are now clear to the smallest detail, as I am again the Spectre and the Spectre is again Hal Jordan.

WOOF WOOF WOOF WOOF WOOF WOOF WOOF WOOF WOOF WOOF WOOF WOOF!

Jade had been waiting for twelve minutes. Her key was in her hand. She wasn't sure she wanted to use it.

This was her home, too. A place she'd shared with Kyle for quite some time. Their relationship was what it was, but Jade recently discovered a dimension she hadn't realized existed. A whole new reality, where Kyle was apparently having a different relationship than she was having. Like the mystery dirt you find when you pull your refrigerator away from the wall, Jade discovered things between them that had always been there but she had not seen. What frightened her was, perhaps she didn't want to see them. Perhaps she couldn't handle seeing them. And, yet, there they were: her having lunch with Eddie Roach, the exterminator guy, and Kyle asking her to marry him because of it.

Marry? Is that why you marry somebody, to keep them from having an innocent lunch with Eddie Roach the exterminator guy? Or was there something more to it? Mystery dirt behind the fridge.

How innocent was the lunch, really? Eddie—whose name really wasn't Roach, it was just fun to call him that—was a handsome guy. A funny guy. *An exterminator guy.* He worked with his hands. And he popped into their lives right around the time Kyle started flaking out on Jade. Right about the time Kyle had started emotionally checking out. Women have a radar about those kinds of things. Women like Maybelle ignore the warning signs. Women like Jade start packing.

Kyle had found an early pregnancy test kit in their bathroom, a discovery that had made Kyle even weirder. The notion of a child should have brought them closer together. Instead, it seemed to Jade that Kyle had started running from her. Reviewing his options. Wondering about their future, about his love for her. Things Jade thought were set in stone.

Being so young and so green, Jade was missing the point that panic is the natural response to men discovering they're about to become fathers. Women—regardless of circumstance—nearly always have some small joy, some great hope about their role in Creation and what was about to blossom in their lives. It takes men a bit longer. Men understand wrenches. Men understand Don Imus. Men understand frolicking with the happening green chick. "Dad" is somebody else. "Dad" has gray sideburns and wears old golf pants. "Dad" listens to Tony Bennett and still mourns the death of Hoss from *Gunsmoke.*

For many women, "baby" means the beginning of "the dispensation of mommy." For many men, "baby" means "the end of naked pizza". It's like getting a chip in your windshield; you know it's only the beginning, that a massive crack will eventually spider-web across the entire glass and the whole thing will need to be replaced. Baby will expose any weakness in your relationship. One minute you're nuzzling someone and whispering your greatest secrets, fantasizing about a long and happy future. The next, he or she has emotionally checked out, become one of the walking emotionally dead we see shuffling aimlessly through shopping malls across America.

Ever see that? That dead look in the guy's eye as he reluctantly sidles along with his wife while pushing the ubiquitous umbrella stroller with the fussy child who came as a surprise to them both; a child who is most certainly loved and, at least in Dad's case, most certainly regretted. His is the mask of desperation. *Kill me. Kill me now. Please.*

Jade could always tell the married couples in a restaurant by seeing who's not talking. If you see a couple, with or without the regretted child, who seem bored and aren't talking to each other, they are most surely married. And, whether they admit it or not, they are both looking for the nearest exit, which is likely to be some stupid, meaningless fight that simply presents an opportunity to end the misery they are both enduring. These are the same people who once couldn't keep their hands off each other. Who used to talk all night long, take interminable walks, who cried and prayed and demanded of God an eternal bond with each other, now rendered mute by the tyranny of pancakes and Simulac.

That was Jade at the door, telling herself she'd just come to pick up a few things and then back to her dad's house in Gotham City. She thought she and Kyle were on firmer ground than that. She thought things were fine. Instead she got the jittery excuses and emotional backup of a man terrified of being more than who he imagined he was. And then the totally half-baked marriage proposal—first behind the business with Eddie Roach, then, after the dust settled, when Kyle needed to prove he wasn't a schmuck by being a schmuck. You don't ask a woman to share the rest of her life with you just to protect your damned ego. It was so wrong and so awful and God, Kyle is such an idiot and what am I doing here, in the hall, listening to the damned dog bark?

WOOF WOOF WOOF WOOF WOOF WOOF WOOF WOOF WOOF WOOF WOOF WOOF!

I'll just get my things. Jade turned the key.

Kyle's apartment appeared to have been robbed. Virtually everything had been turned over and destroyed. Books, paintings, drawings.

Drawings of Jade. Everywhere. Torn. Ruined.

"Kyle," she whispered, figuring this for some fit of rage on Kyle's part. I mean, who'd want to rob *that* joint?

She scooted down and started organizing some of the chaos. Tears hit some of the papers in her hand before the emotional edge of it cut her. Things were going bad to worse. *We were fine,* she thought. *Everything was fine.*

But she knew, if that were true, she wouldn't be there, alone, picking up the ruined pieces of their life together.

Kyle Rayner had ruined a perfectly good lie.

Jade collected stacks of things and began organizing them into general categories of Junk Kyle Really Should Have Thrown Out Years Ago and My Stuff. She couldn't stop crying. Now she needed a tissue, so she made her way through the chaos to Kyle's drawing board and grabbed a Kleenex from the box. The TV was still on blue screen. Kyle's desk lamp was on, and there was a fabulous drawing of a duck that had somehow survived the carnage. The duck did its job—it made Jade smile. At least for a moment.

She plopped down among the debris, becoming part of the chaos. She thought about visiting Eddie Roach in the sanatorium. Yes, Eddie's encounter with the happy couple had left him clinically insane.

She didn't want to see Eddie so much as she wanted someone to touch her. *My God, please touch me.* She wanted the world to make sense again.

She wanted the lie back.

Jade wasn't pregnant. Wasn't planning to be pregnant. The early pregnancy test hadn't even been opened. Why? Because it belonged to someone else, her friend Sonya, the Czechoslovakian model. The woman had spent the night instead of dragging herself all the way back to Brooklyn after day one of a two-day shoot a few months back. She thought she might have been pregnant so she bought the test but ended up leaving it behind, unopened. She was, after all, a model. And blonde.

Then Kyle found the test and the wheels just came off the wagon. Jade chewed her lip, getting angry now. She needed to find Kyle. Not that they needed to talk so much as she needed to vent. It was "me time," the certain self absorption that puts women well on the road to becoming Maybelle. But anger was better than hurt, so Jade balled her fists and decided she was going to—

—Jade stopped in her tracks. Though she had seen it several moments before, *what* she had seen finally registered in her head:

Kyle's Green Lantern ring in the soap dish.

Jade sprang up, suddenly at Red Alert. She suddenly realized this wasn't about a lover's spat—this was an attack—

—which was when a trio of Sleepers burst into the apartment.

Eddie Roach had been a Sleeper—possessed and converted by the Sinestro Ring given to his grandfather back during World War II. One Sleeper. And he nearly destroyed the solar system, all by himself.

Now Jade was battling three Sleepers, by herself. She didn't recognize them—they could be Kyle's neighbors or the Comcast guy or the Mail Carrier—didn't matter. All that mattered is they all had Sinestro Rings and were firing at Jade as she dodged and fired back, manifesting the emerald plasma energy she'd inherited from her father, Alan Scott, the original Green Lantern.

The battle was fierce and swift, blowing holes in the walls and bursting windows, glass raining down to the street below. Jade was hit by one of the Sleepers' blasts, knocked through a wall into the bedroom, the wind knocked out of her as she returned fire, keeping the Sleeper at bay.

But it was a losing battle. These Sleepers were not as far along as Eddie had been—they had not been completely changed to Sinestros yet. Even so, there were three of them, and only one of her, and she was hurt.

Jade decided to make a strategic retreat, blowing a hole in her bedroom wall—

—only to find three more Sleepers waiting on the other side, bursting into her bedroom from the adjacent apartment. The mutated Cody was with them as they pounced on Jade.

"Nooo!" Jade screamed as she unleashed her power at full blast, hurling the dog and two of the Sleepers back, but they were racing back toward her before she reached the bedroom door.

Jade ducked into the living room, diving for the floor, and the Sleepers in there were hit by antimatter bursts from the Sleepers pursuing her from the bedroom, buying Jade precious seconds to reach the door. Near the door, she turned and fired back a huge blast for good measure, then whipped the front door open—

—to find Carol Ferris aiming her pistol at her.

"Down!" Carol ordered. Jade ducked as Carol fired off a wide-angle neutrino burst. Several Sleepers screamed in agony and collapsed as several more raced out of the bedroom, aiming their Sinestro Rings—

—and were hit by a barrage of incoming arrows. Jade whirled to see Green Arrow, holding his longbow and now wearing his costume and mask, racing out of the bedroom, having entered the apartment through the wall.

"Got us a problem, here," Arrow said, thumbing behind him.

Cody, the mutated Sinestro-Dog, galloped through the bedroom and leaped at Green Arrow. The dog had several arrows stuck in him but showed no signs of slowing.

"Jeeez!" Ollie snarled as he was bowled over by the massive beast. Carol had given G.A. special arrow tips designed to emit neutrinos on impact. Three of them should surely have severed the link between the parasite and the dog.

"Why isn't this working?" Carol exclaimed as she fired her plastic gun at the dog.

I ran into Kyle apartment, still wearing the humiliating orange prison jump suit, hoping not to get myself killed. "The neutrino emissions are severing the connection to the parasites," I said as I tried to pull the dog off, "but he's *still a really big dog!*"

"Little *help*, here!" Arrow snarled as he barely evaded the massive maw, a dozen pairs of eyes focusing on him. "And get this mutt a breath mint!"

Jade blasted the dog, the force carrying the dog, Ollie and myself backwards, the three of us slamming into a wall.

And then, quiet.

Ollie, pinned under the unconscious dog, snarled at me. "So," he said. *"This is your big move?"*

"We need to get to the JLA Watchtower," I shot back. "To the *moon*, Arrow! Now, I don't know of any way to do that without outside help!"

"Aquaman told you Kyle was wearing a Sinestro Ring," Carol said. "We needed to find out what happened here after Hal left."

"Well, here's what happened," Arrow sneered, "a *giant dog fell on him!!*" He struggled against Cody. "Get this thing off me!"

"Excuse me, gentlemen," Carol said as she removed the Sinestro ring grafted to Cody's paw, dropping the ring into another of her containers. "I've got the rest of the rings."

"Yeah, well," Green Arrow said as he finally managed to extract himself from Cody, "looks like you're gonna need a whole lot more containers."

"Not if we get this done," Carol said. "All Kyle had to do was emit a neutrino pulse, which would cause the rings' antimatter signature to, well, bleep or something—it'll help his power ring locate them."

"Yeah," G.A. said, dusting his costume off, "and *then* what?"

"Then you lock in and bring all of the rings to you at once," Jade said. "You just command the power ring to do it."

"Then a trip to the sun, and take out the trash," I said, still a bit annoyed that Kyle hadn't managed to accomplish something so simple.

Arrow started backing toward the door, his bow at the ready. "All righty then, let's get to it. The longer we stay, the more of these things we attract."

"Good deal," Carol said. "Jade—did Kyle leave his real power ring here?"

Jade was a little puzzled by the question. "How did you know? Who *are* you?"

"A friend," I told her. "Jade, Kyle was taken over by these things. He's in the sick bay at the JLA Watchtower. He's all right, but he was wearing a Sinestro Ring, not his own power ring."

Jade grabbed Kyle's ring out of the soap dish, "Well, we'd better get up there, get his ring to him—"

"Jade—there's no time for that," Carol said. "The JLA transporters are off-line and the Watchtower is in a special lockdown alert mode. Getting in will take some time."

Jade turned toward her. "What are you saying?"

"I'm saying that Aquaman is dying and we don't know Kyle's or John's status. I assume the rest of the League are on their way, but every minute we delay hundreds more Sleepers—*each* with the power of Sinestro—are activated. We've got to act now."

Jade whipped out a cell phone. "All right, then, I'll call my dad—"

"Jade," Carol said, softening, "your father is welcome to help. But we need to move even faster than that." Jade instinctively knew where Carol was leading, but didn't want to even consider the journey. "Jade, we've got to put that ring to use *now*."

Jade looked at the ring. She began to put it on, "I haven't thought of myself as a Green Lantern in a long time—"

"Jade." Carol was firm. "Kyle's ring has security lockouts that prevent others from using it. The only person who could possibly use it...." Carol searched for the right words, "...is the ring's original owner."

Jade stared at Kyle's ring. She wanted no part of Carol's suggestion. It was Kyle's ring. *Kyle's ring.*

Jade clenched the ring in her fist. "Absolutely not," she said.

Carol tried to draw her out, "Jade—"

Jade pointed at me, "That man is a killer. A destroyer. A murderer."

I bowed my head a bit, stung by the words. Words I'd said to myself a million times, but they still did damage when uttered by someone else.

Jade sneered at me. "He betrayed his oath. He destroyed the entire Corps! And now you want me to just *give* him Kyle's ring? *Give* him Kyle's power—Kyle's future?"

Carol grabbed Jade's arm and looked her in the eye, "Jade—there won't BE any future if we don't shut these Sleepers down. Kyle battled *one* Sleeper and almost lost the solar system. We're facing *thousands.*"

Jade sneered as her eyes welled up. She wasn't nearly there, yet. Not nearly ready to even stand in the same room with me.

"Listen, gals, love that Oprah crap, but time's a'wastin'," Ollie said, looking over his shoulder for more Sleepers.

Jade looked down at the defeated Sleepers at our feet. The virus was dying off, turning to scabs. "This wasn't *that* hard," she said. "We could still get the ring to Kyle, and—"

"And maybe he's fixed and maybe he's not!" Arrow exclaimed. "Lady—the fate of the whole danged planet is hanging on your soap opera! Give Hal the goddamned ring already!!"

I protested a bit weakly. "Jade—" It sounded so insincere I didn't believe it myself. "Do what you think is best."

Jade shot me a hateful look. A tear streaming, now. "What *I* think is best?"

"Yes. We'll do this any way you decide."

Jade felt played. She hated this, hated being there. *Why did I come here?*

She sneered at Ollie, who sneered back. *Screw you, kid.*

She looked hatefully at Carol, who gave her no energy.

And back to me. The very last thing she thought she'd be doing today was handing over Kyle's future to a mass murder. She stepped over to me, standing very close now.

"Promise me you won't go insane and destroy entire planets again."

I gave her The Look. "I can't."

"Promise me this plan of yours will work."

"I really can't." I had no promises for anyone. I didn't want Kyle's ring any more than she wanted me to have it.

An alcoholic doesn't want just one drink.

Jade held the ring up to my eye level. "This," she said, "belongs to the man I love. He will be expecting it back."

Our eyes locked for a moment before she placed Kyle Rayner's power ring in my hand and headed into the hall.

"Let's move, kids," Green Arrow said from the hall as he followed Jade.

Carol touched my arm as I stared at the ring in my hand. I looked up from the ring and into Carol's eyes where, for the first time in many, many years, I saw compassion.

And, perhaps, a bit more than that.

"We'll give you a moment," she said. She followed Jade and Ollie—

—leaving me standing among the ruins of Kyle's apartment, staring at the biggest mistake of my existence.

I wasn't sure this was entirely a good idea. In theory, all I'd need was a few minutes. A half-hour at most. Then the threat would be diminished, and I could return Kyle's ring and get back to spooking people as the Spectre.

But, things rarely work out the way you expect.

I turned the ring over in my hand, wishing someone would tell me what to do.

No matter what you do, Martin Jordan won't be home for dinner.

"Lantern," I said. It was a whisper. Nearly a prayer.

Across the room, Kyle's power battery shimmered into this plane of existence. I walked toward it.

I prayed for wisdom. *Please...don't let it happen again.*

I slipped the ring onto my hand.

Aiming my fist at the polished bell of the power battery, I looked for the courage of my convictions.

In brightest day...

I pulled my hand back. This was an incredible mistake. An alcoholic takes a sip.

I started to call to Carol—we'd just have to find another way. But, then I looked around at the unconscious people at my feet. People who may never be fully human again. There was a legion of Sleepers out there, the certain destruction of Earth and possibly all Creation.

There simply was no time. And that was the excuse that worked for me.

I aimed my fist at the battery once again. I swore the oath. I *meant* the oath.

In brightest day
In blackest night
No evil shall escape my sight
Let those who worship evil's might
Beware my power...

Green Arrow, Jade and Carol waited together on the street below. No words were spoken. Ollie looked about furtively and Jade tried to contain her anger. Carol's eyes drifted skyward, and a yearning deep within her threatened to burst through her chest. God, how she missed it. How she *needed* it—the power of Star Sapphire. Being stuck there, on the ground, like some...some...mortal...was damming to her, especially now, when she could make a real contribution, make a real difference. Especially now that, slowly descending from high above her, was a vision of everything she once had...and everything she'd lost.

Green Lantern.

I was Green Lantern again. Born again. In love again.

I was home.

14

I*'m too sexy.*

Waiting there in the shadows, Guy Gardner's eyes narrowed to a menacing glare.

I'm too sexy.

His power ring sparkled with emerald energy, ready for anything.

I'm too sexy.

The Green Lantern seal on Guy's stylized jacket was eclipsed by the ambient light.

I'm too sexy.

Guy's oversized mountain boots were firmly planted in a battle stance.

I'm too sexy.

His sparkling white teeth clenched as he prepared for the ordeal before him.

I'm too sexy.

Guy's sublimely athletic buttocks flexed and clenched.

He was ready for action. "Bring it," he hissed, fists clenched.

The massive drum beat pounded out of the subwoofers beneath him as the stage lights flashed and a bright strobe overhead got the audience to their feet. Guy flexed and clenched and brazenly undulated, putting his athletic posterior to work as the song thundered out of the loudspeakers.

I'm too sexy for my shirt too sexy for my shirt
So sexy it hurts
And I'm too sexy for Milan too sexy for Milan
New York and Japan

The largely female audience went wild, leaping and clapping, as Guy spun around to face them, an arrogant, warrior's grimace on his face as he heel-toe-stepped forward of the lights and commenced his dance routine.

And I'm too sexy for your party
Too sexy for your party
No way I'm disco dancing

But Guy was indeed disco dancing. And, horror of horrors, he was actually good at it. Men dancing came in two basic varieties: the wildly effeminate and the laughably bad. Only the best dancers—the Fred Astaires, the Gene Kellies, the John Travoltas and, yes, the Michael Jacksons—could find that mystical, evanescent middle ground between the two, where a man could actually dance and not look stupid. Guy Gardener, the one, true Green Lantern (according to him, at least) had found that zone. In fact, he was mayor of the zone.

I'm too sexy for my car too sexy for my car
Too sexy by far
And I'm too sexy for my hat
Too sexy for my hat what do you think about that

Women were screaming and falling over themselves. A very attractive young woman bolted on-stage to dance with Guy, and Guy never missed a move as he incorporated the curvaceous beauty into his routine. Then a second woman joined him onstage, and Guy made it a Guy sandwich, never loosing his determined warrior's expression as he gracefully—and 'graceful' is never the first word you think of to describe Guy Gardner—floated through elegant jazz and modern dance moves, to the utter delight of the overflow crowd at Club 86.

A gregarious and often obnoxious extrovert, dancing was actually fairly serious business for Guy Gardner. He took jazz and modern dance classes as part of his physical therapy after he was disabled in a school bus accident. To become fluent and graceful after fearing, for months, that he'd never walk again, was a major victory in Guy's life.

An extremely macho individual with a short fuse, Guy held a Masters in Developmental Studies from Morgan State and served several years as a social worker before earning his teacher's certificate and dedicating his life to teaching physical education courses for developmentally challenged students.

Rowdy as a sailor, he was, nevertheless, Saint Guy, a deeply committed and, ultimately, deeply serious and sincerely noble person, who used cutting sarcasm as a defense mechanism. If you took away Guy's self-parody and sophomoric layers, beneath you'd find the soul of a hero.

But that would require peeling a lot of layers.

The stage was ultimately not big enough for Guy, who leaped onto a nearby table and began unbuttoning the jacket of his self-styled Green Lantern uniform while undulating to the disco beat. Now women were trying to shove cash into his belt, and the crowd was going absolutely crazy, which—for a man like Guy—was like a heroin rush.

For reasons I could never understand, Guy had a big hole in his center. Some kind of inferiority complex that forced the ridiculous party boy persona to the surface while masking his true value. Guy needed external validation. Needed to be told he had value and meaning. That he was handsome and brave. The women screaming were intoxicating to Guy. It was a drug fix, a real high for him. Though his face showed almost no interest—a mask of macho indifference—inside, Guy was eating this up. He was having the time of his life.

Which allowed him to miss the point that his ring was glowing because I had sent him a message. Learning, well after the fact, what Guy had actually been up to while we were trying to warn him didn't help endear the man to me.

I'm too sexy.

The trip to the moon took nearly eight minutes. *Eight minutes.* Did I *really* move *that slow* when I was Green Lantern? The joy of returning to my beginning—to myself—was tempered by just how limiting the inane restraints built into the ring's software were. Things designed to protect mortal sanity now worked the opposite way for me, driving me out of my mind. A mind that had been enlightened and in touch with all Creation, now shoved back inside flesh and bone. It was a bad fit. I was out of sorts. Sitting through a movie I already knew the ending to.

Jade flew next to me in silence. She could have used her powers to communicate with me through my—through Kyle's—power ring, but she chose not to. She just wanted to get this over with. Ollie and Carol rode along in a ring-generated facsimile of Carol's X1010—which she had dubbed the "Arrow-plane" as an incentive to get Ollie to suit up. Neither could be of much help in the vacuum of space, but Jade insisted they see this thing through, if for no other reason than they both have enormous emotional influence over me and can, hopefully, keep me from destroying the universe and everything in it.

Which was, ironically, the farthest thing from my mind. The Green Lantern power ring—the most powerful weapon in the universe—felt completely limiting and completely cheap. Destroy the universe? With *this* trinket? Omnipotence and omniscience is a really tough check to cash in. Wisdom and an expanded consciousness had made it simply impossible for me to repeat those past errors, as I now knew where I had gone wrong and how. Jade worried over nothing: let's take out the trash and go home.

I looked at the stars as I crept toward the moon. Their beauty and majesty, once so taken for granted as I blithely traveled around the galaxy, humbled me all the more now that I was once again mortal. *Beloved,* I thought. *I will never take you for granted again.* The beauty, the vastness, the architecture—it was all worth defending. The Green Lantern Corps was a noble calling. A worthy thing to commit your life to. Kyle and I would need to have a talk once this was over.

Even if one of us actually had a transport key, we could not use the JLA transporter once the Watchtower was put in lockdown mode. Nobody in, nobody off until the lockdown was released. None of us were active JLA members, so none of us knew how to release it, but we assumed Aquaman's distress call would have brought the cavalry running by now. By the time we crawled, slowly, to the moon, we expected to find things well in hand.

I halfway expected to find Guy Gardner—the one remaining Green Lantern on Earth—to be waiting for us. I attempted to contact him through his ring, but Guy either wasn't wearing it or ignored my signal. Carol left a message on Guy's cell phone warning Guy of the imminent threat from the Sleepers, and instructing him to use his ring to contact me immediately. Being the single-minded megalomaniac that he is, I doubt Guy would bother contacting me, but would instead race to where the action was. Guy loved a good fight.

Of course, I didn't know that, at the time, Guy was otherwise occupied. Backstage at Study 86, Guy's cell phone flashed with a message reminder as the dance music continued to thunder out across the audience. Guy was table dancing now, slinging his shirt around like a flag while women doused his bare chest with wine.

I'm too sexy...

We entered the moon's orbit at about seven minutes, thirteen seconds into our flight—a completely arbitrary time period the ring had set to make me feel the distance traveled in a visceral way. It was so annoying. The ring was certainly powerful enough to simply blink us to Tycho, rather than drag us through this arduous foot-shuffling. I briefly wondered if there was a way to update the software in the ring for advanced and cosmically aware minds like mine.

Complex calculations necessary to keep us from becoming disorientated and hopelessly lost in the vastness of space—such as the moon's 5.145 degree orbital inclination to ecliptic and 6.68 degree equatorial inclination to orbit—were the least significant components of that software, which included complex, detailed star charts of hundreds of galaxies and included complex instruction sets on modifying the auto-generated life support force field to process a proper atmosphere under the prescribed conditions. Surely, technology that sophisticated could include a mode for advanced users.

Arcing around the southeastern rim of *Mare Serenitatis*, we could see Taurus-Littrow, Apollo 17's landing site, in the dark deposit between massif units of the southwestern Montes Taurus. The Lunar Roving Vehicle, a kind of dune buggy for the moon, sat abandoned near the descent stage of *Challenger*, Apollo 17's Lunar Excursion Module. We turned south over the Cayley Plains, soaring across the breathtaking Descartes formation before hitting the barren plains leading toward Tycho.

Ollie was bored. This was stuff he'd seen on the Discovery Channel by accident while surfing for Broncos scores. Carol chewed her lip a bit. Coming along had been a mistake, she now realized. She was suddenly jealous of Jade, who was flying by my side—a place Carol wanted to be. Not necessarily with Hal, she told herself. Just...*out there*. No space suit. No clunky, steel rocket. Carol closed her eyes, trying to ignore the anxiety building within her, but that only empowered her imagination, enabling the movie playing inside her head. A film starring Star Sapphire.

It's not fair. Something deep inside Carol writhed and twisted. *He has his power back.* Carol shook her head, trying to shut it out. Shut *her* out—Star Sapphire. But the clawing only got worse. The *need.* Something deep within whispered to her. *I'm still here...*

As we closed in on Tycho, the horizon line gave way to the angular spire of the JLA Watchtower—which had been nearly destroyed. There was massive damage to the main structures, evidence of explosions and fire damage. Ice covered most every surface as some incredible event had apparently torn through the base's cryogenic plants. There was no power evident, no lights in the Watchtower as we banked around it. Only evidence of what appeared to have been a battle to the death, one the JLA's majestic headquarters had apparently lost.

"Everybody on your toes." I immediately wondered why I said things like that. More reflex, I suppose. "Jade—take up a perimeter and watch for Sleepers. They could be massing on the other side of the moon." I banked around, towing my glider behind me, "Where's the front door to this place?"

"Hell if I know," Ollie responded. "This is no longer my outfit, remember? The once or twice I came here, I took the transporter."

There was the problem. I could use my ring to, perhaps, burst through a wall but, not knowing for certain how connected the Watchtower's systems were, I might cause more problems than I solved. "There has got to be an airlock someplace—"

"Won't do you any good if there is, Hal," Carol offered. "If the Watchtower's been attacked, then surely the lockdown protocol has either saved Aquaman and the Lanterns—"

"—or everybody's dead in there," I concluded. "Either way,

those protocols are still in place, which means every access point is likely fortified against attack. That gives us a slim hope for our friends."

"Yeah," Ollie chimed in, "but it also means you might bang at the door all day without getting anywhere. We need a back way in."

Executing concentric turns around the perimeter, neither my power ring nor Jade could detect any Sleepers—which didn't mean they weren't merely a heartbeat away, hiding in the plain sight of the vastness of Creation. But, there was no "back door" to be found.

"Hal," Jade said, "I remember my dad saying something about an artificial river underground...a highly pressurized salt tank that runs for miles around Tycho."

I commanded my power ring to scan for salt water, finding Aquaman's sea run beneath the Moon's crust. "Got something. The tank appears extremely fortified as well—"

"Yeah," Carol said, "but it is water—under extreme pressure, right?"

"Just like fish-face's brain..." Ollie muttered.

"What if you—"

I aimed my fist down at the lunar surface. "Cranked up the pressure, yes?"

"There *must* be tectonic plates below the surface," Jade said. "Try shifting those around."

"Wrong, kids. The moon is dead," Carol said. "The most recent signs of volcanism here are a million years old."

"Not quite," Ollie interjected. "Equipment left on the moon by Apollo astronauts detected a series of 'moonquakes' during the last decade. This place isn't *completely* dead, but the lunar crust is twenty-five miles deep, so Hal really needs to bring it to get a quake going."

There was a brief moment of silence as we all stared at Green Arrow.

"What?" he finally said, "Oh, only *you* people get to know stuff?"

That's when it hit me: I'd really, really missed him. Missed *us*. I allowed myself that moment and then got on with it.

Creating a gravity well with my power ring, I was able to use the moon's gravitational field to press down against the tectonic plates deep beneath the surface, creating an ad-hoc tractor beam. The tractor beam forced the massive plates to shift only slightly—

—which was when I started second-guessing myself. After all, moving those plates an inch too far in either direction could cause an earthquake so massive it would destroy the Watchtower and perhaps a great deal of the moon with it. It could be Coast City all over again.

Things I took completely for granted as Spectre—an inscrutable being under providential guidance—I locked up on as the mortal and flawed Hal Jordan, a man who had played God more than once with tragic consequences.

Of course, my hesitation, my second guessing, could cost us all our lives. I was wearing the costume, but not the soul of the man I once was. Green Lantern, in his hopeful naiveté, would have just moved the damned plates. Instead, with lives held in the balance, I hesitated.

"Hal?" Carol stirred me from the moment. Ego won out over conscience as I didn't want her to know how far I'd fallen, how nervous I was to even wear the damned thing.

I fired the ring.

The ring's energy shifted the tectonic plates mere fractions of an inch, but that was enough to create a massive earthquake just below Aquaman's salt water tank, which in turn caused a destabilization of the ultra-pressurized environment.

The resulting explosion was completely silent. A fabulous ice show, a fireworks display frozen in the moment, materialized before us as the water in the tank exploded through a rupture and immediately formed a stationary, crystalline geyser arcing 200 feet above the moon's surface.

"Okay, we're in," I said before I could stop myself. "Jade, watch the perimeter while we—"

"No," Jade said bluntly.

I stopped, annoyed. I really didn't have time for this, "What?"

"I gave you his ring," Jade said, angry. "Don't ask me to just hang around out here while you see if the man I love is dead or alive."

In other words, *how do I know I can trust you?* After all, I had Kyle's ring. I had Kyle's power, his future. How would she ever know that I didn't just let him die.

Carol interjected, speaking to her through her link to my ring. "Jade—we don't know what we are up against. Either you or Hal needs to cover our backs out here."

"And *he's* your boyfriend, right?"

Carol snarled at her, "He's the most experienced, Jade. If you really love Kyle, Hal is his best chance."

I didn't wait for Jade's decision. She would either stay or not stay. Time was wasting and, frankly, I didn't want to wear Kyle's ring one moment more than I had to. "Do whatever you want," I said. "We're going in."

I dismissed the ring-generated Arrowplane and narrowed Green Arrow and Carol's life support bubble into a tight oval as I dragged them behind me.

Jade, furious, pursued us for a moment, but broke off just before I smashed through the gleaming crystal sculpture, sending twisted ribbons of ice arcing across the lunar sky as I used the ring's power to drill through the ice geyser's diamond-like sur-face and burrow down into the salt water tank. Behind us, Jade banked around in the lunar sky, turning reluctantly in a patrol orbit to keep us safe.

The dance number completed, Guy, his chest glistening with perspiration and white wine, struck his most macho, most serious warrior pose as the auctioneer opened the floor to bids.

"Now, ladies—how much am I to bid for this prime specimen of manhood? An academic scholar with a Master's Degree from Morgan State, former member of the Justice League, and famed member of the Green Lantern Corps! Do I hear a thousand?"

He did.

And the bidding became ferocious from there, moving quickly to five and then ten thousand. Guy struck another pose, turning his head to give the ladies a heroic grimace. Tom Cruise. Mark Walberg. Usher. Batman.

The women went wild. Some of them would have taken out second mortgages to afford a date with Guy Gardner. The number spiraled as Guy flexed and pouted. This charity auction was, for Guy, the best of both worlds, feeding both his narcissism and his innate nobility. Not only would he raise a lot of money for a local children's charity, but he'd get to have hot chicks fighting over him.

I'm too sexy.

Beneath the moon's surface, I found a great deal of the sea water had been lost to our penetration. Nearest our point of entry, I found water frozen solid as granite. Burrowing through required intense focus of will, but it had to be easier than trying to break through defenses designed by the likes of The Martian Manhunter and Steel. Aquaman's tank extended several miles in a wide loop before it turned back toward the Watchtower, and there was absolutely no light in the tunnel. Aquaman being used to leisurely swims along the ocean floor, the darkness posed no particular problem for him. But I had never been inside this tank before, and was only marginally familiar with the layout of the Watchtower itself. The ring illuminated our path as we traveled ever farther through the near-empty tunnel, none of us knowing what was waiting for us in the blackness at the other end.

And, I suppose that's the truest dynamic of heroism. Green Arrow would as soon cut off his left nostril as admit he was afraid, but he had to be anxious about what we were getting into. I had enough confidence in the power ring—limited though it may be—to protect me, but, even so, a part of me obsessed with the potential for losing my humanity after having only regained it a day before.

Heroes defy the strongest human instinct—self-preservation—in the name of a greater good. Our greater good was saving the lives of our friends and defeating an enemy that threatened all of our existence. And, it was the pursuit of that greater good that made burrowing deep into the heart of a dead citadel—built and maintained by the most powerful beings on the planet, that had nonetheless been all but destroyed by enemy attack—seem both reasonable and rational.

The tunnel led to a decompression chamber separated by a double-hatch system. Rather than explode up from the freezing depths, I first commanded my ring to scan the room from below, the three of us emerging from the pool only when I had confirmed we were, for the moment, safe.

I flooded the tank bay with neutrino emissions, just in case Sleepers were hiding in the shadows. There were none. The bay, like the rest of the Watchtower, was completely black. My ring illuminated the room in subtle green hues as I asked Ollie which way.

"Which way to where?" Green Arrow asked.

"To sick bay—where John and Kyle are."

"And, you are asking me this *because?*" Ollie asked, sarcastically. "Hal—I've been here, what, once or twice? And I was always following Plastic Man's silly ass around. How would I know?"

"There must be a schematic, a diagram of some kind," Carol suggested as she looked around.

"What, 'You Are Here' with a big arrow?" Ollie said, devolving into Ollieisms. "Not a shopping mall, Carol. And, if there *were* a panel like that, watch me now, it'd be shut down like everything else."

Aiming my fist at the ceiling, I exhaled loudly, annoyed at my suddenly too-linear thinking, "Locate King Orin of Atlantis." The power ring projected a schematic of the Watchtower on the ceiling, displaying our location and Aquaman's several levels above.

"You-are-*here,*" Carol snarled, pointing at the schematic. Green Arrow let that one go.

"Getting from point 'A' to point 'F' won't be a cake walk," Arrow offered. "The trick is to deliberately set off certain booby traps while avoiding others. And—"he pointed at my hand"—you probably need to take that thing off."

I paused a moment, Green Arrow being no scientist, and asked, "Why?"

"Because the Watchtower's security system is looking for metahumans—super-powered invaders." Carol answered. "The more human you seem, the more effectively we fly under the radar."

"Yeah," Ollie agreed. "What she said."

Staring at the ring on my finger, I was suddenly consumed by my own hypocrisy. Despite the soul searching about putting the thing on, truth was, I didn't want to take it off.

"Hal?" Carol said.

"Yes, yes of course," I said, removing the ring as the bright orange Warren County Jail jumpsuit replaced my Green Lantern uniform. "There. Three humans."

Green Arrow pried an access panel off. "Let's get this done, kids."

At Club 86, the bidding for a date with Guy Gardner slowed at an unprecedented $24,700, and the auctioneer began to gavel in the final bid.

It wasn't good enough. Guy wanted $25,000.

"Hey, c'mon—what's another lousy three hunnert?" Guy demanded, flexing his well-toned biceps. "I mean, *look* at this? It's a thinga beauty and a joy forever, ladies!"

Twenty-five thousand.

Guy turned around and flexed his moneymaker, "Four hours a day on the Stairmaster, honies!"

Twenty-seven five.

Guy turned again, giving the ladies his best devilish glare. Guy actually had a pretty good one. "A car this fine don't pass your way everyday, ladies," he said, devilishly. "Don'tcha wanna ride?"

Twenty-nine two.

Guy displayed his power ring, which was glowing brightly, grinning, "And you won't *believe* the places I can tickle you with *this,*" Which was the first time Guy noticed his ring was trying to signal him.

Frowning, he turned away from his adoring fans, activating his ring, thinking, *Kyle, you twit, can't you see I'm workin', here?*

No connection was made. Either Kyle was no longer interested in talking to Guy, or something had happened to Kyle. Narcissism was Guy's first line of defense. *Feh. I'm sure it's nuthin',* and he turned his attention back to the bidding, which was now a whopping $30,000 for the Special Kids Fitness and Health program.

"*Sold!*" The auctioneer shouted as he gaveled in the winning bid of $30,575 to a tall, athletic brunette in a form-fitting dress. Guy was absolutely beguiled as the ravishing beauty approached him, check in hand, her shoulder-length hair falling gently across her amber skin.

"Honey," Guy said as he leaned forward to kiss her, "prepare for an experience!"

The woman smiled as she moved to kiss Guy, "Funny, I was about to tell you the same thing..."

Ssszzzaaaaaaacckkk!

Guy was suddenly and violently propelled across the room, smashing through tables and bowling over many of the women bidders, their bid paddles flying across the room.

Picking himself up off of the floor, Guy shook it off, narrowing his eyes as he wondered what the hell just happened. That's when he saw his winning bidder, the tall brunette, walking purposefully toward him, her fist extended. And, on her finger—

—a Sinestro ring. Firing.

Guy was propelled back through the wall of the night club, taking most of the club's façade with him as he smashed into a passing bus, splintering the windows and creating a huge dent in the side of the bus. Guy had no idea whatsoever what was going on. Shaking it off, he threw up a force field—

—which the incoming yellow energy sliced through effortlessly, slamming Guy again, this time through a deli's storefront window, Guy ending up sprawled in cold cuts.

That did it. Guy was ticked.

"All right, sister—you wanna *dance?*"

Shrugging off his disorientation, Guy propelled himself across the street, his ring at the ready, his force field fully up now, and plowed back into Club 86, tackling the Sleeper, chivalry be damned.

Guy pounded the woman into the floor, even as club bouncers raced to pull off the bare-chested hero. "Get *off* me!" Guy snarled, hurling the massive bouncers back, before grabbing a fistful of his winning bidder's hair, snarling and menacing her with his fist and power ring.

"Who the hell are you? And, are we still going out?"

The Sleeper smiled as the Sinestro virus ate away her beauty, replacing it with the red hues of the eternal sworn enemy of all Green Lanterns. "You will die at my hands, Guy Gardner! You and *all* Green Lanterns!"

Guy didn't get it. She was such a groovy chick a minute ago. Now she was beginning to resemble...*nah. Couldn't be...*

Guy was nailed broadside by a massive energy discharge, knocking him clear into the stage as patrons and club staff raced for their lives. Guy shook it off to see three more Sleepers moving toward him—two men and another woman. All had Sinestro rings and all were in various stages of transformation.

"What in hell's bathroom is goin' on, here?" Guy wondered, his mind suddenly shifting to the classified JLA security briefing, marked URGENT, that he'd received some days before, which he'd used, unread, to prop up a wobbly sofa in his bar.

Before he could find any answers, Guy was blown back through the club, through the kitchen and smashed into the rear wall—embedded, Wyle E. Coyote style, in the brick, Guy smiled an evil smile and borrowed a line from his favorite *Loony Tunes* character:

"Of course, you realize, this means *war.*"

Guy Gardener exploded out of the bar, flying at full speed, snarling with rage, dragging all four Sleepers with him, caught in a ring-generated giant net. As the Sleepers slashed through the plasma construct, they were caught in a hail of gunfire from Guy's ring-generated 50mm machine gun. Firing plasma "bullets" faster than the Sleepers could react, Guy cut through their defenses, nailing the Sleepers, who collapsed on the sidewalk before Guy dropped a ring-created piano on them, smashing them through the pavement.

Guy then created a ring-generated cement mixer and dumped plasma "cement" into the crevasse in the sidewalk, incapacitating the Sleepers while he reached in and yanked rings off of their hands as they reached out of the goop.

"Yeah, yeah, yeah," Guy muttered as he yanked their rings off. "Ya mutha."

Guy looked at the Sinestro rings in his hand. "Don't know what this means, but it prolly ain't good," he said. His opponents were all unconscious now, the Sinestro virus retreating, turning to dead skin and scabs. "Oh, *yumm*," Guy sneered.

Just as Guy thought, *Well, I'd better start checkin' my messages,* he was hit with another blast, sending him spiraling, the Sinestro Rings now tossed in the air as Guy was blown backward.

Landing on his rear several yards away, Guy wiped his mouth with the back of his hand, snarling ferally, his eyes narrowed. "All right, you punks," he demanded, *"bring it!"*

And they did.

Guy looked out over the New York skyline to see Sleepers flying toward him.

Hundreds of them blacking out the sky.

CHAPTER

15

O*rin.*
Black Mantis's elliptical onyx helmet shimmered out of the black. Before his appearance, there had only been black. Only been silence for the dying king.

You can hear me, can you not?

King Orin of Poseidonis scowled in the darkness. The anti-biogens used to destroy potential bio-threats were harmless to humans but toxic to him. His voice was nearly gone and he had almost no energy.

"I...hear you..." Aquaman hissed at his most hated enemy.

I'm glad we could spend these last moments together, Orin. To achieve...closure.

Aquaman had absolutely no interest in achieving closure with the murderer of his infant son. Black Mantis was a damning reminder of Orin's erratic history of victories and defeats.

What is your dying wish, O King?

"My hands..." Aquaman said, his voice cracking from dehydration, "...around your throat...one last time..." Aquaman spat at his devil, the man who'd cost him everything. Mera, Aquaman's wife, had gone insane after their child died. He lost everything he loved, and eventually he lost everything he was. Rebuilding his world had been an imperfect and difficult process.

He hadn't quite gotten to the point where he was satisfied with his life's achievements. He wasn't ready to die.

King Orin's life was ending much the way it began, abandoned, gasping for breath, naked and alone in a strange place. As an infant, Orin had been left by King Trevis to die on Mercy Reef. He now faced his journey's end trapped in a sealed compartment near the sick bay in the JLA's headquarters on the moon. The Watchtower's anti-biogens had long since dissipated, but their effects were still toxic to Aquaman's unique body chemistry. He needed to return to the sea and quickly, but the lockdown protocols had shuddered a dozen emergency bulkheads between him and his saltwater tank below.

The power was now off. There would be no more emergency calls or radio transmissions. There would only be the encroaching cold as the Watchtower's life support dwindled down to frozen death. Orin faced his end with grim stoicism, bearing the burden of the many ghosts coming to pay their last respects.

He had already been visited by King Trevis, Porm, the dolphin who had raised him from infancy, and Arthur Curry, the kindly lighthouse keeper who'd eventually adopted Orin and raised him as his own. So many faces, so many ghosts had found him there, between those bulkheads, dying in the blackness. Now, just as Aquaman would breathe his last and close his eyes forever, this torture...

Orin.

Aquaman sneered at Mantis. "Go away! Go away and be damned!" Shouting nearly finished him. He became dizzy and almost passed out.

Mantis refused to leave.

It is your curse, he said. *The Curse of Kordax.* The ridiculous superstition that led Aquaman's father to abandon his own son. *We will be together soon.*

Aquaman gave his last moments to spitting a curse at Black Mantis, who had long overstayed his welcome.

Orin...

"Damn...you..." Aquaman snarled.

Orin...

"Begone...hateful spirit..."

It was about then that I realized: Aquaman must be hallucinating.

Carol Ferris, Green Arrow and I were trapped in the very cramped confines of the power junction between sick bay and the monitor womb above. We actually ended up having to go several levels past sick bay in order to safely double back without being stopped by the Watchtower's automatic defenses.

But, now we were caught between the rock and another rock, and Aquaman was apparently hearing someone else. "Orin!" I called, knowing he could hear me through the bulkhead.

"Be damned! Damned, I tell you!" Aquaman hissed from the other side. His voice was scratchy and fading and he was coughing. There was no time.

Sandwiched into the power junction, all three of us would be vaporized, instantly, if the main power came on-line, which would surely happen the minute the rest of the Justice League arrived. I reached into the pocket of my bright orange jumpsuit and looked at the Green Lantern ring. Normally, it would be so simple to power up and punch through the bulkhead. But I was certain Martian ingenuity had anticipated every super-villain attack. Powering up would definitely put us on the radar, and then *game over.*

I needed Aquaman to release the bulkhead manually. I needed him to snap out of it. "Orin, dammit!"

"Spawn...of...evil—" Aquaman spat as he began to pass out.

No, no, no. We were too close to lose them now. "Orin—it's Hal! Hal Jordan! I need you to focus!!"

A strategic blunder. Aquaman struggled to become more alert. "H-Hal?"

"Yes, it's me! Now, I need you to—"

"N-no..." Aquaman hissed. "I will...I will stop you...with my dying breath..."

Aquaman thought I was still Parallax. Still the enemy.

"Orin, no, I'm *me* again—human! I'm not a—"

"Dammit, fish-face, open the hatch!" Green Arrow screamed from below me.

I looked down at him. *Thanks for helping.*

Oddly enough, it worked. Aquaman became just a bit more lucid, "Ollie? G-green A-ar-row?"

"Yeah, you smelly sardine-head! Now *focus* before we all *die*, ya got that?"

Aquaman used his waning strength to sit up. He tried to focus there, in the black. "W-what...do I do..."

"The main power is out, so you have to release the bulkhead manually," Green Arrow said. "We can't open it until you give the all-clear. Look for a release handle somewhere near the floor!"

Every move was agony, every breath labored as the king slowly felt around in the dark unto his hand rested on an over-sized manual release handle. The bulkheads had to be opened from the other side, but as a safety precaution they could not be opened unless the protectee inside—Aquaman—gave the all-clear by pulling the manual release.

"Got...got it..." Aquaman said as he took hold of the handle with both hands. The handle was a forty-pound throw, normally nothing to a man as powerful as Aquaman. But in his desperately weakened state, pain ripped through every fiber as he strained against the handle.

"What's he doing?" Green Arrow asked.

"Not sure," I said. "I don't know how much strength he's got left."

It felt as if Aquaman's arms were being pulled out of their sockets. His lungs began to fail and he couldn't breath. His heart racing, gasping for breath, Aquaman gave the handle his final moments.

A mechanical panel slid open in the crawl space, changing a red panel to a green panel. The all-clear. "Hang on!" I said as I used my entire weight on the bulkhead release, and the emergency bulkheads surrounding Aquaman slid back into their open positions.

Aquaman was passed out on the floor as Carol, Green Arrow and I squeezed out of the power junction. Sick bay was only a few doors away, but, without the code to shut down the emergency system, it was a few doors too far.

"Orin!" Green Arrow shouted at Aquaman while giving him firm but therapeutic slaps. "C'mon...wakey-wakey! We need the code, Orin—to shut down the emergency system!"

Aquaman was drifting toward death. Blind, he could barely hear Ollie.

"*Fish-face! C'mon!*" Ollie shouted. "The *code!*"

Orin winced with pain. Turning his head, he mumbled, "S—snap—"

Arrow gave us a quizzical look. "Snap? Snap *what?* Snap *who?*" But, it was too late. Aquaman slipped into a coma.

I placed Kyle's power ring on my finger. "I can power up the comm-panel Aquaman was using, but, the moment I do, expect the Watchtower's back-up systems to detect us and trap us in a force field."

"So," Carol concluded, "we'll only have one shot at entering the code."

"Yes."

"And Aquaman only gave us a fragment of the code."

"Apparently."

"And, if we enter it wrong, we'll be trapped here and Aquaman will die."

"That's about the size of it," I said, aiming my fist at the comm-panel. "Ollie, you ready?"

Green Arrow rubbed his chin, "I dunno, Hal—it's a big leap. I mean, Fin-head could have been delirious."

"No time, Ollie," I said. "I'm going."

Ollie braced himself. He wasn't the greatest speller. "Oh...oh what the hell."

I fired the ring.

Emerald energy shot into the comm-panel and it instantly came to life, even as a series of sophisticated force fields slammed down in place, trapping us inside the hall. Within seconds, the onboard sensors would likely analyze the source of the power and conclude it was a Green Lantern—likely a rogue Green Lantern like Sinestro—and would dispatch resources to neutralize my power ring.

All of which was to say: Ollie had better get it right the first time.

On the comm-panel, Ollie tapped into the touch screen: SNAPPER.

As in *Snapper Carr,* the team's mascot in the early days.

Nothing.

"Dammit!" Arrow exclaimed, "I told you! I told you this was stupid!"

"Wait!" Carol demanded as she lunged forward, hitting the ENTER key on the touch screen.

Still nothing.

And then, suddenly, the force fields clicked off, and emergency lighting flooded the hall. The Watchtower was secure from lockdown.

Ollie sneered at Carol. "Teacher's pet?"

I carried Aquaman as I ran toward sick bay, "Move!"

Sick bay was a disaster. A terrible fight had left most of the equipment mangled and twisted. The main power was offline so only limited emergency power was available. Kyle Rayner and John Stewart were still unconscious, but they showed no signs of the Sinestro virus.

"Looks good," Carol said as she flooded the room with neutrino emissions. I hooked Aquaman up to a special breathing unit filled with saltwater while Green Arrow lifted the comatose Green Lanterns into medical bays.

"We need to get Aquaman down to the saltwater tank below," I said, covering the monarch with a triage gown. "How about those two?"

Green Arrow was reading medical data from screens mounted above the comatose heroes. "If I hadda guess—looks like some kinda severe shock to their central nervous systems. My guess is they'll be out for a while."

"We haven't got a while," I said, using the power ring to ditch the hideous orange jumpsuit and restore my Green Lantern uniform, while trying to mask my relief that Kyle remained, for the moment, out of commission. "Something or someone attacked this station—and my money would be on Sinestro."

"Hal—you've got to shut those rings down—now!" Carol demanded. *Well, no kidding.* The human ability to state the obvious was grating. Carol handed me a pack with several vials inside: the captured Sinestro rings. "Go!" she ordered.

"I'll get Sardine-face downstairs," Green Arrow offered.

"I'll keep an eye on the guys," Carol said as we moved out.

"*Hey!*" a voice crackled over the comm. We turned to see Guy Gardner snarling at us, "Anybody *awake* up there? I got me a situation!"

I leaned in to speak, "Guy? Guy—what's going on?"

"Hal? Hal *Jordan?* Geez, how long have I been sleeping?"

"Guy—"

"You're supposed to be an all-knowing, omniscient spook, rattling chains and the like, and *you're* asking *me* what's going on?"

I had no time for this. "Guy—"

"Look, there's a buncha guys with power rings that look just like Sinestro's. In fact, the guys are startin' to *look* like Sinestro!! And they're right on my six!"

Carol interjected, "They are Qwardian Sleepers, Guy—pre-programmed by the Qwardians!"

"Oh, yeah, *now* ya tell me!!"

"How many do you see?"

"How *many?"* Guy asked, incredulously.

"Looks like *all* of them!"

Guy Gardner soared across Manhattan, pursued by hundreds of Sleepers who were firing at will as Guy did his best to evade them. Guy was no longer bare-chested, having used his ring to recreate his uniform.

Banking around Midtown, Guy poured on the speed as Sleepers fired their rings at him, hitting the Met-Life Building and the Waldorf Astoria. Glass and debris rained down on Manhattan from multiple blast impacts on buildings as Guy barely evaded his lesser-trained adversaries.

"Guy, get out of the city for God's sake!" Carol screamed over the comm-link. "The Sleeper rings are programmed to attack Green Lantern—*any* Green Lantern! They'll follow wherever you lead!"

"No," Guy shouted back, "ya *think?"* Dozens of blast impacts ripped through buildings as Guy made a dash up 52nd street. Getting out of town was, indeed, his plan, but he was a little busy running for his life at the moment.

Rocketing toward Broadway, Guy was broadsided by yet more Sleepers, hammered by a massive energy surge that sent him sprawling backward through the seventh floor of a publishing house, editors and clerks diving for cover as glass exploded everywhere and Guy tumbled back through several walls of sheet rock.

Landing in the publisher's spacious and lavish corner office, Guy sucked wind as he scrambled to a low crouch, "Get *down!*" he ordered the shocked publisher, who didn't know what to make of any of this.

Through the publisher's ruined interior office wall, Guy saw a Sleeper walking into view, the golden Sinestro ring glowing with energy, evil in the Sleeper's eyes as virus microbes ate away his flesh.

"What the hell is going on?" the publisher demanded.

"Best I can tell, pal? The Apocalypse," Guy sneered, bracing himself.

A second Sleeper stepped into view.

And then a third. A Fourth. Until more than a dozen Sleepers, each with the power of a Green Lantern, had massed in the hall, facing Guy through the ruined wall.

"Feets, don't fail me now!" Guy cracked as he turned toward the glass wall behind the publisher, meaning to take the man to safety through the wall. Only, hovering outside both glass walls of the corner office—Sleepers. Dozens of them. Their power rings held at the ready.

"Uh, kids," Guy said across his comm-link, "beam me up!"

"Impossible," Carol said as she worked at a data station in the sick bay, trying to acquaint herself with the Watchtower's systems. "Main power is still offline, and I wouldn't know how to run the transporter anyway!"

Back on Earth, Guy smiled. If he was going out, then, dammit, he was going out fighting. "Peachy," he said. "well, then, give my regards to Broadway—"

Carol interrupted him, "Guy—hit them with a wide-angle neutrino pulse!"

"A *what?*"

"A wide-angle neutrino pulse!" she repeated.

"And, I do that *how?*" Guy sneered.

In the Watchtower, Carol snarled. *Morons.* The Guardians of the Universe gave out rings to *morons.* "By your *will,* Guy!" she said, annoyed.

"Hey, britches, don't get all sassy with me! I'm no rocket dentist, you know!"

Back on Earth, the Sleepers closed in, walking ominously toward Guy, aiming their fists at him. "How do I fire the Wheatina pulse deal if I don't understand it?"

"You don't *have* to understand it, Guy," Carol yelled across the comm. "Just *do it.* Command the ring to emit a wide-angle neutrino pulse *now!*"

Faith. Carol was talking about faith. Trusting in things we do not entirely understand.

It amazed me how a lunchbox like Guy Gardner could depend on the ring to allow him to fly without understanding how the ring works, while questioning something as simple as an energy pulse. He needed things *selectively* explained to him.

The Green Lantern power rings worked by force of will. Simply willing something into being was all that was required. I did not need to know, for instance, precisely how a bulldozer is built in order to command my ring to create one. The *ring already knows.* The data is already programmed in there. All the ring's owner needed was simply the will to make it so.

Faith.

In New York, the Sleepers powered up their rings, dozens of flashes of brilliant yellow energy. Guy was a dead man.

"*Aaaaaahhhhhhhhhhhh!*" Guy screamed his best macho

Braveheart roar as he fired his ring, loosing a simple cluster of harmless sub-atomic particles—

—that momentarily interrupted the hold the Sinestro virus parasites had on their Sleeper victims. The Sleepers froze in place.

"Hah!" Guy shouted, climbing to his feet and jabbing a finger at the Sleepers, who were collapsing to the floor, "Yeee-eah, bee-yotch! Just *like* that!"

"Guy—"

"I owe you a kiss, Carol. *Tongue.*"

"Guy!"

"What?"

"You have, maybe thirty seconds before they recover. You need to get to work."

Guy was annoyed. The bad guys were defeated—what else *was* there? "What are you talking about?"

In the Watchtower, Carol was monitoring me as I rendez-voused with Jade in orbit. "The *rings,* Guy. Get the *rings* before they recover."

"Oh, sure," Guy said over the comm. "I knew that."

"Take up a position around 10,000 feet and cover the entire city with neutrinos, then command your ring to bring all the Sinestro rings to you. Meet us at the Watchtower ASAP," Carol said.

Guy snarled in the monitor screen, "Y'know, that sounded an awful lot like an order!"

"How about that." Carol said, clicking Guy's obnoxious face off of the screen. The monitor went black, leaving only the faint mirror of sick bay as Carol sighed, grimacing, trying to hold things together. The monitor was still black when she looked up again, only, reflected in the glass—

—Star Sapphire.

A moment I missed, at the time, because I was arcing across the lunar sky, I came alongside Jade, who was near-hysterical.

She hadn't expected to see *me*.

"He-he's dead?" she asked, using her own emerald power to communicate through my ring, "My God, he's *dead?*"

My patience with these people was fading fast. The chronic self-absorption. Her *neediness*. Things she confused with love but had nothing to do with love. It was about her. About her unfinished business. About Alan Scott, her father and the original Green Lantern. Maybe he dropped her on her head too many times as a child. Maybe he didn't hug her enough. She was such a Maybelle.

Whatever it was, I didn't care. I needed her to focus. "He's fine, Jade—"

"Then *why are* you *still Green Lantern?*" She began screaming, *"Give Kyle his ring back! I knew it! I knew you'd pull this!"*

I grabbed her by the shoulders. A frail, flesh-and-bone girl. A *child*. It was all I could do to resist blasting her out of space.

"Jade—I need you to focus. *Focus*, dammit!"

Jade looked at me with hatred and contempt. I represented loss to her. The Grim Reaper. It was a role I knew well. "You...let him die...to keep his ring..."

Kyle's ring.

Kyle's ring.

It was *my* ring, dammit. Mine. The sole remaining Green Lantern power ring after I destroyed the Corps. Ganthet escaped with it and tossed it to some kid in an alley, and now this...this...*child*... wants to make it Kyle's damned birthright.

She couldn't possibly understand how much farther I'd evolved. How much more I'd seen. How utterly limiting Kyle's precious bauble was to someone who had existed on an entirely different scale, who had communed with all Creation.

I wanted to shove the ring down her throat. Let her choke on the thing. But, for now, I needed her.

"Listen to me—Kyle is fine. But he is still unconscious. He's in no condition to use the ring now. Jade—"

I took her beautiful face in one hand, her eyes blazing with mistrust and contempt. "I need you now. Please help me."

Jade froze in the moment, boiling in her contempt for me.

"Tell me what to do," she finally said.

"Tell *both* of us," Guy Gardner's voice boomed through my power ring's link. Jade and I turned to see Gardner soaring toward us, dragging a ring-generated Santa Claus bag full of Sinestro rings—*"Whoa*—what happened *here?"* he asked, looking down at the ruined Watchtower.

"Our guess is Sleepers," Jade said. "We haven't found them yet, which probably means they are massing for an attack somewhere."

"More Sleepers?" Guy exclaimed. "I pulled all of the Sinestro rings I could find," Guy said. "How many of 'em *are* there?"

"Thousands," I said, stoically. "Scattered across time and space. And we've got to shut them down *now.*"

"'We?'" Guy remarked. "'We' *who?*"

I dropped the rings I recovered from the Sleepers at Kyle's apartment into Guy's bag as he, Jade and I settled into a triangular formation. "The Sinestro rings have antimatter signatures that will react to simple neutrinos. Once we've located them, we draw them to us by force of our will power."

"From all over the Earth?" Guy asked.

"From across time and space," Jade said, in her twelfth-grade understanding of the matter. Space and time, when used to describe events, can't be clearly separated. Space and time are woven together in a symbiotic manner. Having one without the other has no meaning in our physical world. Without space, time would be useless to us and without time, space would be useless, as any occurrence in our universe is an event of space and time.

I could have spent seven hours explaining that to Britney and Spongebob, or we could just get on with it. "I need you to join your power with mine," I said.

Now Guy was giving me the skunk eye as well, "Say again?"

"If we combine our power, we can reach that much farther."

"Yeah," Guy said, annoyed, accusing, "and *you* get to be Super Lantern! Memo to Parallax: ya didn't do so good with that last time around!"

"Guy's right," Jade said. "Hal—you can't expect us to trust you. You can't."

I chewed on it a moment, resisting the impulse to choke them both.

All Creation at stake, and these two want to squabble about past mistakes. Somewhere, on some level, I certainly understood their point. But it was a very deep level and I had no time for this.

"I am not asking anyone to trust me," I said calmly. "I can't possibly. Tell me what 'Plan B' is, and I'll do that."

"Well," Guy started, "first, I think Greenie, here, should strip naked. That'd be a start—"

"Fine!" Jade snapped, repositioning herself within the triangle.

"You'll do it?" Guy snickered.

"Shut up, you lame-o!" Jade shot back. "Let's just get this over with!"

My sentiments exactly.

The sooner we linked up, the sooner we could locate every Sleeper ring in existence. The sooner we did that, the sooner we could draw them to us. The sooner we drew them to us, the sooner they could be destroyed. The sooner the Sleeper threat was destroyed, the sooner I could give Jade Kyle's precious ring and get back to being *so much damned more than these people could ever conceive of.*

We took up formation, Guy and I firing our rings toward Jade, who, in turn, fired her emerald energy back at us.

The bond was formed.

"I am sending out the pulse," I said, preparing to saturate all of spacetime with a massive neutrino pulse, which would act much like a radar grid or LoJack device for the Sinestro rings.

My ordeal was finally about to be over.

Ssssthhraaakkkttt!

We were suddenly attacked by a massive discharge of anti-matter—greater than anything we'd encountered so far. The discharge smashed through our energy bond, propelling us backwards through the vacuum. It took me several revolutions to regain attitude control and regroup, my eyes focusing on our new enemy, the ones who had nearly destroyed the JLA Watchtower.

It was the JLA.

Superman, Batman, Flash, Wonder Woman, The Martian Manhunter, Plastic Man—closing in on us, ready for battle—

—*all Sleepers.*

16

The battle was over.

Standing amid the dead and dying, he loosened the drawstrings on his field utility sack, giving it a good shake, rattling the metal pieces inside. He reached a dirty, battle-scarred hand into the sack and drew out a handful of rings. Fool's Gold, someone called it. Dime-store fakes that kids win with a pack of gum. The metal cool against his flesh, he looked down at the Sleeper rings in his hand, many more left inside the sack, hundreds of them, and he considered the atrocities those rings committed. Then he looked at his own ring, a sterling, polished emerald metallic, and gravely considered the atrocities *that* ring had caused, and his own role in it.

Recovery efforts had begun in Iwo Jima on March 17, 1945, with dozens of small boats ferrying wounded to ships anchored in the lagoon. The dead would be last, so, for the moment, brave men suffered the indignity of lying where they fell, scattered across the sand and the hills of the volcanic island. Standing among them, his great and tattered cloak billowing in the wind, was Green Lantern.

Green Lantern had survived the final battle entirely on the strength of his sheer will. This was his baptism of fire, the moment he moved from being Alan Scott, a young engineer with no direction in life, to a matured sober man of purpose.

His hand full of Fool's Gold, he realized how close, how *very, very close,* he'd come to losing not only the battle, not only the war, but the entire world to a threat of unimaginable power. And how the margin between victory and defeat hinged entirely on his lack of focus: his failure to understand his purpose, his role in Creation.

The handful of rings, stained by blood and decaying human tissue, some with parts of fingers still attached, brought Scott the focus he needed. Finding the magic green railroad lantern wasn't an accident. It was fate. Destiny. For reasons he'd never fully understand, he was chosen to serve. Chosen to protect. His life was no longer his own, he had *purpose.*

Dropping the Sleeper rings back into the sack, Green Lantern surveyed the battlefield. The dead soldiers—Allied and Axis alike—bore silent witness to his new birth—his new beginning. Beneath his mask, his eyes narrowed into a grim glower: a sober determination. No longer a neophyte getting trapped inside bank vaults and what have you. No longer a sideshow to Doiby Dickles and other carnival acts.

There, among the dead, his cloak helping create a foreboding, wraith-like figure, Alan Scott truly became Green Lantern. *I will honor you,* he vowed. *I will fight evil wherever it arises. I will be the best hero I can be.*

A glint of emerald metal caught Scott's eye. He walked several paces through the reddish-brown mud, finding the crushed remains of an antique railroad lantern half-buried in the sand. It belonged to him, but he had discarded it, taken it for granted. Scott knelt, pulling the ruined lantern out of the muck.

It was covered in mud and blood.

Realizing the fool he'd been, Alan lost control, dropping his head and weeping bitterly, as he brushed the sacrifice of brave men off of the near-flattened lantern. As his emerald ring brushed against it, the lantern suddenly reconstructed itself, filling out and re-forming into its original shape and design, polished and glistening. Though no wick had been lit, the lantern glowed with light and bristled with power.

Standing again, Scott held the now-mighty lantern aloft, considering it, considering his own destiny, his tattered cloak again billowing in the breeze. *An omen,* he thought, to find the lantern again was surely a sign, a confirmation of his calling. His purpose.

Scott touched his ring to the polished metal of the lantern's bell, and swore an oath he would keep for the rest of his life.

And I will shed my light over dark evil
For the dark things cannot stand the light
The light of...the Green Lantern!

An enormous explosive green flame ignited around Scott, engulfing him in an emerald pyre that swept skyward, momentarily halting the rescue and recovery efforts as everyone turned to see this mythic force. Was it a volcanic eruption? A new attack?

The flame swirled, life-like, around the figure inside, growing in breadth and height, until the flame propelled itself skyward, racing toward the heavens, leaving in its wake—

Green Lantern: fully restored to health, his uniform repaired, hovering high above the awed servicemen, glowing with ethereal energy.

The servicemen studied him with awe, not quite knowing what they should do. Green Lantern's eyes now shone with a glower, his cloak swirling about him, before once again becoming engulfed in a fearsome green flame—

—and then he was gone.

The intercom buzzing was lost to Alan Scott as he stood in front of the huge, multi-paned vintage gothic sunray arch window in his office at Gotham Broadcasting. His hands clasped behind his back, Scott cut an ominous figure in his custom-tailored Brooks Brothers suit and Bruno Maglia shoes, a purposeful and focused man of power and influence in the world of broadcasting. Before him was all Gotham, an eclectic train wreck of undisciplined architectural aegis that regularly frightened pets and small children. Despite the tourist bureau's best efforts, Gotham came to have the same mythic quality to it as, say, Transylvania. Which was not to say tourists didn't travel there, but that they usually came for the ghoulish dice-roll of seeing if the could live to tell the tale. Try as they did to gloss over a cityscape dominated by glaring stone gargoyles and cryptic, menacing archways, where the symbol of a bat was projected regularly and in huge dimension high above the menacing spires, Gotham's strongest selling point was also its most obvious descriptor: Mickey Mouse doesn't live here.

Batman lived in Gotham. Other heroes did as well, but Batman had become such a polarizing presence, he was what most anyone thought about when the words "Gotham" and "city" were paired up. Which suited Alan Scott just fine, as he was happy enough for Green Lantern to operate well below the radar. Over the six decades Scott had served as Green Lantern, he'd learned his purpose, his role in Creation. It was enough for Scott to simply *be*. He didn't need to compete with a man so emotionally scarred that he strapped on rubber bat ears and went around punching people.

Gravity was the very first and best attribute one observed when meeting Scott: a certain self-awareness and sense of purpose. Though logging in at an athletic 210 pounds, Scott's sheer presence—his *gravity*—made it seem as though he weighed a ton. An unmovable, monolithic *guy*. Scott was such a *guy* that everything seemed to orbit around him. Around Scott, even Batman, the Faux Spook himself, was just another mask waiting his turn.

At thirty-seven, Scott had the confident manner and practiced demeanor of a man twice his age. That was, perhaps, because Scott truly was twice his age, and then some, having mysteriously regained his youth by means of the mystical Starheart—the source of his emerald energy. He was, in many ways, a father living in the body of a son. As a father, as one of the original "super" heroes, many of the most powerful beings on the planet would regularly sojourn to Gotham to seek his advice and expect that advice to be sage and somehow more insightful than what you'd get in the back of a Gotham City taxi. It was a burden he'd grown accustomed to, men and women with the power to save the planet or destroy it looking to him for counsel. He was, in many ways, regarded as the father of super-heroism, as if simply having survived so long counted, in and of itself, as wisdom.

As most every other hero did, I looked to Alan on many occasions for wisdom, for guidance. There wasn't a man I trusted more, nor was there a man who accepted me—as Parallax, as Spectre, as Hal Jordan—so unconditionally as Alan Scott. Briefing me on his encounter with the Sleepers, Alan told me he had, by this time, assumed the crisis was over: the evil defeated, Alan now paused to reflect on his recent battle and how it connected to battles fought decades before.

Gotham's night lights cast angular lines across his face as he glared at the city through the sunray arch, Alan's noble eyes narrowing. *It's time,* he thought, looking out over Puzzle City, the Bat Signal casting gloom across the skyline. Intuition a sense of ill-at-ease. The whole world seemed somehow out of sync.

"The world's going to hell," a familiar, fatherly voice offered.

Scott did not need to turn around, continuing to survey No Man's Land beyond the office window. "And all of us with it, Commissioner."

Scott knew the quiet authority of his old friend, James Gordon, when he heard it. "Jane got tired of buzzing you. I told her I'd let myself in."

Scott continued with his back to Gordon, "The Bat-signal's been on quite a while tonight."

"Yeah, well, he's funny that way. Does what he does when he does it and for his own reasons. Sometimes he'll show, sometimes he'll make us wonder why we ever installed the damned thing."

"He's not going to show," Scott said, his eyes narrowed. The Look. Looking for that needle in the haystack somewhere down Broadway. "Something's brewing tonight."

"That a newsman's instincts?"

"It's indigestion. Egg Fu Young."

Scott finally turned to discern what had brought his old friend around. "So, you got a story for us, Jim?"

Gordon, in comfortable tweed and Boston Craft loafers, rubbed his chin, looking for the right words. "No. Actually, I've come to place you under arrest."

For reasons Scott could not immediately identify, this didn't surprise him. "Uh-huh," he offered, nudging Gordon to get to the point.

"Some dandy from the Department of Homeland Security. He's got a court order and an arrest warrant—neither of which is terribly difficult for his department to get their hands on."

Scott wasn't connecting to what Gordon was saying. He was connected to Creation. To just how out of joint things were. "Okay," he said. "This guy thinks...thinks I'm a terrorist?"

"They don't tell me, Alan," Gordon said, reaching for a pair of handcuffs. "Which is what makes my job so great."

Behind Gordon, Scott could see Gotham police and FBI agents swarming through the bullpen, demanding his reporters and staff stop working while seizing documents and computer drives.

Gordon waited on Scott, gesturing with the handcuffs, "This is merely regulations, Alan."

The moment distracted Scott, taking him out of the zone, his awareness now being limited by his circumstances—the cold metal of the handcuffs fastened around his wrists. Gordon cuffed his hands behind him as detectives and police officers poured into the offices of Gotham Broadcasting Group.

"Look, Alan, get your lawyer to meet us downtown, you'll be home in an hour. We're ready to process you right through.

"I doubt they actually want you. Whatever they're after, embarrassing you is probably just a tactic to get at it—"

"I wouldn't be so sure, Commissioner," a spindly voice cracked as a gaunt, red-faced bureaucrat sauntered into Scott's office, flashing government credentials, "Jack Summers, Homeland Security. And you, sir, are going to jail."

Gordon groaned, "Dammit, Summers, I told you I'd handle this."

"Yes, and I run the task force. My ball, my rules. You—"Summers jabbed a finger at Scott"—have been aiding and abetting enemies of the state, disseminating classified inform-ation to terrorist cells!"

Scott was now so distracted, he'd lost focus on the important thing—on Creation, and what was off about it. "Are you out of your mind?" he asked Summers.

Summers displayed an arrest warrant. "We'll soon find out, won't we? Alan Scott, you are under arrest on suspicion of espionage against the United States of—"

Before Summers could finish, Alan pivoted on one leg and kicked Summers flush in the mouth. Summers caromed off of Alan's vintage Chippendale desk while spitting out teeth and blood, his arrest warrant now fluttering toward the carpet.

"*Alan!*" Gordon shouted, "You're only making things worse—"

"Get out of here, Jim!" Alan shouted.

"Alan you know I—"

"*Get out!*" Alan screamed, just before he was blasted by a massive discharge of antimatter plasma, propelling him, wrists still cuffed behind his back, through the sunray arch, hundreds of small panes exploding outward over the dire Gotham miasma as Scott fell to his waiting death.

"Summers, what the devil—" Gordon shouted at the ersatz Fed, who was wiping blood from his mouth with one hand, his other hand clenched into a fist, extended toward the smashed window—and wearing a Sinestro ring.

"The Devil indeed, Commissioner," Summers sneered as viral maggots ate away his flesh, transforming him into Sinestro. "In the moments you have left, pray to your gods, for, this day, your world shall end!"

With that, Summers propelled himself forward and, astonishingly, took flight, flying through the ruined glass—

—only to become consumed by a massive discharge of green flame. Summers shrieked in agony, dying a demon's death as the green flame utterly destroyed the Sinestro virus and Summers plummeted to earth, passing in his descent—Green Lantern. Having transformed to Green Lantern in free-fall, Scott flew back up to the Gotham Broadcasting executive office, finding a stunned Commissioner Gordon.

"What? Green Lantern?" he stammered. "What the hell is going—"

"Not now, Commissioner!" Scott barked while using his ring to encase Gordon inside a force field just before a dozen Sleepers burst through his office wall. Gotham Police, FBI Agents, parcel delivery men, secretaries—people from all walks of life. The Sinestro virus ate away their humanity as they blasted Green Lantern with the rings.

The immeasurable blast of the combined Sleepers blasted out the entire side of the building, but Green Lantern hovered amid the explosion, encased in a form-fitting force field. Scott was aware of Kyle Rayner's recent battle with a Sleeper and had hoped that was an isolated incident. Still, he was not completely shocked to see them again.

Having battled them before, Scott knew how to modulate his force field's properties to cancel out the antimatter plasma of the faux Green Lantern rings. Though not a permanent solution, his battle experience made him a much tougher opponent for the hapless drones, buying Alan the few seconds he needed.

"I see you people are back," Lantern said. "Well, then, allow me to welcome you accordingly." And, with that, Scott unleashed hell—a massive wall of green flame, which consumed absolutely everything in his office. A torrent of horror engulfed everything and everyone, a massive death strike as the Sleepers screamed in agony as the flame utterly destroyed the parasites controlling them.

Gordon winced and heard himself screaming before he could adequately invoke his dignity. Had Green Lantern lost his mind? Was he now some kind of mass murderer? Having worked with Batman, or at least served Batman's purposes, Gordon was used to being thrown into larger-than-life situations. A "hero" utterly incinerating his adversaries—no matter how vile—seemed excessive and frightening to Gordon. It was a side of the original Green Lantern—a homicidal rage—Gordon had never seen.

Gordon slumped to the carpet as the green flame swirled into a controlled whirlwind and was drawn back into Green Lantern's ring. As Gordon flattened on the carpet, more than a dozen Sleeper rings dropped to the floor—all that remained of the Sleepers.

"Good God, man—did you have to kill them?" Gordon asked.

Green Lantern stoically picked up the golden rings. He was now back in the zone, back looking at the Big Picture, and Gordon was a bit off of the map. "They are not dead, Commissioner. They are"—he searched for the right word as he continued picking up the rings—"*detained.*"

Detained? Gordon thought. "When will you return them?"

Green Lantern soared out of the ruined office and banked across the city of gloom, "When I'm ready," he said, having no time to explain himself.

Alan Scott was often mistaken for a member of the Green Lantern Corps, bound by covenants and rules of engagement prescribed by the Guardians of the Universe. But Scott wasn't part of the Corps and, while aware and respectful of our ethical and procedural boundaries, Scott was his own man and accomplished his mission his own way. He was a unique component of the universe, and did not alter himself to fit some arbitrary definition of what "Green Lantern" should be.

A war veteran, Scott had his own rules of engagement and had far less anxiety about using lethal force than most Green Lanterns did. The enemy was the enemy. Protecting life was what he did and he lost absolutely no sleep over sending the evil and the guilty straight to hell.

Completing a graceful and majestic turn over what had become hell town, Scott positioned himself in tandem to the massive, foreboding Bat-signal projecting on Gotham's smog cover. He used the power of the green flame—the emerald energy that was his power source—to tap into all Creation, to become one with the universe. While not as cosmically aware as I was as the Spectre, Scott was indeed practiced and knowledgeable about the universe. Patient. Wise. He didn't just run around punching people in the head. He asked the right questions. Hovering high above the city, Scott extended his arms in messianic fashion, his great cloak billowing in the night air. He looked into Creation, feeling the oneness of it all, and in so doing he could sense what was wrong with it.

As Lantern communed, 876 Sleepers, flying in formation,

banked out of the clouds. The night sky and ghoulish radiance of the Bat-signal made this army all the more ominous as they turned toward Scott, who seemed so disconnected from reality that he was unaware of the approach of a veritable army of drones, each with a power ring commensurate to Scott's own.

The Sleepers closed in for the kill, aiming their faux power rings.

"Die, son of the Guardians!! Die at the hands of Sinestro!" The Sleepers shouted in a deafening unified roar as they unleashed enough power to split the city in half.

The massive discharge struck Scott, illuminating him with a blinding flash that surely must have been interpreted as a nuclear explosion from a human perspective. In his oneness with Creation, Scott was not at all concerned about dying. His living and dying were matters of predestination. His concern was *purpose*—his role and place in Creation. Sixty years of battle had hardened his resolve and strengthened his will to the point where he truly was fearless, and his will truly was indomitable.

The stronger your will, the stronger the power ring's abilities. Alan Scott's will was not to be denied, which made him, potentially, the most powerful Green Lantern in existence.

"Fools," Scott scowled within the maelstrom. "The evil who spawned you died a fool's death. And now, so shall *you.*"

And, with that, Green Lantern redirected the massive power blast back at the Sleeper armada—engulfing them in their own blast. The inexperienced drones did not know how to compensate or rechannel the excess energy and were decimated by the powerful blast, which scattered them across Gotham as Lantern flew into a wide arc, his power ring blazing with emerald fire.

Lantern's will—and, thus, his force field—was so strong, he'd managed to not only contain the Sleepers' blast but redirect it at his will. Without completely understanding the science of it, or even the logic of it, Alan Scott fully and unconditionally trusted the promise of the emerald lantern. Without doubt, without hesitation—

—Green Lantern incinerated Gotham City.

Massive billows of green flame incinerated everything and everyone in its path as the fireball engulfed the entirety of the old city, catching men and women and children and elderly and saints and sinners and pets and ants and microbes—every living thing—in its wake. In a holocaust of unprecedented proportions, Lantern engulfed the city in the kind of epic retribution usually reserved for gods.

Moments later, with a grand gesture, Scott withdrew his wrath. He recalled the massive flames, which reduced themselves hundreds of times over before being vacuumed back into his power ring, leaving the city seemingly untouched as though nothing had happened.

However, to Green Lantern's left, 876 Sinestro rings, torn from their unwitting owners, were held in stasis.

Scott deposited the Sleeper rings in a ring-generated facsimile of his old World War II drawstring field utility sack as he took flight, leaving Gotham now, heading toward the horizon. Not knowing much at all about neutrino emissions or antimatter signatures, Scott had used his will to command his ring to destroy the Sinestro virus and recall the faux rings. His power ring's software already knew how to accomplish it. All Alan Scott required was the will to make it happen.

"Jennifer!" he called, speaking into nothingness.

"Dad?" Jade's voice returned to him from the void.

"I'm on my way to New York," Scott said. "I need to find that boyfriend of yours. Something terrible has—"

Zipping across the surface of the moon at full speed, Jade was barely evading a Sinestro-controlled Wonder Woman, who had both the power of the faux ring and her own Amazonian strength, speed and skill. The ring replaced Wonder Woman's natural ability to ride wind currents, making her more maneuverable and faster in the void of space. The moon erupted from massive blast impacts as Wonder Woman fired her Sleeper ring at Jade, as Jade banked and rolled to evade.

"Yes, Dad, I know—the *Sleepers!*" Jade exclaimed while trying not to get nailed. "We've got a Mayday alert up here—bring help!"

Scott changed course, now heading toward space. "You are at the JLA Watchtower?" he asked, having already sensed his child was on the moon.

"Yeah!"

"And Kyle's with you?"

"Yeah, but, Dad, he's out cold! Hal is using his ring!"

Scott, now rocketing into the upper atmosphere, took a moment to process that. "Hal? Hal *Jordan?*"

"Yes!"

"Hal—is Green Lantern again?" Scott asked. He needed to confirm this.

"Yes! Dad, hurry! We need help *now!*"

Alan Scott had never heard his daughter sound quite so desperate. Her life must have truly been on the line. And, if all hell had broken loose in the stronghold of Earth's mightiest heroes, Scott was certain everything in the universe was, likely, at stake.

Which was why he broke off his rush to the moon and, arcing back toward Gotham City, abandoned his daughter to her own fate.

CHAPTER

17

Superman's fist caved in the side of my face as the Martian Manhunter hit me with a massive body blow. I coughed blood and saw, suddenly, only the white light as my personal force field buckled under the stress of the pounding it was taking from two of the mightiest men in all Creation. Possessed by the Sleepers rings, their superior immune systems had apparently kept the Sinestro virus at bay. Superman at least *looked* like Superman, albeit with the evil glower of my most hated enemy.

They kept in close, not using the power of the rings but the near immeasurable strength of the host bodies, pounding me relentlessly, employing both the superior strength and rapid speed of the two titans. The Green Lantern I once was, even at the height of his arrogance, would not have thought to battle these two men at once.

Smashing through secondary support structures near the Watchtower, we were a tangle of limbs, a blur of fists, as the two super-Sleepers kept me off balance, knowing that allowing me even a fraction of a second to focus would shift the battle precipitously. My collapsing force field allowed me to experience excruciating pain as these two heroes landed blow after crushing blow, forty, seventy within a second. Losing consciousness would mean losing the war and losing the war would mean losing all Creation to the evil Qwardian plot, the ultimate revenge of a man long dead.

The irony was, I'd always wanted to go a few rounds with Superman. The last son of an obliterated planet, Kal-El's parents imposed their own sense of order over that of the universe by deliberately transporting their baby to a primitive and less developed planet. While I'm sure they were hopeful the boy would grow to become an asset to the less-powerful terrans, there was absolutely no guarantee he would not become the most dire evil the universe had ever seen, a conquering despot crushing all humanity beneath his heel. Sending a super-powered infant to Earth was, in many respects, the ultimate act of selfishness. Chaos ruining the orderly and natural progression of Creation.

While arguably on par in terms of our power and abilities, I'd always found Superman just the slightest bit arrogant. While I often struggled to know the right choice and the right thing to do, Superman rarely, if ever, doubted himself or his choices. He was the kid who went straight to the front of the class, the one we, the most powerful heroes on Earth, turned to for leadership. The man who set the standard for the rest of us. And I, in my cowardice, was content to let Superman lead. To let him decide. After all, if he made the hard choices, I wouldn't have to. I'd have somebody to point to if things went bad.

John Jones, on the other hand, was much more of a mystery. In many ways Superman's equal, John—or "J'Onn" in his native Martian tongue—often deferred to Superman, Batman and others. His was the quiet spirit of a philosopher or, say, an economics professor with an Oreo cookie fetish. Always a bit enigmatic, J'Onn was hard to know but easy to like—perhaps because of the very lack of ambition I found so puzzling. If anybody could pin Superman's ears back and take him out for a walk, it was

J'Onn. But he never did. He was content to serve, comfortable with his place and his role in Creation.

Caught in a relentless barrage of blows strong enough to drop mountains, clinging to consciousness, the entirety of my will was focused not on defeating them but on staying alive. On keeping up my dwindling force field. And, even as my hold on life began to slip away, I couldn't help but admire those two men. To have so much power and yet not become megalomaniacal dictators surely required the kind of character legends are written about.

Some miles away, Jade was out-maneuvering Wonder Woman, which was the only reason she was still alive. Like all Sleepers, the parasite dominating Wonder Woman lacked extensive experience with the Sinestro ring, and Wonder Woman's flight abilities were severely hampered in the slight lunar gravity. The Wonder Woman Sleeper, therefore, relied on the ring's capabilities to maneuver, which made her just a bit slower and less maneuverable than Jade, who fired on Wonder Woman at every opportunity while desperately trying not to be pinned down by the mightiest woman alive.

Still trapped in a finite and linear human mindset, Jade was thinking quite two-dimensionally. Run, throw zap bolt, hide. Whoever gets in the big punch wins. Which was precisely the problem with her, with me, with the League. There was absolutely no reason a collection of beings this powerful should ever be reduced to these insipid bar brawls. But, throughout its history, the JLA has led the super-hero's call to arms: *C'mon, folks—let's go punch somebody in the head!* Conflict resolution by violence, imposing our sense of order over that of the universe; playing God.

Wonder Woman herself was, perhaps, the worst example of someone being out of sync with their purpose in Creation. The homeless soul of an unborn child trapped for untold years within the Cavern of Souls on the mythical Amazonian island of Themyscira, Diana was endowed with special gifts and abilities by the Amazons' patron gods and then gifted with a mortal body molded out of clay by her mother. Diana was the child of promise: a new life and new vision of hope for the women of Themyscira. But, upon her first glimpse of a male—a pilot who'd crash-landed on the island—Diana's curiosity about the world beyond the Amazonian utopia ultimately led her to leave, journeying to America to teach mankind the principles of the Amazonian race. How she fulfilled that calling by punching people in the head was beyond me. Love, peace, joy, happiness—all principles espoused by her people, and so few of them manifested in Diana, a warrior princess. A woman whose entire mission became a paradox: fighting battles in the name of peace.

The lunar gravity made lasso throws impractical for the Sleeper-controlled Wonder Woman, the reduced speed making the rope easy to avoid. The "magic" Lasso of Truth, forged from the girdle of Gaea, compelled anyone tied with it to obey Diana and to speak only truth. But Jade was too fast and stayed out of reach of her pursuer, even while failing to use her direct command of Alan Scott's emerald power to snap the hold the Sleeper ring had on the warrior princess. Jade's mode was *escape and regroup,* linear thinking at its most tragic.

Which brought my notice to Guy Gardner.

Years ago, Guy squared off with Batman and ended up chewing floor after only one punch. Guy was finally getting a rematch. "Yeah," he sneered at the Sleeper-controlled Batman, "let's *dance,* baby."

Sleeper Batman and Guy Gardner exchanged a flurry of super-powered blows as Guy swore at and cursed the man who'd repeatedly humiliated him. Guy was indifferent to the fact this was not Batman so much as a symbiote who'd possessed him, and Guy had also seemingly forgotten time was not on our side.

The Sleeper Justice League attack was, doubtless, more of a delay tactic than an actual attempt to destroy us, although killing us would be a definite bonus.

Being the poster child for linear thinking, Gardner reveled in his chance to one-up Batman. Now Batman was taking on Guy on Guy's terms, or at least that's what Guy told himself as he generated a pair of fifteen-foot wolves with his power ring and set them against Batman, who retaliated by attacking Guy with a horde of Sinestro ring-generated yellow bats that Guy's force field would be vulnerable to.

It was all so stupid.

If I had a breath, an eye blink, to collect myself, I would have both Superman and the Martian Manhunter on the ropes while I told Jade and Guy what utter wastes of chromosomes they were.

I later learned that, as the battle raged outside the Watchtower, Carol was on her back in sick bay under the command station, trying to reroute a few key conduits and restore main power to the Watchtower. Carol was hardly a technician, but it was impossible to sit in on meetings run by testosterone-crazed flight jockeys without at least learning the difference between a live wire and a ground. And, truthfully, the inner workings of the Watchtower were deceptively simple, using color-coded gel packs and artificial intelligence bio-neural ROM chips that would anticipate what you were trying to do. Fixing the entire Watchtower from the sick bay was unlikely without the cooperation of the Watchtower itself. Carol's process, therefore, was about getting the station to like her. To that end, she fed in retinal scans, palmprints and other biogenic data with which the Watchtower's security computer could process through the monitor womb and find Carol's security file. Unfortunately, much like a mediocre credit score, her profile had both the good and the bad, notably the bad—her former life as the villainous Star Sapphire. Thus, the Watchtower regarded her with suspicion and analyzed every change she made under the counter. But it was slowly getting the idea that she was trying to restore main power—which the Watchtower permitted—so, things were progressing when Carol spotted a man in the shadows.

"Ollie?" she asked.

A hundred or so feet below, Green Arrow looked up from his observance of Aquaman in the saltwater tank to answer Carol. "What?"

"Where are you?"

"Where I *said* I'd be—down here watching Doctor Scales take a bath!" Green Arrow was no fan of either Aquaman or baths. He'd found Aquaman's spare uniforms stored below, so the comatose monarch was once again properly adorned, much to Green Arrow's relief. Ollie was pretty bored, considering, so far as he knew, the main crisis was over. Which accounted for his not seeing the strange, misshapen human shadow moving behind him.

Carol shrugged it off as paranoia and went back to negotiating with the Watchtower's artificial intelligence. "Nothing, I guess," she said. "Hey—think I'm getting the hang of this—"

Star.

A whisper sent a chill down Carol's spine as Ollie responded. "Whooptie-doo for your Subaru. I'm hungry."

How I've missed you...Star... the voice hissed again.

"Shut up, Ollie!" Carol barked.

"What?" Green Arrow asked as multiple streams of waxy ribbons shot across the wall behind him, racing and fluttering like mercury spilled from a thermometer.

Carol was suspicious now, sliding from under the console, "Just give me a minute," she said. "Something...not right up here..."

Star...

Carol whirled to see a man in the shadows. *"Jeez!"* she screamed, nearly jumping out of her skin until she recognized the white reflective emblem sparkling in the low light. The emblem had a gold lightning bolt running through it. "Flash! Geez, you scared the snot out of−" She looked again, and the man was gone.

It's time...Star... Carol spun around, the voice behind her now. In a far corner of the room, draped in shadow, the stranger in red. The lightning bolt on his chest. The ghostly figure extended his hand toward her. *Come to us, Star...*

"Ollie," she said, her teeth set with determination, "think you better get up here."

Green Arrow fumed as he clambered to his feet. "What? What! Can't a man watch another man take a bath in peace?"

Suddenly, Green Arrow was swarmed by dozens of elasticized ribbons, jetting at him like whips, each hit ripping his uniform and drawing blood as Arrow, whipped forty times before he could draw breath, sank to his knees, the enigmatic bands wrapping around him, mummifying the archer and cutting off his breath.

Carol reached for her neutrino-emitting pistol, but it wasn't there.

Looking for this? The voice hissed evilly out of the darkness. The Flash stood in the shadows, displaying her weapon. He tilted his head somewhat and smiled evilly before slamming the pistol against the bulkhead some 3800 times in a heartbeat, the impact sounding very much like a drum roll as the weapon shattered−Carol's hope of breaking the Sleeper hold on Flash shattering with it.

Now it is just us, Flash hissed. *Just Wally...and Star...*

The eerie, malleable ribbons released the comatose Green Arrow from their grasp, dropping him to the deck near the salt water tank, before rapidly recoiling and re-sorting themselves into the human figure of Plastic Man. Bereft of his trademark grin, Plastic Man glowered at the defeated Green Arrow, displaying a clenched fist that bore a Sinestro ring.

Carol turned back to the open compartment, hoping to get the Tower back up, but as she turned she saw virtually all of her work had been undone, the panel was a mass of ripped wiring and wrong turns. She whipped around, turning back to face the Flash, "You son of—" but he was gone.

Carol turned to scramble to her feet, and, suddenly, Flash was behind her, *How I have missed you, Star...*

Flash viciously backhanded Carol, who recoiled from the blow, slamming her head into the edge of the console. Flash grabbed a fistful of Carol's hair, dragging the stunned and semiconscious woman toward him. He then shoved his hand up under Carol's jaw, squeezing it and forcing her mouth open and head back as the Flash, smiling evilly, forced a Sinestro ring into Carol's mouth. *Welcome back, Star...*

Below decks, Plastic Man made a show of transforming his arm into a double-edged sword as he sneered down at the comatose Green Arrow. "What—no witty repartee? No hollow bravado, old friend?" he asked, closing in for the kill. "I only wish your brother, the accursed Green Lantern, could watch you die."

Plastic Man suddenly shrieked in horror as his mind virtually imploded, filled with unimaginable pain. He staggered back, losing all control of his elasticity, his limbs extruding in dozens of directions and forming dozens of objects before Plas collapsed on the deck, unconscious, his limbs gradually forming back to normal human proportions.

Aquaman climbed out of the saltwater tank, having just blasted Plastic Man with a powerful telepathic burst. Orin wasn't a hundred percent, but there was no time for waiting.

Now it was his turn to wake up Green Arrow. He slapped Ollie. He *enjoyed* slapping Ollie. Ollie started to come around but wasn't coming fast enough, so Aquaman hit Green Arrow with a telepathic *wake up!*

Green Arrow sat up suddenly, annoyed and complaining. "Ya don't have to *shout,* dammit!" Ollie nursed his head, "Gah—what happened?"

"You got dropped by Plastic Man," Aquaman said.

"Very funny. Seriously, what happened?"

Aquaman removed Plas's Sinestro ring, displaying it to Green Arrow. "My guess: Plastic Man was curious about this thing—the original Sinestro ring Kyle Rayner recovered from the Sleeper he fought. If the ring took Plas over—"

"—Plas coulda gotten to the others...one at a time..." Arrow offered.

"Perhaps aided by Kyle once he was taken over. The JLA answered the emergency call, and were likely ambushed by their own teammates—"

"Damn," Arrow spat, climbing to his feet, "the whole blasted *League* could—*Carol!*" he called.

Up in sick bay, Carol Ferris, groggy and disoriented, pulled herself up to the control station. "Y-yeah—still with you, Ollie..."

"Carol, listen, the whole damned League may be Sleepers—"

"Little late with that news, pal," Carol said, unsteady. "The Flash is in the Tower...watch out, he could be anywhere...and everywhere."

"Like the fuel cells," Aquaman snorted, pointing to a display. Located at several points near the base of the tower were enormous fuel cells, airplane hangar-sized massive batteries that supported the Watchtower's ECLS system—Environmental Control and Life Support—by combining hydrogen and liquid oxygen to create electricity. The panel display was showing a Code Red at fuel cell storage banks one, two and three.

"If he explodes the cells," Aquaman warned, "all that hydro-gen—"

"H-bomb," Green Arrow said, cutting to the chase. "Well, kids, here's where it gets fun." Green Arrow reached into his quiver, giving Aquaman a few of his arrows. "These arrows have those arrowheads Carol gave me—they release neutrinos on impact. You just gotta hit Flash with one to break the Sleeper hold on him," Ollie said, as though hitting Flash with anything at all wasn't a real stretch of the imagination. "Carol!"

Carol was already running for the access ladders, "I'm on three," she said. "I'll see you down there."

Aquaman and Green Arrow were on the move, splitting up to go stop the Fastest Man Alive. "Copy that, Carol," Arrow said. "Me and Flipper, here, will tackle the others. Keep that neutrino pistol of yours handy—Wally could be anywhere!"

"Understood," Carol said as she hurried down-ladder, the pit in her stomach growing ever more threatening.

CHAPTER

18

Morning.

Like I was noticing it for the first time.

"Ad Deum qui laetificat juventutem meam."

To God, the joy of my youth, I heard a gentle voice say.

"Emitte lucem tuam et veritatem tuam: ipsa me deduxerunt et adduxerunt in montem sanctum tuum, et in tabernacula tua."

I turned to see the Spectre. The Spirit of Vengeance. Now, finally, come for me.

"Send forth thy light and thy truth: for they have led me and brought me to thy holy hill"—I said to the Spirit—"and thy dwelling place."

Without walking, without moving, the Spirit of Vengeance came to me. Without speaking, he told me it was time to pay for my crimes.

For the murdered Guardians and Green Lanterns, for the trillions of lives in the galaxies Parallax destroyed. For atrocities too numerous to name and to heinous to even recall.

As the Spectre drew nearer, I relaxed, relieved to finally have an end to the burden. *Yes,* I thought. *Enact your vengeance. Free me from this pain.*

The Spectre and I were now face to face as the wraith reached a bony hand to his hood, pulling it back to reveal fourteen-year-old Marie Tunnelly. Who became Janelle the store clerk. Who became Tavares the drug dealer. Who became Maybelle the housewife.

Who became Martin Jordan.

My father glowered at me. Gave me The Look.

Martin Jordan won't be home for dinner.

Pain ripped my head open and I heard myself screaming.

That was when I opened my eyes to see the Martian Manhunter. The Manhunter showed no emotion, his deep-set eyes hidden by the shadow cast from his inhumanly oversized brow. Despite having worked hard to kill me, the Manhunter was his usual collegiate self.

"My apologies, Green Lantern—it was not my intent to harm you, but I needed to bring you around quickly," he said, apologizing for using his telepathic ability to jump-start my brain.

We were hovering near the now badly damaged Watchtower. J'Onn was cool as a cucumber as he held off Superman with one hand locked around Superman's neck, effortlessly holding the Man of Steel aloft while he saw to me. For his part, Sleeper Superman was concentrating his heat vision on the Martian Manhunter—who had a psychological susceptibility to fire—but J'Onn was, for the moment, screening it out, maintaining an unnerving stoicism.

"It's good to see you again, Hal," J'Onn said. Not many of my old friends have said that, or at least said it convincingly.

I nursed my head, still blinking, "Yeah, J'Onn—you, too."

The Manhunter gestured at Superman. "Hal, if you wouldn't mind—"

I blinked out the pain long enough to notice J'Onn was under attack, and blasted Superman with a neutrino pulse, snapping the hold the Sinestro Ring had on him. J'Onn removed Superman's Sinestro ring and handed me two—Superman's and his own.

"The Qwardian Sleeper rings are fairly sophisticated," Manhunter coolly stated as Superman collapsed, unconscious, the three of us now hovering near the Watchtower. "Still, the Qwardians did not fully appreciate Martian mysticism. Though the ring controlled my physical being, my spirit—my *Mvaugne*—remained beyond its control.

"Fighting off the Sleeper ring required time to study its algorithms, but once I did, I was able to find a security hole I could exploit to break the ring's control."

There was a time that, whenever J'Onn started talking about his religion, his faith, it made me uneasy. That a being as intelligent and advanced as he, could get caught up in ghost stories unnerved me. Of course, that was before I went to work for the Boss. "What about Guy and Jade...?"

"Well, Jade"—J'Onn turned from me, pointing to Jade who was flying toward us, towing a comatose Wonder Woman by her own rope—"eventually used a bit more strategic thinking, ensnaring the Sleeper within Wonder Woman's Lasso of Truth, and forcing The Sleeper to remove the ring.

"As for Guy"—the Manhunter pointed toward the lunar surface, where both Batman and Guy Gardner lay unconscious—"I would have to call that one a draw." Flying to his position, I fired a neutrino pulse at Batman before stripping him of the Sinestro ring and encasing him within a life-support shield.

"J'Onn, get the Leaguers inside the Watchtower and get the mains back on line," I said, taking command—as though the Martian Manhunter had any reason at all to take orders from me. "I'm going to put an end to this."

I flew off into space as J'Onn and Jade collected the fallen Leaguers, bringing them into the crippled Watchtower.

This had gone on far too long. A simple errand—so simple a *child* could have done it by now—had become a major aggravation and embarrassment. Approaching Earth, my mind desper-

225

ately searched for someone to blame but, ultimately, that responsibility rested only with myself. I, after all, have the superior, more evolved mind. I am the one more in tune with the universe, in harmony with all Creation. The finite limitations of my humanity—as sweet as it was to regain—were now terribly annoying. How could I have ever lived this way? How could I have ever been *so small?* Like those small people down there, on the planet.

Ending the Sleeper threat would end my commitment to this "heroism" and allow me to return to the life of the damned. Not that becoming a wraith again was a particularly inviting prospect, but the level of awareness and centrality to the universe was something I sorely missed. Hovering there, high above what was now, to me, a very small planet, I felt incredibly lost and alone. As the Spectre, I was assigned there, to Earth, but I was aware of and in tune with *billions* and *billions* of worlds—cultures, civilizations, art—across the cosmos. Hal Jordan, Green Lantern, had one obsession: this little puddle of insignificance. Capable of greatness, surely, but squandering it all on hatred and war and evil. Evil that cried out for vengeance. For the darkness awaiting me at my journey's end.

Oh, well, just get on with it, I thought as I prepared to summon all of my will, all of my existence, to flood the Earth with neutrino emissions before pulling every last goddamn Sinestro ring off of the planet. Guy Gardner and, hopefully, John Stewart, would surely be awake by the time I was done with Earth, and we could then link up to tackle farther distances and time periods.

But, first things first. I summoned up the entirety of my being and prepared to unleash the full potential of the power ring—when, suddenly, a burst of green flame, an enormous conflagration, appeared before me. My flesh was startled by the massive, hundred-foot fire burst, even though my intellect instantly recognized that trick. It was a favorite of Alan Scott, the original Green Lantern.

The flame swirled and reduced itself as it was drawn into Alan Scott's lantern, revealing Scott, in glorious costume and flowing cloak, in an ominous stance, holding forth his lantern like a signalman. It was an ominous and eerie sight, Scott selling spook to me, making my human flesh crawl just a bit. I found it annoying—not Scott's arrival so much as that, try as I did, I could not help but feel a wave of anxiety from his dramatic entrance.

"I heard you were back," Alan said. "It's good to see you." I wasn't entirely sure he meant it.

"A little busy, here, Alan. Maybe we could do this later—"

"We'll be doing this now," Alan said, grimly, "because you are about to destroy everything in existence."

Again was what he meant to say. *You are about to kill us all again.*

Now I was annoyed. Alan Scott was a great man, but he was a great man half a century ago. Much as I would have liked to have patronized him, I had a job to do. "Look, I really don't—"

"Hal, what are you doing here?"

I exploded, "What's it *look* like? What do you people *think* I'm trying to do, old man? I'm trying to shut down Sinestro's damned Sleepers!!"

"You're not following me," Alan said, grimly. "What are you doing *here?*"

I had not the slightest notion what Scott was talking about, and my patience was just gone.

"Alan, I respect you, I value your service to mankind—"

"—but you're tired of carrying me and humoring the Old Man and get out of your way, right?"

"Alan—"

"Hal—you are not a Green Lantern anymore. This isn't your job anymore."

I briefly wondered if Alan had been talking to a squirrel.

"You are way out of step with your purpose, your place in the universe."

The sheer arrogance of the man, to tell me—*me*—the most evolved mind he's ever *met*. The damned *arrogance* of this puny, flesh and bone *insect*.

"Your plan will end us all. If you were still communing with the universe, you would know that. Because you're cut off at present, you're kind of bulldozing your way through. And, how has that worked for you so far?"

He was working me. I thought seriously about just laying the Old Man out, but I couldn't help but wonder about his question.

I defied the Boss to accomplish one small thing—one bit of business that should have taken, what, fifteen minutes? A half hour?

"I'm betting things have gone from bad to worse to utterly ridiculous," Alan said.

I glared at him. I gave him The Look. He didn't care.

"The Hal Jordan I remember—the *Green Lantern* I remember—was a noble, honest, peaceful, balanced man. He inspired me. He *trusted* me. You?" Alan concluded, his words damning, "I don't even know who *you* are."

My patience with this insignificant *nothing* of a man was completely gone—when I realized the voice in my head wasn't Hal Jordan's. *Insignificant nothing* was not a phrase Hal Jordan would be capable of ever uttering.

"Oh...my God..." I said, the horror of it overwhelming me.

And, then I whispered, "...this...this is how it starts, isn't it..."

Alan glowered, still holding the lantern. A signalman. "You tell me."

I couldn't.

I looked at the ring on my hand. The one I'd made a dozen excuses to put on and still more to keep on. And I knew, in my heart, that I would never, and I mean *never,* surrender that ring to the likes of Kyle Rayner—which was when I knew I had to.

Seizing the window of clarity, I tugged at the ring, meaning to give it to Alan, but Scott waved me off, "Not yet," he said. "There is one mission you must accomplish first."

Now the old man was *really* irritating me. "If this is not my role—my purpose—then how—"

Alan closed the gap between us, still holding his vintage railroad lantern. "Hal Jordan—the *real* Hal Jordan—trusted me," he said. "If you—whoever *you* are—are serious about redemption, serious about achieving your oneness with and purpose in all Creation"—he handed me his lantern—"you'll take this to Sector Four."

I held the antique lantern, curious about it, fighting my demons.

Sector Four was a forbidden zone, a prison the Guardians of the Universe set up for a single prisoner—a most deadly and unhinged creature who posed a threat to all life in the universe. "I don't understand," I said, stalling. "Sector Four is hundreds of thousands of light-years away—"

"Qwardian dissidents—*good* men—terraformed a planet in that sector, unaware of the threat the Guardians had imprisoned there. They built transformer bridges between that planet and Earth."

"Kyle shut down all of the Qwardian transformer bridges," I said, still stalling. "Even at maximum speed, by the time I got to Sector Four and back here, you'll all have been dead for hundreds of years."

"Hal, years ago, long before this current Sleepers business, you were once trapped in Sector Four where you battled the menace imprisoned there—a madman named *Malvolio.* Malvolio wore a power ring he'd stolen from his own father—who had been the Green Lantern of Earth—when he killed him.

"During your battle with Malvolio, he destroyed your power ring. Truthfully, he made you *believe* he'd destroyed it, so you would, in turn, take *his* power ring and use it to get home, and in so doing, provide Malvolio with means to escape his prison.

"For years after, you used that power ring—Malvolio's power ring—as your own. Your ring, which had once belonged to Malvolio, became the sole surviving Green Lantern ring and was ultimately given to Kyle Rayner."

I looked at the ring on my hand, having all but forgotten it had, years before, belonged to Malvolio.

Alan continued, "That ring on your hand—Malvolio's ring—your ring—Kyle's ring—are one and the same."

Abin Sur's original power ring had no star charts programmed into it for Sector Four, but Malvolio's power ring did. Using his ring, I was able to chart my way home from Sector Four to Sector 2814 using black holes and temporal rifts, arriving in my own time period before twenty-four hours had passed for me—before my ring's charge expired. It was the most frightening journey of my career.

For reasons he would not divulge, Alan Scott needed me to return to the Guardians' prison sector. And, since Kyle had destroyed all of the transformer bridges, there was only one way to get back there—retracing the steps I'd taken years ago when I'd used that very same ring to escape Sector Four.

Because Kyle's ring would work only for me, Alan knew I was the only living being in all of Creation who could find his way there. He knew this was my *purpose.*

"Alan..." I began, hedging.

"Hal, what you do is up to you. These Sleepers? There are three other Green Lanterns here who can tackle that threat. But this journey is one only you can make."

Alan saluted me, "It's up to you now," he said, vanishing in the same dramatic way in which he'd appeared—leaving me floating in space and wishing I had listened to the squirrel.

19

G reen Arrow crouched inside the emergency access to fuel cell bank two, his bow in his hand, ready for anything. His gaze narrowing to a snarl, Ollie cursed under his breath. *What the hell do I know about fuel cells?* Looking around the dim chamber, where massive tanks of hydrogen and massive tanks of liquid oxygen towered some twenty-five feet high, Ollie wondered whose nightmare idea *this* was, to power the JLA Watchtower with the equivalent of a hydrogen bomb. If the entire system went up, it could take an enormous chunk of the moon with it, possibly even affecting the moon's orbit, which would, in turn, cause massive ecological disasters on Earth. Ollie cursed under his breath and wished I was there; not that I'd know any more abut fuel cells than he did, but I had "that damned magic ring."

An unapologetic liberal, Ollie likened the JLA's ECLS system to the massive tanker trucks and railroad cars that traverse the United States every day without any manner of security or monitoring system. A railroad tanker loaded with liquid oxygen or chlorine gas could be perverted into a terrible weapon. Any religious fanatic with a Laws rocket could kill most of the population of Washington, D.C. But we take for granted the safety of those containers, underestimating the lengths desperate people will go to to have their petitions aired. Ollie thought, *Leave it*

to men in tights to build their tree house on the damned moon,
of all places, and power it with an H-bomb.

Ollie was missing the point that, massive as they were, the
fuel cells were only a back-up system. The Watchtower's primary
power and life support came from alien technology courtesy of
the Martian Manhunter.

Ollie realized hunting the Flash was a complete and utter
waste of time. Wally West could move faster than the human
eye could follow. Faster than we could even *think* about looking
for him. Thus, the Longbow Hunter needed to jerry rig something
right quick. Ollie notched one of his small-diameter field target
shafts—a custom-tooled 450 grain, laser matched, CX *Medallion*
multi-directional carbon shaft—to his custom-designed 70-pound
draw emerald metallic Matthews *Conquest* hunter's bow, and
locked in, effortlessly holding the 70-pound draw taut.

In silence.

His breath gone shallow.

For long minutes.

Without moving a muscle.

The discipline and sheer strength—the *will*—required to lock
up a bow that heavy was beyond the abilities of even the most
seasoned archers. Not many men on the planet could do it
without their arms shaking involuntarily from the strain, and
those who were capable of it could only hold it maybe a minute
or two before the enormous tension cramped up their back and
made them see double.

Ollie could stay there all night if he had to. Ollie was a hunter.
Patient. Utterly silent. Aware of even the slightest movement,
Ollie could lay in wait for ninjas and even the best trained and
most heavily armed special forces, dropping them before they
had any inkling at all he was there.

His *Medallion* was fitted with one of Carol's tricked-up
arrowheads, designed to emit neutrinos on impact. As satisfied

as he could possibly be that he was, for the moment, alone, Green Arrow released the *Conquest*, which instantly placed the jerry-rigged *Medallion* in a wall some fifty feet away—in total and complete silence.

Faster than most humans could even think about it, Green Arrow notched arrows two and three and fired in two other directions, setting up a triangulation of embedded arrows releasing neutrinos into the chamber—Ollie's mousetrap for the Flash. Should he bring his super-speed butt into fuel cell bank two, the link between the Sinestro virus and the Flash would be broken.

Satisfied that he'd done the best he could at the moment, Green Arrow hustled through the massive and imposing chamber, arriving at the master control junction, which was threatening a massive overload. The Flash had, apparently, programmed a cascade failure into the housekeeping computers that managed the Watchtower environmental control and life support system. Ollie bravely removed the panel from the main controls and stared blankly at the mass of wires, color-coded gel packs and artificial intelligence bio-neural ROM chips.

Studying the problem, Ollie came up with a solution: he banged on the unit repeatedly with his fist.

Nope.

Oh well, he thought, *I gave it my best.*

Aquaman fitted the remaining bio-neural ROM chip into place in fuel cell bank one while keeping his keen senses honed for any sign of the Flash. As with Green Arrow, Aquaman was certain he'd be dead long before he was even aware the Flash was in the room, and he allowed himself the thought of *what if* Wally ever turned on them, on the League—how great a threat would he be? A terrible one, Aquaman concluded, which was why the League should have a file, somewhere, on how to beat the Flash and, for that matter, each one of them. Given Aquaman's own ups and downs, his victories and crushing, devastating defeats, he was keenly aware that alliances shift and that *anything* was possible. Hal Jordan being the prime example: there should be, somewhere in that Watchtower, a Green Lantern Neutralizing Kit. How, the monarch wondered, could we be sure about any of us?

Aquaman successfully shut down the ECLS failure in bank two by communicating, on some rudimentary basis, with the computer's artificial intelligence. Aquaman's telepathic ability—greatly enhanced since his becoming one with the Clear, a very similar concept to my own communing with all Creation—enabled him to communicate either telepathically or empathically with a variety of species. While not exactly Shakespeare, Aquaman's JLA active duty status enabled him to go deeper into the Watchtower's systems than either Ollie or Carol, and by crudely talking to the computer, he explained what the problem was, and it shut down fuel cells 1-20 there in bank one.

Which still left the Flash at large. Aquaman narrowed his eyes to scrutinize every inch of the chamber—looking for even the slightest vibration. Nothing.

Carol Ferris was getting nowhere fast in fuel cell bank three. She barely knew what she was looking at inside the master control, and now the computer was arguing with her. Flash had apparently shorted out the networking between the fuel cell banks, so Aquaman's successful shutdown of bank one was of no help to her there in bank three.

Carol was defenseless. Her neutrino-emitter destroyed, she was weaponless and alone. She knew her race down to bank three was most certainly a one-way trip, but what choice did she have? If the cells exploded, the Watchtower—and everyone in it—would be instantly vaporized. So, as desperate a gamble as it was, she needed to find some way to—

Star...

Carol jumped out of her skin as she heard the Flash hiss out of the darkness. He was nowhere to be seen. "I'm not her!" Carol called back. "I'll *never* be her again!"

Not true, the voice shimmered. *We were allies once...sharing the same vision...*

Yes, both Sinestro and Star Sapphire hated the Guardians of the Galaxy, hated the Green Lantern Corps. But Star Sapphire was dead, severed from Carol Ferris and ultimately killed by the demon Neron. The Spectre later brought Carol redemption, placing the powerful sapphire gem in her hand, where Carol herself had crushed it—forever ending the curse of her dual persona.

Still here, the voice taunted her, as Carol feverishly worked the computer controls, getting nowhere fast and knowing the Flash could un-do whatever she did in less than an eye blink. "No," she said, "she's gone. Gone forever."

The feeling in the pit of her stomach told a different story.

Green Arrow's hands were bruised and bleeding from pounding on the computer and screaming at it. He thought about firing an incendiary arrow into the casing and blowing it to kingdom come, but that would, likely, also affect the cooling system down there and *boom goes the neighborhood.*

Ollie snarled as the hairs on the back of his neck stood up. *He's here.*

Ollie whirled, firing off three smoke arrows, filling the chamber with a light, effervescent fog that revealed the radiant pattern of the neutrino emitting arrows. Neutrinos, of course, are far too small to be seen with the naked eye. The light show Ollie was seeing was a kind of static discharge from the jerry-rigged emitters.

The fog enabled Ollie to track Flash, who laughed at him as he moved effortlessly about the chamber, much faster than Ollie could actually *see*, but the archer could see where Flash *had been* by the shape of the mist. the Flash was actually moving faster than the static discharge light show, neutralizing Ollie's slim advantage while hammering Green Arrow into the wall with 70 haymakers in an eye blink.

His eyes closed, Aquaman *felt* the Flash disturb the harmony of the Clear before he actually saw him. Truthfully, Aquaman—whose eyes can focus in the blackest darkness at incredible depths—was likely the only Leaguer who *could* actually *see* the Flash when he was moving at super-speed. Flash vibrating through the twenty-foot thick hardened concrete walls separating fuel cell bank one from fuel cell bank two, created a shimmer not unlike a rock skipping on a pond, so much so that Aquaman actually turned—himself moving many times faster than a human could—and evaded the Flash's murderous lunge while launching a telepathic attack, filling the chamber with a psionic blast against which the parasites controlling the Flash had no defense.

The Flash shrieked in agony, but, before the parasites released their victim, the speedster grabbed Aquaman and dragged him with him, accelerating to near-mach speed, and ran right through the wall of one of the massive liquid oxygen units, vibrating both himself and Aquaman through the sheer wall and inside the liquefied death awaiting them at -297.31 degrees Fahrenheit.

Fuel cell bank three was beyond saving. Carol furtively worked the computer but now the knot in her stomach was more like a roaring fire. In agony, she tried to throw up, spit out the damned ring the Flash had forced her to swallow, even as the chamber prepared to blow.

With only seconds to spare, Carol changed tactics: if she couldn't convince the damned thing to shut down, maybe she could convince it to eject the fuel cells.

Green Arrow turned over, half-conscious, bruised and bloodied. His fog was lifting, and there was no sign of the Flash, but fuel cell bank one was at the brink of cascade failure. "Dammit!" he exclaimed, staggering over to the main terminal. He considered punching it again, but realized the jig was up. "That does it," he muttered, grabbing a fistful of wires. "I got nothin' to lose, now! I can't figure out how to get this damned thing to *shut down!*"

The computer core shut down.

Ollie, still holding a fistful of wires, snarled at the computer. Waiting long moments, agonizing over his own stupidity.

"You *heard* me, didn't you?" he asked the computer.

Affirmative, the Watchtower replied.

"You know...you know who I am?"

Oliver Queen. Code name: Green Arrow. Member status: inactive.

Inactive member status, but either Steel or the Martian Manhunter had indeed included Ollie in the databank. Ollie slumped on the floor next to the master control. "Computer," he said.

Ready.

"Let's...let's keep this our little secret, okay?"

The Flash's eyes popped open in shock deep inside one of the massive liquid oxygen cells inside fuel cell bank two. Disoriented and on the verge of blackout, he had no idea how he got there or why he was there, but he knew, instinctively, that should he stop vibrating at the ultra-high frequency, he and Aquaman would be dead in a *nanosecond.* Wally West's central nervous system was going into shock as the Sinestro virus parasites released their hold. He used his very last fractions of a second of consciousness to drag Aquaman through the viscous horror—which, at such an extreme sub-zero temperature would have actually *burned* them both to death.

Aquaman and Flash emerged from the tank, collapsing to the deck. Before he passed out, Aquaman removed the Sinestro ring from Flash's hand—and suddenly felt the deck shaking as a massive explosion rocked fuel cell bank two. Aquaman, his own body going into shock from his ordeal, realized what had happened.

Outside the Watchtower, powerful rockets ignited as fuel cell bank three cracked apart and, exposed to open space, blasted away from the moon—taking Carol Ferris with it.

Carol's eyes went wide as she gasped for air, her lungs expanding and blood freezing with the exposure to space. Death came quickly for her as her body went fully into shock while the massive chamber sped away from the moon faster than a bullet fired from a gun. The sheer inertia of the ejection flattened Carol to the deck, her internal organs shutting down, her body going numb now, sparing her the horror of the unimaginable pain of her blood freezing and skin crystallizing.

Within seconds, fuel cell bank three nearly vanished from view, becoming but another pinhole in a vast ocean of pinholes dotting outer space, traveling hundreds of miles in mere seconds—before lighting up Creation in a display nearly as brilliant as a supernova. All space went white for ten minutes as the massive hydrogen tanks exploded in eerie silence, only to then dissipate over long moments, allowing first oranges and then navy blue and then the inky blackness to return.

And, moving through that darkness, a pinhole among trillions, racing back toward the Watchtower at incredible speed—

—Star Sapphire.

CHAPTER
20

I t took me a long time to realize it, but I was weeping.

Overwhelmed by the kind of remorse a motorist feels when he accidentally hits a child playing in the street. The self-loathing an alcoholic experiences from a sober glimpse at the lives he's ruined. The morbid fatalism of a cigarette smoker who'd set the house on fire.

I was shocked to discover that, despite my arrogant claim to superiority, *he* was still inside me. *Him.* Parallax. The finite mind corrupted by the infinite. The arrogance that had led me to impose my order for Creation's plan, my wisdom for that inexplicable mix of random fate and divine plan.

In my human lifetime, I'd met many people who'd gone from being drunks to becoming the most insufferable, pushy know-it-alls I'd ever seen. Somewhere along the twelve-step program, they developed tools for managing their disease and, having found them, appointed themselves God—immediately pointing out deficiencies in my life and my choices. *Here's a pack of gum lemme show you how to chew it.* The same people who, weeks before, were passed out behind the wheel of the car they'd just wrapped around a tree were now passing judgment on what method I used for lacing my shoes because they'd found their truth and, like a religious zealot cornering you with a handful of pamphlets, they felt qualified and appointed to fix me and tell me, in excruciating detail, how to live my life. To my immeasurable horror, I suddenly realized that's what I had been doing, too.

There really is a huge difference between a recovering alcoholic and a dry drunk. A recovering alcoholic or recovering narcotics abuser is someone who has come to terms with the fact he or she has a disease. This implies not only a change in heart but a crack in the ego, in the *id,* that allows them to see the world—see all Creation—perhaps for the first time. Having spent months or years or however long seeing only himself, only his own microscopic piece of an infinitely bigger puzzle, the recovering abuser trained himself to see with better eyes. To listen with better ears. Not to dissolve into self-loathing, but not to put himself on a pedestal, either.

The arrogant and insufferable dry drunk is someone still focused on himself. Someone who turns every conversation toward himself. Someone using "I," "my," and "me" with mind-numbing alacrity. Someone you hate to see coming because you know, much like your mother or Maybelle, the dry drunk is going to find fault with something you're doing and offer to correct you. This is not someone in touch with reality. This is not someone communing with all Creation. Not a recovering alcoholic. He's a dry drunk, still missing an enormous chunk of himself and using you to fill it.

Sometimes it takes a powerful mirror to see yourself. Sailing through wondrous nebulae and magnificent star clusters, daunting solar storms and collapsing stars, the wonder of it all was rather lost on me. Churning in my stomach, Parallax was annoyed that I'd run from the battle. That I *still* had not, simply and easily, done away with the Sleeper threat. Hal Jordan, on the other hand, was relieved to have been sent on the journey to Sector Four, to have postponed the humiliation of coming to terms with the horror of his own mistakes.

The first time I went to Sector Four, years before this current crisis, I was simply transported there by accident. Having never been there before, my power ring lacked the proper programming to navigate the sector, but I discovered faint trace energy from a Green Lantern power ring and followed it to its source, a planet seemingly ruled by a massive and imposing Green Lantern named Malvolio.

I later discovered Malvolio was never an actual Green Lantern, but had stolen his father's power ring after first having committed patricide. And Malvolio's "planet" was not a planet at all but was a sophisticated illusion his ring had created. Malvolio was a prisoner in Sector Four, an entire section of space the Guardians of the Universe reserved specifically for him, to keep him far enough away from living beings that he could do no harm.

I barely escaped Malvolio's prison with my life, wearing his power ring—which had mapped Sector Four and, therefore, could chart my way home to Earth within my proper place in the space-time continuum before the ring's charge expired.

Now heading back to Sector Four, my heightened awareness realized that, of the trillions of immense calculations my power ring was making every fraction of a second, if even one of those calculations was even a *fraction of a decimal point off,* I would be lost for all eternity. The ring not only had to get my navigation *exactly* right, it had to also calculate an infinite number of celestial events and gravitational changes since my last journey and constantly adjust my life support force field to operate properly under conditions that changed as many as a billion times per second.

Not to mention that my human understanding of the ring required it to be charged at least once every twenty-four hours. Though similar to my own, Alan Scott's power battery—which I'd transported with me, cloaked within a dimensional rift—was incompatible with my ring's software and thus could not charge it. And I'd left Kyle Rayner's power battery sitting on his cabinet because, in my arrogance, I didn't think I needed it. I assumed it would be virtually impossible for my mission—destroying the Sleeper rings—to take more than fifteen minutes.

My first trip to Sector Four left me powerless before an enraged Malvolio—a creature who did not understand the limits of the Green Lantern ring and, therefore, *had no limits.* By the time I reached Sector Four it could be thousands of years in the past or thousands of years in the future but, for me, for my—for *Kyle's*—power ring, twenty-four hours will have passed. I would arrive in Sector Four just in time to either die or to, once again, find myself powerless before an infinitely powerful madman.

None of which actually bothered me as much as realizing the error of my ways. That, in pursuing my humanity—selfishly seeking Janelle's light, the novice from Balmerino Abbey, or, for that matter, haunting Carol—I had unearthed a great flaw in the plan, the purpose for my being. Soaring through uncharted, inexplicable points in Creation, I realized that wasn't Hal Jordan reaching out for the light...it was Parallax. Destroyer of worlds. Agent of chaos. The ultimate embodiment of hatred, loathing and conceit.

The dry drunk.

And, in my arrogance, I'd set out to turn the dominoes my way. A simple, fifteen-minute assignment had instead ruined lives and threatened all Creation.

I had to complete my mission—whatever it was—quickly, so I could find some means of getting home and relieving myself of that burden. Or, perhaps it was indeed my fate to end my days trapped there, in Sector Four, once my ring's energy was depleted.

Whatever destiny awaited, I humbly prayed for the strength

to face it as Hal Jordan, submersing Parallax as long as I possibly could.

I exploded out of a cosmic string and banked around Sector Four at about 73 times the speed of light, moving quickly around the space sector as my ring had, perhaps, twenty minutes charge left to it. Turning toward Malvolio's cosmic prison in a remote corner of the sector, I grit my teeth for the next run-in with that moron, when, suddenly, my ring picked up another power ring's trace energy.

Malvolio, I figured. He'd managed to escape his confinement again.

I pursued the energy signature, yielding to whatever fate was in store for me.

Nearing the threshold of my ring's power failure, I arrived at a strange planet. Of course, calling any planet "strange" was more human arrogance, but this tiny world seemed an unlikely place for Malvolio to hang his hat. An intemperate, humid planet with a thick, gaseous atmosphere, it was conceivable that humans could survive down there, but they'd likely need to burrow far underground and filter out the harsh atmosphere.

I tracked the radiant energy to its source, the ring properly calculating my angle of insertion into Planet Hell to prevent me from either burning up in the toxic atmosphere or skipping off of it toward an icy death in deep space.

I slowed to supersonic speed, surveying the small planet at Mach seven, taking in a quick survey in the waning moments of my ring's power. All around me were signs of what must have been a magnificent civilization. Towering spires and awe-inspiring architecture. Roads, lakes, oceans—there once had been *oceans* there—lush valleys. Plan, purpose. *Art.* Now, all destroyed, lying in ruins and covered with ash and the misery of the planet's extreme atmosphere.

What happened here? I wondered. Some solar event? Another planet exploding, perhaps shifting this one's orbit? Could this system have had two stars, and one went nova? I rocketed over the horizon, saddened by whatever act of Creation had brought down so noble a place.

Zeroing in on the energy signature, I looked for Malvolio, but saw only gaseous winds and shifting sands and immense, eerie ruins—half-destroyed entombments of the life that had once flourished here.

I landed, looking around at the towering, half-destroyed buildings. Squinting through the wind and gas, my eyes watering as my life support shield began to fail, I actually thought I saw something...scrawled across a half-ruined wall...in...spray paint?

SHAMROCKS RULZ

Shamrocks? What would an alien people know about...about a shamrock? I began coughing, my shield now down to less than fifteen percent. I blinked at what appeared to be street gang graffiti, done by "taggers"—graffiti artists. "Shamrocks" was the name of a ruthless street gang—gun runners and drug dealers with ties to radical factions in Ireland. As Green Lantern's costume faded, replaced by the bright orange jumpsuit of the Warren County Jail, I couldn't help but remark that Planet Hell was an awful long way from home for gang bangers—

—which was when it hit me: the architecture. I'd seen it before. The ring totally failing now, I spun around. Hal Jordan, millions of light years from home, was surrounded by ruins designed by Qwardians.

Qwardians. An evil society from an antimatter universe. Sinestro, the rogue Green Lantern and sworn enemy of the Corps, was their god. A race whose value system promoted evil over good, Sinestro was tailor-made to be their ruler. His death made all Qwardians despise both the Green Lantern Corps and Earth that much more.

As revenge for their leader's death, the Qwardians designed a prototype of Sinestro's counterfeit Green Lantern ring and programmed an invasive virus into it—the Sinestro virus. They made thousands of copies of the ring and scattered them across time and space, knowing many of the rings would end up in the hands of unwitting beings who would, some day, become their agents—Sleepers—and destroy the Green Lantern Corps and all mankind.

Sinking to my knees in the swirling maelstrom, I realized I couldn't possibly be on Qward. Even without the ring's advanced programming, I'd recognize Qward if I saw it. No, this planet had been some kind of colony—a world terraformed by the Qwardians for some unknown purpose.

My head smashed against the sandy soil as my lungs worked overtime to process the hellish atmosphere. *Planet Hell*, I thought. *I dub thee Planet Hell.* My eyes glazed over as a rail thin man hurriedly approached me. As he kneeled by my side, I saw, with my dying moments, the face of my enemy—the enemy of all Creation.

The man was a Qwardian.

CHAPTER

21

Lord Malvolio, Master of the Green Flame, had crushed Alan Scott's arm. The limb now useless, his power ring having exhausted its charge, Scott was near totally defenseless against the hulking, seven-foot 500-pound mass of muscle who had patterned his appearance—his hair, his costume—after Scott himself. Malvolio had pursued the war era Green Lantern throughout the elegant Gotham City townhouse Malvolio had co-opted from a well-to-do couple by twisting their heads off of their shoulders.

Learning these events from Scott himself, I finally realized why the Malvolio I'd meet decades later so resembled the Golden Age Green Lantern—a Green Lantern who was, at that time, far from the revered elder statesman sharing these events with me.

Scott threw a fire hatchet, snapping a weak leg beneath a table supporting a massive, decorative globe of Planet Earth, which in turn rolled into Malvolio, ramming him back into the roaring fireplace.

"O foolish soul," Malvolio said, swatting the massive globe, "thou doth toil in vain!"

The massive globe hurled toward Scott faster than he could avoid it, the globe smashing mere inches from Scott's face, sending Scott tumbling to the priceless Oriental rug.

Indifferent to the fire, Malvolio climbed to his feet and

marched purposefully toward Scott, glowering, his teeth set. Scott recalled a Malvolio who spoke to him in plain English, but I remember a hulking Elizabethan era blowhard, preaching in the King James version.

"Worlds die and galaxies flicker to dust. Armies rise and even the mighty, yea even the meretricious, find their end as providence's immutable grace showeth favor to whom she will; granting dispensation and revelation unto the As Promised—mighty men of valor and purpose, justified by imminent domain and purified within the crucible of blood!"

In agony, Alan struggled to his feet as Malvolio stalked him, wondering if Malvolio would crush his skull like an egg or merely talk him to death. Malvolio loved to talk.

"As the dawn dost herald the death of the past and birth of the future, as peace dost herald the death of war and the newness of liberty, as love dost prescribe the precipitous death of hatred, so now, therefore, doth the heavens and, yea, verily, all Creation, trumpet the triumphant and beneficent ascension of him who is the As Promised, him who is the As Written, he who shall bring light to darkness, peace to war, future to past; he who is the As Wise, who is the As Knowing, he who is the Power, the Glory, The Dominion—the Trump of Power and Lord of All Evermore—" Malvolio built to a throaty, phlegmy frenzy, now shouting in a stentorian thunder that shook the house's very foundation—

"—*Malvolio! Lord of the green flame!*"

Scott had assumed that Malvolio was, apparently, a fellow Green Lantern. Befriending him, Scott quickly realized how utterly unbalanced Malvolio was but, by that time, Malvolio had already begun imitating Scott—changing his hair color and even wearing a modified version of Scott's Green Lantern costume and mask. *Mask.* Why would someone built like a Sherman tank *wear a mask?* As if no one would realize who he was?

Their alliance having gone south over a woman's affections, Malvolio had finally concluded he had learned all he'd needed to learn from the puny Scott and, grabbing Scott by his ring hand, Malvolio crushed the bones in Green Lantern's hand while raising him several feet off of the ground.

Malvolio sneered as Scott writhed within his grip. "O piteous man, how lost thou art," he lamented. "Him who is the As Promised set before thee darkness and light. Yet thou, in thy piteous iniquity, chose neither of the twain. Choosing, by such virtue, nothingness."

Malvolio chilled to an iron stoicism. "And so, thou art nothing."

Malvolio dropped Scott to the floor. "Take heart, my former brother, that death shall be both quick and painless. However–" Malvolio stooped to rip the power ring from Scott's broken finger. "–this dost belong to he who is–"

Scott suddenly lunged, moving past Malvolio, and leaped into an elegant closet some feet away. Energy crackled and spat out of the closet door as Alan Scott vanished in a flash of light.

Alan Scott, the original Green Lantern, lay in the dust on the gaseous planet. Opening his eyes, he saw what seemed to be a sky, but was far too orange and muddy to be anyplace he'd ever seen before. Pulling himself up to a seated position, he nearly blacked out again from the pain of his injuries. Malvolio had beaten him nearly to death.

He coughed blood onto his crimson shirt. *Bet that's not good,* he thought.

Squinting, he looked around while laboring to breathe whatever passed for air on the muddy rock of a planet. Having never left the Earth before, Scott had no reason to assume this was anything worse than perhaps the smoking ruins of the townhouse wherein he'd battled Malvolio. But, all around him, the ruined structures told a different story.

A structural engineer, Scott had an eye for architectural design. He didn't understand how any of the ruined structures he saw could ever have been structurally sound. Odd angles, uneven and inconsistent supports—it didn't surprise Scott that so many of those buildings now lay in ruins.

Scott looked at the power ring on his hand. Its charge had been exhausted. It was now a gaudy piece of jewelry. And Scott was stranded...wherever he was...

Squinting through the haze, Scott saw a man approaching. A good Samaritan, perhaps. A passing car who had, perhaps spotted him there in the ghost town. Scott wanted to wave to the stranger but one arm was crushed and the other hurt too much. He wanted to call to him, but the thick and gritty air choked and burned his lungs. He could only sit there, waiting, as the stranger drew closer and closer—

—until horror flashed up Scott's spine. There, on the stranger's chest, was the emblem of the Green Lantern.

Dammit—it's another one! Scott thought as he defied both pain and logic to scramble to his feet, adopting a wobbly battle stance, his tattered cap cascading over his ruined shoulder. His teeth set in a determined grimace.

"All right, you bastard!" he shouted. "Do your worst!"

As I approached Scott, I had absolutely no idea what he was talking about, "Excuse me?" I said.

"Kill me! Go on and kill me if you can!!" Alan taunted.

I stopped, turning to look behind me, my freshly-charged power ring at the ready. *Was Malvolio behind me? Sinestro?* I scoured the muck for signs of an enemy.

"Go on!" Alan shouted. "Get it over with!"

Which was when I finally got it: Alan was talking to *me*.

"Oh, no, " I said, smiling, "I'm not here to—"

"*Liar!*" Scott screamed, as he charged forward and punched me, landing me on my back.

On pure adrenaline, Scott pursued me, attempting to ball his ring hand into a fist, but not quite making it. "You may kill me, but, damn you, I'll take you with—"

Without even using my ring, I swept his leg with mine, dropping him to the ground. Scott impacted, sending a cloud of soot into the atmosphere. Great, just what we needed, more soot.

"I'll—I'll!" Scott was sucking in soot, trying to yell epitaphs, but not quite making it.

"Stop talking, Alan," I said. "Just breathe slow."

"Don't try and trick me you—you—" Alan started choking.

I sat up in the dirt, smiling. "Told you." I gave Alan a moment to cough up phlegm and blood before continuing, with a smile. It felt good to smile. It had been a very long time. "Welcome to Planet Hell."

Alan looked at me, Though we sat in the dust like two kids in a sandbox, he still distrusted me. Which was when I finally realized why—he had never *seen* another Green Lantern before.

Alan Scott and I had never met. This must be Alan Scott from some time period very early in his Green Lantern career.

"I'm Hal Jordan," I said, still smiling for no other reason than that it felt good. I'd been a Spook so long, I feared the muscles had atrophied.

"Did Malvolio send you?" Scott said.

Scott must have had some kind of run in with that 17th century lunatic. I shook my head *no*.

"I don't believe you!" Scott barked. "And, after I'm done with you I'm going to go find Malvolio, so you might as well tell me now who you are!"

"His name is Hal Jordan," a voice from behind Alan said.

Alan whirled about to see The Qwardian, a bi-pedal humanoid with an oversized head and enormous eyes.

It was Scott's first alien.

"*Get back!!*" he demanded, instinctively raising his ring, which was dead, "Get back or I'll kill you!" The Qwardian scampered back so fast he, too, fell into the sand.

And then there were three kids in the sandbox.

"Alan," I said. Scott's gaze was fixed on the petrified Qwardian. *"Alan"*–I persisted–"he's more scared of you than you are of him."

Finally hearing me, Scott snapped his head around. "How–how do you know my name?"

I was really getting into this 'smiling' business, "You introduced yourself. Like, ten years ago."

Alan gave me a quizzical look. *Surely this man is insane.* "Ten years ago, I was fourteen."

I scratched the back of my neck, searching for an answer that would make sense. "Yeah, uh, look, Alan, most of what I could tell you to explain wouldn't make any sense to you yet. But someday it will."

Scott was becoming convinced he was either hallucinating or dead. But even hell couldn't possibly be this ridiculous. He pointed to the Qwardian, who had regained some of his composure. "Who's he?"

"A friend," I said, smiling, "a member of an alien race from the planet Qward. His actual name is unpronounceable, so I named him 'John'."

"I am John Q," the Qwardian offered, glowering menacingly. Qwardians always glowered menacingly, it was their natural state.

Alan couldn't possibly know that. "Keep away from me!"

"Alan–John feels much the same way about you."

"You wear The Sign," John Q said, pointing to Alan's chest emblem, "The Sign of The Green Flame!"

Alan looked at his bloodied shirt. "Green Fl—you mean *Malvolio?*"

John Q screamed and cringed, dropping his face to the ground.

"No—no, wait—" Alan offered, "—I'm not like Malvolio! In fact, he tried to kill me—that's why I'm here!"

Didn't help. Alan had spooked poor John Q half to death. Alan turned back to me, regarding my own Green Lantern uniform.

"What about you? You one of Malvolio's cronies?"

"Man tried to squish me like a roach," I said. "Trust me—he's no friend of mine."

Scott looked at the meek, harmless John Q, turning back toward me now, "Qwardian?"

"Yes. Qward is a planet that exists in parallel with Planet Earth, only in a different dimension of space."

"'Dimension'...?"

Oy. I scratched my head a bit, "Let's just call it, say, Over There Space for now. So Qward is Over There and we're Over Here. To Qwardians, evil is good, left is right, night is day, truth is a lie—"

"It's all...backwards?"

"Yes. So there was this Green Lantern named Sinestro who was once the greatest of all Green Lanterns until pride caused him to want to take control of the Corps. He was censured by the Guardians of the Galaxy, and he bolted in disgrace, eventually ending up on Qward where Sinestro's evil was, to them, the ultimate virtue. Sinestro ruled Qward with an iron hand, plotting his revenge against the Green Lanterns while also plotting to bring Qward from Over There to Over Here.

"Sinestro was eventually killed, and the Qwardians' hope of escaping Over There Space died with him. Furious, they enacted a final revenge, creating thousands of fake power rings—colored yellow because, Over There, everything is backwards, right? They flung these rings across time and space, knowing the rings would end up in the hands of unwitting sentient beings who would some day be marshaled into an army of Sleepers the Qwardians could use to avenge themselves on the Green Lantern Corps and the planet Earth. You still with me?"

Alan blinked, "You mean, there are *other* Green Lanterns?"

Derailment warning: Alan was going to sidetrack me. "Yes, but let's just put a pin in that for now, okay?

"Anyway, finding out their people had plotted such an evil revenge, Qwardian dissidents decided to flee Over There Space and colonize a world Over Here where they could leave peacefully. And, since everything Over There is backwards, Qwardian rebels, like John Q over there—"

"Are *good* people?" Alan offered, again glancing at the alien.

"Glad to have you with me," I said, smiling. "The dissidents journeyed to this remote sector and terraformed this planet to make it compatible with their life requirements from Over There. What they didn't realize, was, this is Sector Four, a restricted penal colony set up for one specific criminal—"

"—Malvolio," Alan concluded, still lost, but the pieces were coming together.

"Yes. And, thinking Malvolio was a Green Lantern—*which he's not*—the Qwardian dissidents—the *good* Qwardians—welcomed him with open arms. Malvolio became their hero and defender, but ultimately became their dictator and oppressor, as he began pressuring the Qwardians to build a transformer bridge to carry Malvolio home to Earth."

"'Transformer bridge'?"

"A star gate—a means of instantaneous transport over vast distances. It's how you got here—passing through the star gate in Gotham City."

Alan gave that some thought. The closet. He realized I was talking about the closet.

"When the dissidents refused, fearing Malvolio would destroy Earth the way he was oppressing them, Malvolio became enraged. He laid waste to the Qwardians' new world, killing everyone on the planet—"

"Except John Q," Alan offered, looking again at the alien.

"Malvolio left John's family alive and threatened to kill them if John did not program a transformer bridge to take him to Earth. John gave in—"

"John Q failed," the alien lamented.

"—but Malvolio killed John's family anyway before escaping Sector Four for Earth," I concluded. "And that's where Planet Hell came from."

Alan painfully climbed to his feet. He had his second wind, now, his tattered cloak carried by the nauseating, thick atmosphere as he surveyed the alien vista.

"So, we're stuck here," he said, stoically.

"Not exactly," I smiled. *"Lantern,"* I commanded, and Alan Scott's emerald power battery shimmered into existence, my fist gripping the mounting ring.

"A lantern!" Scott exclaimed, "Just like mine!"

"It *is* yours, Alan."

Alan didn't understand. "Malvolio crushed my lantern back on Iwo Jima—"

"Yes. And it's still there," I said.

"So, then, how can this be the same lantern?"

I continued smiling. "Let's put a pin in that, too."

Alan Scott did not quite know what to make of the benevolent stranger, nor did he particularly trust me. But some instinct told him I was, indeed, a friend, and he staggered toward me, wracked with pain, to limply touch the ring on his broken finger to the lantern's polished bell.

And I will shed my light over dark evil
For the dark things cannot stand the light
The light of...the Green Lantern!

Scott was suddenly consumed by an enormous, emerald pyre, the fames billowing and consuming his flesh, obscuring him from view. John Q screamed and ran back as the flame twisted and flowed and ultimately funneled into the sky before exploding in a climactic flash, leaving in its wake, hovering high above us—*Green Lantern.*

"I suppose I should thank you," GL said.

I smiled up at him, "No, actually, you're the one who saved me."

Scott looked down at me grimly. Now fully healed and restored, his costume in pristine condition, his ominous, dark cloak blowing in the breeze. "How?"

Smiling, I hesitated a moment before figuring, *what the hell.* "By sending me here."

"*I* sent you here?" he asked, maintaining his stoicism.

I struggled for words before Alan himself bailed me out, "I know, I know—we'll put a pin in that, too.

"Okay," he continued, "now what? How do we get home?"

"Well," I said, "your transformer bridge is recharging now. It'll be awhile before you can step through it to get home." I rubbed my chin, "Wanna take a run?"

Alan's recollection of these events differs somewhat from my own, but they tell the same story: two men, both lost and on the verge of defeat, sharing a moment in time that rejuvenates and empowers both of them.

Taking the original Green Lantern out for his first romp around outer space, Alan Scott was like a kid at Disneyland. We'd escaped Planet Hell's atmosphere and darted out across Sector Four. Alan was wide-eyed with wonder: never, *never,* in his life had he even dreamed human beings were capable of moving beyond the planet.

"Y'know," Scott said, "since I found that lantern on the train, I've spent most of my time wondering about my place in the world and my purpose. I think you may have helped me with that."

I used my ring to more or less tow Alan—even though his ring would indeed protect him, he was still far too inexperienced to navigate space on his own. Besides, he was enjoying the view, enjoying being a passenger.

"What my greater purpose is remains to be seen. But, right now, I know I have to stop Malvolio—but I'm not sure I can."

Alan became very grim, his boyish glee eroding, now. "He's very powerful. He doesn't doubt himself, and he's absolutely ruthless."

His words warmed me. Genuinely and in a real way, not the stolen moments with Janelle or the Balmerino novice. I felt something I had not felt in far too long—*joy*. The giddiness that came from giving of yourself, of your spirit. From loving your neighbor. For sacrificing some small part of who you are to enrich and enlighten others.

Now I couldn't stop smiling. I was the village idiot. "Alan—none of that matters. That ring on your hand is powered by sheer conviction—by your *will power*. The stronger your resolve, the more powerful you'll be."

Alan was distracted now, his mind on the battle ahead. "Which means *what* to a guy like Malvolio?"

We were moving at several multiples of the speed of light, but there was little point in explaining that to Scott, who was fully immersed in the new experience. *Space*. He couldn't wait to get home—to share this grand adventure with Irene.

"Alan, at the end of the day, this conflict will be about resolve—about whose *will* is strongest. Everything else about

Malvolio is smoke and mirrors. Alan—you've got to get in the game. You absolutely must stop second guessing and doubting yourself. Malvolio is just a suit; he knows *nothing* about the Green Lantern Corps and he's *not* a Green Lantern. He's a four-year-old with a power ring."

We plowed through a nebula, finding wonder in the brilliant hues of noble gases and carbon compounds, before winding through a plasma storm and into a singularity—our power rings somehow compensating for the mass needed to overcome the Oppenheimer-Volkoff degeneracy pressure limit. The area around us warped, Alan and I becoming cosmic anomalies as light could not overcome the acceleration of gravity within the singularity but, paradoxically, the Green Lantern light could function.

"Malvolio doesn't doubt himself because he's *insane,*" I continued. "He is *unaware* of his own limits, therefore he has no limits.

"You, old friend, are being reasonable and taking a rational approach to a threat that is neither reasonable nor rational. You've got to learn to do what Malvolio does: not doubt yourself. You need to learn to speak Malvolio's language."

Emerging from the singularity, I then flew, faster than Alan thought we could or *should,* through an asteroid belt, banking and dodging majestic chunks of rock the size of small cities.

Alan kept his determined expression as he processed this. "Malvolio...is all *will.*"

"But he's an idiot," I said. "He thinks linearly and two-dimensionally. You have to start thinking on a whole new level, less about *power* and more about *will.*

Escaping the asteroid belt, we caught up with a comet, racing it across all Creation as ice and steam bled off of the pivoting frost giant.

"In this fight, you'll be the only one with both will and

intellect. I promise you, Alan"—As I concluded, Alan's sober expression told the whole story—"you *can* do this. You *have* to."

Alan Scott's transformer bridge had completed its duty cycle by the time we again touched down on Planet Hell. I had been careful to shield my power ring's energy signature from Kyle Rayner—who was on the other side of the planet, near the SHAMROCKS gang graffiti, waiting for his own transformer bridge to carry him back to Gotham City in what we consider our "present" day.

Alan shook my hand, regarding me with an intense glare: a hint of the man of gravity he would someday become. "In the future...who are you to me?"

I smiled, life flowing through me. Parallax banished to some far reaches of my being.

I was Hal Jordan.

I was Alan Scott's friend.

"Let's just say we're close," I told him. "And, if we survive this Sleeper stuff to meet again, it'll be because of you."

Scott glared at me for a long moment before summoning the Green Flame, which consumed him in dramatic fashion before the swirling maelstrom was drawn through the transformer bridge, leaving me alone on the barren planet.

"Hey, Green," Spire Raines, the Green Lantern of Space Sector 2814, said in his sprite-like fashion as he came in for a landing, "Things jack okay, Fud?" Raines had a...unique vocabulary. He was my successor from thousands of years in the future.

"Jack okay, yes," I said, sounding very Dad.

The sprightly Raines twirled like a top as he came in for an energetic touchdown, a wide grin on his face. He was human, early twenties, and his uniform was, I suppose, what all the kids were wearing in the 45th century.

"Thanks again for saving my life," I said, perhaps a little too flippantly.

"Plish!" Raines dismissed, "Fellow green well met!"

Which was his way of saying he'd found me, marooned and powerless on Planet Hell, and allowed me to charge my ring using his battery. He then moved me out of range of Kyle Rayner's detection, Kyle being the man this future Lantern had been waiting for.

In fact, Kyle had *sent him* there. But that's another story.

"Spire," I asked, "do you know how to set the controls on these transformer bridges?"

Spire made a kind of snort and twirled a bit. I supposed that to be *no.*

"But what dif matters, Jack okay?"

What the hell did he say?

Raines aimed his Green Lantern ring at the transformer bridge. "When you would be like?"

What time and place, he was asking me. I started to tell him the exact time I left Earth, but then it occurred to me—what if I arrived back a little before that? And convinced Kyle he needed to leave *that minute* so the Sleeper threat would have been dealt with? Or—

—even farther, if I went back to where Kyle saved the planet Saturn and, in so doing, the entire solar system? I could simply tell him about the Sleeper threat then, and avoid everything that followed.

Raines looked impatient, "Fud...?" His word for *buddy.* But I was considering the alternatives—

—going back to before I sought the Spectre's destiny. Or, before that—

—before the Spectre.

Before Parallax.

Before Coast City.

Before—

—the thought paralyzed me. *Before Martin Jordan died.*

I could change things. I could un-do so much damage, right so many wrongs. Save so many *countless* lives. Put things right, dammit. And this time, this time for *sure,* I'd get it right—

—oh God.

Horror cut through me. *Oh...my dear Lord...*

I was doing it again.

I sank to my knees in the sand, in the swirling maelstrom, and wept.

Raines continued waiting, not knowing what else to do. If I waited too long and the transformer bridge shut down, Kyle would short out all of the bridges once he returned to Earth, and I'd have to again find my way home on my own. I considered not ever going home. I'd done more than enough damage there.

"So," a familiar voice said, "do you get it *now?*"

I looked up from my self-pity to see Martin Jordan standing near me, wearing his best flight suit, his helmet cradled under his arm.

Dad smiled at me. "I'm tempted to say, *Merry Christmas."*

This angered me. "I liked you better as a squirrel," I sneered.

I stood, walking away and waving "Dad" off, "No, don't do this. This is just too cheap—way too *Field Of Dreams. "*

"Yes, but it gets right to the point, doesn't it? Jordan, you're a man who's had chance after chance after chance not to blow it. And you came to us, remember? You said you deserved your fate—becoming the Spirit of Vengeance and doing our bidding.

"It's this other part of you—this 'Parallax' creature—that continues to trip you up. You'll need to come to terms with that. That's the demon you need to put to rest."

"And you allowed my fall from grace to teach me this lesson?"

"I allowed nothing. I don't interfere with free will. Your destiny is, ultimately, what you make of it."

I scratched my neck, clenching my chin a bit, swallowing my pride, "Yeah...as this...debacle...proves..."

"*Post hoc, ergo propter hoc,*" Dad said, smiling. Words I knew well.

Glaring out at the horizon, I translated the Latin phrase, *"After therefore, because of it."* One thing follows the other, therefore it was caused by the other.

"In the cosmic scheme of things," Dad said, "all it takes is one skateboard left near one staircase to send the dominoes toppling."

One skateboard.

One *magic ring.*

I looked at the ring on my hand. The wrenching emotional pain of what I had to do seared into my mind. I felt paralyzed. Resentful. Angry. My mind flipping through excuses and loopholes and finding none.

"So, what—we head home now?" I asked Dad.

"Dad" turned and walked toward the horizon, slowly becoming engulfed in the thick, acrid atmosphere. "'We' don't do anything. It's your life, Jordan. Clean up on your way out."

And then I was alone. Staring at the ring. Caught at the crossroad.

And running out of time.

22

O ld Man Ferris went to a stockholder's meeting.

And, so it was that his young daughter and newest pilot trainee ended upstairs in her room watching *Rocky and Bullwinkle* in their underwear. Well, Carol was watching it. I was too serious for any of that. And too noble to understand the actual point of cartoon-watching at Carol's place. I thought I was actually there to *watch cartoons.*

So I brought my homework with me. ACM—air combat maneuvers—charts and complex jet design formulas on which old man Ferris would be quizzing me in the morning. I was also writing Carol's college papers for her, learning business administration courses on the fly as Carol talked me through it. Carol was wearing a sunny yellow bra, tube socks and white panties with little ducks on them. I propped my notes on her firm backside, tapping my calculator while mumbling to myself.

Which was precisely why I struggled as a test pilot. In those days, long before Green Lantern, I was so squeaky clean I could have been canonized. I was nowhere near arrogant enough and I had the mating instincts of a fern.

Carol turned away from the flying squirrel, a concept I considered dismissive. "You having a good time back there?"

I murmured something while fretting over a formula I couldn't prove.

"Hal—I can get the old man to give you another couple days."
I continued fidgeting.

"Hal. *Hal.*"

I finally looked up, a bit disoriented about where I was.

"I can help you with that," she said.

I seriously doubted it.

Which was when she swept all of my things off of her down-filled comforter, dumping several of her overly-cute stuffed animals with them. "Hey!" I objected.

Carol rolled over, now lying next to me, staring at her ceiling, smiling. "Hal—I want to do something great in my lifetime. Something more than just being Carl Ferris' kid."

I was distracted, looking at my papers over the side of the bed. They were wrinkled now. Now I'd have to start over. Presentation was everything. "Being Carl Ferris's daughter has worked for you so far," I muttered.

"There's more. There has to be. Something inside me...just screams it."

I thought, *That's the evil screaming.* I knew Carol was evil but loved her anyway. She had an odd duality that made her the perfect, spoiled, scheming id to my superego. Much as her evil streak irked me, I knew messing with the formula would just ruin the magic that was Carol.

"How about you, Hal?"

"Me?" I was still obsessing over the papers. "I just want to be Carl Ferris's daughter."

Carol tugged on my tee shirt, rolling me over on top of her, finally getting my attention. "No you don't. You want to be Marty Jordan's son."

"And, what luck, I already am."

"Yeah, but you want to *beat* him. Surpass his achievements. Make him proud."

"I want to win the Nobel Prize. Or be the seventh Jackson brother."

"Hal—"

"Carol, I don't *do* 'fate.' I don't stare up at the sky and wonder. I *study*. I *research*. I believe what I can touch, what I can prove, what I can hold in my hand."

"All evidence to the contrary," Carol said, drolly.

"Carol—stop rushing. We've got nothing to prove. I'm not going anywhere."

Carol exhaled loudly, pushing me off of her. She wasn't in the market for what Saint Hal had for sale.

"Carol," I said, "if this is love, I mean, if that's what we're doing here—we'll have the rest of our lives to, ah, to—"

"Watch cartoons."

"Yes. You sacrifice a little now, it pays off later. Life without discipline is chaos."

"Who told you that, the Fun Police?"

"Carol—"

"All right, fine. But, mark my words, Hal Jordan—*greatness* awaits us. We need to start planning now. Y'know, for when we're great."

I smiled at Carol, stroking her cheek gently while looking into her eyes.

"Maybe you're right," I said. She cheered up, hopeful now.

"I'm always right," Carol said. "That's the rule."

"Hey, you know what I wanna do *now?*" I mischievously asked.

Carol smiled at me. "You wanna go get your papers."

I scrambled off of the bed, diving for the papers on the floor, hoping some of them could be salvaged.

Carol turned back to the moose, dreaming of what was to come.

The Justice League Watchtower was under attack.

For the second time that day, major explosions rocked the headquarters of the world's greatest heroes as Star Sapphire, reborn to her former glory, arced around the citadel, targeting the heavily reinforced fuel cell storage banks.

Star was laughing. *Laughing,* while doing her level best to cause catastrophic damage not only to the installation but to the moon itself and, by extension, planet Earth. Her Zamoran Sapphire—a highly advanced energy weapon much like the Green Lantern power rings—was fully restored and hers once more. The raw *power* of the Zamoran jewel flooded through her, making her delirious and drunk with it. Having been so long denied the *esprit,* the sheer liberation, near-limitless power can bring, Star Sapphire was lost within joy as she hurtled around the complex in wide turns at a fierce rate of speed.

This was no Sleeper. No crude automaton, no bacteria eating her brain and forcing her to unspeakable acts. This was Carol Ferris—the *need* within her, the *evil* that had always been there—finding its voice. The shattered mirror of her darker half—of Star Sapphire—brought to the surface by virtue of having pushed Carol beyond human extremes. At the threshold of death, Carol reached a depth she believed had been excised from her forever, finding that smallest piece of herself that was still Star Sapphire. Coupled with the evil power of the Sinestro ring inside her, Carol's psyche split once again, banishing Carol Ferris to some nameless prison within her own mind as Star Sapphire became a reality once more.

Instantly, the newly reformed persona used the power of the Sinestro ring within her to summon the fragments of her des-troyed crystal from where the Spectre had consigned them, and, in the heart of the massive hydrogen explosion, fused the terrible sapphire together again.

A consequence of the jewel's dark power was the creation of

an entire alter ego. Star Sapphire was, in fact, a wholly different person from Carol Ferris, her twisted, evil other, a person who hated Hal Jordan because her other half loved him so much. Carol Ferris indeed thirsted for and longed for the *power* of Star Sapphire, but she never wanted to lose control to the Zamoran queen, as she now had; Carol Ferris now having been banished to the farthest recesses of Star Sapphire's evil psyche.

Star Sapphire could have turned and escaped within the explosion, and no one would have been the wiser. She could have ridden the cosmic winds to wherever adventure took her, or tracked down her long-missing Zamoran subjects. She could have conquered worlds or defended galaxies from evil invaders. She could, simply, have vanished, bided her time and struck down her enemies when they least expected it. She could have done most anything she wanted to. But, try as she did to separate herself from Carol Ferris, the fact was Star Sapphire and Carol Ferris were not two separate people. They were one and the same.

A badly battered Justice League, huddled aboard a barely operating Watchtower, was far too tempting a target for Star Sapphire. And the Justice League, battered or no, might have been Carol Ferris' last hope. After all, if Star Sapphire used the explosion as cover and rocketed off to Andromeda, Carol would be lost forever. Thus, for two completely different reasons, two completely different personalities shared the same driving impulse—get to the Watchtower.

"I'll go," Superman said as he painfully raised himself off of a sick bay exam bed. Sick bay was full to overflowing anyway, and Superman's heightened invulnerability made him the first to shake off the traumatic shock of having the Sinestro ring removed. But he was far from a hundred percent, groggy and still a bit wobbly as he lurched toward the sick bay hatch while the Watchtower quaked from Star Sapphire's relentless attack.

The only Leaguer on his feet was the Martian Manhunter, who discouraged Superman from taking on Star Sapphire. "You should wait, my friend," he said before altering his density to pass through the bulkhead. "I'll call if I need you."

The only other heroes on their feet were not active JLA members. Green Arrow and Jade saw to Flash and Aquaman—who were still in shock from their exposure to liquid oxygen—and Batman, Wonder Woman and Plastic Man—all sedated and recovering from extreme trauma.

The Green Lanterns—John Stewart, Kyle Rayner and Guy Gardner—were having a better go of it. John and Kyle were breathing on their own, and Guy was coming around with a monstrous headache. "Oh, mama..." he whined. "Somebody get the plate of that truck..." The fierce tremors slamming the Watchtower sent Guy sprawling back onto his exam bed.

"Dad!" Jade cried out.

Nearly a quarter million miles away, hovering high above the Earth, Alan Scott was still standing, arms outstretched, his imposing cloak floating in weightless space. All around him were thousands and thousands of Sinestro rings—a veritable sea of fool's gold floating all around him.

By the sheer force of his will, Alan was channeling the lantern's power to draw every Sleeper ring from the planet Earth to himself.

"Dad!" Jade's voice snapped via their shared power link.

"Stand by," Alan said, locked in the zone. He extended an upturned palm, which contained the small drawstring sack within which he'd stored his Sinestro rings. With a gesture from Alan, the sack created a massive vacuum effect, drawing the countless gold rings impossibly into itself while growing no bigger. While it appeared to be magic or mysticism, Scott was merely opening a portal to an alternate dimension, keeping the enormous volume of the sack there. "Go, Jade."

With the JLA Watchtower transporters still down, Jade flew through the winding corridors, looking for an airlock. "Where *are* you? What's taking you so long? Star Sapphire is attacking the Watchtower! We really need you, Dad—and bring help!"

Alan Scott moved out of his stationary position, leaving Earth's orbit and soaring toward the moon. "Honey—by the time I get there, it will all be over."

"Dad!"

"Jade—just do what you can, and trust me. These things have a way of working themselves out."

Jade's father's benign indifference angered and frustrated her, as did *this incredibly complex stupid clubhouse with no damned doors.*

"Jade—" Scott called to her.

"What?" Jade snapped back.

"Where are you supposed to be?"

In sick bay with the man she loved. That was the point Dad was trying to make. Stick to your role, your place in the scheme of things. Instead, Jade snapped back, "Protecting my friends from that crazy woman."

The Watchtower rocked from yet another huge explosion, and the lights flickered out. Jade increased speed, zipping through corridors looking for a way to get into the fight, her own emerald energy illuminating her way.

"Jade."

"Dad, please go be Zen somewhere else!" Jade snapped as she flew down an access shaft, heading into the lower decks.

"Where are you *supposed* to be?"

Jade reached a dead end. She pivoted in midair, stopped in the dark of inter-connecting shafts, frustrated by the rat maze of a headquarters. Her fists clenched. She wanted to blow a hole in the wall to get out of there, but even in her agitated state, she realized how ridiculous it would be to destroy the Watchtower in order to save the Watchtower.

Her father's voice echoed in her mind. *Where—*

Jade was suddenly slammed with an eviscerating, crippling pain, cutting from her skull right through to her feet. Pain so sudden and so intense, she couldn't manage a scream or even a cry for help. Her body locked up as her muscles knotted and nerve synapses shorted out. Sheer, crimson agony raced through her spine, shutting down her central nervous system and throwing up roadblocks between her body and her mind.

She could not think to process what was happening to her, but instinctively she realized she had been ambushed by Star Sapphire.

"Hello, Jade," Sapphire purred as she leapt out of the blackness, her demon Sapphire jewel firing yet another blast of midnight blue agony, this time slamming Jade against a bulkhead, sparks flying off of her body as the radiant energy interacted with the metals in the bulkheads and deck plates. "I need you to do something for me," Star said as she closed the gap between herself and the emerald heroine.

Star Sapphire grabbed a fistful of Jade's hair. Jade was going into shock and could do nothing to stop her. "A little thing, really. But, a purpose you alone are uniquely suited for," Sapphire said. With her fist in Jade's hair, she gruffly pulled Jade's face to hers, whispering in her ear, "And, you *will* keep this our little secret, yes?"

An ornate Zamoran ceremonial dagger appeared in Star Sapphire's free hand, a construct of her dark power. She kissed Jade lovingly on the cheek, Star closing her eyes, nuzzling Jade as a comfort offering. "Such a sweet girl."

Star then savagely slammed Jade's face against the bulkhead, and whipped her blade around in a savage backhand gesture, slitting Jade's throat as Jade rebounded off of the wall.

Jade slammed to the deck at Star Sapphire's feet.

Star Sapphire ran her blade along her tongue, wiping the blood, smiling evilly. "I need to distract your father for a few moments, Jade. I appreciate the help."

Alan Scott lost his connection to his daughter.

"Jade?" Rocketing toward the moon, Scott called to her. He tried to feel her presence. *"Jade!"*

Scott increased speed, focusing now on his daughter rather than his mission. It was one thing to have faith. Having that faith tried was another matter entirely. Scott tried to reach out to any of the Green Lanterns, but none would respond.

Something had gone terribly wrong. Alan Scott stepped outside of his role and purpose to deal with the pain now exploding in his chest. *"Jade!"*

Star Sapphire burst through a wall on a lower deck of the Watchtower, again banking around the JLA base and firing on the Watchtower's fuel cell banks. They were much better shielded than she'd thought, but it was only a matter of time. Star had given herself over to the passion and bloodlust, so much so that nearly all logic and reason escaped her. She was firing largely on impulse now—both sides of Carol Ferris's split personality having been drawn to the Watchtower.

Only Hal Jordan's voice could penetrate her hatred. "Carol."

Star whirled about, enraged, her fists balled, her deadly jewel glowing with deadly energy, as Green Lantern flew toward her. Hal tried to talk her down.

"Look," he said, trying his best not to seem menacing. "I'm the one you want. I'm the cause of your anger, your rage—deal with me and let the League survive."

"Well, well, well," Sapphire hissed, "it's been so very long,

Hal. You tried to destroy me. Neron, that morose demon, gave it a shot, too. You both missed the point, though, lover."

Hal moved in closer, hands up in a yielding position, trying not to antagonize the crazy woman. "Your point being...?"

Star snarled, lurching forward, firing a massive plasma blast at Green Lantern. "The point being I can *never die!*"

Hal threw up a force field milliseconds before being vaporized by Sapphire's blast. His shield cracked and splintered, but held as Hal winced and braced against the massive shock.

"I am *forever* part of her, don't you understand? So long as she lives, *I live!!*" Star hurled another blast at GL, battering him back, followed by a volley of additional blasts as Sapphire attempted to finish Green Lantern off.

"No one wants to kill you, Star!" Hal said as he returned fire, trapping Star inside a ring-generated cage. "We just want you to be whole again—complete!"

"Yes, with *her* in charge!" Star screamed while easily rending GL's cage. "And me imprisoned in the depths of her pitiful, finite human mind!"

The cage had done its work. GL closed in, grabbing Star Sapphire by the shoulders and trying to get her to listen to reason. "Carol—please!"

Star smiled, "Are you pleading with me, Hal? Should we go back to my father's house—strike a new bargain?"

Hal was stoic. "There's no going back, Star. For either of us."

Star smiled, caressing GL's cheek. "Very well then, lover—where do we go from here? What *shall* we do?"

She drew Hal to her. Hal leaned in for a kiss—

—and then blasted Star with a massive bolt of Martian Vision. Martian Vision was a unified radiant energy beam generated by the Martian Manhunter's eyes. The blast not only carried the wallop of a force beam, but the telepathic "blindfold" of a psionic blast. It was so powerful, in fact, that it was capable of dropping even the most powerful villains in their tracks.

Blinded and enraged, Star's head shot back from the force of the bolt, which knocked her sapphire loose from her Zamoran tiara. Star sailed back, her mind losing focus, blinking through thousands of channels.

Green Lantern morphed into the Martian Manhunter—a shape-changer from an ancient mystical race—as he soared across the void, reaching out for the eldritch crystal. The Manhunter had used his telepathic abilities to create the illusion of Green Lantern's power ring functions.

Reaching for the Zamoran jewel, he was a fraction of a second too late.

"Nooooo!" Star shrieked, as, gesturing toward the jewel, she commanded it to fire a massive energy discharge. The Manhunter evaded the energy blast, which vanished from view as it propelled itself into the inky darkness, heading toward the Earth.

"I'm afraid you'll have to come with me, madam," the Manhunter said as he grabbed Star Sapphire's evil jewel in one hand, and the woman herself in the other.

Alan Scott was racing to the moon when Star Sapphire's shriek reached across the cosmos, all Creation seemingly wrenching as the psychic shriek momentarily deafened him. Alan covered his ears, wincing as the sound melted his mind, his panic over Jade and this sudden woman's shriek distracting him *just enough...* that Scott never saw the Sapphire blast hit him.

Star Sapphire's massive energy blast ripped through the vintage Green Lantern, catching him almost completely defenseless, tearing through the dimensional pocket he'd set up, tearing through the small pouch of Sinestro rings allowing thousands upon thousands of pieces of evil gold to be spewed from the ripped dimensional pocket like water from a burst pipe.

The rings attached themselves to Alan all over his body, forming one on top of the other until he was cocooned up to the eyes by the doomsday weapons—with thousands more to come. Not even Alan Scott's indomitable will could break out of the massing of so many Qwardian artifacts, and, within seven tenths of a second, Scott was completely entombed inside a humanoid-shaped mound of golden rings—rings that began glowing with evil power and increasing in mass, changing shape, transforming their unconscious captive in the process.

I burst out of the final black hole some eighty-seven seconds away from Earth's moon, blasting across the Sol system at three or four times the speed of light before dropping to sublight speed, lest I overshoot the moon and end up on the other side of the solar system. I'd returned, as instructed, with Alan Scott's lantern hidden in a dimensional pocket as I made my final approach to the badly damaged Watchtower. By that time, the Martian Manhunter had activated an airlock, and a bright beacon flashed to show me the way in.

"Hey—there he is!" Kyle Rayner cheerfully announced as I entered sick bay. Though still clearly weak from his experience, Kyle was shaking it off, ready to get back in the game. Which was what I'd expect him to do. I admit I'd been harder on Kyle than he deserved. While I'd like to blame Parallax for that, the truth was my humanity was envious of him. Jealous of the life and love Kyle Rayner so took for granted.

"Hey, partner—it's been a while," John Stewart said, cautiously welcoming someone who was once the greatest threat the universe had ever known.

I smiled. I was getting good at it.

"Good to see everybody," I said. And I meant it. "What's our status?"

"Our status is we've been holdin' down the fort while you've been takin' the A-tour of the galaxy!" Guy Gardner baited. *Babbitt buys a power ring.*

"The Watchtower is secure, main power has been restored," the Martian Manhunter reported.

"Alan Scott just called in. He reported that he's recovered all of the Sinestro rings from Earth," Kyle said. "He sent coordinates for all Green Lanterns who are able to meet him."

"That's all *Green Lanterns,*" Guy sneered. "Not *nutty power-mad reanimated corpse ex-GL's.*"

"I believe this belongs to you," the Manhunter said as he handed John Stewart his Green Lantern power ring, recovered from space. John kissed his long-lost friend, relieved to have it back.

Which made me glance over at Kyle. Kyle seemed a bit embarrassed, unable to look me in the eye. It was awkward for him to complain about my using his ring, or to even ask for it back. The ring was, after all, *my* ring, given to him.

There was an uncomfortable pause, things unspoken, now suddenly thunderous.

All Green Lanterns.

Alan wanted *all* Green Lanterns to leave immediately. Guess there'd be no time for a ceremony.

I took one last look at the power ring on my hand, and I smiled again: this time because I had absolutely no problem removing the ring—and handed it back to Kyle Rayner. Kyle exploded in relief, a smile spreading on his face.

I stepped back toward Superman, who was preparing to leave. My Green Lantern costume faded into the bright orange Warren County jail garb.

"New fashion trend?" Superman asked.

I sensed Superman's reservation; the emotional speed bumps in all of my close former friends, now anxious around me and full of suspicion.

"Alan Scott suggested I go planetside," Superman said. "We seem to be secure here, and our base-to-Earth communications are still out, so I'll make a quick patrol of the planet and report back."

He wasn't asking my permission so much as making a graceful exit while several of his teammates remained unconscious, recovering from severe shock.

"Well, kids, time t'go to work!" Guy said, pushing past me like I didn't exist. "Sorry—no feebs allowed!"

Kyle smiled at his ring. He didn't need to say it—he was relieved to have his life back. With some effort, Kyle stood to his feet, never taking his eye off the ring, and, in a flash of emerald light, Kyle's costume was restored.

"Hey—where's Jade?" he asked.

"Patrolling the perimeter, last I saw," Guy said. "You can blow her a kiss on the way out, scrapper. Let's saddle up already!"

Guy, John and Kyle left to rendezvous with Alan Scott in deep space and complete their mission of destroying the Sinestro rings. J'Onn went below to continue station repairs.

Leaving me with absolutely nothing to do. No purpose. No point to my existence.

A monitor panel displayed the trio of Green Lanterns leaving the moon's gravity. I allowed myself the human emotions of envy and jealousy as I stood there in the ridiculous prison uniform.

I realized it was time to go.

Time to return to the loneliness, the emptiness, the *coldness* of my existence. I closed my eyes and breathed in deeply—enjoying what would surely be my last breaths. My last moments of a beating heart.

Green Arrow's hand on my shoulder interrupted that "Hal—" he said, as I turned toward him. "It's Carol."

Deep in the bowels of the Watchtower, Jade lay dying. In some obscure junction of access tunnels, Alan Scott's mortally wounded daughter struggled to breathe, forcing shallow breaths far and few between as her emerald glow dimmed and the blackness swept over her.

The deck felt cold against her cheek, her eyes glazed, her pupils fixed and dilated.

"...K-Kyle..." she said weakly.

She felt no pain. She was far beyond that now. She had no expression as her control over her facial muscles had shut down as well.

"...Kyle..."

Jade was not lucid enough, not alert enough, to focus her will on the Starheart energy inside her. Though the power resided within her, it was miles beyond her reach.

"K—"

And the black consumed her.

"Fools!! You will all dieee!!" Star Sapphire screamed from within her ecto-plasma detention cell. Absent her crown jewel—which the Martian Manhunter had stored in ultra-secure stasis—she was merely an enraged mortal woman.

I sat nearby, on a stool, still wearing the ghoulish prison garb, my head in my hands, while she ranted obscenities. This side of Carol—this evil—had been split off and killed. I didn't understand how brain cells regenerated, how this *other person* lived inside Carol's psyche. Cut it out all you want, the evil was bound to return eventually.

We were a lot alike in that way.

She was my mirror. Perhaps I was hers.

I had to go. I'd learned my lesson: I needed to be where *I* needed to be. My days as a hero were behind me. My days of loving Carol were long gone as well. Defying that logic had nearly cost everyone everything—again.

But, this I wanted to fix. This last thing. This one thing. If I could just put Carol back where I'd found her—then I could go back to being the Spectre without terrible guilt hanging over my head.

But, meddling was what had put us there, in that room, in the first place.

I struggled with what to do. Hal Jordan wanted to fix this. Parallax *demanded* to fix it. The Boss's voice, ringing in my ears, told me to go home—wherever "home" was.

As Star Sapphire cursed and shrieked, I took precious moments to wallow in indecision. I allowed myself a moment: the small dignity of regret.

Which was why I was still on the Watchtower when it was destroyed.

CHAPTER

23

The lights went out and the entire Watchtower pitched sharply as sparks arced across the detention cell and components smashed to the floor. All hell was breaking loose as the main power went out once more, then the backups, plunging us into pitch blackness as Star Sapphire bolted from her prison cell and vanished into the black.

"Come!" Sapphire commanded, and her deadly Sapphire jewel obliterated the Martian Manhunter's stasis cube, which had lost cohesion during the attack. The jewel reattached itself to her Zamoran tiara as she leapt down an access shaft, taking flight once again.

"What the hell did you do *now?*" Green Arrow said as he staggered into the holding area with a lit flare-arrow, casting the chamber in ominous emerald hues.

I scrambled to my feet, trying to walk the sharp incline. "Hell if I know!" Ollie and I lurched through the Watchtower, which shook and rocked violently, until we made it to an observation port and looked outside.

Sinestro.

Easily 300 feet tall, he was a massive, raging figure of pure evil. Sinestro grabbed the JLA Watchtower in one hand—and hurled it to the Moon's surface, smashing it into the dust.

Sinestro, sworn enemy of both the Green Lantern Corps and

of all humanity, was now reborn as a giant. Towering like a small mountain, Sinestro aimed a massive fist down toward us. On each finger was a yellow Sinestro ring.

He fired them all.

The crippled and ruined Watchtower was smashed by enough energy to split a planet in half, which drove the structure several hundred feet into the moon's crust, wedging it deep inside the Tycho crater.

Sinestro glowered down at us. "And so Hal Jordan dies," he said grimly—

"—and *Sinestro lives.*"

Sinestro then turned, taking several massive steps, causing quakes to unsettle the moon's foreboding landscape, before taking flight. The towering monolith now headed toward the destination for his final revenge: Earth.

Inside the Watchtower, the roof had buckled and almost everything was smashed. Moving about was difficult and dangerous work. There was no light.

"Why aren't we dead?" Green Arrow asked—tempting fate, I suppose. "Why aren't we *dead?*"

I wished I had an answer for him. As sound a structure as the Tower was, nothing should have survived a strike like that. It was as if—

—I stopped moving. Ollie rammed into me. "Dammit—*tell* me when you're makin' a short stop like that!"

"The lantern," I mused, barely audible.

"All of the GL's went to meet up with Alan Scott," Green Arrow reminded me.

"No, Ollie, " I said, working through this, "the *lantern*. I hid Alan Scott's power battery inside a dimensional pocket, but it's still here. I'm betting the lantern's automatic protection prevents it from being destroyed!"

Ollie sneered in the blackness. "And, since we just *happen* to be inside the same structure, it protected us, too."

I smiled. "That's about the size of it," I said. Then I called it forth, *"Lantern!"*

Alan Scott's vintage power battery shimmered into view. Its lens glowed brightly with emerald power.

"Okay," Arrow said, "now what?"

"Now," I said, scrutinizing the battery, "I hope she's a friendly gal."

"'She'...?"

"Lantern—your master, Alan Scott, has been co-opted by the demon Sinestro!" Which was my best guess.

There was no response from the lantern.

"Recognize Hal Jordan, Green Lantern of Sector 2814."

No response.

Alan Scott's lantern was carved from a meteor that had landed in China and originated in an entity called the Starheart. While its emerald power was indeed some off-shoot of the Guardians' power battery, Scott's lantern was rooted in mysticism more so than science. It was not programmed to respond to Green Lantern Corps protocol.

"Lantern!" I commanded. The lantern glowed brighter—I had its attention.

"I summon forth the Green Flame of Life!" I said, as Ollie gave me the skunk eye. "That I may defeat the Evil One—and preserve the Master of the Starheart!"

Nothing.

Ollie whispered, "Maybe if you buy it dinner first—"

Suddenly, the cramped, crushed chamber erupted in flame. Green Arrow and I were instantly consumed by a raging fire that enveloped the entire chamber.

"Aaaahhhhhhh!! Turn it off!! Turn it off!!" Ollie screamed.

The flames swirled and diminished, reducing themselves to

our feet, leaving in their wake—Green Lantern. The lantern had obeyed me, creating a Starheart-powered facsimile of both my costume and ring.

Kyle...

I suddenly heard Jade's voice in my head.

...K-Kyle...please...

I winced, trying to sort this out. A trick from Star Sapphire?

...love...you...

"*What,* already?" Green Arrow demanded, I waved him off, looking at the science of it; a comm-channel built into Scott's lantern?

"C'mon!" I shouted, using the Starheart ring to carve my own airlock into the bulkhead. Throwing a life-support shield over Green Arrow, I burst out of the crippled Watchtower, Ollie in tow, and sped toward the Watchtower's base, which was now nearly three football fields away.

In the distance: the monstrous Sinestro, headed to destroy Earth.

"What is this, a *pit stop?*" Green Arrow demanded as we landed near the base of the crippled station. "In case you haven't noticed, Red Boy's about to eat China!"

"The Starheart!" I exclaimed, losing Ollie altogether. "Alan Scott's lantern is powered by an entity called the Starheart! He and his daughter draw from this energy and share a bond!" I used my ring to carve a way into the mangled labyrinth of the lower decks.

"Which means we *don't* wanna stop Sinestro from eating China?"

Inside the lower decks: blackness. A tangle of ramps and catwalks, access tunnels and maintenance shafts. Wires and pipes, all smashed, everything lying on its side. Which made less difference than it might because, on those decks, the artificial gravity and life support had gone to hell anyway.

"Which means I can't leave her here," I said bluntly, aiming my power ring at the source of the Starheart's message—Jade, lying in a corner. I enveloped Jade in a life-support force field, using the ring's Starheart energy to jump-start Jade's own, and the field operated independently of me. Which did not guarantee the girl's survival.

"She's lost a lot of blood, but she's still with us," I told Ollie. "Find the Martian Manhunter and get her to sick bay—fast!."

"Hey—*hey*—where *you* goin'?"

"To pick a fight," I said grimly.

"Hal—need I remind you, screwing around is what got us all here in the first place? You need to alert Kyle and Guy—let them deal with Sinestro."

"Not this time," I said. "It's possible the other GL's are all dead, or almost certainly trapped."

"Hal!"

I took a moment to reassure an old friend, placing a hand on his shoulder, smiling. "I know. I *know,* Ollie," I said. "But it's me or nothing."

Which implied I was the right person at the right time in the right place in all Creation. This mission was my purpose.

Green Arrow kept his guard up, regarding me grimly as long seconds ticked past, finally dismissing me with his benediction. "Don't get us all killed."

I could make him no promises.

Soaring at best speed to Earth, Sinestro was still thousands of miles ahead of me but was already impossibly huge, well over 500 feet now. I'd dispatched a warning to the other Green Lanterns, but Sinestro—somehow impersonating Alan Scott—had faked them to a remote corner of the solar system. Assuming they hadn't been trapped or killed, it would take them nearly fifteen minutes to reverse course and get back to Earth, given the clunky limitations of the Guardians' power rings. By that time, the entire deal would be long over.

Though the Starheart-generated ring resembled my own, I seemed to be moving much, much quicker. The timespace buffers were either far less severe or did not exist, as I closed the gap on the monstrous Sinestro in a matter of seconds.

I did not need to announce my arrival.

Without turning, Sinestro made a casual backhand gesture, firing off planet-destroying blasts of antimatter plasma.

I accelerated to faster-than-light, approaching certain obliteration in mere fractions of a second. At the last possible moment, I opened a dimensional rift—the same way I hid the lanterns—and flew through it, emerging from the rift a few thousand yards farther in, evading Sinestro's blasts while unleashing hell of my own.

"*Sinestro!*" I shrieked, firing off a massive discharge of the Starheart's Green Flame.

The burst slammed the monster, who shrieked in pain, turning now, firing beams from both fists—from ten massive power rings.

I could have likely evaded even those blasts, but they would have ripped the moon apart—which would, in turn, cause massive death and destruction on the Earth. No choice—I placed myself directly in the path of the antimatter tsunami.

The blast raged toward me, some 300 feet high, nearly a mile wide, racing at the speed of light.

Certain death, flashing toward me.

Will, I heard myself say. *This contest comes down to whose will is strongest.*

My guess was Sinestro hadn't *impersonated* Alan Scott—he indeed *was* Alan Scott, somehow co-opted by the thousands of Sinestro rings he'd recovered. But volume—the number of rings—was meaningless. Size—how huge Sinestro seemed—played absolutely no role in whether or not the Starheart power ring would save me.

I'd reverted completely to type: resolving conflict with my fists.

Stop punching people in the head, I heard myself say.

Rather than construct some elaborate defense, I hovered in space, arms outstretched.

I looked into Creation.

The massive, planet-killing energy wave passed harmlessly through me and lost cohesion on the other side, never striking the moon.

"Damn you, Jordannnn!" Sinestro shrieked, firing off an even greater blast before turning toward the small blue planet before him. With a dramatic gesture, he aimed both fists at Earth's atmosphere. "You destroyed everything I had! Everything I *was!* Everything I could be!" Sinestro ranted.

"And, now," he concluded, "my revenge is *complete!"*

Sinestro discharged the full power of the thousands of Sinestro rings at Earth, which would certainly reduce the globe to cosmic ash.

I didn't care.

I mean, I *cared,* but I didn't care.

I accepted what was. I observed the order of things. I became one with all Creation.

If it was, indeed, Earth's time to die, then so be it.

However, if we were *meant* to go on, then—by my *will,* I siphoned *all* of the Sinestro energy into myself.

The massive energy wave coming toward me clung to me as lightning seeks the rod. Simultaneously, Sinestro's planet-killing burst skimmed around the planet's atmosphere and was redirected toward me, Sinestro whirling about as his massive reserve of power left him.

"Noooo!"

I waited. Patient. In harmony with the galaxy. Arms out-stretched. Making no hostile moves. Punching no one in the head.

I simply *was*. And that was enough for me.

Space turned sheet white as power of an unimaginable scale raced toward me. Sinestro, having expended all of his power, dissolved from a flesh and bone entity to a mass of thousands of golden rings in the outline of the giant.

At the center of the great mass of rings: Alan Scott, apparently unharmed but comatose.

As the power mass raced to me, I briefly considered what to do with it. Absorbing the power—if that were indeed possible—would put me well on the way toward regaining the sheer, raw power I'd known as Parallax and the Spectre. But with that power came corruption—the evil still not expunged from me: *Parallax*. Alive, somehow, within me. Power on that level would surely call him forth, and then I'd be back where I started—out of control, empty, seeking salvation by destroying everything I loved.

The wave was upon me now, filling the void. White space. Null space. I waited patiently, peacefully—and, finally, took off.

The mass of Sinestro rings became caught in my space warp, the golden rings forming the tail of the comet as I charged across planes of reality.

As I raced along, the energy wave caught up with me, eventually creeping up my body and engulfing me within its massive power. The rings began clinging to me—as they'd done to Alan Scott. Piling more and more on, covering every inch of my being.

Propelled both by the Starheart and the antimatter discharge, I bulleted into "denied speeds"—theoretically impossible speeds that warped time, space and all reality with it. I was moving so fast, I was in several places at the same time, my essence beginning to fill vast ranges of spacetime.

I criss-crossed the universe, summoning all Sinestro rings to me by my sheer force of will. An irresistible and undeniable magnet, recalling the doomsday weapons in much the same manner as they'd been scattered across existence.

Trailing across time, space and dimensions, I passed through all that was and all that would be, catching only glimpses of a universe too vast for my finite mind to even consider. The enormity of it all was too much to sort out, entire worlds and civilizations processing through my finite human mind as so much static and radar chatter.

I began glowing white hot, becoming a rogue star as I journeyed through all Creation, reaching out into her—into the universe—and asking the question: *is this all there is? Is this all I am?*

Finally satisfied that I had, indeed, retrieved all of the Sleeper rings detectable within the universe, it was time to complete my journey. Making a turn, at that speed, took 88,125 light years and crossed hundreds of gravitational lines in hundreds of galaxies, which may have shifted hundreds of planetary orbits, potentially causing untold numbers of deaths or creating untold varieties of new life.

I accepted both. I did not choose one over the other, but merely existed within Creation. Arcing through hundreds of galaxies, I realized the Boss had set me up. He'd stripped me of the Spectre's power because of my continued meddling in the order of things. But, I finally realized, even that choice, even my rebellion, was, itself, part of the plan. That, ultimately, all things, all choices—even random or wrong ones—inexplicably added up to *order*. To the tapestry of the universe, to the *art* of it.

As the last vestiges of humanity burned away, my essence

elevated into a celestial body, a living star. My flight was, indeed, my *purpose*. Even my failures, even my rebellion, added up to a predestined order. I was exactly where I was supposed to be. I was doing exactly what I was supposed to be doing, and *he knew it*. The Boss knew it. But he let me stumble and suffer and doubt because those things were needed to equip me for the journey. For that moment.

I smiled.

Which was probably why I did not notice Star Sapphire until she drove massive, ornate energy swords into my back.

24

Star Sapphire had pursued me from Earth and had been caught in my wake as I had progressed throughout the universe. She, too, had absorbed vast energy and now she, too, had become so much more than human and so much more than Zamoran.

Her weapons of choice were crystal Zamoran short swords, generated by her dark power that was now enhanced to an indefinable degree. She'd calculated the precise temporal vibration the swords would require to cause me enormous pain.

I screamed, losing focus on my purpose, on my plan, and, suddenly, I was careening across the galaxy, a rogue star out of control.

"Well, Hal, you've really done it this time!" Star shrieked as she plunged the swords again and again, hacking off pieces of my energy cocoon. "And that's what we'll engrave on your memorial: *'Hal Jordan: the Guy Who Didn't Get It.'*" With each blow, massive energy shot off from our path, smashing through planets and obliterating stars.

Chaos.

"It's your chief failing, your major blind spot," Star continued, "that you know everything about everything and nothing about yourself, about the pathetic, small, impotent little life you've lived!"

All Creation cartwheeled wildly out of control now.

"You've always lived in a world, in a universe, of your own creation, of your own imagination. A storybook world where good triumphs over evil, where fairness and honesty were the order of things and where you, Hal Jordan, are the self-appointed king of the donut shop. Donut *emperor*. Defending the meek, the innocent, the needy—all of whom think you're a joke!"

Star Sapphire repeatedly plunged the blades into me. Suns collapsing now. Planets imploding.

"Meanwhile, everybody who loves you just kind of clears out a No Reality Zone—a space in their lives where the fools afford Hal Jordan his illusion of goodness, justice and mercy, while they quietly pity this weak, pathetic gum drop of a man stumbling through life with blinders on while suffering selective amnesia!"

I did my best to lock in, to regain focus, but I no longer knew where I was. A heartbeat had cost us a thousand light years. Traveling far faster than light could keep up with us, I was navigating by instinct but could no longer hear the universe's song. I was no longer communing with Creation.

"They've been laughing, Hal. Laughing at you, all your life. Laughing at the boy scout, the chivalrous and ultimately clueless white knight so pathetically out of touch with reality that he's only a few I.Q. points away from orthopedic shoes and the short bus—believing in Neverland, Santa Claus, and Oswald in the book depository—rambling off ditties about duty and honor from *Pinafore* and *Penzance* while the rest of the planet was doing body shots and going out for ice cream!"

Panic tore through me as I realized it was happening again:

my very best and most noble intention had now cost untold lives.

"It's all been a lie, Hal—all of it. Your values, your beliefs, your insane worship of your father—a man who cared much more about flying jets than raising kids! You've got this movie playing in your head, Hal, this G-rated optimism that keeps you on the treadmill, running at full speed but going nowhere while suffering the slings and arrows of people just beyond the welcome mat of Hal's House of Martyrs, who, having never read the script, were nevertheless on the same page—holding in contempt the Galactic Policeman who risked all and gave all to save the lives of people who, by their life's examples, mock his values!"

My God, I thought, *it's happening again...*

"You can't be rid of me, you idiot! You'll *never* be rid of me!" Star ranted, plunging her blades over and over. "You *love* me, Hal. And it is precisely that love that empowers me! That keeps me alive! So long as that love is there, so shall I be also!"

Destroying the universe...*again...*

"Watch those planets die, Jordan, because they are only the beginning!" Star kept plunging her blades into me, wiping out entire solar systems as, with each blow, massive, planet-killing energy was released. "The universe shall die, *again,* by your hand! And then I shall absorb your power into the dark jewel and, finally, restore my people—the Zamorans—to their rightful place as *rulers* of the Universe!"

From my experiences as Parallax and Spectre, I had detailed information on billions of planets throughout the universe. I knew the names of even the smallest child of the most distant and obscure alien race, and knew exactly how many hairs that child had on its head. How many fingers, how many toes. How many souls were being obliterated because my focus had shifted from all Creation to Star Sapphire's attack.

"Stop fighting me, Hal! The wheels came off the wagon long ago!" Star was chuckling now, drunk with passion, insane with power. Wholly indifferent to the mass carnage her attack on me was causing. "This is the end—your end, *our* end, lover! This is the *greatness* to which we've aspired all our lives!"

But I had the power—vast and incredible power—to fix things. I could move back through time and un-do the damage Star was causing. I could mend those systems and heal those planets. Or, I could simply wipe them out and start again, recreating them from scratch.

Star raised both swords, where were spattered and crossed with discharged plasma—symbolic blood. Smiling, delirious with power, Star prepared to deliver the death blow. "You should've listened to me," she said, now fully Maybelle to my pitiful Sid. "Now the entire universe will have to pay for your lack of vision!"

And she was right.

I needed to stop worrying about her, worrying about the damage she was causing, about the untold numbers of death screams in my head, the calamity of a thousand stars going super-nova, of planetary bodies smashing into one another, moons crashing into cities—I needed to simply turn it off.

In the grand scheme of things, none of that actually mattered. It was what it was. And, whatever happened was, ultimately, part of the plan. I needed to trust that, and stop thinking like a damned super-hero.

Elevating my mind beyond the confines of Hal Jordan's humanity, I dismissed Star Sapphire with a simple gesture, drawing her power and elevated mind away from her with a simple impulse, stripping her of her immortality and leaving the mortal, temporal Carol Ferris—now in the presence of a god.

Her attack ended. I did not struggle to regain control of my direction. Rather, I simply communed with all Creation, and once my focus was no longer on speed and angles and gravity—becoming more about art and design and *purpose*—I accepted that I no longer *needed* to be in control of my speed or direction—Creation was.

We were now moving so fast we no longer seemed to be moving at all. Moving so fast, I was in nearly all places in Creation at the same time. My humanity now long lost, my human emotion burned off in the crucible; Carol Ferris existed to me only slightly more than Hal Jordan did.

"G—geez, Hal, " Carol stammered, wincing from a nightmarish hangover, "what have you done?"

Ejecting the JLA Watchtower fuel cells was the last thing Carol remembered. For all she knew, we were still near lunar orbit. "Is the Watchtower still—I mean, is everybody—"

Carol gasped, alarmed that she seemed to be standing in the vacuum of space as the cosmos swirled around her and galaxies flew past. She had not yet realized the exact opposite was true, that we were hurtling across time and space at speeds beyond human comprehension.

I chose to ignore her. Of course, I could *hear* her, I could hear everything, every*one,* in all Creation. But she was simply beneath my notice. I was busy. I had a mission to complete.

"Hal!" Carol cried, as the inky void morphed into hues of teal and cobalt, the two of us now effortlessly breaching trans-mixed hypothetical boundary states. "Hal—what's happening to us?"

Nothing Carol saw made any sense to her. The last thing she remembered was ejecting the Watchtower's fuel cells. *Blue space,* she thought. *I'm in blue space.*

Then it hit her: space wasn't moving, *we* were moving. And the blue color was likely gaseous anomalies or—

"—The antimatter universe!" she exclaimed, with surprise and annoyance. "You—you're heading for the planet Qward!"

295

It wasn't so great a leap for her, as Star Sapphire had surely explored that far.

"You're taking those Sinestro rings back where they came from!"

I was.

"You're going to release all this power—all the energy you've built up and multiplied by criss-crossing the universe—by firing it at Qward!"

I was.

"Hal—this level of power could destroy the planet! Could destroy their entire *universe!*"

Yes, it could. And it was not my concern. Order was my concern. Restoring the balance by returning the goddamned Qwardians' rings to them.

Cleaning up on my way out.

Carol grabbed my shoulders, trying to get my attention. I didn't look at her. Around us, chaos became order once again as we crossed into the antimatter universe, a realm of blue space and black stars. A realm I knew fairly little about beyond the fact that Qwardians lived there.

"Hal, you've got to stop this," Carol demanded. "I know they're evil—I know they've got it coming—but, Hal, it's not your call! It is not for you to decide!"

I gave her nothing. Put nothing of myself out in the universe. I simply *was.*

"Hal, don't you see? It's happened again! By absorbing all of that power, you've become *him* again—Parallax!!"

She was wrong.

"Hal—you are not a murderer! You are not a destroyer!"

She was *very* wrong.

"You can't possibly destroy an entire universe!"

An alcoholic doesn't want one drink.

"And you are not God, either!" Carol demanded.

Ad Deum qui laetificat juventutem meam.

"Hal!" Carol grabbed a fistful of my Green Lantern costume, which, by that point, was more conceptual than fabric. "Snap out of it! This isn't you!"

Wrong.

"Hal Jordan is a decent, a moral and honest man! Someone who taught me his values—a patient man—"

Hal Jordan was weak. Hal's nobility was also his greatest inadequacy. I learned that from a squirrel.

"Hal!"

I gave her nothing.

"Hal, dammit!!"

Absolutely nothing. Carol began pounding on my chest with her fists.

"—I watched cartoons with Jack!" she screamed.

I already knew. Hal wasn't nearly as naïve as he seemed.

"Hal!" She was screaming now, a tear running down her cheek. Not that Carol gave one whit about the damned Qwardians. She simply recognized the town drunk bellying up to the bar. Once I'd wiped out the antimatter universe, she knew what would come next. "You've *got* to stop! You *have* to—the man I love could never act out of selfish revenge!"

That got my attention.

A simple word, piercing through a billion storms raging in my head. Through a hundred trillion voices, all talking, all screaming, at once.

I actually turned and noticed her.

Love.

Suddenly vulnerable, Carol searched my eyes, letting me in now, risking everything.

Love.

Her hand on my cheek now. My eyes sunken in shadow, a stony mask.

I never once, not ever, believed Carol Ferris loved me. Carol was in love with Carol. Carol did what she thought best for Carol. Hal Jordan served some utilitarian purpose for Carol, but it was ultimately all about Carol.

For Carol, love meant weakness. Emotionally crippled by old man Ferris, love was something Carol buried so deep, she'd let people walk out of her life before ever admitting it was there. But, there it was. The façade cracking. The Iron Lady melting. It was, for her, an act of bravery.

I, of course, loved her. Loved her from the moment I had laid eyes on her. Loved her months before she ever realized I was alive and drawing breath in her father's pilot training program. Loved her long after I realized she and I could never be—that she was simply incapable of giving me what I needed; warmth, trust, affection. *Love.* All of those things were buried somewhere with old man Ferris.

I caressed her cheek and a tear streamed from her eye.

"Yes, yes, Hal, that's it," she said, coaxing, "Come back to me, now." I considered her the way one considers a stranger. All around us, the blue universe convulsed and shook as we secured from light speed on approach to Qward, a planet with mere seconds left to live.

She was so beautiful. It was the kind of beauty Carol only exuded when she was sleeping and unaware that she was being watched. In those quiet times, those vulnerable moments, she let her guard down and revealed the smallest glimpse of her grace, her uniqueness in all creation.

I was never a fool to love her because I knew that side of her, existing only in fleeting moments. That person of nobility and integrity and warmth Carol expended so much energy to hide.

"Please," she whispered, placing my hand on her heart as she pulled me closer, *"touch me."* I was suddenly aware of her heart beating. Her warmth, her humanity—her *light.* Not a stolen

moment or a desperate one, but a fellow soul reaching out for mine. Offering, giving herself to me.

She was trying to *save* me. The way I'd saved her.

As the planet Qward loomed largely before us, we kissed.

I kissed Carol, my first love, as we expanded into infinite space—existing in all places and all times at once.

I looked into Creation and all Creation opened to me—

—*An impatient Carol Ferris tossing my research papers off her bed while* Rocky & Bullwinkle *played on her television.*

—*A smiling Marty Jordan saluting me before climbing aboard the X17 Stingray.*

—*A noble Abin Sur extending his hand as his power ring flew off of it.*

—*Myself, becoming Green Lantern for the first time.*

—*The Justice League taking its first formal portrait.*

—*Green Lantern and Green Arrow battling ecological terrorists while arguing over Washington's domestic agenda.*

Smiling faces, now:

—*Old man Ferris.*

—*Thomas "Pieface" Kalmaku, my mechanic at Ferris Aircraft.*

—*Barry Allen, the Flash.*

—*Ganthet, the last Guardian of the Universe.*

—*The Black Canary.*

—*Guy Gardner, hoisting a beer at his bar.*

—*Alan Scott, the original Green Lantern.*

—*Aquaman, coming as close to a smile as he does.*

Janelle at the inconvenience store.

Claudia in her crib.

Carol smiled through her tears, "Hal."

I was smiling. I was Hal Jordan. I was with the woman I loved.

Carol embraced me, holding me tight, "Thank God...thank God..." she said, "Thank God you're back."

And, I was. Which was why, with the merest gesture—

—I expelled all of the evil Qwardian energy at the planet.

"Nooo!!" Carol screamed as the massive energy discharge left us.

"What have you done?" She shrieked.

I wanted to explain, but there was no time. The energy ruptured all time and space, and we were caught in the wake of a universe rending at its core. Color and sound beyond description threatened to drive Carol insane, but by my will and the Starheart ring, I shielded us both from the utter destruction of the antimatter universe.

Hal Jordan. *The mad god Parallax,* Carol surely thought. The power alcoholic fallen off the wagon. *It's happening again,* she thought. *He's going to kill us all.*

She was wrong.

Going about my mission, it occurred to me: the universe would survive or it wouldn't. There wasn't much I could do about it either way. Rogue stars created life and destroyed it a thousand times a day. Destiny, fate, God—whatever you want to call it—had already designed the course of all Creation eons before any of us ever took breath.

It didn't matter to me whether I succeeded or failed. Whether I lived or died. Those were matters for someone else. All that mattered to me was my *purpose.* My role in the scheme of things and my place in all Creation.

And, soon as I made peace with all of that—

—I let go.

Let go of all of it. Of the guilt. Of Parallax. Of the anger. Of the bitterness. Of the need to prove myself or avenge myself. In that moment, I released my human limitations. I simply *was*.

Which, finally, was sufficient for me.

Blue space congealed into a reddish brown space. Burnt sienna space.

Carol, cringing, opened her eyes to see...the planet Qward. Completely intact and, apparently, unharmed. In a stable orbit around a blue star somewhere in maroon space.

The vast energy I'd absorbed was completely gone now. I was simply Hal Jordan. A Green Lantern on borrowed time.

"What—what happened?" she asked, wiping a tear.

"I changed the gravitational constant of the universe," I said. Which was *precisely what I'd told Kyle to do in the first place.*

Carol's feminine softness hardened back toward the Dragon Lady, "You *what?*"

I smiled at her. I was really going to miss her. "I moved Qward from a medium density region to a low density region."

"You moved Qward from...a red state to a blue state...?" Carol didn't like sounding stupid. Which made this all the more enjoyable for me.

"The rules of matter and gravity—the way things in existence work—are vastly different, here. While, in our universe, an energy discharge on that scale would certainly have destroyed everything, energy reacts differently here because the rules are different."

Carol blinked, putting on her annoyed face to mask the fact that she'd spent her last college semester making me do her science papers. "Which means *what?*"

I smiled, caressing her cheek. She allowed that only because she wanted something from me. The Carol Ferris Affection Barter System. "It means I changed the rules enough so the power I'd absorbed could move Qward into another dimension. At their present technology level, it may take them thousands of years to discover the proper vibrational frequencies to find their way back to our dimension."

"You—*moved* the planet?"

"Yes."

"To a place so far away they'll have a hard time threatening us again?"

"Well, 'far' has no real meaning in this example, but, yes, sort of."

"So, you never planned to destroy them?"

"Thought about it," I admitted. "But, the way I figure, if they keep this up, eventually, they'll destroy themselves. They won't need my help."

"So...you were never completely out of control."

"Not completely, no. The Qwardians understood the Guardians' technology, understood the rules of the Green Lantern Corps. This"—I showed her my temporary ring—"is not a GL Corps ring. It doesn't have identical encoding and, thus, was immune to much of the Qwardian rings' programming." Alan Scott, distracted by Jade's distress call, was caught off-guard by Star Sapphire's attack. Once he blacked out, the Qwardian rings were able to co-opt him. And, Scott was right: had I pursued this matter wearing Kyle's GL Corps ring, I'd have likely become Parallax again.

"But you were tempted."

"By you? Every day," I said. caressing Carol's cheek. But, it was too late. *That* woman was gone, Carol now fully locking down the armor.

"Hal—"

Yes, of course. It was late. Far too late for us. For things left unsaid.

I didn't care.

I hugged her, whispering, *I love you.*

She allowed that. Allowed herself to be overwhelmed by relief.

Allowed a passionate kiss.

Tears—hers and mine.

There, in an untold time and place, we allowed ourselves that moment.

The simple dignity of regret.

25

I got my job back.

Having passed the Boss's test—and learned my lesson—the spirit of Hal Jordan was once again fused with the fierce Spirit of Vengeance to form the composite being known as The Spectre. Most of the blanks—things Hal Jordan didn't or couldn't have known while I was temporarily mortal—were instantly filled in as I spoke to Creation and Creation revealed those details to me.

Several weeks had passed since the destruction of the Justice League Watchtower. Superman, Martian Manhunter, Flash and Green Lantern had already rebuilt two-thirds of the lunar base. I would have offered a hand—but I was no longer in the offer-a-hand business.

I was the Spectre.

I motivated myself to Planet Hell, where, standing amid the chaos, the Spectre's great cloak billowing in the viscous, thick atmosphere, I let John Q see me.

"Hello, John," I said.

John smiled. I was no longer capable of such things. "The crisis—over, yes?"

"Over, yes," I said, grimly.

"Qward—destroyed?"

"Unfortunately, no. The energy—enough to lay waste to a

galaxy—changed its composition in the antimatter universe, losing a few protons and neutrons along the way. The blast all but obliterated the Qwardian central command, but the planet's still there."

John looked very sad.

"If it makes you feel any better, it's going to rain there for the next 80 years," I said.

Didn't help.

John Q lived alone, completely alone, on a planet in a forbidden system. He had no ship. No people. And, with the Qwardian transformer bridges all shut down, ultimately, no way to get home. I wanted to help him. I wanted to feel something for him.

I could do neither.

"Farewell, John," I said, grimly.

"Be well, friend Lantern," John said sadly, as he turned and vanished in the mist.

The wind had just about ruined Carol's hair by the time her husband, Gil Johns, stepped off of the Ferris Aircraft corporate jet out on landing strip seven. Carol wore her usual "serious executive" DKNY suit, but she tried to look hopeful and happy. She'd forgotten nearly everything that had happened after she ejected the JLA Watchtower fuel cells, and the League thought it best to keep the rest from her for now.

Gil smiled as he walked across the tarmac in relaxed French-casual dress. He really did love Carol, and that was all of Carol—all anyone—really could hope for. But Gil wouldn't be fighting aliens or teaming with a curmudgeonly archer anytime soon, so Carol had her doubts about their future.

She'd chosen Gil for much the same reason she'd chosen me: he wasn't the kind of man her father was, he was the kind of man her father wanted for *her*. Gil was Carol still trying to please daddy.

He gave her a pleasant kiss. He was a pleasant guy. What Carol wanted was to get dragged back on that plane and flown off to some dangerous adventure where villains fired guns at them and they'd end up running from giant rolling balls and so forth.

Gil made dinner reservations instead.

I stood about twenty feet away, near the X1010, from which Carol's people had spent days scraping off bright yellow paint. I didn't let them see me.

Ollie's landing at the Warren County Jail had generated so much publicity for the X1010 that McDonnell Douglas came to the table with billions in licensing fees—essentially a buy-off to prevent Ferris from competing for their military contracts. Fighting off the big boys would have cost Ferris Aircraft truckloads of money, and a government contract was by no means a lock. At least the deal meant the company would remain solvent to fight another day. It wasn't the happiest of endings for the X1010, but that was generally how business was done: pay the other guy to *not* build a better mousetrap.

Were I capable of such an emotion, I'd have been happy for Carol and, likely, jealous of Biff.

I mean, Gil.

But all of that was behind me. I simply *was*.

I'd finally learned my lesson.

Between Cody barking and Kyle snoring, Jade wasn't about to get any sleep at all. She lay across Kyle's chest, her eyes fixated on his Green Lantern ring, her hand fussing with the bandaging around her neck while Jay Leno cracked jokes in the background. Thanks to her own Starheart energy and the Martian Manhunter's advanced science, she had survived her encounter with Star Sapphire.

She was content. She loved Kyle. But marriage had to go back on the shelf. The Sleepers crisis had pulled scabs off wounds and deficiencies neither realized were there. There was much work to do.

Jade was back home. Back where she wanted to be. But it was back to the first rung on the ladder.

Jade rested her head on Kyle's chest. The audience applauded.

I sat at Kyle's drawing board, looking at the duck.

I didn't let her see me.

Alan Scott gazed across Gotham City. They were shining that damned Bat Signal again. It was like a nut magnet. Scott estimated fully half the costumed bozos Batman ran around punching in the head came to Gotham *because* this was a town that flashed a giant bat image on the night sky. *Crazies welcome.* Scott's strategy for fighting crime? Ditch the Bat Signal and massively re-decorate.

I stood behind Scott. The Death Angel. A wraith even more terrible than Batman. I didn't let him see me, but he knew I was there. He was in touch with the universe in his own way.

I wanted to admire him, his iron will, his dedication, his *gravity.*

But I didn't allow myself to. Keeping that side of me in check was the only way to bury Parallax for good. Today it's rescuing kitties out of trees, tomorrow I'm ripping apart the fabric of existence.

An alcoholic doesn't want one drink.

Alan was content that, for now, things were fine. He wasn't thrilled about Jade moving back in with her boyfriend, but that battle was for another day.

For this day, for this night, he was content to simply *be.*

Something I considered a lesson well learned.

A video arcade opened in Heart Attack's old, ratty store. I passed through the place once or twice but I did not hang out there. No longer craved the touch—the light—of human contact. The arcade preyed on the neighborhood in a different way—poor kids getting poorer by tossing dozens of quarters and dollars into a few minutes' diversion from the misery their lives had become.

I passed through the crowd without being seen. Without being touched.

I backed up briefly when I spotted someone I recognized. Someone on my *list*.

Heads up, pal. I'll be visiting you soon.

Maybelle got twenty years.

Claudia was adopted by the Reynolds.

Acknowledgements

Thank you, John Broome, Gil Kane and Joe Giella for this hero. For a lifetime of looking to the stars.

Thank you Denny O'Neil for the long walks through Greenwich Village while you explained Hal Jordan to me. Thank you MD Bright, my partner in crime, for co-creating many of the characters and concepts this trilogy is based upon. Thank you Dan Raspler for giving our hulking Victorian blowhard a name—Malvolio.

Thank you Byron Preiss and the staff of Byron Preiss Visual Publications for your support and enthusiasm for this project. Thank you Howard Zimmerman and the staff of ibooks for your hard work and patience.

Thank you Paul Kupperberg for 27 years of keeping me off the ledge.

Thank you Mike Baron and Michael S. Ahn for your wonderful contribution to this series.

Thank you Bala Menon, Dave Van Domelen, Greg "Elmo" Morrow, Ph.D., Rick Jones, Kevin J. Maroney, Hosun S. Lee, Jerry Franke, Marc Singer, Max Chittister, Denise Voskuil, Sidne Gail Ward, and Michael Chary, Esq., for timely research assistance.

Thank you to Sheriff John Ariss, Captain John Newsom, Lieutenant Barry Riley and the men and women of the Warren County Sheriff's Office in Lebanon, Ohio for your enormous help, good humor and assistance.

Thank you to my friends Stan Lee, Jeanette Kahn, Jim Shooter and Paul Levitz: I've learned from the best.

Thank you Mark Waid for being the very best of the very best, giving me something to aim for. And for being a better friend to me than I've been to you.

Thank you Brian Augustyn for refereeing the battles in my head. Thank you Bob Greenberger for more than I have space to articulate. Thank you Willie Schubert for your friendship and professionalism. I want to be just like you when I grow up.

Thank you Tom Brevoort for still loving comics and for being the best guy making them.

Thank you Denys, wherever you are. Thank you Dwayne McDuffie for profound and lasting lessons, for your excellence and friendship. Thank you, Michael Davis for putting humanism over capitalism and for showing us what a real pro looks like.

Thank you Reggie Hudlin for your consistent support, friendship and encouragement. *Marrr-cus, darling!*

Thank you, Joy, for the sanity. Brace yourself. Thank you Laurice and Colleen and my daughters—Jhammel, Tierra, Erikka, LaShante, Ashley and Joannastacia. I love you. Now stop bothering me.

Thank you, Cody, for letting me get this manuscript done. Thank you John and George.

Thank you Henry for being what a pastor should. Thank you Tevin and Quonnu for being the best sons Henry (or I) could hope for. Thank you Christine for making sure everybody wears matching socks.

Thank you, Promise, for being the brother I never knew I always needed. Thank you, Juanita, for what seems to be limitless patience with me (and him).

Thank you, Sam, for being fabulous. I love you.

Thank you, Darryl and Neil for literally keeping me alive.

Thank you, Kelli, just because I feel like thanking you. Yeah, it's *like that*.

Thank you Larry.